Growing up near the beach, **Annie West** spent lots of time observing tall, burnished lifeguards—early research! Now she spends her days fantasising about gorgeous men and their love-lives. Annie has been a reader all her life. She also loves travel, long walks, good company and great food. You can contact her at annie@annie-west.com or via PO Box 1041, Warners Bay, NSW 2282, Australia.

Jackie Ashenden writes dark, emotional stories, with alpha heroes who've just got the world to their liking, only to have it blown wide apart by their kick-ass heroines. She lives in Auckland, New Zealand, with her husband—the inimitable Dr Jax—two kids and two rats. When she's not torturing alpha males and their gutsy heroines she can be found drinking chocolate martinis, reading anything she can lay her hands on, wasting time on social media or being forced to go mountain biking with her husband. To keep up to date with Jackie's new releases and other news sign up to her newsletter at jackieashenden.com.

Also by Annie West

The Desert King Meets His Match
Reclaiming His Runaway Cinderella
Reunited by the Greek's Baby
The Housekeeper and the Brooding Billionaire
Nine Months to Save Their Marriage

Also by Jackie Ashenden

His Innocent Unwrapped in Iceland

Three Ruthless Kings miniseries

Wed for Their Royal Heir
Her Vow to Be His Desert Queen
Pregnant with Her Royal Boss's Baby

Discover more at millsandboon.co.uk.

HIS LAST-MINUTE DESERT QUEEN

ANNIE WEST

A VOW TO REDEEM THE GREEK

JACKIE ASHENDEN

MILLS & BOON

First published in Great Britain 2024
by Mills & Boon, an imprint of HarperCollins*Publishers* Ltd,
1 London Bridge Street, London, SE1 9GF

www.harpercollins.co.uk

HarperCollins*Publishers*, Macken House, 39/40 Mayor Street Upper,
Dublin 1, D01 C9W8, Ireland

ISBN: 978-0-263-31991-0

01/24

This book is produced from independently certified FSC™ paper to ensure responsible forest management.
For more information visit: www.harpercollins.co.uk/green.

Printed and Bound in the UK using 100% Renewable Electricity
at CPI Group (UK) Ltd, Croydon, CR0 4YY

HIS LAST-MINUTE DESERT QUEEN

ANNIE WEST

MILLS & BOON

To those readers who adore a desert romance
and asked me for more.

There are too many of you to mention individually,
but I want to thank you so much for your enthusiasm!

Zamir and Miranda's story is for you.

CHAPTER ONE

Zamir pinched the bridge of his nose as he stepped from the air-conditioned luxury of the hotel foyer into searing sunlight that heightened his hammering headache. Only then did he realise he'd forgotten his sunglasses.

The last few days hadn't been long enough to fit in all he needed to do. But—the thought shimmered like the promise of life-giving water in the desert—by the end of today it would all fall into place.

He breathed a sigh of exhausted satisfaction. The last weeks had been hell but he hadn't allowed himself time to mourn. He'd had to be strong for his family and his country. Now he was on the cusp of achieving everything he'd promised his dying uncle.

Securing the crown and therefore the stability of his homeland, Qu'sil.

And paving the way to reunify Qu'sil and neighbouring Aboussir into one nation.

There'd be celebrations across both countries when it was done. Even the most diehard nationalists in both places had agreed this was the way forward. But negotiating a balance that gave equal weight to both sides had been time-consuming and tough.

Now there was just one last item to tick off and everything could proceed.

The most crucial item of all.

Without breaking stride, holding his phone to his ear as his finance minister detailed an unforeseen budget problem, Zamir strode to the waiting limo.

The car door was open, held by a chauffeur standing to attention. Zamir's brow twitched as he wondered why his hosts should insist the driver wear gloves, unnecessary in this heat, without ensuring his uniform fitted. Even his hat seemed too big, shadowing his face.

But Zamir had other things on his mind. With murmured thanks to the driver, he got in and focused on his minister, stretching out his legs and reaching for sparkling water.

A few minutes later he ended the call and took one from his head of royal security. Hassan hadn't liked him travelling without his usual escort in a foreign country, even on this short trip from the hotel. But that was the point. For Zamir to show complete trust in his hosts and the people of Aboussir who would, once the legalities were completed, be his subjects.

'Relax, Hassan. I'm on my way. I'll see you soon.' He looked out at the crowded, narrow streets of the old city, where traffic moved at a snail's pace. 'Don't worry if I'm a little late. The roads here aren't as streamlined as at home.' A small laugh escaped. 'At least they won't start the ceremony without me.'

Ending the call, he frowned at his phone then pressed the button to lower the privacy screen between himself and the driver.

Despite the tinted windows, the sunlight made him squint. The medication he'd taken for his headache hadn't yet kicked in. He took another long swig of water. He should have taken time for a proper breakfast but despite all the preparations, his uncle's death had meant a flurry of work.

But soon… After today, Zamir could at least take the night off.

'My phone battery is low,' he said to the driver. 'I need to charge it.' Something he usually did before sleeping but there'd been no sleep last night.

'Of course, sire.'

Sire? Such an old-fashioned word but then Aboussir was more traditional than his country. There most addressed him as sir. Soon, after being formally acclaimed Sheikh and Head of State, it would be Majesty.

Zamir's mouth tugged down. He'd known that day was coming, that his uncle couldn't last for ever, yet he missed the old man.

'If you pass me the phone, sire, I'll see to it.'

The man's voice was light, very young by the sound of it.

As long as he knew the way, that was all that mattered. But he manoeuvred his way deftly between vehicles, livestock and pedestrians.

'Thank you.' Zamir passed the phone over and sat back, closing his eyes against a sudden swimming sensation. He really should have snatched some rest. 'How long till we get there? Fifteen minutes?'

'Longer, I'm sorry. There's been a major accident. We'll have to detour off the main road. But I'll get you where you need to be.'

Zamir nodded but didn't open his eyes. This appointment was vital. He'd power nap now, ready to be at his best.

Even as she drove the air-conditioned vehicle, Miranda's skin was clammy, not from the temperature but nerves.

Nerves? More like outright terror!

Even for her, the one labelled so often by her family as volatile and irresponsible, today's actions were beyond the pale.

How had she ever thought she'd succeed? It had been an act born of desperation. Not her desperation but her cousin's. Miranda couldn't turn her back on Sadia in her distress.

When she'd come up with the plan she'd been more than half joking but Sadia had jumped at the idea. For once her timid cousin wasn't concerned with propriety or repercussions.

Why would she worry when you're taking all the risks?

That was unfair. Sadia couldn't do this. She'd have been missed if she'd sneaked out this morning. Anyway, if this came undone they'd both pay.

Correction, they'd both pay anyway, whether Miranda succeeded or not. There'd be no hiding what they'd done.

Her breath caught, her brain atrophying at the thought of what would happen if they succeeded. Even her fertile imagination couldn't picture it.

But if they succeeded it would be worth whatever repercussions were meted out. To sit idle and let Sadia down was impossible. They'd been friends all their lives, even through the years of Miranda's absence from Aboussir.

Swinging the big car through an archway into the new part of the city, she glanced in the rear-view mirror. He looked asleep, shoulders resting against the cushioned backrest, long limbs sprawled and head to one side.

He was the most imposing man she'd ever seen. The photos didn't do him justice, even though they showed a broodingly handsome man. There was something about him in the flesh, a confidence, an aura of—elemental masculinity were the only words to describe it—that turned the air around him electric and made her janglingly aware of her own sex.

Given that she'd spent so much time around men, often good-looking men with never a qualm, that awareness shocked her.

A shiver scuttled down her backbone. It was one thing to hatch this outrageous plan, huddled in Sadia's room at midnight. It was another to carry it out.

Her courage had taken a battering when she'd read about Sheikh Zamir's sharp intellect and his prowess both in government and in any athletic endeavour. The press painted him as someone who could look after his country and himself, no matter what the circumstances. It wouldn't be easy to best such a man.

Her cursory research last night had left her worried, wishing she could pull out of this hare-brained scheme. But Sadia was desperate.

Miranda felt guilty, wishing Sadia hadn't left it until the last minute to seek help, knowing she'd be almost thankful if the plan failed. But it hadn't and she'd found herself frozen with a dreadful mix of fear and excitement as Sheikh Zamir strode out to the car.

Her heart had risen to her throat as she took in the big man's lazy yet purposeful gait. The breadth of his shoulders beneath his traditional robe. His well-shaped, powerful hands. And the glitter of ebony eyes in a hard, handsome face that made her insides squirm.

Miranda's stepfather was handsome, like many of his polo-playing friends. She was used to good-looking sportsmen who moved as if they owned the world.

But Sheikh Zamir was in a class of his own.

Ignoring the heat coursing through her at the thought, she turned onto the main road out of the city, casting a quick look in the rear-vision mirror, but he hadn't moved. Her heartbeat quickened as she accelerated, waiting for that deep voice to ask why they were heading away from their destination.

No protest came. Maybe he really was asleep.

Yet she felt nauseous with worry.

They left the built-up area. Another look in the mirror and this time she caught him moving, not sitting up to demand where they were going but snuggling deeper into the leather seat. The contrast between his severe, ultra-masculine features and that tiny movement, as if seeking comfort, sent a spiral of something unfamiliar through her middle.

Her breath escaped in a gusty sigh of relief.

She checked the time. It felt as if she'd been driving for hours but if she turned the car around now they'd hardly even be late.

Setting her jaw, Miranda focused on the road and all the reasons she was doing this.

Because she hated bullies. Because Sadia was too precious to be treated this way. Because, come what may, disgrace, international incident, maybe even imprisonment, what this man planned was wrong. It might be Sadia's father actually forcing her to comply, but it was at the behest of *this* man. If no one else had the courage to stand up to him, Miranda had to.

The car approached an intersection of three highways. Miranda darted a look towards the back seat then opened her window a sliver. In one quick move she grabbed his phone and dropped it out.

There. If someone tried to locate him using his phone, they'd have no chance.

If only she'd thought to do it while they were in the city. Then anyone pursuing them wouldn't know if they were still in the metropolis.

Miranda smiled shakily. She'd make a mental note.

In case she ever kidnapped a royal sheikh again.

CHAPTER TWO

ZAMIR'S MIND FELT dull and there was a bad taste in his mouth. That medication! He'd used it only once before, years ago, and had forgotten how lethargic it left him.

At least his head wasn't pounding any more. He'd take that as a win.

Then he realised the car had stopped. He snapped his eyes open, disliking the idea of being found dozing instead of alert, ready for this important occasion.

It took long moments to digest what he saw.

There was no chauffeur, no welcoming host, no familiar faces from his entourage. Instead of the entrance to a palace and eager faces, he looked onto stony ground that dropped down to a plain. There were no buildings and the only road a gravel track that disappeared around a hillock.

His nape pinched tight and he tensed. Clearly they'd left the city but where he was, he had no idea.

He strained to hear any telltale sound. A voice, a footfall. A gun being cocked.

The height of the sun told him hours had elapsed since he left his hotel. Whatever had happened, the driver had been part of it. At least the man had left the car open and the windows down, in the growing heat.

He swung his head around and realised the vehicle was parked in the shade. Behind rose a tall stone wall with high, shuttered windows.

Zamir's heart thudded. Where was he?

Uncoiling from the car, he rose, balanced on the balls of his feet, only a little unsteady, ready to face an attack.

None came. He stood listening, but there was nothing except the sigh of an afternoon breeze rounding the massive wall. What was this place?

More to the point, why was he here?

He allowed himself a single flicked glance at his watch, confirming what he knew. He was hours late for his appointment.

Hassan would be frantic. Not just Hassan. The whole machinery of the royal court would swing into emergency mode when he didn't arrive.

Bending to the front window, he confirmed what he'd feared. His phone had disappeared. Nevertheless he searched thoroughly. Nothing.

Zamir's jaw set and his gut curdled as he considered the consequences of missing today's appointment. It was catastrophic.

What enemy of the state had planned this?

Why leave him, alone and unharmed? This bizarre situation turned stranger by the moment.

Swiftly, keeping in the shadow of the building, he ran silently down the length of the wall, pausing at the corner. Still he saw no one but on this side was an entrance. A huge arched entrance with stout wooden doors, studded with iron and ornate, antique hinges. The sort of doors designed to keep marauders out. His own palace had something similar, though grander and in better repair.

The notable thing here was that one of them stood open. In invitation or oversight?

Scooping up a fist-sized rock from the barren ground, Zamir moved forward.

Miranda's hands shook so badly even now that she had to pause and take deep breaths.

He'd be okay. He was just asleep. Yet when she'd tried to wake him he hadn't moved.

Because you barely dared touch him.

Because, once he wakes, you'll have to face the consequences of what you've done.

It worried her that she'd had to leave him outside in the afternoon heat, because her genius plan hadn't factored in his sheer size. Well over six feet and strongly muscled, he was too big for her to move.

She gripped the bench and told herself he'd be fine. It wasn't midsummer, when the temperatures rose lethally in the desert. There was a breeze passing through the car and she'd take water and a wet cloth to cool him.

As soon as her fumbling fingers managed the stiff catch on the bathroom cupboard.

She'd never expected he'd sleep so long. With every kilometre out of the city she'd expected him to wake and demand she turn around. She'd never believed the plan would work.

At least Sadia was safe. Miranda tried to convince herself that was all that mattered.

She swiped damp hands down the bulky uniform jacket and reached again for the cupboard. Finally she managed to open it and reached in, when the flesh between her shoulder blades tingled and her breath stopped.

She wasn't alone.

There'd been no sound but she *felt* the difference.

'Withdraw your hand slowly and turn around.'

Fear rose to a point just this side of panic at the harsh authority in that rough voice.

Heart hammering, Miranda turned her head.

It was the Sheikh, very much alive. He bristled with energy, narrowed eyes glittering in a way that made her breath stop then start again, painfully as if her lungs forgot how to work.

His obsidian-black gaze raked her, her flesh stinging as if he'd grazed it. Didn't they make razor-sharp knives from volcanic obsidian?

She swallowed convulsively, the movement painful as she felt that sharpness in her throat.

His handsome, brooding features were set like a granite thundercloud. His eyes were narrowed, his mouth grim and nostrils flared disdainfully.

His shoulders filled the doorway and even from a couple of metres away he mastered the space, sucking the oxygen out.

Every protective instinct urged Miranda to run or hide. Except there was nowhere to hide and he blocked the only door.

She drew a shuddering breath.

Time to face the music.

He ruled a kingdom, would soon rule two, and no doubt was used to having his every wish obeyed. He was powerful and incensed. She could hardly blame him, after what she'd done.

'I—'

'Let me see what you've got in your hand. Slowly.'

Miranda nodded, the too-large cap slipping further down her forehead as she pulled her arm from the cupboard. But the braid at the wrist snagged on that troublesome catch, stopping her. She lifted her other hand to free the fabric.

She was still struggling with it when something collided with her, pivoting her back against the wall.

Stunned, she felt the world dim, blocked out by the tall body pinioning her. She dragged in a desperate breath, discovering it scented with cedarwood and warm spice.

Then she heard that same deep voice, muttering something she couldn't catch.

There was movement, the weight against her eased a fraction, resolving itself into the solid torso of Sheikh Zamir of Qu'sil as he pulled back just enough to survey her.

Miranda sucked in another lungful of desperate air. She'd thought him imposing and haughty. This close she discovered something else in that austere face that made her, for one confusing moment, forget they were enemies.

'A woman?'

There was no need to answer. He knew the shape of her breasts and hips now just as she knew the breadth of his chest, the jut of his narrow hip bones and the power in those long, encompassing legs. The ferocious heat of him seared into her.

Miranda blinked up at a jaw so sharply squared she was mesmerised. Or maybe that was shock. She'd imagined the Sheikh as a distant figure, a problem to be overcome. Not a man, potently alive, whose body against hers evoked unaccustomed responses.

'I was kidnapped by a woman?'

He plucked off her cap. For a pulse beat, and another and yet another, he stared at her cropped curls.

His narrowed eyes flared.

Slowly he loosened his grip on her wrist. Pins and needles prickled, making her gasp and flex stiff fingers.

'You were going to attack me with a *towel*?'

He unwrapped the towel she'd been holding when her arm got snagged and she used his distraction to try wriggling free. But he was having none of that, holding her where she was with disturbing ease.

Miranda gulped. There was nothing sexual about what he did. Yet a single spark of heat swirled through her pelvis and remained there, warm against the chill enveloping her.

She cleared her throat. 'Of course I wasn't going to attack you. I was getting a towel.'

'There's no of course about it.'

His eyes met hers and her breath went AWOL again. Fear could do that. It had nothing to do with the strange *awareness* she felt.

Of them not as kidnapped and kidnapper, but as male and female.

Her breathing quickened and he eased back a little more.

'Where are your accomplices?'

'I don't have any.'

It wasn't a lie. Sadia knew the plan, had helped devise it,

but it was Miranda alone who'd carried it out. Even now she could barely believe she'd got away with it for so long.

Maybe she hadn't. Maybe this was a crazy dream and she'd wake soon.

Except this man was too real. Even her fertile imagination couldn't have conjured up someone like him.

'What are you smiling at?'

'I'm not smiling. I'm dazed.'

His forbidding expression didn't ease. 'That's my line. I'm the one you kidnapped. What were you doing here?'

Miranda chewed the corner of her mouth. 'I worried when you didn't wake. I was getting water for you and a towel to wet.'

'Tending to my needs? You're a regular Florence Nightingale, aren't you?'

Miranda held his fulminating stare. 'I was worried you might be unwell.' She swallowed hard. 'But I'm not sorry I kidnapped you.'

Zamir watched her chin lift in an attitude of defiance that should have been laughable.

It wasn't. Instead it intrigued.

He might even have labelled her absurd attitude engaging if it weren't for the catastrophe she'd caused.

He felt her runaway pulse yet she kept her cool. She was brave, he'd give her that.

But how dangerous was she? And who else did he have to contend with?

'If you wouldn't mind, I'd like to stand alone now.'

There it was again, that courageous insouciance as if she weren't bothered by the fact that she was now at *his* mercy.

He scrutinised her, from the gaping collar of her obviously borrowed or stolen uniform to the nimbus of mahogany hair like a sexy, dark halo. Her skin was fine-grained, a pale olive-gold that contrasted bewitchingly with eyes of light grey-blue.

Bewitchingly? That medication must be impairing his thoughts.

Her features were unremarkable yet pleasing. Or they would be if she hadn't single-handedly destroyed everything he and so many others had worked for.

On a surge of furious energy Zamir stepped back, watching as she straightened her jacket and moved away from the wall. He could have frisked her to be completely sure she had no concealed weapons, but he'd touched enough of her to believe she was no immediate threat.

Nevertheless, he positioned himself beside the open doorway where he could see anyone approach. 'Why are we here? Who are we meeting?'

'We're not meeting anyone.'

She arched her back, one hand to her shoulder blade. The movement thrust her breasts against the jacket, reminding him, as if he weren't already fully aware, that she was a young, attractive woman.

Assassins and fanatics came in all shapes and sizes, he reminded himself. He was attuned not only to her movements but to the silence beyond this room, anticipating the arrival of her partners in crime.

'Then why are we here?'

'I needed somewhere to take you that's off the grid so you can't get back quickly to the city.' She stood tall. 'There's no phone. I know you won't believe me, but it's true. I threw yours away.'

Zamir would indeed check for himself. 'And now you have me here? Who's making the ransom demand?'

Dark eyebrows pinched above those bright eyes. 'There is no ransom demand. I've done what I set out to do.' She looked at the man's watch on her slender wrist. 'You've missed the ceremony and it's too late to return, that's all that matters.'

She was right. That was all that mattered.

Even now Zamir couldn't believe how such a promising day

had ended in disaster. The headache that had plagued him this morning began pounding anew. If he had time to waste he'd berate her over the unthinkable damage she'd done.

But she knew what she'd done. It was there in those wary, pewter-bright eyes.

'Who are you working for?'

His country didn't have enemies as such but some were jealous of its phenomenal financial successes. Perhaps too, some envied its stability and social harmony and the way it was held up as an example to others. That success would increase when Qu'sil and Aboussir rejoined.

Except that reunion might no longer be possible. Time was running out. Thanks to this woman. He gritted his teeth.

'I told you. No one.'

His pulse drummed painfully in his temple as he clung to a veneer of patience. Exhaling slowly, he held out his hand. 'I'll have the car keys now.'

She swallowed and moistened her bottom lip.

He'd swear it was an instinctive gesture, and it made him revise his assessment that her face was unremarkable but for those eyes. Now her cupid's bow mouth and especially her fuller, sensual bottom lip held his gaze. His body temperature hiked up a couple of degrees.

'You can't. The first thing I did was throw the keys down the well in the courtyard. I can't afford for you to get back to the capital today.'

She didn't sound defiant now. Was she belatedly realising how vulnerable her position?

Yet she must have some protection apart from sheer bravado. She clearly expected his wrath after what she'd done.

The ruler of Qu'sil outwitted and abducted by a woman in her early twenties!

It was laughable. Preposterous.

Cataclysmic.

Because it wasn't simply his pride on the line. It was his nation's future.

Zamir stepped forward and she shuffled back, bringing him up short.

Not so brazen now. Uncertain, but trying not to look it with her chin still angled high.

'How far to the nearest habitation?'

'Too far to walk. It would be dark before you got there and you'd probably lose the track and get lost. I doubt there are any torches here. Not that you'll believe me.'

He nodded. He didn't believe her.

But the view through the window behind her seemed to confirm what she said. Nevertheless he'd have to try. After he'd checked for a hidden phone. He couldn't imagine she'd come here without some form of communication.

Zamir folded his arms. This *was* an ideal place to hide a captive. He suspected they were in the remote area near the border of their two countries. But instinct told him there had to be another reason she'd brought him here.

'What is this place? *Whose* is it?'

'It's mine. But I haven't been here in years.'

In a day of surprises she still managed to confound him. 'Yours?'

The size of the place and the faded grandeur he'd seen so far pointed to it being an old fortress palace, albeit neglected.

She nodded, seeming to find his collar inordinately fascinating. Because she was, finally, realising she no longer had the upper hand? But then, as if she were reading his thoughts, her head snapped up, those startling, misty eyes meeting his.

He dismissed the zap of energy he felt as their gazes locked.

'I inherited it from my father but no one has lived here for a while.'

Zamir rocked back on his heels then forward. 'How convenient to have somewhere isolated enough to hold a kidnap hostage.'

She scowled. 'You're not a hostage. And I didn't *know* I was going to kidnap you. It was only last night—'

She stopped and bit her lip.

'It was a last-minute plan?' His eyes narrowed. Could it be true? Had he been outwitted by a woman who'd acted on the spur of the moment? He refused to believe it. 'Ms…?'

'Fadel. Miranda Fadel.'

Zamir stiffened, his scant amusement at her lies fading. He knew that name, knew it very well. If she were indeed from that family…

'You're related to Sadia Fadel?'

She nodded, her features taut. Her expression persuaded him this at least was no lie. 'She's my cousin. We grew up together.'

She licked her lip again as if her mouth were dry. Once more Zamir felt an echo of heat low in his body but was too shocked to focus on it.

'You're also related to the Sheikh of Aboussir?'

It was the Sheikh, with Zamir's uncle, then Sheikh of Qu'sil, who had proposed today's ceremony. If he'd changed his mind he would have told Zamir, not concocted this outrageous kidnap.

'Distantly. The Sheikh's cousin had two sons. Sadia's father is the elder and my father was the younger.'

Zamir nodded. He knew the family tree. The fact that the Sheikh of Aboussir had no children made his cousin's children his closest relatives. That had been one of the reasons he'd felt free to support an amalgamation of their countries. Sadia's father, the Sheikh's distant, surviving male relative, wasn't considered suitable to rule. The two royal Sheikhs and their governments had agreed that Zamir would rule both nations, once his position was confirmed with his marriage.

The marriage that had been due to take place today.

Because the laws of his own nation decreed that the royal Sheikh, if not already married, should wed within three weeks of his predecessor's death or be passed over in favour of a married man.

An arranged marriage between himself as heir to one throne and Sadia Fadel from the royal family of Aboussir had been devised. Both royal families would combine to create a new dynasty to rule over the new nation.

The original plan had been for the wedding to take place in several months' time with the blessing of both ruling Sheikhs. Except Zamir's beloved uncle, ill for so long, had suddenly taken a turn for the worse, dying mere weeks ago.

The last thing Zamir wanted now was to consider marrying. His grief and his nation's were enough to cope with. Except it *had* to be done, quickly, and the wedding had been brought forward to today.

'Why?' He glared. 'Why wreck what we've all worked towards?'

'All? Don't you mean you and Sadia's father, my uncle? *He's* the one who wanted this wedding. He wants his daughter married to a powerful sheikh. He can't rule so he wants to be close to the man who does. All this is just about personal power and influence.'

The repugnance in her tone matched the curl of her lip and Zamir was torn between disbelief and fascination. His character, hard work and dedication were known to all. He was a man of principle who'd devoted his life to his country, not for personal gain but because it was his duty.

'What can I possibly have done to warrant that sneer?'

He should be pressing for more details of the plot, yet he was distracted by her dismissal. The insult to his integrity was like a sneaking stab to the gut.

What did she think gave *her* the right to judge *him*?

'You really don't know?' She shook her head. 'You try to force a woman into marriage and think it's all right? Because you're greedy enough to want to rule two nations instead of one.'

'Force?' Zamir strode closer, compelled into movement by

her outrageous suggestion. 'I've used no force! You'll have to produce a better lie than that. What's your real motive? Who do you work for?'

Instead of being cowed as he towered over her, the woman had the nerve to stare right back, jaw set and eyes flashing. Only the quick rise and fall of her breasts beneath the drab uniform betrayed her disquiet.

'Of course it was to be a forced marriage.' She paused. 'Your bride told me.'

CHAPTER THREE

MIRANDA SLUMPED BACK against the wall, knees drawn up to her chest and mind racing.

She didn't wear a watch so couldn't be sure of the time, but it seemed hours since they'd heard a vehicle approaching. That had galvanised Sheikh Zamir into action. He'd hurried her through the building until he found a bare storeroom with a solid lock.

At one point she'd heard voices, deep male voices, but then they moved away and there was only silence.

What was he doing? Why had he left her here so long? And who had arrived? No one knew where they were.

Miranda recalled the Sheikh's expression when she'd called him out for forcing Sadia into marriage. Indignation and fury, and something else that had looked almost like surprise.

She'd put that down to the fact no one had ever had the temerity to confront him about his methods. Yet when he'd questioned her again and she'd confirmed Sadia herself had told her she was being forced into the marriage, that she was petrified at the prospect of marrying a stranger and becoming a queen, he'd looked astounded.

Again and again she circled back to that moment, unable to shake the conviction that something was wrong.

Apart from the fact that you kidnapped a head of state and now have to face the consequences?

Her mouth turned down as her blood iced. She could barely imagine her uncle's ire.

But it wasn't her uncle she needed to worry about, not yet. In her hasty planning, she'd had no time to think about what came next. She'd been so focused on achieving the impossible, delaying the Sheikh long enough to prevent the wedding, that she'd been hazy on the aftermath.

She'd assumed that once they arrived here she'd hide the car keys and, when enough time had passed, she'd drive them back to the city. That was before she saw Sheikh Zamir in the flesh and realised only the most drastic action would keep him from his appointment.

His boldness, his air of determination and unmistakable power had made her rethink.

Miranda had realised she could take no chances. She'd ditched the car keys where he couldn't retrieve them, just as she'd had to dispose of his phone.

Which meant she was trapped here as he was.

Her thoughts snagged on the memory of his hard frame pressing her against the wall.

Never in her twenty-three years had she been so close to a man, so *aware* of him. It had been the strangest sensation, anxiety mixing with something that even now made her blood pulse quicker.

Pinpricks had peppered her body and she'd assumed it was reaction to his anger. But she'd faced anger before. Her uncle had never approved of her and had found fault with her since childhood. Yet Miranda had never experienced anything like today's phenomenon.

Her thoughts began another, useless cycle of regret, fear and determination, when she heard the key grate in the lock. By the time the door swung open she was standing on wide-braced feet, her back to the wall.

A strongly built man in a dark, tailored suit surveyed her, his expression blank.

'His Highness will see you now.'

His Highness. Whoever this man was, he was an ally of Sheikh Zamir. So much for her fragile hope that the new arrival was someone who might help her.

She had no allies. No powerful ones anyway, though she had a few friends back in the city. Her parents were dead and though she'd spent most of her early life in Aboussir it had been years since she'd lived here.

Miranda swallowed, her mouth dry and throat scratchy, and felt the wall press against her shoulder blades. Then she gathered her tattered courage and stepped forward. He waited until the last moment to allow her to exit.

He shadowed her every step, a forbidding gaoler.

It was almost reassuring to enter one of the sitting rooms and see the familiar figure of Sheikh Zamir standing with his back to her, looking out the window.

The fluttery sensation of relief was surely misplaced. He was her enemy.

He turned swiftly, robe flaring wide, frowning eyes homing in on hers. She was reminded of a hawk, its wings outspread, piercing gaze already locked on its hapless prey.

For long seconds he pinioned her with that fierce stare, making her wonder how far this man would go for revenge. One thing was for sure, he wasn't used to being crossed. He was used to ordering and being obeyed.

He'd ordered a suitable bride and expected her meek compliance.

The thought of Sadia settled her churning stomach a little. Miranda knew he'd make her suffer for what she'd done but it was worth it if Sadia remained free.

'You can leave us, Hassan. You have things to organise and Ms Fadel and I have matters to discuss.'

The other man turned away, his footsteps silent.

That was a feat Sheikh Zamir had managed too. She tried to ease her tension by telling herself it was something they must teach in Qu'sil. Yet her heart beat too fast and she felt the panicked urge to run from his gimlet stare.

When her nerves had finally reached screaming point he spoke.

'Sit.'

He gestured to a low divan while he sank onto its mate near the window.

Miranda was tempted to say she preferred to stand but her wobbly knees might give way. She refused to let him see how stressed she was.

For a second she considered making a run for it. But where would she go? Besides, for all his air of stately command, she'd come in close contact with his fit, powerful body. He'd reach her before she escaped the room. Plus there was his hulky bodyguard. She'd never evade them both.

On stiff legs she crossed to the divan and sank creakily, every joint stiff. She hadn't slept last night, had spent the previous day travelling back to Aboussir, and stress had finally hit her like a sledgehammer.

Stress and fear. She was about to face the consequences of her actions.

She recalled, almost with fondness, the way her uncle used to rant at her reckless actions as a kid. He'd bluster and lock her in her room and take away privileges. But this was different. She was no longer a confused kid and, apart from his disapproval, this man was nothing like her uncle. He didn't rant, just surveyed her with a hooded, intense gaze that made her wonder exactly what the legal penalty was for kidnapping a sheikh.

Miranda tried to divert her morbid thoughts. 'He works for you, I take it?' Her voice was unsteady. 'How did he find you?'

For a second she thought he wouldn't answer, then his mouth flicked up at one corner in cool amusement.

'What you didn't realise when you tossed my phone was that the car was one supplied by His Majesty the Sheikh of

Aboussir for today's ceremony. All royal vehicles are fitted with GPS trackers, though it took some hours before Hassan learned that and was able to follow.'

A while. How long?

She looked at the patch of sky beyond his broad shoulder. It was almost dark. Surely there was no time to return to the city and force Sadia into marriage.

'You claim you acted alone. You also claim your sole purpose was to prevent your cousin being forced into marriage.' He grimaced on the word *forced*. 'What about the other consequences of your actions?'

'Other consequences?'

Wasn't it enough that she'd stopped the wedding?

She *hoped* she'd stopped the wedding. When the Sheikh didn't arrive there'd be uproar and in the aftermath Sadia would hopefully persuade her parents it would be better if she left until the scandal blew over.

The Sheikh leaned back against a row of silk cushions and it struck Miranda as ominous that he didn't seem in a rush to leave.

Given the luxurious setting and his semi-reclining pose, he should have looked like a louche sybarite. But those hawkish, handsome features were too intent, too focused.

He'd always attract women. No doubt he had them queuing for his attention, not simply because of his wealth and power but because of his undeniable charisma. It horrified her that she noticed. More than noticed. She felt an undercurrent of sexual awareness tug her lower body.

Miranda froze, pulse skittering at her body's betrayal. It was so wrong. The man was her enemy.

'The crown of Qu'sil.'

She shook her head, trying to focus on his words. 'Sorry? What about the crown of Qu'sil?'

One hand lazily stroked a crimson silk cushion but there

was no softening of his expression. 'The fact that I need to marry in order to become Sheikh.'

Miranda started. 'I don't understand.'

Silence reigned. A silence in which those black eyes bored into hers as if reading every weakness, every doubt.

'Who persuaded you to kidnap me? It must be someone with political ambitions to control my country.'

'Not that again. I told you I acted alone.'

'You'd have me believe it's sheer bad luck that, because of you, I'll be unable to become Sheikh of Qu'sil, the position I've trained for since the age of ten?'

She scowled. 'But you *are* the Sheikh.'

Slowly he shook his head. 'I'm acting in the role, have been since my uncle's illness took a turn for the worse. But I'm not officially Sheikh yet. Nor will I be unless I marry.'

'Oh.' She sat back, her mind spinning. 'So today's wedding wasn't just about taking over Aboussir too.'

It was amazing how eyes so dark could glitter so brightly. Yet despite his banked fury, his voice was cool. 'You make me sound like a power-hungry desperado, instead of the man chosen by both nations to be leader.'

That was news, but then Miranda had been living overseas, not following politics here. All she knew was what Sadia had told her. Which, she began to realise, wasn't much.

'So, you need a bride to become Sheikh.'

It seemed implausible but he clearly wasn't joking. Hauteur turned his features grim. Grim, coldly angry and still undeniably sexy.

Miranda shivered and told herself she was imagining things. Maybe she was sickening with something. A fever might explain the heat coursing through her body, the trembling, the fact that even now, about to face whatever punishment he meted out, she couldn't keep her tongue between her teeth. If she could pretend to be meek and biddable, or at least apologetic, things might go more easily.

Who was she trying to kid? Easy wasn't in this man's lexicon. And to be duped by a lone woman, that must be a blow to his precious pride. She wasn't naïve enough to expect mercy.

A taut smile curled his mouth. He spread his arms wide, resting them on the back of the cushions, the image of ease. Except for those burning eyes.

'Fortunately I have a back-up plan, since time is of the essence.'

'It is?'

Why was he sitting, telling her this when he could be driving back to the capital? The more she pondered, the less she liked this situation. Her nape drew tight, prickling with foreboding.

But how could this situation get worse? She'd already been caught red-handed.

'Yes, a new Sheikh of Qu'sil must be married or, if not, must wed within three weeks of their predecessor's death or abdication.' His smile deepened yet Miranda discerned no amusement in it. 'To secure the succession, you understand.'

Mutely she stared back. She wished he'd just tell her what her punishment was and get it over.

'Today is my deadline.'

His words fractured her thoughts. She blinked, turning them over, trying to read another meaning into them. 'You mean,' she said slowly, understanding dawning, 'you have to marry *today*? Or you can't be Sheikh?'

He inclined his head, his mouth flat.

Miranda's eyes locked on the sky through the window, now turning indigo.

What had she done?

It was one thing to save her cousin. She couldn't regret that. But had she changed the course of politics? Could she have denied this man the chance to rule his country?

Last night she'd tried to discover what he was like as a person. She'd got the impression he'd played a key part in his country's recent successes and modernisation. He was supposed to be capable and powerful. He didn't suffer fools and he had a reputation for aloofness but also competence.

She waited for him to say she misunderstood.

He didn't. He sat there, still and dour and judgemental, and her heart sank.

'You're serious.' She swiped her tongue around dry lips and swallowed. 'I had no idea. I'm sorry. I—'

'It doesn't matter whether you're sorry.' He didn't raise his voice. He spoke softly and low yet the sound chilled her to the marrow. 'What matters is fixing this before it's too late.'

'You're serious? You really do have a back-up plan?' She frowned. 'Why are you here talking to me? Why aren't you heading back to do whatever needs to be done?'

'There's no need.' She heard a thread of satisfaction in that deep voice. 'The final scene in this catastrophe will play out right here.'

'Your man, Hassan. He's organising it?' Whatever it was.

'Very astute of you, Ms Fadel. He is indeed. In another hour it should all be done.'

She racked her brains. 'You're marrying here?' She looked around the room that hadn't been redecorated in decades. Once luxurious, it was faded and dusty.

'It's appropriate given the connection with my bride's family.'

Miranda shot to her feet, wobbling on unsteady legs. 'You're going to force Sadia, even after all this? Even knowing she doesn't want to marry you?'

No mistaking the flash of distaste on his aristocratic features.

That was why he'd taken the time to explain it to her. He wanted her to understand what was happening and know she'd failed.

He got to his feet in a single, graceful movement that brought him too close for comfort, yet she refused to step back.

'It was agreed I'd marry into the royal family of Aboussir. That's why your cousin Sadia was chosen. And before you make any more accusations let me reiterate there was no force involved. I asked and she accepted.'

Miranda snorted. 'You might have chosen Sadia but she didn't choose you. As for asking her, what choice did she really have?'

Dark eyebrows shot high on that bronzed face. 'Your cousin is an adult and perfectly capable of saying no.'

He'd touched a nerve. Miranda would never have allowed herself to be railroaded into a marriage. But Sadia was completely cowed by her father.

'As if! With her father breathing down her neck? You've no idea how he's always bullied her and how little autonomy she has.'

His eyes widened and she thought she read shock, even dawning horror there. But the impression was gone before she could be sure. '*If* you're to be believed. For all I know you had your own motives for the kidnap. Jealousy, maybe, that *you* weren't chosen as a royal bride.' Miranda gasped, stunned at the notion. She itched to set him straight but knew it would be pointless. 'But you're nothing like your cousin.' He sneered. 'At twenty-three you're so confident that you've already embarked on a career of criminality and kidnap.'

Her mouth snapped shut, her conscience in flames. Until she processed everything he'd said. 'How do you know my age?'

'Hassan and his team brought phones. We've done a little research, confirming your identity among other things.'

She didn't know which she disliked more. The idea of them poking into her private life, or that Hassan had brought reinforcements. No doubt the place was surrounded, so any fragile hope of escaping grew more tenuous.

She drew a shuddering breath and shoved her hands behind her back, clasping them where he wouldn't see how they shook. 'Sadia is on her way here, then.'

'No. I've made other arrangements.'

Miranda sagged in relief.

Annoyingly, this man made it sound as if he had a bevy of willing women ready to marry him.

But then his wife would have riches, luxury and status. Some women would see a loveless marriage to a cold-hearted man as a small price to pay for all that. It would have destroyed Sadia, who'd already suffered at the hands of her dictatorial father.

'You've changed your mind about marrying into the royal family?'

Yet in that case, why keep her here to witness the event? Why not send her off to prison now?

He folded his arms, the movement emphasising the power in his tall frame. Miranda shivered again, remembering how it had felt to be pinned against him.

To her consternation, the memory wasn't wholly negative.

'I've already explained it's vital I marry into your Sheikh's family.'

Miranda scowled at him, mind racing as she mentally flicked through the leaves of the family tree. She didn't know all the distant relatives as well as she might because she'd spent so long overseas. How many unmarried females of marriageable age were there?

'It's not my bride coming here, it's the cleric who'll officiate at the wedding and a representative of her family to witness it.'

Revelation was a glare of searing light even as Miranda's vision darkened at the edges. Her breath rattled and she had to drag in more oxygen before attempting to speak.

He beat her to it. Gleaming eyes held hers. He didn't bother concealing his mockery.

'I see you finally understand. How fitting that my bride should be the woman who tried to steal my throne from me and destroy everything our governments have worked for. Who caused this mess in the first place.'

He leaned in so she inhaled that intriguing aroma of cedarwood and virile man.

'*You* will be my bride. We'll marry in an hour.'

CHAPTER FOUR

MIRANDA WANTED TO protest he couldn't mean it. It was impossible that they'd marry.

But the implacable light in those dark eyes spoke of sombre determination.

Even so she heard herself saying, 'I'm sorry. Really sorry about that glitch in your plans.'

Not for disrupting the marriage to Sadia but…

He stood so near she *felt* the vibration of his deep voice as a ripple through her belly. 'It's too late for apologies. The damage is done.' His nostrils flared as if he reined in impatience. 'You should have thought before you acted.'

Her shoulders hunched high at the familiar refrain.

Her uncle had spent years castigating her for being thoughtless, impulsive, a disappointment. Even when she tried to live up to family expectations, feigning interest in domestic skills that bored her to tears. Trying to hide her exuberance behind a prim façade that always cracked.

'But I didn't know about your coronation. I was just trying to save my cousin.' His jaw flexed on the word *save* and she hurried on. 'Surely there's another way—'

'If there were another way, I'd take it.' She felt the waft of his breath on her face. He spoke slowly, branding every word deep. 'I wouldn't be in this ruin waiting for a makeshift wedding I don't want. And—' his stare skewered her '—I definitely wouldn't choose to marry someone like you.'

His venom was understandable, yet she winced inwardly at his lashing disapproval. She was stunned to discover that, far from wearing it as a badge of honour, she didn't like it.

Why should it matter what he thought of her?

Miranda had a lifetime's experience of disapproval and had learned to appear unmoved despite how that hurt.

Her foreign mother hadn't fitted into this country so her daughter had had little chance of being accepted. When Miranda's father had died young she'd spent years shuttling between visits to her mother, in whichever country she was working, and here. Miranda had never fitted anywhere, especially in conservative Aboussir. She'd never blended in.

Surely that was the key to her salvation now.

Instead of retreating, she stood her ground. As if dealing with a furious sheikh, who looked as if he'd rather toss her into a dungeon than marry her, were no more difficult than breaking in a spirited horse.

She must be woozy from stress and dehydration. For a moment her wayward brain actually wondered how Sheikh Zamir would respond if she stroked his lean cheek and whispered that he was a good boy, as if he were a highly strung stallion.

How would that square, bronzed jaw feel against her palm? Would the animosity in his eyes soften to something else?

Miranda ducked her head, biting her lip to hold back a bubble of hysterical laughter. And something that wasn't laughter. A sensation low in her body that made her want to shift restlessly and press her thighs together. She blinked and cleared her throat.

When she looked up again, his disapproving scowl had been replaced by a look that might almost hint at concern. It caught something high in her chest. For two whole seconds, as he surveyed her and she couldn't look away, heat crept along her chilled bones.

The feeling was so unfamiliar Miranda actually debated feigning illness. Anything to escape this situation and this man.

She'd never fainted in her life but if he believed her to be ill, he'd have to drop his farcical plan.

Or maybe whoever he brought in to officiate wouldn't care if the bride was comatose. This wasn't a normal marriage but a dynastic necessity.

Besides, Miranda wasn't that good an actor. More importantly, she had too much pride to pretend. Whatever happened, she wanted to be awake and aware.

'Of course you shouldn't marry someone like me. I'm totally inappropriate.' The words tumbled out so quickly she had to catch her breath. 'I'm rash and reckless. It would be a disaster if you married me.'

No one in their right mind would think her a suitable royal bride. Even she couldn't imagine it.

One expressive eyebrow climbed that broad forehead. 'True. But not as much of a disaster as if we don't.'

Miranda shook her head. 'You don't understand! I'd be a complete embarrassment. Even if I didn't mean to do the wrong thing, I would.' She saw no softening in his expression. 'Just look at me!' She gestured to her ill-fitting and now dusty uniform.

'Since you insist.'

With deliberate slowness his gaze travelled to her short, dishevelled hair, then down her body, not missing anything, before lazily rising again, igniting Catherine wheels of fire that twisted and flared under her skin.

Miranda had never experienced anything like it. She *knew* he'd done it to discomfort her and he'd succeeded. But his languid survey had been so thorough her flesh burned in mortification.

Not because there had been anything overtly sexual in that look. On the contrary, he might have been sizing up a horse he was considering acquiring, or a sports car, assessing whether it would meet his rigorous standards.

No doubt she failed those standards miserably. Not just because of the borrowed uniform. Her body compared unfavourably with the lush curves of her beautiful cousin. She'd never be the demure, self-effacing yet competent sort of woman that, according to her uncle, men sought in a wife.

But the horrifying fact remained that this man's slow perusal ignited sensations that were more than mortification. They felt like…arousal. Unwanted and inexplicable, especially given his obvious contempt.

She firmed her mouth and glared, hating the way he'd dragged old insecurities to the surface in such a short space of time then piled on new ones to torment her.

The man was dangerous.

'It's not an attractive outfit,' he murmured, 'but clothes are easily changed.'

Miranda scowled. Was he being deliberately obtuse?

'As for embarrassing me by doing the wrong thing…' He shook his head. 'No chance of that. I have no intention of letting you run amok without supervision. I've seen the damage you can do. You'll be closely monitored at all times.'

She swallowed, discovering her throat was tight and gritty. Anger and lack of water, she told herself. Not hurt.

After all, he just echoed what she'd said. What was obvious to anyone. Sooner or later Miranda always messed up and let people down.

Zamir watched her colour fluctuate and her eyes turn glassy. Just like a few moments ago when he'd felt an unaccustomed scrape at his conscience, as if he'd gone out of his way to hurt her.

He shifted his weight, not liking the feeling.

Was he being deliberately cruel?

This woman had all but destroyed every carefully laid plan not only for his marriage but his accession to the throne. And she'd done it with all the finesse of a shotgun blasting through flesh straight to his ego.

Beyond her obvious crimes, what really rankled was her appalled, dismissive tone when she'd spoken of his plan to marry her cousin. She'd acted as if he were some monster!

The notion left an unpleasant, metallic tang in his mouth.

Had Sadia really detested the idea of marrying him?

Never for one second had that occurred to him. Sadia had been sweet if quiet on the two occasions they'd briefly met. She'd shown no hint of reservations about their marriage.

Arranged matches had been the norm in royal families for generations. He'd assumed that she, like he, accepted the arrangement as a duty. The idea that she was so desperate to avoid their marriage she'd turned to her cousin in distress… Why hadn't she told *him*?

Despite the desperate urgency of today's events, that notion made Zamir feel wrong inside. He'd spent his life building himself into the man his people needed. Reliable. Decisive. Honourable.

Now this silver-eyed adventuress not only disrupted his plans but made him feel… Less.

Yet despite his justifiable annoyance, he didn't like the hurt he'd glimpsed in her either. But Miranda Fadel's feelings weren't his priority. He had a nation to think of. Two in fact.

He felt better when her chin tipped up again and her eyes narrowed. He preferred her argumentative to that suspicion of vulnerability.

'Even with the right clothes and the right minders, I wouldn't make a suitable wife.' Her voice was husky. With emotion, or was that her natural tone? Why did he even notice? 'I'm restless and impatient. I don't like sitting for long periods. I'd be no good at…' She waved one arm. 'Whatever royal wives do.'

'On the contrary, that energy will be useful. Being royal is rarely about sitting in one place for long.'

Zamir refused to let his thoughts stray to other directions where he could channel her restless energy. Yet he felt a stab of awareness in his tightening groin.

It was inexplicable. Miranda Fadel was a pest, a sow's ear that he'd have to turn into a silk purse and present to the public as a suitable wife. Because she'd left him no choice.

She was a thorn in his side and this spark of awareness must be the result of instant dislike. She was defiant and brash. She was Trouble with a capital T.

Yet he couldn't deny a piquant fascination at the prospect of knowing her better.

His breath banked up in his lungs and the torsion in his belly grew as he remembered her body against his, breasts and hips and slender thighs moulding to his harder frame. Her sweet breath against his throat and the vibrant energy that seemed innate to her sparking off something in him, reminding him that he was first and foremost a man.

A man who'd been celibate too long while he shouldered the burdens of the sheikhdom as his uncle declined.

'You don't understand.' Her eyes flashed and it struck him that, for a woman who should be pleading and persuasive, she was crackling with impatience. 'I don't...' She shook her head. 'It's not just the clothes, though I warn you I don't even own a dress. It's me. I'm not...'

'Not what?'

Zamir was intrigued to find her lost for words. She had no hesitancy spelling out *his* supposed flaws.

A knot formed in the centre of her forehead. 'I'm not...' Her voice dropped. 'Feminine enough.'

Of all the objections she might have raised, that hadn't occurred to him. Not feminine enough? Even when she spat fury he couldn't help noticing the provocative, natural pout of her lush mouth. The way, when she smiled, albeit sarcastically, her lips curved a little downwards, and appeared all the more kissable.

Then there was the memory of her definitely feminine body against his.

'Women in my uncle's family are expected to blend into

the background. Not voice strong opinions or make their own decisions. Not wear their hair short or work in jeans. They're supposed to look and be—' she gestured vaguely with one hand '—sweet yet alluring, as if butter wouldn't melt in their mouths.'

Zamir couldn't prevent his huff of amusement. The notion of her sitting quietly, never voicing an opinion, was too much.

To his amazement he saw a flash of hurt cross her face. Did she think he couldn't imagine her as an alluring woman?

It seemed impossible. If she lost the pugnacity he could readily imagine her cutting a swathe through any men in her vicinity. Those stunning eyes alone were mysteriously enticing.

Before he could respond, she continued. 'Then there's the issue of my birth.'

'Pardon?' Zamir didn't recall anything about that, but then his research into her background had been necessarily brief.

'I could never be a king's consort.' She paused then went on quickly. 'I'm what my uncle calls half-blood, didn't you know? Only my father is from Aboussir.'

Zamir inhaled sharply. 'That's not a term I use, nor anyone in my court.' He shook his head. 'Qu'sil is a melting pot of people from many places. For centuries it's been a crossroads for trade routes between east and west, north and south.'

She stared back stonily, as if unconvinced. 'Perhaps Qu'sil is different from Aboussir but I think it unlikely.'

Zamir was angered that her own family had considered her less because of her parentage. He felt his jaw firm.

'You're related through your father to a royal Sheikh. You're a member of his family.'

'But my mother was an American singer.'

He inclined his head. 'Whose own mother was Swedish. That's an asset, an instant link with the US, one of our key trading partners, and with a significant European country.'

She opened her mouth then closed it again, as if bereft of words. For a blessed few seconds, silence reigned.

He should have known it wouldn't last.

'You're twisting things. Trust me, you really don't want to do this. It would end in disaster and if you think the Sheikh of Aboussir would approve, you're wrong. He wouldn't want me representing the country. I'm the relative the family prefers not to mention.'

Zamir had heard enough. 'You're wasting your breath. This is happening as soon as the appropriate person arrives to officiate.'

He heard, as if conjured by his words, the distant throb of a chopper's rotors. Just in time.

'You created this mess, Ms Fadel, so you'll help resolve it. Don't look for a reprieve from me. I'm simply doing my duty and it's time you stepped up and did yours.'

Her face flushed and her eyes sparked. 'But you don't want me and I definitely don't want you!'

He'd have labelled her reaction childish, except there was nothing childlike about her. Even in that badly fitting uniform she was all vivacious woman. How had he, even for a moment, been taken in by her disguise?

The fact that his lack of attention had contributed to this appalling situation only added to his disgruntlement.

'You think I *wanted* to marry your cousin Sadia?' He paused, watching her eyes widen. 'This isn't about what I *want*, or about what *you* want. It's about what needs to happen for the sake of our countries. Therefore it *will* happen. And as for your Sheikh not approving of you as my bride…' He strode to the window to see the helicopter landing. 'Who do you think arranged for the cleric who has just arrived from the palace?'

Miranda's heart fluttered high against her throat. Her mouth dried. 'The Sheikh knows?' She waved both hands wide in a gesture that encompassed the musty room. 'He knows about this? About me and—'

'He does. And he agrees it's the only solution.' Sheikh Zamir looked down his imperious nose. 'I'm not the only one with a vested interest. He and my uncle instigated arrangements for the original marriage, and for the union of our nations.'

Miranda shook her head, trying to take it in. 'But surely he doesn't approve of me as a replacement for my cousin. As a representative of his family and our country.'

True, the Sheikh himself had never specifically voiced his disapproval of her, but her close relatives, particularly her uncle, had made it clear that she let the family down in multiple ways and was only accepted out of family loyalty.

'On the contrary, he thought it an excellent solution. Which is why he's sent the appropriate people to ensure the wedding goes as it should.'

Miranda barely heard anything after his first few words. The idea of her stepping into the limelight as a royal bride was impossible!

But she heard the helicopter and knew he wasn't lying. He had the smug arrogance of a man about to get his own way.

The roar of the chopper melded with the roar of her thundering pulse and she shuffled her feet wider, trying to steady shaky limbs.

'No one will believe it. Royalty marries in front of a huge audience, not in the middle of nowhere.'

Dark eyebrows rose in a look of almost pitying superiority. 'Your cousin didn't tell you? I and my country are in mourning for my uncle so the ceremony was to be private. There will be time for a public celebration later, after the period of mourning is over and I'm crowned.' He paused, his gaze piercing. 'All we need today is the actual, legal ceremony.'

'Oh, if that's all then clearly there's no problem. Unless you count a forced bride!' Miranda's hands landed on her hips.

'You really think you have the right to do that? It's illegal. It's wrong. It's—'

'Happening.' His gaze pinioned her to the spot. When he spoke again his voice was silky with threat. 'I *will* marry today, and my bride *will* be from your family. There's no other option.'

As she looked into that unblinking gaze, Miranda's stomach dropped. She'd intended to refuse his outlandish scheme, no matter how he blustered. After growing up in her uncle's household she had no desire to put herself under the control of a powerful man.

Except she suddenly recalled one obvious fact that in her stress she'd overlooked. Sadia had a younger, unmarried sister. If Miranda refused to cooperate there was still time to fly Amal here before the Sheikh's midnight deadline.

All the fight bled out of Miranda. She couldn't save Sadia and then let Amal potentially take her place.

An inner voice protested that the Sheikh hadn't mentioned Amal. Surely he wouldn't stoop to that. But the truth was she didn't know him. She had no idea what he was capable of.

You're the one who created this situation. You'll have to be the one to step up.

'I despise you,' she whispered in a voice rough with anger.

Those gleaming eyes narrowed and his mouth tightened, but of course something as negligible as her hatred wouldn't sway him. If anything his hauteur only increased.

'You are entitled to your private opinions.'

'You surprise me. Are you sure you're not going to monitor those as well?'

His glare was formidable yet, unlike her uncle, he didn't let his fury leak out. That surprised her.

'As long as they're private, not expressed in public, you're free to believe what you wish.'

As if he had the ability to dictate her thoughts!

She seethed.

'You'd really marry a woman who can't stand you?' Miranda tilted her head, trying to discover what was going on behind that hard, handsome face. Then a thought struck her and dazzling hope rose, making her dizzy. 'But it won't matter, will it? Once all the fuss dies down and the two countries are joined we can quietly divorce.'

She hadn't even finished when he shook his head. 'No divorce. So if you're thinking of trying to get out of this by making a scandal, think again. Our union is a symbol of the union of our countries. Because of that you're needed by my side. You'll remain my wife.'

Miranda opened and closed her mouth but words wouldn't come. It had been her last hope. Even now, in the distance she heard muffled noises. The others had arrived.

This was real. They were going to marry.

It didn't feel real. Her vision blurred and she felt a curious, sweeping sensation in her stomach. Despite her locked knees, the floor seemed to ripple beneath her feet.

Large hands grasped her elbows and he was there, in her private space, towering above her. His eyes looked blacker than ever but instead of familiar disapproval she imagined a softer expression.

'You need to sit.'

She shook her head then regretted it when the world spun. He was right but she refused to acknowledge it. 'I need water. I haven't had anything to drink since I collected you from the hotel.'

'You what?' His voice rose. Funny, when she'd insulted him his voice had gone soft and lethal, not loud. 'Don't you know how dangerous it is to dehydrate in this climate?'

Miranda rolled her eyes as he sat her down into a chair. 'Duh! Of course I know. I was born here. But when we arrived I was concerned about you. I was getting water for you when you ambushed me and—'

'I understand.'

To her amazement she saw colour streak his chiselled cheekbones as if he were embarrassed. For not offering her water after she kidnapped him? It didn't seem possible. It wasn't as if she'd asked for a drink and he'd refused.

Miranda had the creeping suspicion that Sheikh Zamir was more complex than she thought.

'Don't move.' He crossed to the door in a few long strides. 'And don't think of trying to run away. You'd just embarrass yourself.'

He didn't stop to see her reaction but disappeared without a second glance. Naturally Miranda took the opportunity to push up out of the chair, only to fall back.

She told herself she was weak from dehydration. Stupid not to have drunk all day. But it was more than that. Stress, shock and the deep voices from just down the corridor made her, for once, give in. She slumped, defeated, knowing she didn't have the strength to escape.

Defeat was a rusty tang on her tongue.

It was only when his high and mightiness strode back into the room, bringing a tall glass of water and an air of crackling energy, that she straightened her spine and conjured the appearance of aloof disdain.

'Thank you.'

Miranda took the glass carefully so as not to touch his fingers, then drank thirstily, not deigning to meet his eyes. If she was going to be a queen she might as well borrow some of his arrogance. The thought brought a disbelieving laugh and she choked on a mouthful.

Her gallows humour vanished when he moved closer. 'I'm fine.'

She threw up her hand to ward him off, catching his unreadable stare. Just as well. Who would want to get inside this man's thoughts?

'The cleric and witnesses are here. The marriage will take place in the largest sitting room.' His tone was so bland he might have been commenting on the latest stock market figures. Not their *marriage*. How could he be so unmoved by it? 'It's still a sumptuous room, despite the neglect. It will make a good background for the photo.'

'Photo? You're going to take a photo?'

'Just one. To show the happy bridal couple.'

Because it was important to him to share the news the marriage had taken place.

He frowned down at her as if seeing her properly for the first time. She was exhausted, no doubt washed out from stress and the unflattering beige uniform, her face bare of make-up, and not wearing a single item of jewellery. Even without a mirror, Miranda knew she looked nothing like a blushing bride.

She drained the glass then folded her arms. 'People will take one look at me and know there's something fishy about this marriage.'

Let him fix that! Her guess was that he'd arranged the legalities of this union but hadn't given a thought to her appearance.

She couldn't keep the sly satisfaction from her voice as she went on. 'Won't people think it odd that a prince should marry someone dressed as a chauffeur?'

For a second he surveyed her with what might, in another man, be dismay. Then he ordered, 'Undo your collar.'

He marched to a window and reached for a curtain that, even dusty, was lustrous with the sheen of dark blue silk, intricately embroidered with silver thread.

One powerful tug tore it free.

Miranda gasped. It was only a curtain, though an heirloom piece made by hand generations ago. Yet his abrupt, decisive action made her stomach clench.

Here was a man who leashed his emotions instead of flaunting them but who didn't hesitate to act. He was a man who made things happen. For some reason that unsettled her.

He shook the fabric vigorously then turned. 'That high collar's still done up.' He reached as if to rip it open, when she quickly did it herself.

'I don't see what difference the collar makes.'

He frowned, presumably realising his attempt at a makeover wouldn't work.

Then he reached out and flattened the fabric against her collarbone. His touch was light yet she froze and her breath grabbed high in her throat.

Eyes the colour of midnight filled her vision and for an instant she felt…

He flung the heavy silk over her, draping her head and settling it around her shoulders. Instinctively she reached for it as he crossed it over her open collar and breasts. Their fingers brushed and a curious sensation started in her fingers and shot to her stomach.

Instantly he withdrew, his expression as severe as carved stone. Clearly he hadn't felt that odd spark. To him she was just a mannequin to parade in this farce.

'Come. It's time.' He stepped aside and held his hand out. She looked down at his broad palm and remembered the feel of his body on hers.

She could have refused. She could have screamed that this was the biggest mistake of their lives. But his steady look, and the knowledge that her reckless plan threatened to derail the well-being of their countries, stopped her.

She was responsible for that, however unwittingly.

Slowly Miranda rose.

Fifteen minutes later it was done. They were married. The agreement—she couldn't think of it as a ceremony—was witnessed by Zamir's aide, Hassan, the man she'd believed to be a bodyguard, and by her Sheikh's secretary, a distant cousin who'd regarded her with cool courtesy.

A single photo was taken of the bridal couple, Zamir looked regal and imposing in his white robe and she, wide-eyed and solemn but surprisingly bride-like, courtesy of the rich lapislazuli silk with its exquisite silver embroidery. And the richly engraved and surprisingly beautiful golden wedding band on her finger.

Moments later the photo was sent out publicly with a caption that referred to a quiet wedding in the presence of members from both the bride and groom's families.

It was done.

Miranda was married.

To a man she'd never seen before today. A man she'd kidnapped and who had every reason to hate her. A man determined that she should move to his country and play the part of his queen.

If it weren't so unthinkable it might be laughable.

She could only hope she woke tomorrow to discover it had been a bad dream.

CHAPTER FIVE

ZAMIR HADN'T SPENT much time thinking about his wedding night. He'd been too wrapped up finalising the arrangements between both countries and handling the plethora of tasks that fell to him on his uncle's death.

Not to mention wrestling his deep-seated grief for the man who'd raised him and his siblings after his parents died. Zamir had been just ten, Umar and Afifa five and three respectively, so their uncle had been the only parent the younger ones really remembered.

But even if Zamir had had time to think about his first night as a married man, he'd never have imagined this.

It was near midnight and, instead of being tucked up in bed with his wife, he was in a chopper, flying home with a prickly, infuriating troublemaker. The one with eyes that flashed bright as honed steel when she was angry. Or turned misty, dull and haunted when she was worried.

A steel band tightened around his gut as he remembered how she'd looked during the short, all-important ceremony.

She'd clutched the rich fabric to her in a white-knuckled hand and, for a defiant criminal, had looked remarkably fragile. Her eyes had been huge, making her seem younger than the mid-twenties he knew she was.

Yet she'd looked far more than young and scared.

With that drab uniform hidden by gleaming silk, she'd looked…stunning.

The revelation had hit like a blow.

He'd been too distracted to notice earlier, too busy scrabbling to avert the disaster she'd created to see her properly as a person, not an enemy.

To see her as a woman.

Her jaw was more angular than soft, but that only highlighted the sultry pout of her full-lipped mouth.

That mouth. Her lips tilted down at the corners, creating apostrophe grooves in her cheeks when she was amused. They flashed like an invitation to share a private joke, undermining his impatience and making him want to lean down and taste her intriguing mix of obstinacy and disarming allure.

Zamir shifted restlessly, telling himself he was merely impatient to get home.

Yet he couldn't help surveying the woman beside him. Of course she wasn't asleep. She was too determined for that, staring into the night sky as if searching for trouble. He could almost hear the wheels racing in her brain as she assessed her new circumstances.

Was she aware of him watching her? Her shoulder lifted a fraction. Tension? An attempt to put a barrier between them?

Too late for that. They were husband and wife.

The reality slammed into him.

It was one thing to accept marriage to Sadia, the pleasant if quiet woman he'd met briefly.

He'd had no expectation, ever, of marrying for personal preference. A dynastic marriage had been inevitable, his duty to his position and his people.

But a hole-and-corner marriage to a meddling firebrand who was determined to be as difficult as possible…!

Zamir pinched the bridge of his nose, fighting the remnants of the migraine that still hadn't completely gone.

Her recklessness needed to be curbed. Boundaries set. Some sort of understanding reached. For, no matter their personal views on this marriage, it was real and they had to live with it.

Yet more things to add to his never-ending list of urgent tasks.

Zamir grimaced. He had a feeling everything else on that list, like amalgamating the laws and governments of two countries, would prove much simpler than transforming his bride into a suitable queen. He'd have to have her watched constantly and organise lessons on court customs, politics, deportment… no, not deportment. She already had the posture of an empress.

He slanted another look her way, lingering on her profile. She wasn't pretty like her cousin.

She was something more disturbing. His new bride was proud, innately graceful, and possessed a bone-deep elegance that he guessed would improve with age.

Zamir recalled the photo online of her stunning mother. His new wife had that same eye-catching allure, though she hid it beneath bad temper and aggression.

'It's rude to stare.'

She didn't even turn, just looked ahead towards the sprinkle of lights that marked the outskirts of Qu'sil's capital.

'I'm not staring. I'm taking stock.'

Slowly she turned and even in the dimly lit helicopter Zamir felt that distinct buzz of response as their eyes met. Earlier he'd put that down to annoyance. Now he wasn't so sure.

'Taking stock of your new acquisition?' Her top lip curled. 'I'm not a piece of livestock.'

No, she was something infinitely more problematic.

His wife.

The rotor blades slowed as Zamir disembarked and walked around the helicopter. Hassan had already opened the door for his new queen, standing alert in case she needed assistance to alight. Instead she sat, unmoving, gaze fixed unblinkingly ahead.

Zamir looked from Hassan to his wife.

Wife! A phantom punch to the solar plexus accompanied the thought.

'You can go, Hassan, and see to that one matter for me. We'll debrief later.'

Hassan nodded, turning the movement into a bow for both Zamir and the unmoving figure in the chopper.

When Hassan's footsteps died away Zamir moved closer, holding out his hand. 'Come, it's time to go.'

She didn't move.

He squeezed his eyes shut for a moment, trying to conjure patience at the end of one of the longest, most difficult days he could recall. Given what she'd done to him it was tempting simply to upend her over one shoulder and carry her inside. He was tired, his head thumped and another sleepless night beckoned as he arranged to make their hasty marriage appear as a personal and political triumph.

But despite her accusation about him forcing her cousin, Zamir preferred persuasion to force. Besides, when he opened his eyes it was to see her swallow hard, her throat working, her mouth pressed tight.

It wasn't just stubbornness that motivated her.

She'd reaped what she'd sowed, interfering in things that didn't concern her and paying the price. But Zamir knew things weren't usually so black and white, even if in his fury earlier it had seemed that way.

He softened his voice. 'I promise I mean you no harm.'

That jerked her head around, her pale gaze meeting his with the force of a lightning bolt. What was that sensation? Pity at the distress she tried to hide or something else? Something that stirred a decidedly masculine awareness?

'It's been a long day and we both need rest. Things will look better in the morning.'

She gave a strangled huff of laughter. 'You think so?'

'I know so.'

His experience of traumatic events, the loss of his parents to a tragic accident while he was still a child, and the loss more recently of his uncle, had proved that embracing each new day was the only way forward.

'Then you're more optimistic than me.' Her voice had a quality that brushed across his skin. 'But you haven't just had your life and freedom stolen away.'

Zamir drew another calming breath. He wouldn't snap back at her jibe. Though his life, as much as hers, had now changed in unwanted ways.

'You make it sound like a fate worse than death. Many women would envy you. Becoming Queen of Qu'sil is a privilege, not a penance.'

Her dark eyebrows arched high. 'That's debatable, since it comes encumbered with marriage to you.'

So much for détente. The gloves were off now.

'Fine. If you feel that way, stay here.'

He looked at the pilot, still wearing his headphones in an effort to give them privacy, running through his post-flight routine. Zamir had had enough of her effrontery for one night. He stepped away.

'I'll let you explain to the staff who find you here in the morning who you are and why you chose to sleep here instead of in your own suite.'

'My own suite?'

Her whisper made him pause. 'Of course your own suite.'

Hadn't she realised that, no matter how unorthodox the circumstances of their wedding, she was now his wife? Where did she think she was going to sleep? In a broom cupboard?

No, you fool. In your bed. That's where she'd thought she'd have to sleep.

The realisation sliced through him like a sharpened blade. Suddenly her obstinacy in not leaving the chopper took on a whole new meaning.

She'd thought he expected her to spend the night with him…

Zamir's gut spasmed.

He had as many flaws as the next man, though he did his best to rise above them. But as far as he knew no one had ever regarded him as an ogre. Or sexual opportunist.

'A suite by myself?'

He drew himself up straight, meeting her eyes. 'Absolutely.' Then, because he *was* as human as the next man, he added, 'You'll have your privacy. And I'll spend what's left of tonight dealing with the fallout of today's events.'

If he'd thought to make her feel guilty or apologetic, he'd been wrong.

'In that case, I'll come with you.'

Zamir suppressed a reluctant smile. She had the hauteur of a born queen, as if she were doing *him* a favour.

Which he supposed she was. If she were found here in the morning he'd have had to find an explanation for the inexplicable.

She shuffled forward in her seat then rose. Of course she ignored his outstretched hand and climbed out by herself. But her legs crumpled when she stepped onto the tarmac.

Swifter than thought, he swooped down to catch her. Her breath hissed but for once she didn't spit venomous words. Exhaustion, stress, and he suspected the remnants of the dehydration he should have noticed earlier, took their toll for the second time today.

He could support her all the way from the helipad, across two courtyards and into the palace proper. Or he could make it easier on both of them.

He swept her up against his chest, a bundle of enveloping blue silk and accusing mist-grey eyes.

'*Don't* tell me you can walk by yourself when clearly you can't.' He strode towards the palace. 'This will be quicker, which means we'll be rid of each other sooner. Besides, this way anyone who happens to be awake won't see a stranger in blue silk over a pair of men's trousers and boots. If you pull that silk over your feet any observer will only notice *us*, the romantic bridal couple.'

Her silence was loud with unspoken objections, though she did twitch the swathe of fabric to cover her boots.

He sighed. 'Can't we call a truce for now and resume hostilities in the morning? I'm sure you'll find me just as obnoxious then.'

A tiny, reluctant smile curved her mouth and Zamir was surprised by a responding tug low in his body.

As if he enjoyed making her smile.

He must be punch-drunk with exhaustion.

'And you'll find me as bothersome as ever.' For the first time he heard true lightness in her humour rather than sarcasm.

'I'm bound to make decisions you don't like,' he added.

'And I'm sure to make a fuss about them.'

Zamir nodded and, despite everything he'd been through, felt his mouth curl in a tight smile. 'It's good to know where we stand.'

'Absolutely. I've had enough surprises for today.'

'*You've* had enough surprises?' He shifted his hold, carrying her more securely as he took a short flight of steps down into a courtyard filled with fragrant citrus blossom. 'You should try being kidnapped.'

Her huff of breath was a waft of warmth against his chin. 'Remarkable as it seems, since you've made it clear I should be prostrate with gratitude at the honour you've done me, *this* feels like kidnap.'

Zamir shook his head as he carried her through a marble portico. 'On the contrary, you had a choice. It was your actions that led to this situation. And it was you who finally chose marriage.'

He felt her sharply indrawn breath as much as heard it. 'I don't call that choice, I call that blackmail.'

'I call it doing what was necessary to save the future of both our countries.'

'Because no one other than you could possibly rule them,' she muttered, all trace of humour gone.

'They could,' he conceded, 'but I'm the one who's been trained to do it. I'm the one the people and the governments trust. The one who can make it happen without civil unrest or partisan squabbles. Long-term peace and stability are more important than our personal preferences.'

For once she didn't argue. But Zamir knew she was far from conceding the argument. She was tense in his arms as if ready to assert herself at any moment.

As before, it surprised him that a woman who had so much sheer destructive energy should be so light in his arms.

He told himself he was pleased she kept silent as they crossed into the second large courtyard. He was tired of argument, yet those fleeting moments of mutual understanding as they baited each other had felt surprisingly good. Almost like the banter he shared with his siblings.

Except with this woman there was an undercurrent lacking in dealings with his family. An undercurrent of awareness. Sexual awareness.

Finally they reached the side entrance to the palace and there was Hassan, waiting in the shadows.

'No complications?' Zamir asked.

Hassan shook his head. 'Everything is as you asked. There was a maid waiting to look after your bride but I told her she wasn't needed tonight.'

'Thanks.'

With a nod Zamir dismissed him and headed towards the royal apartments.

His bride shifted in his hold, making him all too aware of her soft curves against him. 'Why send the maid away? Because I'm such an embarrassment?'

He looked down into her set features. She was far too ready to take offence.

'Admittedly your clothes would make the staff curious. But

the maid will see them in the morning when she clears them away. Don't worry,' he said when her expression changed to dismay. 'My staff are loyal and discreet, particularly those who work in the private apartments. There won't be gossip outside the palace about what you were wearing.'

Zamir turned a corner, approaching a familiar set of apartments. 'I asked Hassan to send her away because I thought *you* might be embarrassed, arriving in such an unconventional outfit.'

She stiffened and, looking down, he saw the unbelievable had happened. He'd managed to surprise this exasperating woman into silence.

CHAPTER SIX

MIRANDA'S SUITE WAS the size of a house. It contained a sitting room, dining room, study, media room, a walk-in wardrobe big enough to fit a three-seater sofa and copious hanging space, a hedonistic bathroom and the most romantic bedroom she'd ever seen. It combined decadent luxury with a pared-back elegance that made her breath catch.

Her stepfather, Matias, was wealthy but his sprawling Argentinian ranch house was nothing like this. Even the Sheikh's palace in Aboussir, which she'd visited, seemed fussy and outdated by comparison.

Miranda wanted to loathe it. Instead she was seduced by its comfort. The quiet. The unending hot water she used to try washing away her sense of unreality and fear. The lavish banquet laid out just for her that would have easily fed a family. She demolished half of it before tumbling into the cloud-soft bed.

A real queen would have pecked daintily at those delicacies. Whereas she, with her quick metabolism and active lifestyle, always needed plenty of fuel.

There were so many reasons she wasn't cut out to be royal. Why couldn't *he* understand that?

Her last thought before plunging into sleep was that Sheikh Zamir was the most infuriating, stubborn man on the planet.

For the first time in memory she woke late.

The sun was high, revealing she even had her own lap pool.

Its green and gold mosaic tiles evoked the graceful leaves of a date palm. Swimming in that sparkling water would be like taking a dip in a private oasis.

Miranda resisted temptation. Who knew when Zamir would want to see her? She preferred to be fully clothed when they next met. She suspected it inevitable he'd compare her streamlined frame with Sadia's hourglass figure.

Usually Miranda didn't stress about her looks. She'd grown up in the shadow of a supremely beautiful mother and knew she wasn't in that league. Looks were irrelevant in her daily life.

Yet the idea of Zamir, with his austere charisma and his superiority, viewing her as second best compared with the bride he should have had—she didn't want to go there.

Muffled sounds drew her attention and she grabbed the ivory wrap that matched the lacy nightdress she'd worn last night.

Did Zamir have a store of sexy night things for visiting lovers?

She'd been loath to wear the seductive nightdress but had given in, preferring not to be naked. Using that grimy uniform again wasn't an option.

She refused to meet him in her bedroom. Tying the robe securely, she entered the sitting room.

'Madam. Good morning.' A woman in a tailored suit curtsied.

Curtsied! Any lingering hope Miranda had that last night had been some strange dream shattered.

Of course it was no dream. She was in Zamir's palace, wearing the exquisitely engraved, antique gold ring he'd produced at their wedding and slipped on her finger.

The ring he'd planned to give her cousin. But which, in a twist of mocking fate, fitted Miranda perfectly.

The ring she'd meant to remove last night then forgotten.

She put her hand to her throat, trying to still her racing pulse. 'Good morning. And you are?'

The head of housekeeping, it transpired. Here with Qu'sil's top fashion designer and an initial selection of garments. 'Just until your bespoke wardrobe is created.'

Bemused, Miranda stared at the women uncovering wheeled racks of clothes and trolleys piled with boxes. The sight was daunting for a woman who lived her life in jeans or jodhpurs.

Shopping had never been her favourite thing. Miranda had too many memories of her mother finding fault with what she chose then throwing up her hands in despair when the clothes she persuaded Miranda to try didn't suit her.

The housekeeper chivvied her staff. 'Quickly now. Madam has an appointment at midday.'

'Appointment?' Dread settled in her stomach. She knew nothing about being a royal. Sheikh Zamir couldn't expect her to appear in public!

The woman nodded. 'The Sheikh is expecting you.'

Miranda's mouth set mutinously. She had no intention of dancing to his tune.

But there's no point avoiding him. There are things you need to discuss.

Didn't anyone else think it strange that Zamir should make an *appointment* to see his wife on the day after their wedding? But then everyone knew this wasn't a love match but a marriage of convenience.

Inconvenience, more like.

Swallowing her pride, she admitted, 'It would be good to have something suitable to wear.'

Another woman stepped forward, introducing herself as the designer.

'It's a great honour to dress you, madam. And it's such a welcome gesture.' At Miranda's querying look she went on. 'Choosing a new wardrobe designed and made in your new country.' Her smile was warm. 'That decision will be much appreciated here.'

That was the story Zamir was using to explain her need for clothes?

'I'm glad you think so.'

'Oh, it is. There's been a lot of investment in local industry lately but in fields like engineering and robotics. Not fashion or textile production. This will bring welcome interest to our work.'

Not much riding on her appearance, then. Only the hopes of an eager industry.

Miranda stiffened. She suspected she was going to be a disappointment. She knew nothing about fashion.

'I hope I do you proud.'

The designer surveyed her with a practised eye, as Miranda might assess a new horse. 'There's no doubt about that, especially given the way you carry yourself.'

Her posture? The last time she'd thought about that was as a child learning to ride, being told to sit up and keep her shoulders back.

'Now, if I may?' The woman clicked her fingers and a horde of helpers encircled Miranda.

Miranda strode up the wide corridor, thankful the directions to the Sheikh's office were simple.

On the way she nodded to staff who bowed or curtsied. That made her feel like a fraud. She didn't feel royal.

She was a pretender about to be caught out.

No, that was yesterday. Masquerading as a driver. Caught in an abduction. Creating an international incident.

And paying the price.

Still it didn't seem believable. Even wearing this bejewelled tunic of silk so soft it fluttered against her like the touch of butterfly wings. And silver-grey trousers of equally fine silk.

Clothes fit for a queen.

Miranda had seen herself in the mirror and for a second hadn't known herself. She looked so…put together. Glamorous even. The chartreuse green was a colour she'd never worn. The style comfortable yet chic. The stylist had insisted she ditch the stud earrings she always wore and by that stage Miranda had given up objecting. Her new earrings of matching beaded silk and silver looked like delicate, hanging lilies and made her neck seem long and graceful.

Or maybe she just wasn't used to seeing herself in something other than jeans and a work shirt. When she'd insisted on wearing trousers, seeking confidence in familiarity, she'd had no idea she could look like *this*.

She even wore make-up, so light it was almost invisible, but enough to make her eyes look larger and her jaw softer.

Miranda didn't want to be soft. Her weakness yesterday horrified her, even if it had been from dehydration and shock. Today Zamir would discover she was no pushover.

She rapped on the last door and, without waiting for a response, opened it.

'Miranda. Come in.'

It was the first time he'd used her name and it stopped her on the threshold. *Not* because that deep voice sent heat coiling through her middle. That was nerves, or maybe residual anger.

She just hadn't expected him to use her first name. It seemed too intimate for what they shared.

Mutual distrust. Anger. Annoyance. Regret.

And a sizzle of something that felt like electricity building before a thunderstorm.

He sat behind a desk with a neat pile of papers in one corner, a massive computer screen and an old-fashioned blotter on which rested a large parchment. The edges of the parchment were decorated with intricate calligraphy and as she watched, he used a gold pen to sign it with a flourish.

He screwed on the cap of the pen and dropped it, eyes holding hers.

Impossibly, he looked even more arresting than he had last night. So much for hoping stress had exaggerated that.

But Miranda lived and worked in a man's world. She wasn't easily intimidated, either by good-looking polo players who thought they were God's gift to women or by old-fashioned misogynists unused to women working in professional stables.

She pushed the door closed behind her and walked into the room, noticing how his eyes seemed to grow even darker as he watched her.

Was it the unfamiliar heeled sandals that made her hips sway? Or did she deliberately sashay? All she knew was that this wasn't her usual gait.

And the way Zamir surveyed her was unlike the way he'd looked at her yesterday.

Good. The sooner he realised she wasn't going to be meekly browbeaten, the better.

She reached the desk. 'Nice suit,' she murmured to fill the silence.

Not as nice as the body it covered.

Miranda blinked at the unwanted awareness thrumming through her.

So she liked wide, straight shoulders and strong arms. So what? A good body and a suave, bespoke suit weren't as important as a man's character.

'Thank you.' His mouth ticked up at one corner, making that sombre face far too attractive. 'Nice outfit. *Very* nice.'

He didn't ogle. She would have slapped him if he did. But his gaze holding hers ignited heat inside.

She shrugged, aware of the brush of thin silk and, even more, of her new lace underwear.

Maybe that was why she'd strutted into the room. She'd never worn anything against her skin that made her feel so innately feminine. Years living in her mother's shadow had made her defiantly uninterested in sexy lingerie. Instead of taking after her mother and becoming obsessed with her looks and clothes, Miranda had gone the other way, telling herself they didn't matter.

Yet suddenly she was glad for this morning's makeover. She felt not just feminine but assured in a way that was unfamiliar and which she liked very much. Especially when she saw Zamir's Adam's apple jerk.

'You wanted to see me?' She leaned in, resting hands on his desk, tilting her head so one dangling earring brushed her shoulder. Instantly she straightened. She was *not* trying to look coquettish.

'Yes. Take a seat.'

Miranda looked from the empty chair before his imposing desk to the seating area across the room. No way was she going to sit here being lectured like a pupil before a headmaster.

'Thanks, I will.'

Sauntering across the room, she chose an armchair with a view to the coastal city and the deep blue sea.

She took her time studying the collection of traditional ochre-coloured buildings and the cluster of high-rises, some of them clearly works of art.

All the while she waited for his explosion of temper.

Her eyes widened when he strode into her line of sight and dropped into a nearby chair. Partly because *he'd* come to *her*. Partly because that charcoal suit outlined what yesterday's robe had hidden. That the man had the powerful thighs of a horseman. He shifted in his seat and the fabric stretched over flexing muscles.

Miranda's mouth dried.

She couldn't understand it. She was around athletic men all the time. Matias's friends and clients were professional athletes and none affected her like this. She lifted her hand to her forehead, checking for a fever on the pretext of brushing a stray hair off her face.

'You slept well? The accommodation was comfortable?'

'I did, and it is, thank you.'

But I'm ready to go home. I want to end this charade.

Yet she wasn't so naïve. There was no easy way out. If there had been he'd have already taken it.

'How long do we have to do this?'

He frowned. 'Talk?'

'Stay married.'

Horizontal lines grooved his brow, but even scowling the man looked good. Yet another annoying thing about him.

'I told you there can be no divorce.'

Her voice rose a notch. 'But you were just saying that to scare me.'

'I'm not into empty threats. I told you the truth. This marriage is permanent. It has to be.'

And just like that her hope bled away, because Zamir looked as happy about it as she was. Which was not at all.

But Miranda never gave up easily. According to her uncle it was one of her besetting sins. 'Surely, after the fuss dies down, when everything is sorted—'

'We'll stay together. Our union is a vital part of our countries' amalgamation. A symbol.'

'I don't care about symbols. I care about my freedom. Look.' She leaned forward, spreading her hands palm up. 'I'm willing to go along with this for a while. It's a mistake thinking I can play the role of queen long term, but I'll do my bit while the amalgamation happens. A few months.' His expression remained stony. 'A year, max. I know I owe you because of the abduction. It was a desperate thing to do and it had unintended consequences and I'm truly sorry.'

'I'm sorry too. This isn't what either of us planned but we're here now and we'll make the best of it.'

She sat back, stung by his stony-faced rejection. She felt the blood drain from her face, panic plunging like a lead weight in her abdomen.

'Then I won't bother with your cooperation. I'll file for divorce myself.'

'Unfortunately that's impossible.' He raised his hand to stop her words. 'The law forbids it.'

'You have no divorce here?' She didn't believe it.

'We do, but not in the royal family. Royal marriages are arranged for reasons of state. All parties need to be sure there will be no turning back at a later date. There *can* be no divorce.'

Miranda's eyes bulged. 'You really mean it! We're trapped?'

'We are.'

Oh, Miranda, what have you got yourself into?

It was one thing to help Sadia escape an unwanted match. But to trap herself permanently…

She shivered and wrapped her arms around herself. It couldn't be true. It couldn't. Yet why would he lie about something she could check?

'So it's a life sentence.' Her tone was flat.

There'd be no assistance from her family or her distant relation the Sheikh of Aboussir, who'd given his approval. And Matias, while wealthy, didn't have the influence to free her from this.

'You're determined to make the worst of this, aren't you?' Zamir's frown was thunderous. 'Being my queen is a privilege, not a penance.'

'You said that last night but I'm not convinced.' She flicked her finger against her earring. 'Despite the charming fripperies that come with the position.'

Something shifted in his expression. Something that, for a fleeting moment, almost looked like amusement.

That yanked her from self-pity to outrage. She lunged forward in her chair, invading his space. She refused to be the butt of his amusement. 'This isn't a laughing matter.'

'For once we're in agreement. This situation will be catastrophic if we don't manage it properly.' He leaned forward too, so close she saw tiny flecks of light in his inky eyes. His warm breath feathered her as he spoke. 'For the record, any humour was self-directed. I've never in my life met a woman so determined to be unimpressed by me or my status.'

He shook his head slowly, holding her stare, and Miranda had the disquieting feeling that she couldn't pull back even if she wanted to, which, strangely, she didn't.

'It occurs to me, Miranda, that you'll be excellent for keeping my ego in check. If you don't drive me crazy in the process.'

His mouth quirked at the corner. It wasn't a smile, just the merest shadow of a hint of one. And it did something weird to her. Not just that fluttery feeling in her throat. It actually *did* lighten the pall of despair.

Like last night when, for a few precious minutes, they'd exchanged banter like equals. It had felt almost like camaraderie and made her wonder if buried behind the formidable authority and self-assurance was a man she could relate to.

You're seeing what you want to see because it's better than facing reality.

'Gratifying as the knowledge is, it's not the summit of my ambitions to keep your ego in check, or even to make your life difficult. There are other things I want from life.'

'Like what? Tell me, Miranda.'

She shook her head and made to sit back. Except a large hand covered hers and she stilled. She could easily have shaken off his touch. He barely gripped her, yet the sensation of skin on skin and the curiosity in those velvety eyes stopped her.

'Nothing glamorous or high profile. It's much more mundane.'

Zamir inclined his head. 'My role is high profile but most of the glamour is on the surface. It's hard work learning to be leader of a country. A lot of it's mundane, work behind the scenes that few ever know about.'

There it was again, that momentary feeling of connection. Of course it was nonsense. But what could it hurt to tell him? They were stuck with each other for now.

'I'm a horse trainer. I work mainly for my stepfather, Matias Garcia, in Argentina.'

'I've heard of him. He was a top polo player.'

Miranda nodded. 'He's still a phenomenal player but now he concentrates on the breeding side of the business.'

'And you help him?'

She could read no nuance in his tone but was used to people assuming her job was a sinecure while she lived off her stepfather's money.

She sat back so Zamir's hand fell away.

'I work with his animals but with others too.' As well as running initiatives aimed at changing and enhancing peoples' lives through riding and caring for animals.

'You must be very successful to work in such a renowned stable.' Her eyebrows rose at Zamir's comment and he shrugged. 'We're very proud of our horses. Polo has been played here for longer than anyone can remember. I really do know of your stepfather.'

That wasn't what had surprised her. It was Zamir accepting her work as valuable. Or was he saying that to soothe her?

Yet it was better than the casual dismissal she got from some people who believed a 'mere slip of a woman' was out of place in a top-notch stable.

'There are stables here. Excellent ones. Not just for myself but for the mounted ceremonial guard.' Miranda sat straighter, interest piqued. 'You're welcome to ride any time.'

'But not to work.'

Zamir's eyes narrowed. 'I doubt you'll have time to work once your royal duties begin.'

Miranda bit back a protest that she wasn't interested in royal duties. He knew that.

'And when will that be?'

'You'll have a full schedule from now on. It's imperative you learn about our country, customs and ceremonies.' He looked away. 'But you won't go out in public yet. The Queen never appears soon after the wedding.'

That dark gaze returned as his words sank in and heat blistered under her skin.

'You mean—' she cleared her throat, self-conscious but needing to know '—because I'm expected to be exhausted from sharing your bed?'

The trouble was, looking at Zamir, the picture of virility, Miranda found that too easy to believe.

Those wide shoulders lifted. 'Dynastic marriages are about securing the future.' By him getting her pregnant with an heir. 'It's an ancient tradition that should probably change. But it plays into our hands. It means we have time to mould you, ready to face public scrutiny.'

Miranda shot to her feet and across the room. 'I have no interest in being moulded.'

'Bad choice of words. Forgive me. It will give you time to learn about this place and your role so you don't feel daunted or threatened.'

Oh, he was good. Too good. He made this sound as if it were for her benefit, not his.

Yet she saw it made sense. She already felt a complete fraud. How much worse if she didn't understand what was happening around her?

Miranda swung around, clasping her hands behind her back and planting her feet wide. 'We need to get something straight. I have no intention, ever, of sharing your bed, much less bearing your child.'

A shiver started at her nape, tracked down her spine and burrowed down through her middle.

Zamir said nothing for the longest time. Nor could she read his expression.

'Time will tell. We both have sexual needs.'

His bluntness, the way he explicitly yoked their needs together, dried her mouth. Did he *know* about those tiny, forbidden thrills of awareness she suffered around him? The idea was humiliating.

'But,' he carried on before she could protest, 'let me clarify that I'd never force you.' His jaw hardened like honed steel. 'Sex without consent is despicable.'

She breathed out, relieved. Yet her tension remained. Because he'd agreed so easily and she couldn't trust him? Because of his annoyingly offhand 'time will tell' as if she didn't know her own mind?

Or because perversely she'd be happier if he wanted *her*, not just out of convenience but because he couldn't resist her? Because, after a lifetime of being a misfit, she still hated the feeling that she wasn't good enough?

Where had that come from? It was asking for trouble and she already had enough of that. This situation was already dire. She didn't need the complication of him desiring her.

Or of desiring him.

'You really think you're so irresistible I'll end up begging to share your bed?'

Miranda whipped up her scorn but beneath it felt an undermining shiver of fascination at the images the words conjured.

His expression didn't change but she'd swear there was a spark of something in those piercing eyes that matched her own unsettled roil of physical awareness.

'You're doing an excellent job of resisting my fatal charm so far.'

His tone was wryly amused, just short of smug, as if that were exactly what he thought. Miranda's hackles rose but she bit off the argument rising to her lips.

'For now,' he continued smoothly, 'let's concentrate on getting through the next few weeks. And I have a demand of my own.' He rose and paced towards her. Pride dictated she hold her ground, though her shoulders inched high as he neared. 'That you behave, or try to behave, as befits a queen. No deliberate sabotage.'

Reluctantly Miranda nodded. Despite her reluctance she *did* understand how delicate this situation was. There was nothing to be gained by trying to cause a scandal. All she wanted was her freedom. 'Okay.'

'Good.' He thrust out his hand. 'Here's to the beginning of trust between us.'

Trust? It would be a long time before he earned that. But she had a vested interest in not antagonising the man who held all the power here. Miranda reached out and felt his fingers close around hers. It was like connecting with an electrical charge. Energy fizzed through her palm and up her arm, making the fine hairs on her body stand to attention and her nipples tighten.

She made to break contact but his fingers firmed. 'One last thing, Miranda.' He leaned closer. 'Given your penchant for reckless acts, don't even think about trying to run away. You'd be stopped in short order and I'd rather save you embarrassment.'

Her breath seized, filling tight lungs.

Save himself trouble, more like.

Her chin tipped high. 'Am I to have gaolers, then?'

He rubbed his thumb over the ball of her hand, sending a cascade of sparks across her skin. How did he do that?

'No gaolers. But as my queen you'll have an escort when you go out. Bodyguards and, for official events, advisers or attendants.'

Gaolers, in other words.

Indignation flared. He was taking away her freedom.

It's already gone. The moment you agreed to marry, you put yourself utterly in his power.

For a second she felt overwhelmed and that scared her. Usually she was good at looking ahead, rising above barriers put in her way. But not today, not with this man.

It felt disturbingly as if he already knew her too well and anticipated her every move.

Nonsense. That was tiredness talking.

Miranda tugged her hand free and ostentatiously wiped her palm down her trousers, disappointment bitter on her tongue. 'So much for trust.'

She pivoted on her heel and marched out of the door.

CHAPTER SEVEN

'SO, WHAT'S SHE LIKE, my mysterious new sister-in-law?'

Zamir pushed his chair back from the desk and scraped his fingers across his scalp as he shifted his grip on the phone.

He should have known Afifa would be full of questions. Umar might be the documentary maker in the family with a nose for a story, but their little sister could be guaranteed to probe when Zamir least wanted.

'Not mysterious. I told you, she's from the Aboussi royal family but she's been living elsewhere.' He knew some of her background but there was more to learn. Another priority.

'Elsewhere?' Afifa asked.

'Argentina for the last few years but before that sharing her time between Aboussir and the USA, Canada and the UK.'

Was that why she was so different to her cousin? Where Sadia was quiet and placid, Miranda was feisty, reckless, occasionally aggressive, and disturbingly vulnerable.

Disturbing because those glimpses into her softer side played on his guilt at how he'd herded her into marriage.

Herded her? When she'd kidnapped him! And almost destroyed the diplomatic solution their countries had spent years planning.

Her audacity rankled, as did the fact he'd been easy prey to her scheme. No man appreciated such a blow to his pride.

Yet despite that, his curiosity stirred.

What had Miranda's life been like? Her Aboussi family

wasn't concerned about her well-being after the hasty wedding, just about limiting any stain on their good name.

Absurdly, Zamir had felt indignant on her behalf. If anyone had tried to coerce Afifa in that way, he and Umar would have moved heaven and earth to protect her.

He grimaced at the sour tang of remorse on his tongue.

No wonder Miranda viewed him as a villain. But he couldn't regret what he'd done. His people needed the long-term peace and prosperity that would come from joining the two kingdoms. What was one woman compared with that?

Even so, his conscience scraped at the memory of her expression when she'd capitulated and agreed to marry him. He'd been relieved when Miranda had finally acknowledged *she* was responsible to fix the crisis she'd created. Yet that had been mingled with distaste at needing to force her hand.

'She sounds interesting. But she's not the woman you'd planned to marry. This one's Miranda, not Sadia. What's the story, Zamir?'

'No story.' Not that he was ready to tell his little sister. 'Just a change of plan.'

Her laugh sounded rueful. 'You do that stonewalling tone so well now, Zamir. Just like our uncle. Have you perfected the glare he used when someone annoyed him? You know, head up and nostrils flared, eyes narrowed. His don't-bother-me-or-you'll-be-sorry look.'

Zamir stiffened, realising that his nostrils *were* flared and his chin up. He frowned.

'You make him sound like a bully.' His uncle had taken on three orphaned children and loved them like his own.

'We both know he wasn't.' Afifa's voice softened. 'He was special. But you know what I mean. He was charming and caring but occasionally, if someone abused his trust, he went into that superior royal Sheikh mode.'

'He was imposing,' Zamir amended. 'And proud. A sheikh has to have presence.'

'I know. But he has to be approachable too. As he got older and sicker Uncle became more impatient, which made him seem daunting. I'd hate to think that had rubbed off.'

Zamir was about to protest that their uncle had devoted the latter part of his life to the taxing negotiations that would bring Qu'sil and Aboussir together. That his final thoughts had been for the well-being of his people. But it was true that in his later years, especially when in pain, his generous nature had often been concealed behind a stern persona.

'What are you saying, Afifa? That I'm becoming an autocrat? I haven't even officially taken the throne yet!'

'Of course not. You've never been hungry for power. You take duty too seriously for that. But you've got that same drive to do what you believe is right, no matter what. I just hope you don't seem too overpowering.' Afifa paused. 'This change of bride happened quickly. She's not too overwhelmed, is she?'

A huff of laughter escaped as he remembered Miranda several hours ago, leaning across his desk, skewering him with a condescending glare.

She *should* be overwhelmed!

Instead Miranda was confident, challenging and incredibly sexy. From the moment she'd sauntered into his office, all lithe femininity and vibrant sensuality, he'd had trouble keeping the thread of his thoughts. Even his anger had dimmed. He'd found it hard to keep his eyes on her face not her body. She had a combination of flagrant femininity, raw energy and not quite understated sexuality that yanked his libido into full awareness.

He'd already become acquainted with her body. Those memories were vivid. But seeing her in clothes that tantalised with glimpses of her delicious shape had knocked the air from his lungs and left him groping for control.

'Zamir? You didn't answer me.'

'Overwhelmed?' he scoffed. 'Not likely. It would take a lot more to knock Miranda's confidence.'

Like being carried off to a new country where she knew no one.

Like being thrust into a role she didn't know and didn't want.

Like being married to a stranger.

Knowing that stranger had power over her freedom, her life.

Zamir's amusement ebbed. He couldn't forgive her actions but his resentment was tempered by the knowledge she suffered for it now.

'I like the sound of her already. You need someone strong to stand up to you. I only hope she has a sense of humour too.'

He got to his feet and walked to the window, taking in the view of the city, reminding himself he'd acted for the good of his people. He'd had the best motives.

Who had said the road to hell was paved with good intentions?

'She does have a sense of humour.'

He recalled those moments of banter last night when they'd shared dark amusement over their situation.

At the time he'd been reassured, telling himself the situation wasn't too dire if they could laugh over it. He'd enjoyed Miranda's wry humour, feeling they briefly shared an understanding. Since his uncle had become ill and Zamir had taken on more of his role, there were fewer people with whom he could truly relax.

'I'm glad. You need someone to remind you to unwind and since Umar and I are on different continents…'

'How's the study going?'

'Good, thanks. Don't try changing the subject. I'll be back for the coronation so I'll see for myself how things are then. But meanwhile, Zamir, this marriage. Will it be okay? Will *you* be okay?'

It was on the tip of his tongue to say *he* wasn't the one she needed to worry about, but he wasn't that foolish.

'I know you swallowed Uncle's view that an arranged marriage is best for a royal.'

Her voice softened and Zamir knew she was thinking of their parents. Though Afifa didn't really remember them, her belief that they'd been devoted to each other had comforted her when they died and had somehow grown stronger over the years. He and Umar had never contradicted her.

She'd already made him promise not to arrange a suitor for her.

'I want you to be happy, Zamir. I want you to be with someone who will appreciate you.'

Zamir remembered the way Miranda had looked at him as if he were something filthy, discovered on the bottom of her shoe. Because he'd told the truth, that as his wife she would have aides and security staff whenever she went out.

He knew women who'd delight in that proof of their importance.

Trust him to find a spouse who hated the idea.

'You know I married because it was necessary.'

The words spilled into silence that felt stark with regret. Afifa's regret. But her heart was in the right place. She cared for him, the big brother who'd been there through the years of nightmares and distress after their parents' deaths, and later through the growing-up years. He'd always provided a shoulder to cry on, a listening ear, or been a coach, telling her to get up and try again when she failed at something.

'But despite that,' he heard himself say, 'Miranda isn't just a convenient bride.'

'You *like* her?' Afifa sounded eager. 'Really like her?'

Zamir hesitated, caught between the need to reassure and innate truthfulness. It was as he pondered that, he realised there were aspects of Miranda's character he did like.

And her body. Don't forget her body.

Scrubbing his hand across his face, he tried to corral his thoughts. 'She's challenging and opinionated—'

'She sounds perfect for you. If you married a pushover you'd be unhappy. And she's lovely. Don't forget I've seen the wedding photo, though she looked more startled than ecstatic.' He heard excitement in his sister's voice. 'But go on. Tell me, what else?'

'She's brave.'

Her courage, proven in that outlandish abduction, had been misplaced and inconvenient. But mettle was a good thing in a royal and certainly better than weak compliance. A loyal, courageous woman at his side—and Miranda was clearly loyal as shown by the lengths she'd gone to for her cousin—was exactly what he needed.

The knowledge was like a light flicking on in his brain.

'I…admire her,' he admitted finally.

It seemed he'd said the right thing. Afifa began chattering nineteen to the dozen, obviously believing it was only a matter of time before this marriage turned into a grand love affair.

The thought tugged Zamir's mouth into a rueful smile.

For that to happen he'd first have to overcome his wife's disgust. He suspected that if she heard he'd died in an accident, she'd have trouble repressing her glee. It was a good thing the old displays of weaponry had been taken down and moved to a museum when the palace was extended. He didn't fancy his chances if Miranda had access to a sword.

'So how are you wooing her?'

'Pardon?'

'Wooing her! Courting her. Getting her to fall for you.'

He only just stopped himself saying he wouldn't ask for the impossible, when Afifa went on. 'You're strangers but you've committed to spend your lives together. You need to get to know each other. Discover what she likes, make her happy, help her adjust to life in Qu'sil and with you. What are you doing to build on your relationship?'

First he'd have to *begin* a relationship. But out of the mouths of little sisters…

He had to smash the barriers Miranda insisted on erecting between them. For his country's sake, and his own.

'Actually, Afifa, that's something I want to work on this afternoon. It's been great talking but I need to go.'

'You're not going to tell me any more?'

'Not now. Anyway, it's time you got back to work. Watch out for those numbats.'

'You mean wombats. Numbats are in Western Australia not the east and—'

'Bye, Afifa. I really have to go.'

'Bye, Zamir. And good luck.'

He'd need it.

But for the first time today he had a glimmer of an idea how to go forward with this marriage.

He'd spent last night and today putting out potential spot fires caused by his radical change of wedding plans. It was crucial no one suspected their marriage was anything but amicable, stable and successful. Too much hinged on it as a first step to the much-awaited joining of their countries. He couldn't afford to let that fall apart when so many had given up so much to achieve union. His uncle had given his last, failing years to make this happen. Zamir *had* to see this through.

Yet since Miranda's visit to his study he'd been distracted. Not just by the conflicting feelings she'd elicited but by his body's response.

He'd wanted to reach for her, discover if the aura of sparking energy was real or imagined. And when he had, it had merely confirmed what he'd feared.

He wanted her. Badly.

Zamir had told himself the sexual desire between them was good, even if on her part it seemed more like a spark of hatred. Though the way her gaze had clung to his body told him there was more to her passion than dislike.

Nights of frantic work, that dying buzz of a killer migraine, not to mention kidnap and near disaster, had left him below par. Now, thanks to his sister, his thoughts cleared.

It wasn't enough to smooth the way for Miranda as his queen. To have her learn his country's customs and court etiquette. Or to have a suitable wardrobe. He needed to persuade her into accepting this marriage. Accepting *him*.

Persuade or seduce?

He grimaced. That was his ego talking. The ego she'd dented when she'd declared that nothing would persuade her to share his bed.

He'd told himself that was the least of the issues facing them. But statesman though he might be, he was also a man.

There'd be enormous satisfaction in having Miranda eat her words about never sharing his bed.

Who was he kidding? It wasn't words he cared about. It was *her*. That frustrating, tempting bundle of contradictions that was his wife. The sexy woman with the luscious pout and enticing body.

Zamir had no intention of remaining celibate for the rest of his life. Nor was infidelity an option. But for now that could wait. His focus had to be overcoming her negative opinion.

He'd planned to give her time alone to adapt. But after speaking with Afifa he revised that.

Zamir returned to his desk. It was time to make a proper plan.

Miranda had assumed, after walking out on him earlier in the day, that Zamir would be too annoyed to spend time in her company. He was a proud, powerful man. She guessed he wasn't used to being crossed and what she'd done to him had been unforgivable. She understood his fury at being kidnapped. It was how she felt now. And since then, she hadn't pulled her punches, telling him exactly what she thought of him.

But Zamir surprised her. Mere hours after stalking out of his office she'd received a message inviting her to dine with him.

Inviting, not commanding. If it had been an order she wouldn't have obeyed. But an invitation…

That had sparked her curiosity so she'd arrived at the dining room to discover a table set for two and Zamir waiting for her, courteous, calm, the perfect host.

Any thought of resuming their earlier argument vanished when a group of musicians arrived and took up places on the far side of the room.

'Traditional musicians from the mountains of Qu'sil,' Zamir explained. 'I thought you might like to learn a little more about our country while we eat.'

His smile had been charming and her hackles had risen defensively. But logically she had nothing to complain about.

They'd spent the evening as polite strangers, discussing general topics rather than the ones burning for resolution. Gradually she found herself enjoying the music, the food and even, occasionally, Zamir's insights.

The next evening was the same. Except it was a renowned local singer providing the entertainment and Miranda found herself caught up more than once in the beauty and emotion of the music. Enough to let down her guard and admit to Zamir at the end of the performance how much she enjoyed music.

'It must have been a big part of your life, since your mother was a professional singer.'

She nodded. 'There was always music in our house. Even before she returned to it professionally, my mother often sang.'

'And you sing too?'

'You'd think so, wouldn't you? But I can't hold a tune.'

She was surprised to see him frown. 'I heard an expert say everyone can sing in the right conditions.'

She sat back and folded her arms. 'Can you?'

He shrugged and without the least embarrassment launched into the beginning of a well-known ballad. His voice was deep and pleasant and sent a wave of tingling heat across her flesh as he held her eyes.

Miranda's breath stalled but she told herself she wasn't drawn to that dark gaze. Yet she'd swear there was softness in those velvety depths as he sang of yearning and thwarted desire.

'Bravo.' She applauded when he stopped after a few bars. 'You're a man of many parts.'

'Aren't we all? None of us are completely as we seem on first acquaintance.'

Miranda was surprised by that. As if he were a man slow to judge and willing to learn about people. Not an authoritarian ogre.

He leaned forward. 'Have you thought of having lessons since you enjoy music so much? I could arrange—'

'No! Thank you.'

He really *was* trying to build bridges. Miranda didn't know whether to welcome that or resist. But she was stuck here, at least until she found a way out of this preposterous situation. No matter where she ran she'd still be Zamir's wife. Even if she managed to get away from Qu'sil she'd be legally bound to him. He was right. She had to find a way to live with this.

Which meant accepting Zamir's olive branch.

'It wouldn't work. My mother tried to teach me.' Miranda winced at the painful memories. Her mother impatient and frustrated and she blinking back tears because she'd disappointed her mother. Now it was too late to win her approval. 'I'm told my singing sounds like a camel bellowing so I don't try any more.'

Zamir held her gaze and it felt, strangely, as if he saw something more than her sitting at the dining table. As if he saw her younger self, hurting. After a moment he changed the subject and she gratefully followed.

The next day he sent an invitation to afternoon tea. It was actually an invitation she wanted to accept.

'I'm meeting the Qu'sil Ladies' Equestrian Club,' she protested to her assistant. 'Surely I don't need to dress so ornately?'

The invitation said it was a small, private function. She'd been surprised and touched that Zamir should arrange this for her. He knew she was climbing the walls, being incarcerated.

Her assistant was adamant as she fussed over Miranda's stole. 'This is your very first engagement. You need to look both regal and bridal.'

Miranda surveyed her reflection doubtfully. She looked totally unlike herself in a long dress of deep rose pink with acres of gold embroidery on the sleeves and from the hem all the way up to her knees. A matching stole draped her head and shoulders. Around her neck was a heavy gold heirloom piece with a dozen crimson gemstones she feared might be rubies. She wore gold embroidered slippers and at least a dozen beautifully wrought gold bangles jingled on each arm.

Discomfort weighed heavily. And doubt.

All the horsewomen she knew were down-to-earth people. Some might look formally elegant in their dressage costumes but away from the public arena comfort rather than high fashion ruled.

This wasn't high fashion. This was blinding grandeur.

She shook her head, feeling the heavy gold earrings slap her neck. 'I still think I need to tone it down a bit. At least with the jewellery.'

'You don't want to let the Sheikh down, do you?'

Miranda bit her lip. She hated the situation Zamir had forced her into but embarrassing him in public wouldn't make that situation easier. Besides, over the last few days he'd tried to make her feel less overwhelmed. He'd even acquired a horse for her. A gorgeous Arab with excellent manners but enough spirit and energy to present some challenge.

The fact he'd organised for her to meet other horsewomen showed goodwill and thoughtfulness, and a level of trust she hadn't expected. She couldn't repay that by deliberately flouting protocol.

Even her assistant, with her intricately done hair and heavy make-up, was more formally dressed than Miranda was used to. It must be a palace thing.

'Very well.' She loosened the stole and made for the door. She felt more than ever like an imposter but if that was what it took to spend time with other women who shared her interests…

She knew as soon as she joined Zamir in his office that something was wrong. His eyes widened before he looked away to close his computer. When he stood his expression was unreadable.

'Is everything all right?'

Miranda smoothed the folds of her heavy dress then stopped at the jingle of golden bangles. She didn't look like herself and she felt uncomfortable.

He inclined his head. 'Of course. You're ready?' He led her from his office towards the public reception rooms. 'I thought this would be a good way to ease into meeting people. Despite the name, it's not a formal society, but my sister's a member and I thought you'd have a lot in common.'

They approached a room that she knew to be a relatively small salon, merely big enough for fifty. A number of staff entered, carrying trays of food, and she caught the sound of female voices before the door closed.

Miranda stopped, impulsively reaching for Zamir. She only touched the sleeve of his dark suit then hastily let go as her skin tingled.

'You're anxious? There's no need. They all share your passion for horses.'

Miranda nodded. There *were* butterflies in her stomach. She'd never lost the expectation of being an outsider thanks to a lifetime of not quite fitting in anywhere but the stables.

But she never gave in to such nerves. She refused to cower in a corner.

'It's not that,' she murmured, then cleared her throat as she met his eye. 'Thank you, Zamir. Arranging this for me was thoughtful. I appreciate it.'

She couldn't remember the last time anyone had gone out of their way for her like this. It was usually her fitting in with others. This felt significant.

'It's my pleasure. I want you to be happy here.'

His mouth curled in that hint of a shadow of a smile and Miranda felt it as a rush of blood to the head. Would her bones melt if he smiled properly? It felt like it.

She shook her head. At her crazy imagination and at the idea of being happy here. As his wife. Preposterous!

But instead of growing angry, Zamir shrugged and led her forward. 'Shall we?'

Staff opened the door and they entered. There was silence for a moment, broken by a few gasps, then the shuffle of twenty women curtsying.

Women who tried, with varying degrees of success, to hide their surprise at the sight of her. Women in modern clothes, some in trousers and jackets, a couple in summery dresses, all looking stylish but undeniably comfortable.

Whereas she was trussed up like the tinsel-decked Christmas tree Matias always erected in December, the gaudier the better.

Heat rose to her throat and scorched her cheeks.

All her life she'd got the dress-up thing wrong. Her mother had looked effortlessly superb at all times and had eventually given up trying to mould Miranda in her image. Sadia could wear anything from traditional dresses to modern fashion and look totally at home. But Miranda could never pull it off. It didn't matter when she was in the stables, but in a royal court? In the public eye?

She felt gauche, an imposter in this place. Not the bride

Zamir had wanted and, no matter what he said, she knew in her heart of hearts that no amount of coaching would make her fit.

No wonder Zamir had been surprised when he saw her. If only he'd told her how ridiculous she looked.

And what? You'd have raced back to change? It would have taken ages and you'd have been disastrously late.

He greeted the women, thanked them for coming. Then he introduced her and she stood straighter, pushing back her shoulders and fixing a smile that felt horribly false onto stiff lips.

She'd walked into her worst nightmare.

CHAPTER EIGHT

'I'M SORRY, MA'AM, but I can't open the gate.'

Miranda stared down at the uniformed guard whose expression was professionally blank. Beneath her Chico snorted and shifted his weight, lashing his tail as if he, like she, was desperate for a good gallop.

'I won't go far. I know there's a track that leads to a private section of coastline.'

She looked past the guard towards the deep blue of the sea and imagined herself racing along the shore. Exercise and, yes, speed, had long been her way of burning up an abundance of excess energy. Nothing soothed the nerves or overcame impatience like the wind on her face and the thunder of hooves, her heart singing at the sheer joy of uncomplicated physical exertion.

Instead she was cloistered in this palatial prison. It might have every luxury but it was still a prison.

'My apologies, but I have my orders. Under no circumstances—'

'It's all right.' She bit back a sigh. 'I understand.'

It would take more than a request from her to overturn an order from the Sheikh. Yet she stared at the controls for the vast wrought-iron gates. If she had a distraction…

The guard shifted, marching to stand with his back to the controls. Was she that obvious?

Probably. But she felt so hemmed in. Her skin itched with the need for freedom, if only temporary.

Reluctantly she turned away, urging Chico towards the wildest part of the vast grounds. There was space within the palace compound to gallop. It even had its own racecourse. But Miranda needed more, she needed to be away from this place, especially after this afternoon's events.

Her flesh crawled at the memory of her cringeworthy entrance to the afternoon tea earlier. Fortunately Zamir had been right and she'd ended up enjoying herself enormously.

After their initial wariness she and the others had relaxed and she'd been delighted to find herself with so many like-minded women. There was an equestrian trainer, an international dressage competitor, and a whole lot of others who took their riding seriously. Some had even started a programme similar to the one she'd been involved with in Argentina, providing riding opportunities for people with disabilities.

By the end of the session she'd been optimistic, feeling that with time she might find friends in the group.

Yet, as the door had closed behind them and she'd returned to her apartments to fling off her heavy, ornate clothes, she'd felt again that horrible sense of not belonging. What a gaffe, dressing for an intimate event as if she wanted to outshine everyone. Her assistant meant well but Miranda should have overruled her.

Except Miranda didn't trust her instincts when it came to clothes. She hadn't inherited her mother's innate stylishness and never managed to choose the right outfit for the social events to which her mother or her uncle had dragged her. Today reinforced her woeful lack of style. Even with a wardrobe full of designer clothes and a personal assistant she'd still got it wrong!

Her enforced seclusion hit harder than ever. Her guests had left but she alone wasn't allowed beyond the palace doors.

The mere thought of being cooped up made her want to scream and scratch and kick.

She hadn't done that since she was a child, after her father died and her mother left to live overseas. The adults had decided Miranda was better off in Aboussir in a settled environment. She was brought up by her father's family rather than following her mother's singing engagements from one city to another.

Never mind the fact her uncle had treated her like a changeling. An unwanted, untrustworthy foreign child who wasn't one of them.

Setting her jaw, Miranda touched her heels to Chico's flanks as they reached open ground. He leapt forward eagerly as if he shared her impatience.

It was late when they returned to the stables. She knew she'd missed a riveting tutorial on constitutional law. She'd have to apologise to the tutor. But even if she'd attended she'd have taken in little, too on edge to concentrate.

Miranda greeted the head groom, who'd finally been persuaded not to insist that one of the stable hands look after her horse. It was good to be able to do something for herself here. The familiar ritual of unsaddling Chico, rubbing him down, putting up the tack and checking his food and water was soothing.

She held out half a carrot, smiling as he whickered his approval, his soft lips tickling her palm. 'You're a good boy, aren't you, Chico?'

'I thought his name was Zephyr?'

Miranda twisted around at the sound of that familiar, deep voice. She couldn't escape it, even in her restless dreams. Did he have to follow her here too?

Zamir was letting himself into the loose box, closing the door behind him.

The space shrank. That lovely feeling of muscle tiredness and calm that she'd worked hard to achieve disappeared in an instant. Every nerve was on alert, her pulse quickening as it did whenever he was near.

She looked away to Chico, crunching on his treat, almost

wishing he were temperamental enough to shy and rear at a stranger in his box.

Some ally he was.

'That's his name, officially. But he reminds me of another horse I used to know.'

'Called Chico.'

She nodded, not bothering to explain that he'd been Matias's favourite. A veteran mount who'd died last year at a venerable age. Miranda had cried then, for it had felt as if she'd lost a family member. Zephyr's colouring was similar and so was the knowing gleam in his eyes. Miranda had looked at him and felt a rush of homesickness for all she'd left behind in South America. Not just the stables and her stepfather. His casual affection and steadfast trust meant so much. But also the sense of belonging.

'He answers to Chico.' She reached out and scratched the horse's hairy cheek. 'Don't you, boy?'

Chico lifted his head and stamped one hoof. She smiled. But the smile died when Zamir spoke again.

'You missed an appointment.'

'Not an appointment that *I* made.'

He said nothing and she swung around to discover he stood closer than before. Close enough that she had to tilt her chin to meet his eyes. That annoyed her, as if it were a physical reminder of the power imbalance between them.

'We went through that. These lessons are vital. You need to act as a queen. They're for your benefit, so you understand what's happening and can participate.'

'I don't want to participate.'

Miranda knew it was petty. She was in this situation and couldn't get out of it. Even Zamir couldn't get her out of it. But it was easier to argue than confront her new reality.

'You should have thought of that when you kidnapped me.'

Her body stiffened as if at the crack of a whip. That was the worst of it. If she hadn't interfered…

He was right. She had to wear the consequences of what she'd done. But *such* consequences!

It was impossible to be sanguine with her emotions all over the place. Especially when Zamir stood close, all the abrasive feelings she tried to conquer surged to the surface. He made her feel…not like herself. 'I'd rather not talk to you right now.'

'We have to talk some time, Miranda. I'm your husband.'

'In name only. I'm not really your wife. I'm…a chattel. A symbol, didn't you say? A convenience.'

He shook his head, his eyes narrowing. 'There's nothing in the least convenient about you.'

'Good.' She moved closer, thrusting her face into his space, ignoring the rich spice and cedar aroma invading her nostrils. 'I'd hate to make things easy for you.'

She knew she wasn't being fair. She'd brought this on herself. He'd gone out of his way to make things easier for her. Introducing her to those women. Giving her Chico.

But those were just sops to his conscience because he'd trapped her in this appalling situation. He'd upended her life, giving her no choice, and expected her to go along meekly with his plans. Yes, she'd done wrong to kidnap him, but he'd done wrong, forcing her into this fiasco. They were both to blame. Yet it felt as though she was the one paying the heaviest price and she wasn't in the mood to be reasonable.

Zamir's nostrils flared, his eyes narrowing to glittering black slits.

The mere sight of him was a warning to back down. But if she backed down, she'd find it harder to stand up for herself later.

Everything was stacked against her. Even her senses that were enthusiastically cataloguing the sight, sound and scent of this man, as if in welcome, not rejection.

Miranda's head snapped back in horror.

'When will you finally accept that I'm not your enemy, Miranda?'

He lingered on her name, turning the vowels into music that produced a galaxy of goosebumps across her skin and a coil of desire low in her body.

She felt undermined. Trapped in uncharted territory.

'When you set me free. When you stop acting like my own private gaoler.'

Something flickered in those dark eyes. An emotion she couldn't read. His mouth twisted and the sharp planes of his face set like a rigid mask.

He looked daunting, imperious and frighteningly sexy.

'You know I can't set you free. It's impossible.'

He paused, chest swelling on a deep breath. When her glare didn't soften he shook his head.

'If you insist on treating me as the enemy…' His voice grated across her skin, drawing her nipples tight. As if that softly determined tone were instead an invitation to sensual pleasure beyond her imaginings. 'Maybe I should live up to your expectations.'

His hands closed around her upper arms and before she had time to process that, he pulled her to him. Her breasts pressed against his hard torso, her legs were between his, the heat of his groin searing her belly.

Lightning arced through her body, soldering her boots to the ground and turning her mouth arid.

Miranda swallowed and watched Zamir's eyes follow the jerky movement, then lift to her mouth when she slicked her lips.

His stare was needle-sharp. It should hurt her, or at the very least repulse her.

Instead it made her want.

She swayed, her palms flattening on his broad chest. To push him away, obviously.

But then she felt the heavy thump of his heart. Steady and even but quick, almost as quick as hers. Instead of pushing, her fingers curled into his shirt, her short nails raking.

She felt him jump, an infinitesimal twitch of muscles, enough to betray his response to her touch.

That was when it hit her that this was truly dangerous. Not because Zamir had the physical strength to force her into something she didn't want. Despite the disparity in their sizes and the raw masculinity that saturated the laden air between them, Miranda couldn't believe he'd use force.

The real danger was because she *did* want.

So much that it had grown into need. A need for more from this man. A need for something to quell the jittery sensation in her chest and stop the dragging heat inside as if her vital organs were melting on a tide of…

Lust.

The word hit at the precise moment his mouth covered hers.

Her head rocked back. Not with the force of his movement, but in instinctive denial.

She'd weathered kisses before, most unwanted, a few eagerly sought but soon disappointing. This was different. Miranda knew, with the desperate awareness of a hunted animal, that Zamir's kiss threatened her survival.

Yet her rejection was short-lived. So short she wondered if she'd imagined it, a salve to her pride.

Because now the feel of his lips on hers was…

She didn't have a word for it, just felt rising excitement deep inside.

He didn't force her mouth open, demanding submission. He merely slid his lips across hers. Once, twice, three times and that sensual slide threatened to blow the back off her skull.

She gasped, drawing in the taste-scent of hot masculinity and exotic spice.

Even then he didn't press home his advantage, plundering her mouth like a conqueror. To her bemusement he waited. So did she, expecting him to use, if not force, then heavy-handed persuasion.

Instead she felt only the caress of his breath and the surprising softness of his lips on hers. The drumbeat of his heart beneath her palm and the way the muscles in his powerful body stiffened. As if he held himself back.

Whatever game he played, he was better at it than she, but then recklessness had always been her besetting sin.

Unable to prevent herself, Miranda slid her mouth along his, tasting his bottom lip with the tip of her tongue.

Who knew a man could taste so delicious?

That was all it took. This was no longer a challenge or a battle of wills. It was…irresistible. Necessary.

When his tongue touched hers it was as if she'd waited for ever. Her mouth opened like a flower to the sun and what happened next took no thought at all. Their kiss was slow, an unhurried act of discovery. Yet there was no clumsiness, no bumping of noses. None of the self-consciousness she'd experienced when other men had kissed her.

It felt as if she and Zamir had kissed before. As if she'd been born knowing how to kiss him.

Knowing how to elicit that faint groan of approval deep in his throat as their caresses deepened. Just as he unerringly knew how to make her melt with each deft touch.

It was wondrous, addictive, and Miranda pressed closer, almost sighing with relief when those powerful arms encircled her and held her close.

Her hands slid up his chest to the warmth of his neck, fingertips questing into crisp short hair at the back of his head. A quiver of arousal shot through her, just from the friction of his hair against the pads of her fingers.

Or maybe it was from their deepening kiss, mouths fused together as hunger rose.

Zamir cupped the back of her head with one large hand as need became more urgent and she leaned back across his embracing arm.

That made her fully conscious of his impressive strength, the easy way he took her weight. Once the awareness of his greater power would have annoyed her. She gloried in it, arching further, her breasts thrusting against that hard chest. Her thighs braced against his.

Now the kiss held a demanding edge. Something akin to what she'd expected when he'd pulled her to him. But she welcomed it, clutching him close as if she could meld their bodies. Because this wasn't bullying domination. This was shared.

It was utter heaven.

Heat was a volcanic rush from her womb to her breasts, climbing her throat and dampening her hairline.

'Miranda.'

If she hadn't felt the vibration of his voice where her chest pressed to his, she might not have recognised it. It didn't sound like him. It was hoarse, stretched raw, and she loved it.

'Zamir,' she whispered against his lips. 'I—'

Something hit her, knocking her hip and shocking her eyes open to meet Zamir's blazing black gaze. For a second Miranda was lost in those midnight depths. She felt herself spinning out of control, until another knock and a strange sensation against her thigh.

Dragging her gaze from Zamir, she saw Chico's twitching grey ears as he mouthed the pocket of her jeans, pretending to eat it.

The world tilted as Zamir straightened with her in his embrace. For a second longer their bodies were fused from chest to knee. Then he released her, lowering his arms slowly as if to be sure she wouldn't stagger.

Instantly Miranda stepped back, standing tall and gulping in breaths that didn't fill her lungs. Even though, seconds ago when her mouth had been plastered to his, she'd noticed no difficulty breathing.

That's because you didn't care then what he thought. You were too busy being swept away in the moment.

Now reality came crashing back.

'What was that?' she snapped, needing to fill the silence before Zamir did. 'You proving your superior skills as a seducer?'

Chico nuzzled her shirt and she rubbed his head, grateful for the endearingly mundane contact when her brain was spinning and everything she knew about herself turned topsy-turvy.

'Maybe I just kissed you out of curiosity,' she said when he remained silent. 'Did that occur to you? After all, they say know your enemy.'

Disapproval pinched his brow and he seemed to grow taller, towering over her.

It was true that she'd wanted to know what kissing him was like. Yet from the moment their mouths touched it had felt familiar in a way no previous kiss had. More than familiar. Right. Perfect. Her body still sang with the joy of it.

His eyes narrowed but that challenging stare was marred by his slightly reddened lips. Lips that looked that way because of *her*. Even the pulse pounding in the base of his neck was, she knew, at least partly the result of their shared ardour.

He might have initiated the kiss but *she'd* done that to him. They'd both been affected.

That felt like triumph and disaster.

Zamir rolled his shoulders. 'Are you saying you didn't enjoy it? Because if you are—' his stare turned piercing '—I'd have to call you a liar.'

Miranda stepped back, only to come up against the wall. Chico mouthed at her hip pocket, searching for carrots, but she couldn't pull her gaze from Zamir.

'You think you're such an expert you can read my mind?'

He shook his head. 'Not your mind, Miranda. Your body. It speaks the truth you're too scared to admit.'

His glorious mouth, which had led her to the edge of paradise, quirked up at one corner and she felt something—her ego perhaps—crash and splinter. For even that tiny change of expression made her want to return to those moments of bliss in his embrace.

'Your body says you want me. You wanted me a few minutes ago when you were in my arms. And you want me still. *That's* why you're lashing out. Because I made you face the truth.'

For the first time she could remember Miranda was bereft of words. When faced with a situation where she felt out of her depth her defence mechanisms had always been a quick riposte and a defiant act. Taking some risk. Proving her mettle. Showing she wasn't cowed.

This time words deserted her.

Once, long ago, she might even have thrown a punch, aiming to puncture his complacency. But Miranda knew with visceral certainty that if she touched him again, she might just prove the very weakness she wanted to deny.

Zamir shifted his weight, his arm lifting as if to reach for her, but she shrank back and he stiffened, his expression setting in cold, haughty lines.

In anger or disappointment?

'I'll leave you to finish up here.' He patted Chico on the neck and turned on his heel. 'We'll talk later, Miranda.'

When he was gone she wrapped her arms around Chico's neck and breathed in his comforting, horsey smell.

What was she going to do?

Zamir was right. She *did* want him. She who'd never wanted any man enough to take a lover.

She was in desperate lust with her autocratic, unwanted husband.

CHAPTER NINE

'YOU SUMMONED ME?'

Zamir looked up from his computer to see Miranda in the office doorway. Heat gathered in his belly and his pulse quickened as he remembered her in his arms yesterday. Her sweet ardour had subverted his anger.

Miranda's insistence on always painting him in the worst possible light had grown wearing, finally puncturing his armour and making him want to forget the expectations placed upon him as a leader, a role model, a man who strove to do the best for others.

He'd wanted and he'd reached out to take, or at least to stifle her poisonous words. He'd tried to make things easier for her but that seemed to count for nothing.

Yet when he'd looked into her taunting, tense face, his annoyance had dimmed.

'Thank you for coming.' Zamir kept his voice even, ignoring his wayward thoughts and the provocative way she'd used the word *summoned.*

He'd let down his guard with her yesterday. He couldn't afford to do it again, at least not yet.

Would she wear that disapproving pout if she knew it emphasised the sultry invitation of her full lips?

As for her nonchalant stance, one hand on the door she'd opened before knocking, one hip thrust forward in an attitude of feminine challenge…

It made him want to provoke her. He sensed it wouldn't take much to nudge her into reckless action. Confrontation seemed to rouse her fighting spirit. If he exasperated her enough maybe *she'd* initiate their next kiss.

Despite yesterday's scathing words and her disdain now, she couldn't hide the glitter of awareness in her fine eyes, or the way they lingered on his mouth. The air was alive and sparking and Zamir was experienced enough to recognise the charge of mutual attraction.

He punched down a surge of anticipation and stood.

She was a puzzle he needed to understand. Despite her antipathy, she hadn't tried to cause trouble publicly. When he'd rung her stepfather to introduce himself and allay concerns it was to discover she'd already called him. Whatever she'd said, the Argentinian seemed content.

Why had she smoothed things over? Because she'd finally accepted their marriage? Or because she didn't want to worry a man who couldn't change the situation?

'Please, come in and shut the door.'

For a moment she looked as if she might retreat.

That reminded Zamir of yesterday's suspicion that she was a relatively inexperienced kisser. The idea had kept him awake long into the night.

Finally Miranda turned and shut the door with exaggerated care. Did her choice of trousers and a khaki shirt signal she'd made no special effort for him? But the tailored trousers emphasised her toned form and the fine shirt clung to her breasts as she twisted. He recalled in devastating detail how those breasts had felt, pressed against him.

He cleared his throat and yanked his thoughts back to business. 'Please, take a seat.' He waited till she took an armchair before sitting opposite her. 'I need to ask you more questions.'

'Questions? About what?'

'About you.' Zamir smiled reassuringly, but instead of relaxing she sat straighter, fingers digging into the arms of her chair.

'What sort of things?'

Everything. He'd never met anyone so intriguing. He needed to understand her better so she wouldn't be able to take him by surprise or provoke him again. Zamir *had* to be in control, not acting impetuously.

'You've aroused a lot of interest. We need material to release publicly as required.'

'Who is *we*?'

'My team. We have specialists who deal with press releases, public engagements, the media and so forth.' He paused. 'Actually we should have done this as soon as you arrived.'

But for once he hadn't been totally pragmatic. He'd given her time to adjust. He suspected his uncle wouldn't have done so, but despite Afifa's fears, or maybe because of them, Zamir chose a more subtle approach. He'd hoped to win Miranda over with kindness and patience. So far he'd failed.

'You'll tell your staff anything I tell you?'

'Only what they need to know to do their job.' He watched her frown. 'They are there to help us. To manage your public image and pre-empt difficulties.'

'Difficulties?'

'There's enormous speculation about you. You aren't the woman I'd planned to marry.'

She opened her mouth then closed it again, as if remembering she was the reason he hadn't been able to marry Sadia. '*Enormous* speculation?'

He nodded. 'So the team needs to know more.' And because, while Zamir didn't have political enemies as such, there were powerful politicians who weren't above making trouble for the new Sheikh if it meant improving their positions. Disrupting the amalgamation of Aboussir and Qu'sil would be the perfect time. Already they'd tried to pressure him over some major development schemes and they'd love to find a chink in his armour. He couldn't afford for Miranda to be that chink. It was imperative her image, appearances and behaviour were appropriate.

'You're afraid I have scandalous secrets?'

'Do you?' Unlike her cousin, Miranda hadn't always lived under close supervision. Sadia's unblemished character had been part of her attraction as a royal wife.

Miranda held his gaze and he'd swear the air sizzled. He leaned closer, pulled by that same force that had drawn him to her yesterday. He felt the tingle of blood in his fingers, the heaviness in his belly—

'If I had secret scandals, I wouldn't share them with your media gurus.'

She turned towards the window.

Stonewalling wouldn't help. Not if there really was something important. He pulled out the typed pages and proffered them, making her turn back.

'What's this?'

'Your homework. We need answers to these questions. The media team has been bombarded with queries. Your answers will give them something to work with.'

She didn't respond, too busy scanning the pages.

'You need to know about my friends?'

'Once I'm crowned ruler you'll be my queen. With that comes responsibilities. For instance, if in future one of your friends wants to do business here, we want to avoid accusations of favouritism.'

Her eyes blazed more silvery than grey, just as they had in the stables yesterday. Grimly Zamir registered a spark of response deep in his belly. After yesterday's kiss his desire for her was impossible to ignore.

Confident women had always appealed to Zamir. He liked someone who could hold her own in conversation and in bed. Maybe it was a blessing in disguise that the match with Sadia hadn't gone ahead.

Except your wife hates you.

Yet maybe she protests too much.

Miranda had been ardent and enticing in his arms. Walking away from her yesterday had taken all his self-control. If it hadn't been for her horse interrupting, Zamir might have had her up against the wall.

He'd spent a restless night imagining just that.

Would she still be so argumentative if he had? Or would she be enticing him into bed?

'None of my friends would do that.' She interrupted his thoughts. 'Besides, they're not powerful.'

'What about your stepfather and his friends? Wealthy acquaintances you've met through horse training?'

She crumpled the papers. 'You can't expect me to list everyone I've ever worked with!'

'Do the best you can.'

'What, so they can be investigated?'

Zamir held back from saying that at least a cursory investigation of her past was inevitable. No point provoking more outrage. 'Not necessarily.' He rubbed a hand around the back of his neck. Why had he imagined, even for a moment, that she'd make this simple?

'Did you have to fill in a questionnaire too?'

He shook his head. 'There's no need. My life's an open book. I've lived at the palace since I was ten. I've been in the public eye since I was thirteen.'

'You must have secrets.'

He spread his hands. 'Who doesn't?'

'Tell me one.' She lifted her chin. 'Tell me a secret and I'll fill in your form.'

He frowned. 'A secret?'

She nodded. 'Not a state secret. I'm not interested in those. Something personal. Something no one else knows.'

It was crazy. His secrets had nothing to do with this.

But if it meant getting Miranda to co-operate, and, more importantly, winning her trust…

'A secret of mine and in return you answer the questionnaire and a question of mine,' he responded. 'But I won't share that answer with anyone.'

Her eyes widened, then he read a gleam of something there that might have been anticipation. 'No fair. If you want all that, I get to ask another question too.'

Why not? Letting her win this negotiation might help. She must have felt powerless these last few days.

Plus playing Q and A might tear down some of the barriers between them. After yesterday he was even more impatient to overcome her animosity. For the good of the country, of course.

And because he wanted her in his bed. Maybe after that he'd be able to devote his full attention to business.

'All right.'

'You agree?'

Zamir nodded, enjoying her almost comical look of disbelief. 'Fire away.'

She was silent for several moments. 'Why do you want to be Sheikh so much? I understand about the amalgamation of our countries. I don't mean that. I want to understand what it is about being supreme ruler that really appeals to you. What you get out of it.'

Zamir felt the air heavy in his lungs as her words sank in. His flesh prickled at the insinuation he was motivated by personal greed. For wealth, or power. Prestige perhaps. Sourness filled his mouth.

Strange how this proof that she saw him as a power-hungry politician hurt. She'd said as much before but Zamir had hoped she'd begun to understand.

'Aren't you going to answer?'

His vision cleared and he saw her, canting towards him, hands clasped and eyes serious.

The question wasn't malicious. She genuinely didn't understand him.

Whose fault was that?

'I've never *wanted* to be Sheikh. When I was younger I had other dreams. But I grew up. I was made to see the world as it is, not as I wanted it to be.'

Miranda's brow furrowed. 'I don't understand. Sadia said you moved to live with your uncle so he could teach you to be Sheikh. I thought—'

'That I made that choice?' He shook his head. She really had no idea. 'The choice was made for me before I was old enough to have a say in it. When I was ten my parents died and my uncle brought us to live with him.'

In answer to her unspoken question he added, 'Us being my seven-year-old brother Umar and five-year-old sister Afifa. They're overseas but you'll meet at the coronation.'

'That must have been…hard.'

He inclined his head. 'Your father died when you were young too.'

'He did.' She swallowed, her expression softening.

She'd loved him, he realised.

He thought about his parents. Had he loved them?

He supposed so, but he'd never felt close to either. He and his siblings had been brought up by staff, though when they were orphaned, he'd done his best to be a surrogate parent for the others.

He'd learned more about love and nurturing from that than from his parents. Hours consoling Afifa or distracting her with childish games. Nights with one or both his siblings in his bed because they'd had bad dreams. Reading bedtime stories, mopping up tears and encouraging them when they didn't live up to their uncle's exacting standards.

'By the time I was twelve I was well on the way to being moulded by my uncle and tutors to take the throne. I found out later that when my parents died he'd been negotiating to marry again, in hopes of fathering an heir. But he gave that up when he adopted me, with Umar as a spare heir if needed.'

'So this was against your will?'

Zamir shook his head. 'It wasn't that simple. If my parents hadn't died, if my uncle had had a son of his own, then I'd have been happy as a private citizen. But fate set this road for me. There's no point dwelling on what would have happened if my life had been different.'

'Even if you don't want this?'

'It's not a matter of want. This is my duty, my role in life. I've trained hard for it. I'm good at it. Millions of people trust and rely on me. I can make a real difference in their lives. How many people can say that?'

Miranda scrutinised him carefully. 'And that's enough?'

Zamir couldn't hold back a grunt of laughter. Had she gone from believing him to be grasping, to feeling sorry for him?

'There are definite compensations. And yes, there's enormous satisfaction in being able to do good for my country.'

'It never occurred to you to step aside and pursue another dream? Let your brother take over?'

Zamir's amusement died. 'It's not an option.'

Miranda tilted her head like an inquisitive bird, eyes bright, expression intrigued. There was something about having her full attention, not her anger or indignation, but her curiosity and—was he kidding himself?—maybe her sympathy, that appealed.

He should tell her she'd already had more information from him than they'd bargained for. But he'd agreed to a second question. Umar wouldn't mind. Besides, Zamir needed to break down the barriers between them. If she understood his motives it could only help.

'My brother isn't cut out for the role.'

'Aren't you assuming a lot? If he had the chance—'

'He'd hate it. Umar is very bright. He's quick-witted, loyal and decent, but he has a short attention span for anything that doesn't interest him. School was a nightmare except for the subjects he loved. He'd rather be out, making things happen in his own way. The idea of him sitting through long debates or consultations on subjects he's not passionate about, much less putting up with royal protocol…'

Zamir shook his head. 'He couldn't wait to get away from palace life. He's thriving and making his mark in the world, drawing attention to injustice. The thought of him forced to give that up… No, I couldn't do that to him. He suffered enough, trying to live up to royal expectations when he was here.'

'I see.'

Just that. Did she see? Or did she believe, even now, that he twisted the truth to his own ends?

Miranda was reeling but struggled not to show it.

It had been convenient to paint Zamir as a selfish dictator, driven to grab power for his own ends.

But she'd seen his expression soften when he'd spoken of his family. When he'd described his brother, there'd been no mistaking his affection.

Zamir had been raised believing it his responsibility to look after his country, no matter what he personally wanted. That didn't absolve him from forcing her to marry, but it cast a new light on his motives. He wasn't as selfish as she'd imagined. His vehemence in protecting his brother's freedom was real.

In other circumstances she'd admire him. The realisation sucked the air from her lungs. It was difficult enough, fighting this intense physical attraction.

She had an awful suspicion her new understanding of his character would make that resistance tougher.

Miranda shot to her feet, clutching his questionnaire. 'If you want this answered today I'd better make a start.'

'Aren't you forgetting something? You were going to answer a question from me.'

Dark eyes searched hers and there it was again, the feeling he could see deep into her insecurities. Reluctantly she sank into her chair. A deal was a deal. She'd honour their agreement.

Miranda leaned back, crossing one leg over the other. 'Ask away.'

For the longest time Zamir studied her, then spread his hands. 'I'm torn. I should ask if it's likely someone will come forward with a kiss-and-tell story about you that we need to prepare for.'

Miranda stiffened. He wanted to know about her lovers. She had nothing to be ashamed of, making the choices that had been right for her. Yet she shied from revealing her virginity to this charismatic, obviously experienced man who evoked such unprecedented desires.

Not because she was bashful but because it was yet one more area in which he had the advantage over her.

His kiss had undone her and afterwards she'd resorted to anger rather than reveal that vulnerability. He'd sauntered away from that devastating encounter as if unaffected.

He hadn't spent the night unable to sleep for thoughts of what would have happened if Chico hadn't interrupted. *Wishing* Chico hadn't interrupted.

'But I also want to know why you gave up your studies. I know you were planning to become a teacher. But now you train horses instead. Did something happen…something that stopped you finishing?'

His expression was grave and the gleam in his eyes looked like sympathy.

He thinks there was some crisis. That something bad happened that prevented you continuing.

He was concerned on her behalf?

That couldn't be. Yet that really did look like compassion. Did he think she'd had some terrible trauma?

'Is this your way of trying to winkle out answers to two questions?'

His mouth curled in a rare smile that held no cynicism. Its impact was like an earth tremor rippling up from the polished floor, through her soles and shattering another level of her hard-won protective walls.

'Ah, caught in the act. I could point out that you asked me more than one question. But I'll just leave it to you to decide which you'll answer.'

When Zamir smiled he was a different man. As if clouds that had blocked the sun blew away, leaving glittering golden light. Revealing a face so appealing it almost hurt to look at him.

It was on the tip of her tongue to blurt out that he should smile more often and everyone would jump to obey his slightest wish. But they did that anyway.

It was unfair that this man had so many advantages. Power, looks, even charm when he chose to use it, while she had nothing but her wits.

'How did you know I studied to be a teacher?'

'My staff have done *some* background checking.'

She let that pass. Of course they had. 'It's no big secret. I just wasn't cut out to be a teacher.'

'You discovered that when you started your training?'

It would be easy to agree and leave it at that but Miranda felt she owed him honesty. He'd been frank with her, letting her glimpse his private world. Besides, the way he described his brother made her wonder if he might understand better than her family had. She'd been a disappointment both to her uncle and her mother. Only Matias accepted her as she was, never pushing her to be someone different.

Are you really so needy that you want Zamir's approval?

But she owed him something. Despite everything, he'd been kind, arranging that afternoon tea and giving her privacy. He was trying. Pride demanded she accept that.

Miranda looked at the crumpled papers on her lap and smoothed them out. 'I knew before I enrolled. I didn't want to be a teacher. Not in a school anyway. I enjoy helping people learn to ride and care for animals but that's different.'

She looked up. 'I was never good at school, except for sport.

Most lessons bored me and the thought of studying for years just to end up in a classroom again… It wasn't for me.'

She shook her head. 'When you spoke about your brother, I could relate to him.' She hurried on. 'I'm not claiming to be brilliant like him but I like to be hands-on. There are things I enjoy. Like being with animals, training and rehabilitating them after injuries. Helping kids, and adults for that matter, develop self-confidence through riding. But make me write essays? No, thanks.'

'So why enrol?'

'Family pressure.' Like him, she realised. 'My mother had hoped I'd take after her and be a glamorous singer or actress, but she had all the talent in the family.' Her mother had loved her in her own way but hadn't known what to do with a daughter so different to herself. Plus by the stage Miranda left school her mother had met Matias and had other priorities.

'I was living with my Aboussi family and my uncle said I either needed to marry or get qualifications to support myself. I chose the latter. Sadia enrolled in a teaching degree and it was one of the few careers my uncle approved of for us.'

Zamir's mouth flattened. 'He's very old-fashioned.'

Miranda nodded. 'He was almost apoplectic when I withdrew and moved overseas. Later, when he heard I was working in a professional stable, he all but disowned me.'

Gruff laughter scraped her body like the brush of suede on bare skin. 'Think how his nose must be out of joint now that you've married me and will soon be Queen.'

Her lips quivered. 'I hadn't thought of that.' She'd been too focused on her situation to spare a thought for him.

'See?' Zamir's smile did devastating things to her insides. 'There are compensations to our marriage.'

Her mouth kicked up at the corners in answering amusement.

'Speaking of our marriage, we'll make a public appearance in front of the palace the day after tomorrow. It's time I presented you to our people. But don't worry, you won't have to say anything. Just stand at my side and smile.' He paused. 'My staff will talk with yours about appropriate clothes.'

Because she couldn't be trusted to get that right.

Miranda shrank inside.

Despite what Zamir had said about there being no way out of their marriage she'd hoped for a loophole. But once she'd been shown off like some prize acquisition in a no doubt televised event, there'd be no escape.

She'd be Zamir's wife for real.

With difficulty she swallowed over a jagged obstruction in her throat.

The scary thing was that a tiny part of her was excited at the idea of him claiming her as his wife. Because he'd awoken such a longing for intimacy, for *his* touch, that she felt like a stranger in her own body, ready to ignore the negatives of her situation if he'd only ease her growing need.

Miranda shot to her feet. 'I'll go and start on these questions.'

He stood and something in his intent expression warned her he guessed at her weakness. She couldn't bear that.

She stepped out of reach then made herself pause and send him a sideways glance that she hoped looked insouciant.

'As for previous lovers with kiss-and-tell stories…' He stilled, apparently riveted by her words. She shrugged. 'I'm afraid I can't make any guarantees.'

Strictly it was true. She'd never had a lover. Yet she'd heard of people falsely claiming intimacy with public figures, seeking attention or money.

It was a petty thing to do, implying lies about her past. But she was tired of being on the back foot, the inexperienced, gauche one. The one who had to make up ground to be good enough.

With a tight smile she turned and strolled from the room. It was only when the door closed behind her that her shoulders hunched and her mouth flattened at the prospect of what was to come.

CHAPTER TEN

'YOU LOOK STUNNING.'

Zamir's words escaped unbidden, stopping Miranda inside the door of his salon.

Her bright eyes widened as they locked on his and a blast of heat shot through him, settling low in his belly. His pulse thundered and all thoughts of the speech he was about to make fled.

No sign now of the argumentative opponent so ready to take umbrage. His bride looked willowy, womanly and utterly desirable.

Her clothing drew attention to the spare, pure lines of her face, her grace and the lush promise of her mouth.

It took such effort to drag his gaze from her lips.

Her dress was silver, long and embroidered with tight sleeves that widened towards the wrist. Over her dark hair she'd draped a sheer scarf the same colour as the antique pearls that clustered in rows around her neck and wrists.

'You don't need to lie, Zamir. I don't need the pep talk. I'm fully prepared to go out there with you.'

Her tone made it sound as if he were about to lead her into a pit of desert vipers, instead of merely to a podium before the palace where the crowd could see them.

The numbers out there had surprised Zamir. He'd expected a huge crowd to witness the coronation, still weeks away. But it seemed everyone was agog with curiosity to see his bride.

Miranda swallowed and his attention dropped to her slender

throat. She was a confusing mix of vulnerable and determined. Now he noted her tightly clasped hands and pushed-back shoulders. She was anxious and determined not to show it.

Did she really have no idea how she looked? Or how his people would joyfully welcome his bride?

'Have I ever lied to you, Miranda?' His voice was rasping, betraying his growing hunger. For this woman who challenged him, hated him even, but enticed him too.

Hell! He hoped she didn't still hate him.

Yesterday he'd even found himself jealous of her horse! Zamir had wanted her to stroke him and whisper sweet nothings in his ear with as much enthusiasm as she gave her equine friend.

'But I…' She shook her head as if still not convinced.

'Surely you've been complimented on your appearance before.' It was impossible all the men in Aboussir and Argentina were blind.

She drew herself up. 'No. At least, only by men trying to get into my pants.'

His splutter of laughter was unstoppable. The disdainful twist of her mouth said everything.

'You didn't like them?'

What about the ex-lovers she'd hinted might come out of the woodwork now she was famous?

Her expression of regal scorn would have done his uncle proud. 'I don't want to talk about them.'

Zamir was perplexed. Had she really not believed the compliments she'd received? Why? For every new piece of information he had about Miranda he found another puzzle.

'Then we won't talk about them. But believe me, you look marvellous. Every inch the royal bride.'

'Thank you,' she said after a long pause that made him wonder if he'd somehow said the wrong thing. 'You brush up well yourself.'

He wished he could be sure that was admiration in her quick glance. It felt like it.

Or are you so used to feminine interest you're seeing it when it's not there?

No. He couldn't be mistaken, not after that kiss. He'd tapped a deep vein of desire when Miranda had kissed him back. If they hadn't been interrupted…

But royal Sheikhs of Qu'sil didn't have quickies in the stables.

No matter how much they wanted to.

It would have been unbecoming in his new role. More, he owed his bride better than a roll in the hay.

At least the first time.

The memory of their passion, the idea of forgetting decorum and slaking his hunger right there in the stables, stirred his libido. Zamir dragged oxygen into his lungs, pushing away the insidiously tempting image of Miranda, up against the wall with her legs around his waist while he drove them hard to a peak of pleasure.

Deliberately he turned to his desk as if referring to a document there, needing time to collect his wits and force down his burgeoning erection.

His mouth curled mirthlessly. That was *not* how his people needed to see him. He had to remember his uncle's example, the expectations upon him, the responsibilities he shouldered. The gravitas of his position.

When he turned back to Miranda he was in control of himself, at least on the surface. He couldn't afford to betray the desperate lust scrabbling at his vitals like a clawing, caged animal.

When Zamir turned back his expression was aloof. For a second, when he'd called her stunning, Miranda's heart had leapt. Because in that moment she'd imagined he looked dazzled.

Wishful thinking.

She'd had a lifetime of people's surprise when they discovered she was her mother's daughter, but with none of her mother's luminous blonde beauty and charm.

A tomboy, her mother had called her, in a tone that was half laughing, half disappointment.

Of course Zamir hadn't been dazzled. Stunning probably referred to her clothes, not her.

Even if, when she'd looked in the mirror, Miranda had for the first time in her life felt beautiful.

Zamir's gaze skimmed her but didn't settle. Not like a man appreciating a lovely woman. He'd said what he knew she wanted to hear.

He was good with words but his eyes told a different story. She felt a pang, wishing she really were as splendid as her fine clothes.

You are. No matter what anyone thinks, you're special. You've made a rewarding and satisfying life.

Which she'd had to leave behind.

'Are you ready?'

She nodded.

'Excellent. The crowd will be excited to see us but there's no reason to be alarmed. All you have to do is smile.'

Given her stiff facial muscles, Miranda wasn't sure that was possible.

It was as well she didn't have to speak. Her larynx closed and her breath came in quick gasps as she saw the enormous throng surrounding the palace. Her suite was on the far side of the building and she'd had no idea there were this many people in the capital.

The horrible feeling that she was an imposter hit again full force.

She didn't fit here. She hadn't even mastered the art of walking in high heels, much less being royal! Would they see through her? Or would her fabulous clothes be enough camouflage if she stood tall?

'They've been gathering for hours,' Zamir murmured as they walked from the palace into the vast forecourt beyond which the people waited. 'Some have travelled from the furthest provinces.'

A hush descended that made Miranda's nape prickle. It seemed impossible that such a huge gathering should be so silent. Then someone called out Zamir's name and the crowd erupted into cheers and ululations of celebration.

'They like you,' she whispered when she found her voice. This was no orchestrated show of support. This was real and overwhelming.

'They like what I stand for. Stability and good government. Like my uncle before me.'

But Miranda wondered. He said he'd been in the public eye since he was thirteen. He'd spent years deputising for the failing Sheikh. Hearing snippets of conversation among household staff, Miranda knew people admired Zamir because of who he was, not simply because of his title.

They reached a raised platform. Above it an awning of golden silk rippled in the light breeze. Miranda lifted her long skirt a little, needing to see where she stepped in her unfamiliar high heels.

That was when she almost came to grief, her narrow heel slipping sideways on the second step and her ankle turning abruptly. She reached out to grab for a railing that wasn't there but was saved by Zamir.

He gripped her upper arm, holding her steady. She looked up to see him leaning close, concern in his eyes.

Concern that you don't make a laughing stock of yourself and therefore him.

Yet the negative voice faded as Miranda met his eyes.

'Sorry. These stairs need treads and a hand rail. It will be arranged for next time.'

She exhaled slowly and nodded, hyper-conscious of his touch through her gown. 'I'll just concentrate on getting through this time.'

His smile was pure reassurance yet it felt intimate. And it

dragged up all the longing she'd tried to suppress. A longing she shouldn't feel for this man.

They walked up the steps together, Zamir still holding her arm. To her astonishment, when they reached the platform, instead of removing his hand, he slid it down her sleeve and threaded his fingers through hers.

His hand was warm, dry and reassuring, which must be why he did it. He must have seen her tremble and known she was nervous.

Zamir led her to the microphone and addressed his people. What he said was a blur. Miranda concentrated on nodding and smiling in response to the cheers that erupted whenever he paused. And standing firm on her own two feet.

Trust her to have stumbled. Since her mother died she'd made almost a virtue of avoiding occasions where she had to dress up. She should have practised wearing high heels again instead of telling herself she wanted no part of today's event. She'd known she couldn't avoid it but had pretended it didn't matter.

But Miranda couldn't run from this any longer. Zamir and the people who expected so much from him were her reality now. She saw, heard and felt their enthusiasm and trust for him, their willingness to accept her because he'd chosen her.

Being here, basking in the reflected glow of all that positivity made her understand a little of his determination to be the man his people needed. Even made her want to help, or at least not hinder.

She had to face facts. Much as she abhorred their forced marriage, she didn't abhor Zamir or what he stood for. In fact he was proving the sort of strong, honourable yet understanding man her father had been.

Instead of being obstinate and reckless about things she couldn't change, she needed to adapt and learn.

'All done,' he murmured in her ear, the crowd going wild as he leaned close.

Miranda felt that powerful beat of attraction, her attention dropping to his perfectly sculpted mouth. The mouth that had been so gentle yet devastating on hers.

'Shall we go?'

She blinked and saw him survey her curiously, as if he couldn't understand why she was standing there staring with half the country's population and a massive TV audience watching.

'Sounds good. These clothes are getting heavy.' They weren't really. Miranda had found the dress and jewellery surprisingly comfortable and she loved the lustre of the pearls against her skin.

With one last smile for the crowd, she turned and they descended the steps. They were on their way back to the palace when bright colour caught her eye.

At the front of the crowd, not far away, a couple of young children held stems of bright yellow sunflowers, taller than themselves. They saw her notice and beaming smiles split their faces as they waved the flowers.

'Can we go over, Zamir? They must've waited ages and it's such a sweet gesture.'

He paused then squeezed her hand and turned towards them. The handholding was undoubtedly for the benefit of the public but she didn't mind. She rather liked it.

Wasn't that a scary thought?

Maybe that was why she moved faster, needing the distraction of the children. Others joined them now, wriggling between the adults. Children of all ages, one with a football under his arm.

The crowd jostled. There was a cry of alarm and the football shot out from the crowd.

Miranda just had time to see the horror on its owner's face when the ball was on her. She felt Zamir move as if to step in front of her but before he could she lifted the hem of her dress and stopped the ball with one sandalled foot.

A hush fell. She felt it like a weight across her shoulders and prickling on her skin. Thousands of eyes were on her, standing there with her dress of silver tissue hiked up around her shin, balanced on one high heel, Zamir's hand tight around hers.

Miranda didn't look his way, not wanting to see his disappointment that she'd wrecked her image of royal elegance. It was too late for that, so she did what she would have done if she were simply Miranda Fadel. She gently tapped the ball straight back to its owner.

For a second the crowd held silent then a great buzz rose. She couldn't hear what they said but she could imagine. The sort of disapproval her uncle had meted out so often, that she was too tomboyish, too wild, not quietly feminine enough.

'Come on,' Zamir urged. 'They're waiting for us.'

She stumbled forward, grateful for his grasp when seconds ago, concentrating on the ball, she'd had no difficulty balancing.

Fortunately the children didn't notice anything amiss. They were too keyed up with excitement to be judgemental. Gap-toothed grins abounded as eager hands pressed the sunflowers upon her. She heard Zamir greet the children and was grateful he carried the situation so easily. Despite the enthusiasm of the kids, she felt horribly self-conscious.

'My lady, my lady. Will you sign it, please?'

There, before her, was a dusty football.

'I don't—'

She turned to Zamir, seeking guidance and discovered him looking relaxed. He was probably regretting he'd been forced to marry her rather than her decorous and decorative cousin, who could be trusted to behave perfectly in public, but he hid it well.

'I don't have a pen on me. But…' He turned and one of the security staff held out a pen, which Zamir passed to her.

'Thank you.'

Miranda scribbled her name and passed the ball back. She

was kept busy accepting more flowers, until her arms were full and a staff member had to take some. But gradually she found her voice again, responding increasingly easily to the children. She spent a lot of time working with young people and their enthusiasm broke down barriers, even if she was aware of the adults standing back, surveying her. Critically? Most probably.

Finally Zamir took her hand again, thanking the crowd and saying goodbye.

He kept hold of her as they returned to the palace. Some image consultant had probably told him to. Which made her tug free as soon as the large doors closed behind them. It felt wrong that she enjoyed his touch so much when it was just a PR exercise.

From the corner of her eye she saw him frown but he merely led her back through the corridors to the private salon they'd used earlier.

The door had barely closed behind them when she said, 'It wasn't intentional, really. I didn't mean to disrupt everything.'

'Disrupt everything?'

His scrutiny made her blood rush faster, creating a heat far greater than she'd experienced outdoors.

'Stumbling on the stairs. Hoiking up my dress to play football, then being asked to sign it!' She swung around to face him. 'I'm sure you've never had to do that.'

Zamir met flashing silver eyes. They made him think of summer lightning turning the night sky brilliant. That was how he felt, as if a blast of energy exploded inside him. It threatened to scramble his thoughts.

He should be getting back to work. There was so much still to do. Yet all he could think of was Miranda.

'You're right. I've never had that honour.'

The only things he'd been asked to sign were boring legal

documents. Never had he been asked to sign a souvenir like some sporting star.

Yet Miranda didn't look triumphant. When the corners of her mouth dragged down it wasn't in a pout or a tantalising smile, but a grimace. Her breasts rose high and quick as if she couldn't catch her breath.

'I'm sorry. Truly.' Her hands twisted and he realised, belatedly, that she was upset. 'You probably won't believe it, but I didn't deliberately try to sabotage today.'

He frowned. 'Sabotage?'

'By making a spectacle of myself.'

Zamir covered her restless hands with his.

That felt better. Outside he'd held her to steady her, but feeling her fine tremors he'd been hit by remorse.

She wasn't ready for this, hadn't had the benefit of years of training. She'd been thrust into an overwhelming situation with virtually no preparation. The lessons she had on court etiquette, local customs, history and laws weren't enough to prepare for a scene like today.

He rubbed his thumb across her wrist, feeling her racing pulse.

He wanted to ease her agitation. At the same time, just like earlier, he wanted physical contact. He'd been disappointed when she'd ripped her hand away as soon as they'd entered the palace.

'You didn't make a spectacle of yourself.' He peered down into her flushed face. 'You do realise, you were a huge success?'

'Success?'

Had she heard the crowd? Seen the grinning adults as she'd interacted with the children? She acted as if she'd done something wrong.

Then he remembered her dismay when she'd worn that over-elaborate outfit to the afternoon tea he'd arranged. She'd looked aghast, which had surprised him. He'd believed nothing could faze Miranda. Even being blackmailed into marrying a stranger hadn't dimmed her spirit.

The only time he'd heard her sound less than sure of herself was when she'd spoken of her family. Of her mother's disappointment that Miranda didn't turn out to be a glamorous singer like her.

He frowned.

'Of course, a success. Everyone loved you. Not only did you appear like a fairy-tale princess, but you showed yourself to be something much more interesting. You connected with those children. You broke with royal protocol to mingle with them and then you topped it off by proving with that professional stop that, even in heels, you're a football natural. You do realise it's one of our national games, don't you? I suspect there will be a lot of children tonight asking if they can join a local club.'

Miranda scowled. He should be used to it, but this time there was no anger in her stare. He sensed merely confusion.

'I'm glad the costume did the trick.' She swallowed and looked over his shoulder. 'I felt…like an imposter wearing all this finery. But as for breaking with protocol.' Her eyes met his. 'I didn't realise I wasn't supposed to talk to the people. I read the briefing but I didn't see—'

'It probably wasn't in there because I was going to guide you. If anything *I'm* the one who broke with tradition by agreeing when you suggested talking with the children.'

'Why did you?'

Because she'd looked at him with those diamond-bright eyes, eager and excited, and he hadn't been able to resist.

'It seemed like a good idea at the time.'

Her mouth twitched. 'That's what I used to say whenever I got in trouble for doing something wrong as a kid.'

'Did that happen often?'

'Often enough.' Her expression turned serious. 'So what I did really wasn't a problem?'

It surprised him that she still needed reassurance. He released her fingers and stroked his hands up her arms, stepping closer. 'It was a stroke of genius. Our country is a modern one but the rules around royalty haven't changed in a long time. It's time they did. You saw how the crowd reacted at the chance to be near you.'

'Near *us*.'

Zamir shrugged. He was popular with his people but it was she who'd been a hit today. 'You connected with them, Miranda. First you stunned them with your beauty then won them over by being down-to-earth, warm-hearted and real. All the parents watching you interact with their children knew you weren't faking.'

'I…' She shook her head. 'That's one of the nicest things anyone's ever said. About being warm-hearted and down-to-earth, I mean.'

Her eyes met his and there was no attempt to hide her feelings. Zamir felt a rush of blood to his head, dazzled by what looked like joy and gratitude. And more, a glow of pride.

How often had Miranda received compliments? He'd guess not often enough.

'And you're beautiful,' he added deliberately.

Her eyes widened and he felt her retreat a little.

As if she didn't believe him?

Zamir had made his share of mistakes, including with Miranda. He'd come to realise that his bride was *far* more complex than he'd initially thought.

'I don't lie, Miranda. You're one of the most beautiful women I've met.'

She shook her head, that diaphanous stole slipping down to reveal close-cut curls that complemented her vibrant sexiness. She looked fresh and real and enticingly sensual. His fingers itched with the need to stroke those soft locks.

'It's just the fancy clothes. I'm not really—'

'You're not listening, Miranda.'

His fingers curled around her toned upper arms, registering through the fabric the vitality that was characteristic of the woman. As was her refusal to heed what he said.

She frustrated and aroused him in equal measure.

Maybe not equal. For now he drew in her scent—jasmine and warm woman—and arousal outstripped anything else. Except the need to make this absolutely clear.

'You're beautiful, Miranda. Whether you're wearing rich clothes or jeans and riding boots. It's not your clothes or how you wear your hair. Your beauty is in your bones and flashing eyes. In the way you carry yourself. Even in your temper.' He paused, knowing his admission gave her power but unable to deny it.

'It's the sort of beauty that will grow over the years. You'll still look elegant and sexy decades from now.'

'Sexy?'

Zamir's attention dropped to her mouth. Her lips were parted in surprise. Or invitation. An invitation his hardening body was eager to accept. A shudder ran the length of his backbone and down through his belly. A shudder of sexual arousal.

Abruptly he realised how close he held her. And the promise he'd given, that *she* would be the one to initiate intimacy.

'Definitely sexy,' he growled as he released her and stepped back, fingers flexing as if objecting to the fact they no longer held her. 'Too sexy. But I'm a man of my word.'

'You want me.'

He couldn't tell if it was a question or a statement, just knew he had to remove himself from her presence because this conversation eroded his control. 'We'll discuss it later.'

He turned towards the door then jolted to a stop. When her hand closed around his arm.

CHAPTER ELEVEN

MIRANDA LOOKED UP into his set features.

Haughty, she'd have called them a few days ago. Grim. Forbidding.

Ridiculously appealing.

Now she realised something new. This stern look wasn't from anger or disapproval. It was because he struggled against the same desire she did.

He wanted her.

Admired her, even.

He hadn't been buttering her up with soft words to make her more malleable. She'd read his frustration, even indignation at her refusal to accept his compliments.

She'd heard honesty in his voice and read it in the way he looked at her when he described her as beautiful.

That had stolen her breath.

All her life she'd been compared unfavourably with her glamorous mother and beautiful, docile cousin. To the extent that when men *had* complimented her she'd written off their words as flummery, designed to win her over because they wanted sex.

Zamir wanted sex—she'd read that white-hot flash of hunger—but instead of capitalising on his compliment, he tried to walk away.

He was the most frustrating man!

She wanted to learn more. Experience more. She'd been on

tenterhooks for days because, for the first time in her life, she had a genuine crush on a man. On her husband!

And now he wanted to end this fascinating conversation and leave her thwarted and unsatisfied.

From her youth she'd felt comfortable with boys, playing football or hanging around the stables, more at home there than inside her uncle's home, pretending to be a delicate flower. As an adult she'd worked with men, generally managing to downplay her gender by being as competent as them.

And because none of them made her heart race the way Zamir did.

It wasn't because he'd said she was beautiful. Though that had stunned her. For it had been more than a throwaway compliment. She'd seen honesty in his eyes when he'd talked of an intrinsic beauty rooted in character not clothes.

There was something about him that, from the first, had made her aware of him as male and herself as female, stirring up unfamiliar yearnings.

She cleared her throat. 'Don't go.'

He didn't move but nor did he relax. 'It's best that I do. It's getting late and—'

'Are you afraid to be alone with me?'

A muscle jumped under her touch and she watched his jaw flex, a pulse flickering at his temple.

'Afraid?' He shook his head. 'Hardly. I don't have anything to lose here.' He moved closer, right into her space so she had to raise her chin to hold eye contact. 'But you do. You're the one who doesn't want a sexual relationship.'

He was giving her the chance to withdraw.

To run away to her own rooms and pretend Zamir meant nothing to her.

But running away wasn't Miranda's style. No matter how unexpected or inconvenient, she wanted her husband.

'What if I've changed my mind?'

She felt him stiffen, saw his shoulders lift on a deeply indrawn breath. Those inky eyes narrowed. 'I'd ask if you were sure.'

Sure she was doing the right thing? She didn't feel sure of anything. Except that she could no longer ignore the craving that had become a compulsion.

Since she'd met Zamir every dormant feminine desire had grown supercharged. She wanted, *needed*, to share herself with him.

'I'm sure. I want you, Zamir.'

Her words fell into reverberating silence, unbroken so long that her breath hitched and her skin crawled. Had she misjudged him? Had he simply wanted to manoeuvre her into admitting—?

Her thoughts cut off as he leant down, his hands sure yet gentle as they cupped her cheeks, long fingers tunnelling through her hair. Ebony eyes locked on hers and she lost herself in their depths.

His lips brushed hers, once, twice, before settling, his tongue gliding across the seam of her mouth until she opened for him.

Everything changed. Need exploded as he delved deep and suddenly they were devouring each other, heads angling for better access, bodies pressing, hands grasping. She tasted his grunt of satisfaction as she wriggled between his spread thighs, registering the long column of his arousal jutting against her.

Heat saturated from her hairline to her toes, and especially in her womb where a hollow throb started up. She shifted her weight, circling her hips and Zamir groaned.

The sound was so raw that it fed her response. Her peaked nipples pressed against him and between her legs she felt a softening.

He skimmed a hand down her back, planting it against her buttocks and drawing her up against the tantalising hardness of his erection.

Miranda strained higher, dislodging his head scarf, clutching his thick, soft hair. It must be the only soft thing about him.

She moved against him and excitement edged with trepidation shot through her as she realised the size of his erection.

'I want to see you,' she whispered against his mouth.

She wanted to see all of him, experience everything.

He leaned back just enough to meet her eyes. 'I want to see you too. Let's go to my—'

'No!' She needed Zamir. Now. Here. Before she had time to second-guess the wisdom of sharing her body with the man who held all the power in this relationship. 'I want you *now*.'

His mouth kicked up in a smile that dragged sensation through her body like fingers through fur. She trembled.

'I love a woman who knows her mind.' His voice hit a baritone note that somehow heightened her tension.

Before she could protest he stepped back, leaving her body bereft. But he merely strode to the door, locking it.

'Take off your clothes, Miranda.'

She reached for the buttons at the back of her neckline as he toed off his shoes. Eyes holding hers, he hauled off his ceremonial robes, not pausing until he'd stripped bare, and she couldn't repress an awed gasp.

Zamir was tall and well built, broad across the shoulders, narrow at the hips, with strong thighs and a jutting erection.

She swallowed hard, her mouth dry at the symmetry and sheer magnificence of his virile body.

'Do you need help?' He walked towards her and her throat clogged. Instead of answering she nodded, unable to tear her gaze away.

Then he was before her. She was so close to all that bronzed skin, inhaling his distinctive scent, now mixed with something earthy that made her tremble with anticipation. Male pheromones.

'Let me.' Gentle hands on her shoulders turned her around

then he swore under his breath. 'Who put in all these buttons? Haven't they heard of zips?'

His exasperation pierced her breathlessness and a laugh bubbled up. Then she felt him fumble with the tiny buttons as she had and her amusement died. Zamir seemed just as clumsy as she. Wishful thinking? Yet it reinforced the feeling that this was as significant for him as for her.

'It's no good. I haven't got the patience to undo them all.'

The fabric parted and callused hands slid across her upper back, making her shiver with voluptuous delight as the silk slid off her shoulders.

Warm lips pressed her nape then descended her spine, making her arch as sparks of arousal exploded at each point of contact. The bodice of her dress dropped just enough that he could slide her arms free of the sleeves. Then he was cupping her breasts in her bra, pulling her back against him. Miranda felt as if she'd died and gone to heaven.

'More,' she breathed.

'Demanding woman.'

But she heard his approval and when he snicked open her bra and tugged it free, taking her breasts in his big hands, his sigh of pleasure eclipsed hers. The sensation was so amazing, so exquisite, Miranda cupped his hands with hers, holding tight as if afraid he might let her go.

He caught her nipples between thumbs and index fingers, gently rolling them, and it felt as if she flew too close to the sun, cascades of sparks igniting and coalescing to burn bright and hot.

Miranda juddered, sinking back against him, luxuriating in the sensation of flesh against flesh. Even the soft scratch of his chest hair against her upper back undid her.

'More,' she gasped, twisting her hips and pushing back towards his groin.

'I'd imagined our first time being in bed.' His voice was

so thick it took a moment to register what he said. 'But since you're so eager…'

Zamir removed his hands and the loss was so intense it stunned her. Before she could protest though, he lifted her and laid her down on a gilded sofa. The fabric was cool against her upper back and her long skirts still covered her legs. Except now, perched on the edge of the sofa, he slid his hands up her ankles, her shins, knees and thighs, lifting the silvery fabric to bunch around her hips.

'Beautiful,' he murmured. His attention was on the lace covering her mound, then flicked up to her breasts, bare and wobbling with each scant breath. Finally his gaze rested on her mouth and she felt it like a kiss.

A great shudder ran through her as their eyes met again. Falling into that glittering midnight gaze felt even more intimate than when he touched her with his hands or bare body.

Holding her gaze, he touched her again, fingers curling around her lace underwear, dragging it down her legs and off.

Miranda released a breath she hadn't realised she'd held.

Finally. She reached for him but he'd moved. Sliding down the sofa, he planted his palms on her bunched-up skirt and bent his head.

Hot breath tickled sensitive flesh, making her twitch and shift her legs apart. He smiled then, smug, but Miranda didn't mind. She just wanted more.

When he gave it to her, his mouth against her most sensitive flesh, she almost jolted up off the cushions. That slow, lingering touch unleashed something she knew instinctively had the power to devastate her. Something she feared might be addictive.

Before she had time to make sense of that he did it again, and again, and she was moving with him, body undulating. Her breath snagged in her lungs, her hands anchored in his dark hair.

The air changed, thickening and growing heavy as if at the

approach of a storm. Was that the crackle of thunder or an auditory illusion caused by her rampaging pulse? Her heart swelled as if it might burst free from her chest. Finally relief came, searing, blinding white light and sensations of pleasure almost too intense to bear.

Over the thunder in her ears, Miranda heard a high keening sound as she shuddered in ecstasy.

Then finally, Zamir lay over her, his mouth against her, murmuring praise and reassurance, his weight anchoring her to the world again, bringing her back to herself.

Miranda wrapped her arms around his ribcage, holding him close as he stroked the hair from her face and kissed her ear, cheek and neck. She shivered as those caresses set off little aftershocks.

Finally, when the tremors stopped, he lifted his head, eyes glowing, and kissed her full on the mouth. It was a different kiss this time, not so desperate but languorous and thorough, a reminder of where she'd just been and a promise of more to come.

Her body was so limp she didn't think more was possible, until he stroked her bare breast and nudged her knees apart so he could settle between her legs.

Impossible it might be, yet Miranda felt a jolt of shocking pleasure arc between her breast and the apex of her thighs where his arousal rested. Her hips tilted, stroking his engorged flesh. What he'd done before felt fantastic but this…

'I can't wait any longer.'

His voice was rough, almost unrecognisable as he reached between them, the tendons in his neck standing proud and his high-cut cheekbones more pronounced.

Miranda felt a weight between her thighs.

'I need to tell you something,' she blurted, because suddenly it was important he knew. He'd given her such delight she needed to warn him not to expect too much in return.

Zamir stiffened, his body turning to stone under her hands. 'You've changed your mind?'

'No!' How could he think that? She'd never experienced ecstasy like that and every instinct told her there was more, as good if not better, to come. She cleared her throat. 'It's just that I haven't done this before. I might disappoint you.'

His eyes snapped wide. 'You said—'

'I misled you. I didn't want to admit I don't have any experience when you probably have so much. I wanted to…'

'Tease me?'

'No.' She paused. 'I wanted not to seem vulnerable or weak. I've been out of my depth since we met and I wanted, for once, to be your equal in something.'

That made her sound sad and pathetic. A couple of days ago she'd never have admitted it but after what had just happened, her defences were shattered. She wanted him to understand.

But instead of accepting her warning, Zamir reared back as if stung. Her heart plummeted. Had she destroyed the moment?

'When you say no experience, you mean *no* experience?'

Miranda scrabbled to sit up, pulling her bodice over her heaving breasts. 'I've been kissed.' He raised his eyebrows and she shrugged. 'But I've never had sex.'

Zamir scrubbed a hand over his face. 'In that case we'd better not—'

'No!' In a flurry of fabric she closed the space between them, one hand clutching his bulging biceps. 'Don't say we have to stop. Just because I'm a virgin doesn't mean I can't learn.'

'Stop?' His nostrils flared and he shook his head as he stroked her cheek, his fingers trailing from there to her bare breast, revealed by her now-drooping bodice, making her shiver. 'You credit me with too many scruples. I was just going to suggest we move to the bedroom. Your first time shouldn't be on a sofa.'

Relief made her laugh. 'Is that a rule? You can't take my virginity on a sofa?'

His mouth ticked up at the corners in that bare hint of a grin that turned her insides to mush. 'Not a rule. I just think it better that you're comfortable.'

'I'm comfortable here.'

Miranda had an unreasoning fear that if they stopped long enough to move to another room he'd change his mind. It made no sense but her mind wasn't functioning on logic.

She stroked her hand up his arm, her other hand reaching for his groin and that proud erection that so fascinated her. But Zamir grabbed her wrist, preventing her reaching her goal.

'Teach me, Zamir.' She leaned close, feathering a kiss to the corner of his mouth then across to his neck, remembering the shatteringly decadent sensation he'd elicited when he'd caressed her there. 'Show me.'

She grazed her teeth at a spot just below his ear and he shuddered, his big body trembling at her touch.

How strange and wonderful to feel such power. She could get used to it. Except she didn't want power over Zamir. She wanted them together.

Miranda lifted her head and met eyes glazed with desire. His large hands cupped her breasts, his touch firm yet so gentle she felt something dissolve inside. As if a too-tight knot unravelled. She arched, pushing her breasts into his hands, revelling in the febrile heat she read in his eyes as much as the delicious sensations.

He spoke softly. 'You're a headstrong woman.'

'And you like it.'

It was only as she heard the words that she realised they were true. There was nothing but desire and approval in his expression. No matter how they'd argued, he'd never loathed her feistiness the way her uncle did.

'Perhaps I do.' He rolled her nipples between his fingers

and she gasped at the shock of delight that arced from his touch straight to her core. 'Now stop talking and straddle me.'

'Straddle?'

Her brain seemed to have slowed and Zamir finally betrayed impatience by grabbing her hips and lifting her bodily over him. She knelt, one knee on either side of his thighs, facing him, her long skirts bundled up around her waist.

She shifted her weight as something warm and solid brushed her inner thigh. Her breath snared as she realised what it was.

'Absolutely sure?'

Miranda nodded, steadying herself on those broad straight shoulders as he reached beneath the crumpled dress. 'What now?'

Zamir's smile was tight, as if he were in pain. She wanted to query that but kept quiet. There was something she wanted more. She moved her knees wider and felt the head of his erection stroke her again.

'Just sink down, slowly.'

Taking a fortifying breath, because despite everything she *was* a little nervous, she lowered herself, pausing as his flesh notched against her entrance.

Miranda recalled the size of his arousal, perfectly in keeping with the size of the man, but significantly larger than she'd expected. But she wanted this, wanted him, so much, even the prospect of a little pain didn't daunt her.

Biting the corner of her mouth in concentration, she sank down then paused.

'Oh!'

Nothing had prepared her for the strange feeling of fullness as their bodies merged.

'It hurts?' Zamir leaned forward and nuzzled her breast, kissing and grazing it gently with his teeth, making her shudder and her eyes close. Internal muscles softened and eased and without further thought she slipped down further and further until her breath disappeared because it felt as if they'd truly become one. She felt the joining not only in her pelvis but higher, in her chest where her heart quickened and her lungs faltered for a moment at the enormity of this miracle.

'Miranda. Does it hurt?'

She shook her head. 'It just feels…'

She opened her eyes and met his, so close he should be blurry, yet somehow he wasn't. She saw him clearly. The man, not the Sheikh. The lover who'd already brought her such bliss.

Miranda didn't have words. Instead she leaned in and kissed him full on the mouth with gratitude and joy. With all the pent-up yearning she'd battled. With the tattered wreckage of the fear and doubt she'd clung to and which he'd vanquished with his simple, honest praise, turning her tormenting thoughts inside out and offering her a bright new reality.

She couldn't name her emotions as she offered and he accepted, her hands now cupping his face, his arms wrapped tight around her back as if he couldn't bear any distance between them.

She devoured his mouth and he let her, then devoured her right back.

And when he shifted beneath her, bumping his hips so she rode higher, she gasped. For deep as he was, that nudged a spot that hummed in pure delight.

'Lift up,' he urged against her mouth and his hands slid to her hips, grasping and gently drawing her higher till she wanted to protest because it felt like withdrawal. Except then, with a little downward pressure, he had her sinking so they fitted more snugly than ever.

Miranda felt her eyes widen as other parts of her body cheered in awed delight.

Now she understood.

Leaning in to kiss him deeply, she rose again then let gravity do its work, creating more glorious friction as they locked together once more.

This time Zamir's fingers clamped tight at her hips and he

groaned in the back of his throat. She tasted the sound on her tongue, rough and delicious, and wanted more.

She wanted to give him the joy he'd given her.

Eagerly she rose and fell, slowly then faster, excitement feeding off his obvious pleasure.

Zamir's grip turned harder but she loved that, feeling he teetered on the edge of the same ecstasy he'd given her. Meanwhile the friction between their bodies and the amazing feeling of oneness pushed her on. She twisted her hips, learning how to milk pleasure from each movement.

Something changed. The tempo. Zamir's breathing. And Miranda's excitement rose. She felt tremors course through his body and realised he was close to climax. The idea was incredibly arousing, though she knew this time was for him, not her.

Then Zamir slid his hands from her hips, leaving her totally in control. He cupped her breast and leaned forward to take her nipple in his mouth and suck. Instantly she faltered, shuddering as a bolt of lightning hit her.

She'd just found her rhythm again when his hand slid under her dress, warm against her abdomen, thumb pressing down on that most sensitive spot in her whole body.

Miranda's eyes widened. Her body jerked and she felt an answering throb from Zamir.

That was all it took to send her careering out of control, riding him with a desperate, ungainly eagerness that jolted them together and turned their smooth union into a jerky, ecstatic race to rapture.

CHAPTER TWELVE

'MORE, ZAMIR. MORE, PLEASE!'

In the pre-dawn quiet Miranda's voice was a raw gasp, barely audible over the surge of blood in his ears. But he saw her mouth form the words, her lips reddened from passion. Her short nails dug into his flesh and her strong, supple legs encircled his hips, caging him.

As if he wanted to be anywhere but here!

Then thought was beyond him. There was just Miranda convulsing in pleasure, destroying the last of his stamina and drawing him to triumphant climax.

He buried his face against the curve of her neck, drawing in the deep floral and female scent of her while he spilled himself gratefully into velvety warmth. Each climax with her seemed more phenomenal than the last.

Ages later he came to himself enough to think of his weight bearing down on her so, wrapping her in his arms, he rolled onto his back so she lay limp above him, their panting breaths in unison.

He had no perception of time. The world comprised just himself and Miranda. He knew hours had passed. They'd slept a little and, after that first time, they'd bathed in the sunken tub of gold-veined marble that he'd never used because a quick shower was more efficient.

Now he didn't care about efficient. He luxuriated in the physical senses.

Miranda had been a revelation. Her disarming honesty had cut past his pride. She'd revealed doubts and insecurities that surprised him and made him want to protect her, though he suspected she wouldn't accept that. She was so determinedly independent.

And brave. He'd never forget her expression when he'd taken her virginity. How she'd paused, face twisted in discomfort if not pain, nails biting his flesh.

He'd been ready to withdraw, loath to hurt her. But she'd taken stock then simply continued, trusting him to make it good for her. It had been typical of her gallant determination and made him even more committed to making her first time memorable for all the best reasons.

Significantly though, Miranda had also revealed another side to *him*. A pleasure-seeker, determined to wrest every last drop of sensual pleasure from their bodies.

Zamir enjoyed sex but tonight had been different. He felt more…engaged. The climaxes had been more acute, his delight in her arousal an end in itself. He'd given her orgasms, not just because he was a considerate lover, but because her incandescent joy was his too.

There was something different about Miranda.

Something portentous about their coming together.

Instinctively, he shied from the idea, searching for logic to explain the inexplicable.

It's because she was a virgin.

He'd wanted to ensure this was good for her too.

And because she's your wife. You have a vested interest in keeping her happy.

Except this was more than keeping a sexual partner happy.

In the past, when the senses were sated, Zamir had had no difficulty pulling away. He'd chosen partners who wanted short affairs not emotional connection.

Yet all night, after each climax, instead of craving the usual solace of privacy, Zamir had wanted Miranda in his arms.

Their limbs tangled together, as if he cherished her closeness as much as the sex they'd shared.

Gently he stroked her back and she snuggled against his chest. Zamir felt such deep satisfaction at having her here, sprawled boneless above him, that it should shock him. But he'd become inured to surprises where Miranda was concerned.

After that first time he'd decided to hold back for the rest of the night. She was unused to sex and he was a big man. He would let her sleep undisturbed the rest of the night.

For once he couldn't follow through on his decision. The urges of his body undermined his brain.

It was as if he had no control. When they'd left the bath he'd mentioned returning her to her room, because if they slept in separate rooms his resolve wouldn't be so tested. She'd looked at him with huge silvery eyes and his good intentions had dissolved.

He couldn't help but be pleased that his bride enjoyed sex so much. Her enthusiasm belied her inexperience and she learned fast. Already she was frighteningly effective at seducing him. She'd be positively dangerous when she realised the extent of her power.

Zamir frowned. He wasn't afraid of a sexually strong woman. In fact, the idea stirred a libido that should be dormant after their recent activities.

Yet he was unsettled.

Since the age of ten, his life had followed a strict regimen. Every hour accounted for and used to best effect. He rarely took time off and had never been tempted to while away a day in bed.

He was sorely tempted now. In fact he was mentally running through this morning's appointments, trying to persuade himself they could be rescheduled.

Zamir wanted to stay with Miranda. Have a little of the honeymoon that had been denied them because there'd been too many important matters to deal with when they returned from Aboussir. Because it was vital his wife be accepted without question. That she slotted into her role without raising too many eyebrows or causing major scandal. Questions about her suitability as Queen would reflect on him and on the planned merger of nations.

Yet he found it hard to think about politics.

He wanted…his breath locked in his throat as he realised what he wanted most was to be here with Miranda. He wanted to forget his obligations and carve out time for private pleasure.

For sex, yes. But there was more too. He wanted to take her riding at sunset on the coast. He could imagine her grin as they galloped together along the wet sand as the sun turned the water to fire.

He wanted to see her expression when he drove her into the mountain town famed for its ancient houses carved into the rocks. To the hot-air balloon festival when hundreds of colourful balloons rose delicately in the dawn light.

He'd take her into the desert to his favourite oasis, just the two of them. He had a hunch she'd appreciate some of the things he loved about his country.

Since when did you expect or want a honeymoon?

Yours was always going to be a marriage of convenience.

Honeymoons are for people who believe in romance. Not royals with millions depending on them.

A chill wound its way from Zamir's prickling hairline, down his vertebrae and plunged into his belly.

He remembered his uncle's response when he'd begged to be allowed to play football with his friends. The kind but stern voice reminding him he had an obligation to his nation. To learn to be the best ruler he could. To put the nation's needs above his own. And never to forget that.

It had been drummed into him that duty must always come before personal feelings. It was one of the reasons he'd kept going, stoic through bereavement.

Was this, now, him forgetting his responsibilities? Letting emotion rule?

After twenty years of doing his royal duty, was he sliding into selfishness?

You're allowed time off. You're not a machine.

But the way he felt, he'd take an hour for himself and it would become three. A day would become a week. He had to put the brakes on while he still could. Because Miranda threatened to undermine the work ethic that was his core strength. Without it…

He couldn't allow that. He had to be strong, not let selfishness undermine him.

Gently he slid out from under Miranda, rolling her onto her side, and rose from the bed.

His worst fears were realised when he saw the time. He'd noticed the strip of daylight edging the curtains but ignored it. Now he was late for his meetings.

A noise woke Miranda. She lay sprawled in a vast bed. Without opening her eyes she knew it was Zamir's. It smelled of him and of sex. She was boneless with a mixture of tiredness and exhilaration that felt close to heaven. The only thing that would make it better was Zamir.

She opened her eyes and there he was, emerging from the bathroom. He wore a charcoal suit and had just shaved.

She shivered voluptuously, remembering the exciting scrape of his bristly chin along her inner thigh and elsewhere.

Who'd known sex could be so wondrous?

Not just sex but sex with Zamir. Her insides twisted in excitement as their gazes locked. But instead of meeting a heavy-lidded look of sensual awareness, Miranda confronted a cool, unreadable scrutiny. Gone was the warmth, the beguiling invitation, the connection.

The man before her, with his flat mouth and pinched nostrils, reminded her of the haughty enemy she'd first met.

Instantly her lassitude disappeared as she scrabbled for the sheet, tucking it around herself as she sat up against the pillows.

Something flared in his eyes before he looked away. 'Sorry, I didn't mean to wake you. Stay here and rest. There's no need for you to get up, but I have business—'

'Wait!' Miranda didn't know what she was going to say, just that she wasn't ready for him to leave.

Fool. Can't you see he can't wait to get out of here?

If she'd needed anything to remind her that she was the novice when it came to sex, and he the expert, his attitude now proved it. She'd thought they'd shared something glorious and special. He couldn't wait to go. His precious business appealed more than her, now he'd had what he wanted.

Miranda swallowed and jutted her chin higher, striving to keep the hurt from her voice. 'At least tell me how to get back to my room. I don't fancy doing the morning-after walk of shame through the palace.'

That stopped him in his tracks. He turned to face her fully, frowning. 'There's no shame involved. We're husband and wife.'

Her eyes narrowed. 'But that's how this feels. Especially with you…' she waved one hand, searching for words '…dismissing me with a curt couple of words.'

Zamir's eyes widened and his hand went to his perfectly knotted tie. 'Dismissing you?'

He drew himself taller, shoulders back, chin angled proudly, sooty eyebrows forming a deep V, the image of superiority.

Then he shook his head and approached the bed. Gleaming eyes captured hers and again she felt that fizz of connection as if he only had to look at her and she was his. As if she had no pride.

Zamir sat beside her, his arm caging her body as he planted his palm beside her hip.

'I'm sorry, Miranda.' His voice was gravelly, his gaze searching. 'I wasn't thinking.'

His mouth turned down at the corners and his chest lifted on a deep sigh as he raked his hand through his hair. Predictably, it fell back in place perfectly. How did he do that? Miranda knew she looked rumpled while Zamir was as perfectly put together as ever.

He plucked her hand from the sheet, threading his fingers through hers. 'Dismissal was the last thing on my mind.' He paused. 'The trouble was I panicked.'

She'd never seen anyone more obviously in control.

'Panicked? I find that hard to believe.'

With her hand in his, his thumb stroking her palm and his gorgeous scent tantalising her nostrils, Miranda's voice sounded breathless rather than accusing.

'It's true.' He looked at their joined hands then pressed warm lips to her flesh, sending a shiver of reaction cascading through her weak frame.

He murmured something she didn't catch over the thunder of her blood. But she did hear him add, 'This is outside my experience.'

Miranda couldn't prevent a huff of laughter. 'Surely that's my line.'

Abruptly he looked up, amusement creating long dimples in his cheeks, his eyes alight and smile rueful. 'So it is. Though it doesn't feel like it. You undo me, Miranda.'

For a moment he looked as surprised as she felt. *She* undid *him*? Her pulse thudded wildly.

'I'm not used to being married. And before you say anything, of course that applies to us both. What I'm used to are short, discreet affairs away from the palace. My work and private life don't intermingle. I didn't know we were going to spend the night together. I have to work this morning.'

He flicked a glance at the expensive watch on his wrist. 'Instead of having the luxury to stay with you, I have a packed schedule. All important matters that need my personal attention. And I'm already half an hour late for my first meeting.'

'You'd rather spend the morning here with me?'

His look of astonishment spoke for itself. 'How can you doubt it?'

He lifted her hand, pressing it to his groin where she felt a now-familiar rigid length. Heat filled her and her fingers curled possessively.

Zamir wanted her. What had he said? That she undid him.

Relief flooded and that delicious feeling that they shared this attraction as equals. But it was short-lived as he gently pried her hand away.

'Not now.' His voice sounded thick and unfamiliar. 'I have an international trade delegation waiting for me. I can't insult them by being even later.'

This time when he spoke, Miranda saw what it cost him. She felt the fine tremor running through his big frame and the tension in his muscles.

'I came in from the bathroom and saw you awake and knew I had to leave straight away before I did something rash.'

Zamir leaned close, his free hand cupping her jaw, fingertips burrowing into her hair as he kissed her, deliberately, longingly, carnally.

That was all it took to blank Miranda's mind of doubt and indignation. She pressed herself against him, giving herself unstintingly, the floodgates of desire bursting open. She yanked his hand to her breast. Clasping it there, she arched into his touch. A deep growl vibrated from his throat, making her shiver with anticipation.

But too soon he pulled away, capturing both her hands in his and holding them tight. 'This was exactly what I was afraid of. I can't, Miranda. As much as I want to, I have responsibilities that I can't ignore.'

Miranda watched his face, the fleeting emotions, and fastened on the most extraordinary one.

Zamir had been afraid.

It was a common expression, but, combined with his behaviour, she realised he meant it.

She threatened his focus and his timetable. But watching him watch her, she was convinced he didn't say that lightly. She knew how important Zamir's duty was to him. Not for the ego trip but because he genuinely believed his work made a difference.

He'd been afraid she'd tempt him into forgetting that.

Had she that much power? The idea stunned her and she needed time to think it through.

While he needed to work.

'Then you're forgiven. You'd better go.'

His mouth twisted. 'That's the hell of it. I don't want to.'

He lifted her hand to his mouth and kissed her knuckles, sending a shiver of need through her. He only had to touch her and her willpower dissolved. That terrified her. 'You still need to tell me how to get back to my room.'

His smile wound a ribbon of heat around her. 'Didn't you know we have adjoining suites?' He nodded to a door on the far side of the room. 'That goes straight to your bedroom.'

'All this time you've been sleeping just a room away?'

He nodded. 'We *are* married, after all.'

Was it the way his voice dropped to a soft, suede note, or the lambent fire in his gaze that took her immediately back to last night's intimacies? She found herself breathless and dazzled.

Too dazzled. Zamir might have stunned her with his admission of momentary panic because he'd rather stay than attend his meetings. But that was nothing to Miranda's crazy thoughts. She still felt they'd shared something utterly unique and special. Yet logic decreed it was just her inexperience trying to transform physical bliss into something more momentous.

If she wasn't careful she'd read too much into simple sex. On learning their rooms were a mere wall apart, she'd even mentally applauded Zamir's patience in not trying to use their proximity to seduce her earlier. Some men would have.

As if she didn't have the right to abstain from sex if she chose!

But you don't want to abstain. You want Zamir, more even than before.

Last night had changed things. Changed *her.* She needed to regroup and think things through. As it was, she was only slowly coming to terms with the implications of what they'd shared.

'Before you go,' she began. 'We didn't use contraception.'

He nodded gravely. 'Yes. For the first time ever I realised that after the event. But there's no need to worry about an infection. I—'

'I was actually concerned about pregnancy.' She hadn't got as far as thinking about STDs.

He stilled. 'You don't want children?'

Had he simply assumed she would? Miranda wished she could read him better. Through the night it had felt as if they'd connected at such an elemental level that everything between them would simply fall into place, the way their bodies did. Clearly that wasn't so.

'I suppose I assumed I'd have children one day.'

She sat back, pulling her hands from his, realising abruptly how very convenient it would be for Zamir if last night left her pregnant. He'd married to secure the kingdom and, by his own admission, the succession.

Had that been part of the reason he'd wanted her?

'But I'm not ready for a child.' Panic made her voice strident. 'We don't know each other. Except physically. It would be a disaster.'

Again Zamir's expression turned inscrutable. But it wasn't foolproof, for Miranda read his thudding pulse and the tiny firming of his lips. He wasn't happy.

A second later he unfolded himself from the bed to stand,

surveying her from his lofty height. 'Very well. I'll arrange a doctor's appointment today so you can consider contraception options and I'll get condoms for next time.' He paused. 'Assuming there'll be a next time?'

It was on the tip of her tongue to say no because she hated the sudden distance between them, and the feeling it was her fault. But she had no reason to feel guilty. Her stipulation was reasonable.

And what was the point pretending? He only had to touch her and she went up in flames.

'Yes,' she managed, her voice only a little hoarse. 'There'll be a next time.'

For a second they stared at each other, then, belying what she'd believed to be his annoyance, Zamir leaned down and kissed her on the mouth. Not hard but thoroughly, so thoroughly her head was spinning as he pulled back and straightened his tie while she slumped, boneless against the pillows.

'Rest now, Miranda. I'll cancel your lessons for this morning so you can catch up on sleep. You'll need it.'

CHAPTER THIRTEEN

THE NEXT FEW weeks Zamir struggled to get through his work. He kept zoning out, attention straying to his unpredictable, irresistible wife.

Miranda was more challenging than any politician or negotiator. She made him feel things he never had.

He wanted as he'd never wanted before. His continual need for her undermined his resolution to do his job.

Enough even to admit in an unguarded moment how he feared her ability to distract him. Zamir *never* admitted weakness. He'd learned that at his uncle's knee.

Yet though he and Miranda still needed to negotiate some things, he no longer felt they were on opposing sides.

He trusted her.

The more he understood her, the more he liked and appreciated her. He'd rather have her reckless courage and honesty than a bride who simply nodded and agreed with him.

Even if sometimes Miranda wrong-footed him and injured his pride. Like when they'd discussed contraception.

Zamir *never* forgot contraception. Except with her. When he realised, he'd allayed his guilt by telling himself they were married and a child was expected. It was only when she called him on it that he realised how thoughtless that was. He imagined how doubly trapped Miranda would feel if she got pregnant so early in their relationship. He couldn't do that to her while she still faced so many challenges. When she regretted being here.

Knowing that made him feel…wrong. Even if it was too late to end their marriage.

He remembered his parents' relationship. The distance between them and with their children. Zamir didn't want that for any children he might have. He wanted—he realised with sudden certainty—something different to his parents' arrangement.

He wanted children who were loved and knew it. He wanted to be more than a polite stranger to his wife.

Miranda had cut him off at the knees when she'd admitted to insecurities behind her bravado. And *still* she was one of the strongest people he knew.

He'd witnessed vulnerability, obviously rooted in childhood, which made her doubt herself. He'd been sickened that her family had tried to squash her spirit. It made him realise his actions had played into that past negativity.

Because of that Zamir was determined to give his wife the freedom to be herself, to blossom, despite the parameters of royal life. He'd started out needing a suitable queen. But now…

He wanted Miranda to be happy.

It was as simple and complex as that. How thoughtless had been his plan to acquire a wife. As if she'd be two-dimensional, without her own needs and frailties, desires and strengths. After years working with his uncle, listening to the people, arbitrating disputes, hearing their issues and devising solutions, how could he not have anticipated that?

He didn't have to choose between Miranda and his duty because he realised now they were bound together.

Now the man who'd spent two decades adhering to every dictate of royal expectation found himself looking for ways to ease that burden. Not because his wife was weak, but because it hurt to think of all that vibrancy and honesty muffled and unappreciated.

Because she hated formal lessons he'd reduced them and taught her himself in relaxed conversations during sunset rides or over a meal. Until, inevitably, they were distracted by their desire for each other. He ignored the voice of caution warning he was shifting his priorities because of her. For Zamir was assiduous in ensuring he didn't neglect his official duties.

His lack of concentration was at least partly due to lack of sleep. Their sex life grew better and better.

When he wasn't with Miranda, he was imagining how it would be when he was. Her silky skin, her rich, enticing scent, her slender yet strong body matching his, wringing desperate responses that drained him, leaving him bereft of any pretence that he controlled this situation.

On the outside he might look like the man he'd always been but inside he felt different.

His increasing awareness of Miranda's issues made him think more carefully about other things. He found himself revisiting earlier judgements, listening harder to petitioners, and urging his staff to find more innovative answers to complex social problems. Because one size didn't fit everyone. Over the years he and his uncle had introduced useful reforms. But had they gone far enough? Had they been effective and inclusive for everyone? Had there been people left out, distanced and excluded?

Zamir left his last meeting but instead of returning to his office, on impulse took the corridor that led to the back of the palace.

That impulse being the need to see Miranda. He stifled the stern voice of conscience telling him he had a lot of work yet to do.

Surely checking on this new social initiative counted as work? Miranda had been helping at horse-riding sessions for people with disabilities. Each time she'd returned glowing and full of enthusiasm. Instead of complaining about the staff who accompanied her whenever she left the palace, she'd roped some of them into helping.

The change in her, having a purpose again, something she believed in, made him swell with pride and admiration. She seemed more confident too, attending several official functions with him.

Which was why, after she'd presented a persuasive case, Zamir had given qualified approval to a new project here at the palace. A pilot programme working with teenagers who'd skirted the edge of the legal system and who were likely to get into more trouble.

Zamir applauded a scheme to keep youngsters from incarceration and hopefully set them on a better path. Yet he'd wanted to bar Miranda's personal involvement with potentially dangerous young men.

There was that protective instinct kicking in.

He'd wrestled with his conscience, discussed the programme with Miranda and others, including expert youth workers, and finally decided not to interfere. It seemed she was an expert too, having worked with a similar programme at her stepfather's ranch.

His wife was full of surprises. She'd won over Zamir's old-fashioned stable master and not merely with her riding skills. She'd helped several horses recuperate from injury with what the older man called magic hands. She, shrugging, said it was a combination of massage and osteopathy.

His impressed stable master said she'd be able to name her own salary at any professional stable.

Practical, eager to help and with a social conscience yet no sense of entitlement or self-importance. Miranda might at first glance not fit the traditional idea of a queen. Yet she was impressive in so many ways.

The pilot programme had begun three days ago in the royal stables and Zamir had deliberately stayed away, giving those involved space. Besides, Miranda enthusiastically updated him each evening and Hassan was on hand to ensure there were no problems.

'I wondered how long you'd manage to stay away.'

Hassan's softly spoken words stopped him in the shaded colonnade opposite the stables.

Zamir raised an eyebrow. 'The trouble with having a head of security who's known you for years is they think they can read your mind.'

Hassan smiled. He nodded to where several horses stood patiently. 'I had my doubts about this but I'm beginning to wonder if there might be something in it. A couple of the boys stop their tough-guy posturing as soon as they're around the animals. And most pay attention even if they pretend not to.'

They watched in silence as Miranda and two others went up and down the line, murmuring advice and watching as young men undid the girths and lifted off saddles.

At the end of the row one wiry youth had difficulty. He said something and Miranda moved in close to assist. Suddenly the youth lunged, making a grab for her breast.

Zamir was crossing the courtyard at a run when Hassan's hand on his arm stopped him. 'Wait. Watch.'

Miranda didn't even flinch. In what felt like slow motion, Zamir saw her reach for the guy's wrist as she seemed to buckle at the knees, drawing him off balance as she kicked out. A moment later he was flat on the ground and she was standing, looking remarkably unruffled.

A gangly youth hurried to her side, hands clenching, but she shook her head and directed him back to his horse.

'She knows what she's doing.' Hassan sounded admiring. 'I saw her in action the first day. She has obviously faced that or worse before. I might borrow her to teach my team some moves.' He chuckled.

Zamir wasn't amused. He hated the idea of Miranda needing to defend herself. The idea of anyone touching her.

'That kid's out of the programme right now,' he growled, moving forward.

'You think she'll thank you for that?' That stopped Zamir. Reluctantly he turned and met Hassan's stare. 'You'll undermine her authority if you interfere.'

Zamir drew a shuddering breath that didn't fill his lungs. Instinct wrestled with logic. He watched the kid get to his feet, shoulders hunched and, after a quick look around, reach for the horse's girth.

It went against everything Zamir had been taught, everything he was, not to intervene. He ruled and protected, and punished too. He defended the defenceless.

But Miranda wasn't defenceless. She was capable. If he barged in now…

He knew from her own words that she felt out of her depth in Qu'sil, with little autonomy and no control. She'd taken her first steps to establishing both friendships and purpose through the equestrian group. He couldn't stop something so important to her.

More, he owed Miranda his support. She'd been an unwilling bride yet she'd been at his side publicly several times, edgy but valiantly determined to appear as a supportive spouse. She'd been so successful he'd almost believed the image of a contented, gracious wife.

Reluctantly he retreated into the shadows to lean, jaw gritted and arms folded, against the wall. The problem was this was no hypothetical issue. It was *personal.*

He waited till the session ended. A vehicle took the kids away and the staff dissipated, their working day over. Miranda headed into the stable and Zamir followed.

He found her in one of the small rooms at the far end of the now-deserted building, where records and supplies were stored. She perched on a stool, writing up notes at a high bench. A spill of lamplight revealed rich colour in her dark hair.

Zamir leaned against the door jamb. 'How did it go?'

She looked up, eyes lighting, and he had to shove his hands in his pockets rather than reach for her.

'I didn't expect to see you.' She sounded breathless, *pleased*, which made his own breath seize. 'I thought you had meetings.'

'They finished early.' Because he'd rushed through business, fired by his urgency to be with her.

'It went well. It's early days but some of them are responding positively and they're all still participating. I think we're winning their trust slowly. There's one—'

'Who's causing trouble?'

She pushed her chair back from the desk. 'I was going to say, there's one who has really taken to this. He's even volunteered to help a local vet clinic.' She paused. 'What made you think there was trouble?'

'I was here earlier.' Zamir couldn't prevent his harsh tone as the words emerged through gritted teeth.

Miranda's eyes narrowed and she sat straighter. 'Why bother asking how it went if you were spying on me?'

'Not spying! I just wanted to see you. Then that kid assaulted you.'

Wood shrieked against tiles as she shoved the stool back, rising so abruptly it tumbled to the floor. She faced him, chest rising sharply on each quick breath, her face flushed and eyes brilliant.

'*Tried* to assault me. He didn't succeed. He was testing, seeing how far he could push.'

Zamir made himself pause before replying. 'Attempted assault is a crime too.'

Miranda bustled closer, her breath feathering his chin. 'You wouldn't! What do you think would happen to the programme if you brought in the police?'

'It's your safety I'm worried about.' Zamir couldn't eradicate the image of that lout reaching for Miranda.

'You think I can't take care of myself? I'm not even alone!

As well as the other volunteers your security guys are always on hand, trying to look inconspicuous.'

Zamir wrestled with the need to take charge and remove any threat. 'I'd like to see him dropped from the programme.' Miranda was already opening her mouth to argue when he added, 'But I understand your perspective. You can look after yourself and you've taken safety precautions.' He paused. 'If there's a chance this pilot programme can work, it's too important to be shut down before it gets started.'

For only the second time, he saw her speechless. Yet Zamir felt no victory, for the blood still coursed hot and angry in his arteries at the effort of restraint.

Finally she spoke. 'You mean it? You're not going to interfere?'

'I *want* to teach that kid a quick, unforgettable lesson in respect, then eject him from the programme.' Zamir slowly shook his head, pushing down the savage urge for violent reprisal. 'But I won't. If *you* promise to be careful and never be alone with him. And cut him loose if he tries anything like that again.'

'I promise.' Her words were soft.

'Good.' He cleared his throat, feeling a strange, febrile heat as if the emotion in her silvery eyes dug under his skin, which drew too tight. At the same time his lungs atrophied, forgetting for a second how to work.

'You trust me.'

Zamir wasn't sure if her whispered words were a statement or a question.

He nodded. Of course he trusted her. She was obstinate and impulsive but generous and truthful.

She made him feel things he had no name for. No experience of. She made him feel…too much.

But she was *here*, *his*, and there was no going back.

'I trust you, Miranda. And I don't want you hurt.'

Her hands landed on his chest, one palm above his hammering heart, and even that felt wonderful. He'd been scared, he realised, watching her defend herself, his heart in his mouth and a roar of bloodlust in his ears.

Suddenly his arms were around her, hauling her close. Something huge and powerful shuddered through him as he buried his face in her hair and inhaled the scent of woman, jasmine and horse. The perfect combination of alluring and down-to-earth, so typical of his wife.

Instead of questioning or debating, she sank against him, her arms slipping around him and holding tight.

A wave of something crashed through him. Relief. Satisfaction. A feeling of homecoming. As if he belonged here in this windowless room instead of in the palace's lavish, royal suite.

As if none of the accoutrements of power mattered. Just Miranda, safe in his arms.

'I want you,' he groaned, drawing her up against him.

Needed her.

But that was better unsaid. After their first night together he'd betrayed his desperate hunger for her and part of him, the part that had trained most of his life to become ruler, warned it was a mistake to reveal such weakness.

'Good.' Her voice was muffled against his shirt collar. 'I want you too.'

Miranda tilted her head and there it was again, that earth-moving shudder as grey eyes met his and light lanced through his body like lightning racing to earth. It left him trembling with anticipation.

Stepping further into the room, he kicked the door shut, lifting her off her feet, and sat her on the sturdy bench.

Now they were almost eye to eye and Zamir recognised excitement blazing in her features. All the emotion he'd battled to hold in fought for release. Maybe she felt the same. His wife was no milk-and-water miss, submissive and serene. She was feisty, emotional, strong, and their passion always blazed stronger after argument.

'Touch me,' he ordered, uncaring that his gruff tone betrayed him.

Her smile was a siren's as she reached up to undo his tie. That wasn't what he'd had in mind but her hands were deft, already undoing his shirt buttons so she could lean to press her lips against bare skin.

He clutched her to him, his sigh of relief audible. Then her quick hands moved under his jacket lapels, pushing the fabric over his shoulders, and he released her for long enough to shrug free.

'Nice as that is, it's not what I meant.'

He placed his hands around her hips and tugged her close so her knees widened around him. His stirring erection pressed against that sweet spot between her thighs. Syrupy heat thickened his blood as he bucked forward, eyes closing for a moment at how good that felt.

'Did you mean this?'

Her voice was as husky as his as she insinuated one hand between them, fingers curling around his length. Zamir surged into her hold, the air dragging from his mouth.

'More.'

'You're so bossy.' Yet her eyes danced as she reached for his belt. 'But I'll forgive you this time.'

Tension pulled his skin tight as the ends of the belt fell and she undid his trousers. 'Because you want me too, don't you?'

She paused for the tiniest moment and Zamir drew the tension of waiting deep inside. He craved her touch but there was something else he needed. Then she gave it to him.

'I do,' she whispered as if her throat had tightened too. 'I want you inside me.'

His breath shuddered out and he bit down hard on his molars, searching for the control he needed not to spill himself in her warm hand.

Zamir grabbed her wrists, capturing them in one hand as he reached into his pocket before his trousers slid low. His eyes held hers as he tore the packet with his teeth, watching the flare of excitement in her stare. That notched up his own arousal to impossible levels. His hand shook as he fumbled the condom.

'I could do that for you.' She licked her lips as she looked down and he throbbed hard in anticipation.

'Not this time.'

He was too close. In fact, it would be better if he took care of her first in case he couldn't hold on.

He was so distracted he barely noticed her hands slide from his hold. In a few swift movements she'd pulled off her boots, dropping them to the floor, then undone her zip, lifting her hips to shimmy out of her trousers and underwear.

Zamir's chest ached as she opened her legs.

She was beautiful all over. Yet when he managed to pull his attention up to her face he thought he caught a flicker of doubt. How could that be?

'You're gorgeous.' His throat was so raw she'd have to be a lip-reader to understand his words. Yet her slow-growing smile said she got the idea.

Condom on, he teased the downy hair between her thighs, arrowing down to that sweet, fleshy nub and watched her mouth open in a gasp of excitement as she rubbed against his touch.

The sight of her pleasure was addictive. The diamond-bright glint of her eyes, the forward thrust of her breasts as she arched her back, hands on the bench, the restless circling of her hips. His fingers were slick and he smelled that rich, earthy scent of feminine arousal.

Her breathing sharpened, her movements quickening and she was the most magnificent being he'd ever seen.

Then one small, capable hand encircled him as she wrapped her legs around his hips.

Zamir was only human and Miranda was irresistible.

What happened next came without conscious thought. It

was as inevitable and as beautiful as sunrise over the desert. They came together so easily, so perfectly, it felt like destiny.

And pleasure. Instant, all-engulfing pleasure.

So tight and fast it rose like a sandstorm, blotting out the world and leaving the pair of them, gasping, juddering, caught on a point between astonishment and bliss until, hoarse cries curling together in the still room, they collapsed, holding tight as the world tilted and changed for ever.

CHAPTER FOURTEEN

'SADIA! IT'S WONDERFUL to hear from you. I've tried and tried but—'

'It's a relief to hear your voice too! I only just got access to a phone.' Miranda's cousin sounded different, her voice tight. 'I'm sorry. I've been frantic to find out how you are but couldn't get any news. My father took my phone and I haven't been allowed out.'

'Not allowed? What about your classes?' Sadia was a schoolteacher.

'No teaching. I've been under house arrest. Father brought in security guards for the wedding…' Her voice petered out. 'When the marriage didn't go ahead, he kept them on to guard *me*. I've never seen him so furious, ranting about me dishonouring the family and the nation. But,' she said in a firmer voice, 'he's more worried about missed opportunities because he's not father to a queen.'

'Oh, Sadia. We knew he'd be furious, but I never thought he'd lock you up.'

Miranda slumped onto a deeply cushioned window seat, staring at the manicured garden courtyard beyond the private pool. But in her mind's eye it was her uncle's house she saw, with its high walls and beautifully decorative but impenetrable metalwork over the windows.

The only way out, when the house was locked up, was over the roof. Miranda had gone that way herself last time she'd fallen foul of her uncle's temper. But she couldn't imagine decorous Sadia doing that.

'*I'm* all right. *I* wasn't the one forced into marriage.' Sadia's voice wobbled. 'That's all my fault. And I feel guilty too because it's worked out well for me. Mother ended up going to the Sheikh and with his backing I'm moving out of home into an apartment near the school.'

That was what Sadia had wanted for ages, but hadn't been able to push the point with her father.

'That's excellent news,' Miranda said, though she could guess at the emotional price her cousin paid for that freedom.

'Enough about me. How about you? I've been so worried, not knowing how you are.'

'Actually, I'm good. Far better than I'd imagined, though life here is a little different from working in South America.' She laughed reassuringly.

'Oh, Mira. Don't put on a brave face for me. I know what you're going through, or can at least imagine it. Remember, I was the one promised in marriage. Are you really okay?'

Her cousin always had been a worrier. 'More than okay. I'm very good.'

It was true. Life here wasn't what she'd planned, but then she'd never been a great planner. She'd fallen into a career by following her passion.

If anyone had told her she could find happiness in a palace, regularly appearing at formal events and married to a man she didn't know, she'd never have believed them.

But she did know Zamir. And what she knew she liked.

More than liked.

Miranda drew her knees up to her chest and wrapped her free arm around her legs, hugging tight the feelings that had been swelling inside her for weeks now. She wasn't just in lust with her husband. She admired him, liked being with him.

'It's very courageous of you...'

'Not courageous at all. Life here is easy and I get to do a

lot of things I want as well as some things I'd rather not, but then that's life, isn't it?'

She was gradually getting used to being the centre of attention when she appeared in public but she doubted she'd ever get completely used to it. She fared better in informal situations but at least she could hold her own now, after Zamir had spent so much time helping her.

She'd even got used to the minders who accompanied her outside the palace, learning that instead of being disapproving spies they actually had her well-being at heart. Her new assistant was a mine of useful information and wasn't stuffy or formal.

Even dressing up in glamorous clothes could be fun now she'd taken her husband's advice to wear what made her feel good. Her wardrobe had been chosen or made specifically to suit her, so she didn't need to fear appearing as a frump. But what had really overcome her doubts had been Zamir's reaction. Again and again as he took in her appearance, ready for some official function, she read his approval. More than that, blatant desire.

His admiration was more effective than any mirror or well-meant compliment. He made her feel beautiful.

'But it's such an enormous change. Being hemmed in by all that royal protocol and ceremony. And then there's Zamir with his air of authority, his...*certainty.* Don't you find it stifling?'

On the contrary, Miranda found it exciting. Energising. Arousing.

You have a one-track mind.

'We have our disagreements,' she said carefully, 'but we get on well.'

Even disagreements could be fun. Miranda's family had accused her of being impulsive and emotional but she'd discovered an upside to being passionate about things she cared about. Like not being bulldozed into things she didn't want, or like the success of her riding and rehabilitation programmes.

Zamir took her passion in his stride, meeting it with an enthusiasm of his own, never dismissing her views. They debated politics, negotiated her role, sometimes argued, and she'd never felt more alive. More appreciated and valued. She loved the way he was always ready to meet passion with passion.

It was a heady thing, she'd discovered, being wife to Zamir of Qu'sil.

'I see.' Sadia sounded doubtful.

It was Miranda's turn to interrogate. 'I know you didn't want to marry him. But you said he was respectful if distant.' Which was natural between strangers. Knowing Zamir as she did, she saw past his reserve to the admirable, serious man who worked conscientiously for others. 'But there must have been more to it than that.' Sadia had been so panicked she hadn't been totally coherent.

Her cousin was silent for a long time. When she spoke again her voice was flat. 'I was scared about not having a say about marrying. Scared I wouldn't cope with everyone's expectations, especially in public.' Her voice dropped. 'Worried too because Zamir is such a determined, powerful man and you know I've never been able to stand up for myself.'

Miranda's mouth flattened. Sadia had been so cowed, growing up with a tyrannical father. Even now she carried the scars, the lack of confidence, and they skewed her perspective.

Had Miranda's initial view of Zamir been skewed too for the same reason? Of course it had.

'There's a difference between a powerful, determined man, doing his best for his people, like Zamir, and a small-minded despot who gets his kicks from ordering his family around and belittling anybody in the least different.'

That was why her uncle had never approved of her. She hadn't conformed even as a child. Not out of wilful disobedience but because she had an adventurous, questioning disposition, strengthened by early exposure to different cultures and places. She'd never fitted the narrow confines of his petty tyranny. Not because she was intrinsically bad or deficient, but because he didn't have the generosity or wisdom to accept difference.

'Zamir acted for the good of the nation, both nations. And yes, I didn't like marrying a total stranger. But you know what? He's the most decent, honourable, kind man.' Her throat tightened as her chest swelled. 'The only downside is that he's about to be crowned King and that whole royal thing is still a challenge for me, though I'm getting better at it.'

She paused, swallowing hard. 'He's gone out of his way to help me and make life here a pleasure.'

Not just with learning to be royal, but introducing her to people who were fast becoming friends. Giving her leeway to pursue her charitable interests which, while laudable, didn't fit neatly with royal tradition. Trusting her to do them well. And all the while making her feel stronger, more valued, more special.

Then there was his tenderness, his laughter, the way his eyes shone when he looked at her, as if she were as mesmerising as a star-studded desert night.

Her breath hitched. Zamir's touch, from the casual brush of his hand against hers as they entered a formal reception, to the thrilling carnality of his lovemaking, was more powerful than anything she'd known. More wonderful.

'You like him. Really like him. I'm so glad!'

Miranda shifted against the cushions, staring at the still water in their private swimming pool. Just a few nights ago they'd made love there. Even on the edge of the city and at the heart of the vast, sprawling palace, it had felt as if they were the only two people in the world and that together they'd created magic.

Afterwards he'd cradled her as she lay blinking at the stars, wondering at the bliss that seemed to grow stronger and last longer whenever they came together.

Instead of falling asleep or turning away after his climax,

Zamir had told her stories about the stars. Old tales about how they got their names, what they meant, and how to use them when navigating through the desert.

He'd answered every question then laughed with her when she concocted her own alternative story about starry horses and riders racing across the velvet darkness. Laughed *with* her, not *at* her.

'Yes.' Miranda cleared her throat. 'I like him very much. You will too when you get to know him.'

The fact was, Miranda didn't just like him.

She loved him.

Her pulse beat high in her throat and her breathing grew shallow with the realisation. She'd always been impulsive, but falling in love in just a few weeks…

Not a few weeks.

Even that first day when she'd loathed him, there'd been something about Zamir that drew her. Something powerfully magnetic, an undercurrent of excitement and awareness at the most visceral level that called to her.

An excitement she felt now, thinking about him.

It was as if, without knowing his character or his kindness, she'd sensed them.

Why else would she have meekly stayed here in the palace that first night instead of sneaking out under cover of darkness and heading for the border? Yes, she'd been a prisoner but she hadn't even tried to escape, because deep down she'd been too intrigued by her captor.

Miranda blinked and the bright greens, blues and whites outside shifted, as if moving in a giant kaleidoscope, settling into a new, glorious pattern.

'I'm pleased he's good to you, Mira. You deserve that.' Sadia paused. 'It's in his interests to ensure you adapt to life there. He needs a content wife who will play her part well in public. But you know that. You understand it's not personal. You won't break your heart over him.'

Miranda ended the call soon after that. Her initial elation at talking with Sadia had morphed into something else. Something horrible. Worse than her outrage when her cousin compared Zamir with Miranda's uncle.

Sadia was trying to be sensible, even kind. What she said about Zamir's interest in her being happy was logical.

Yet it felt wrong.

Miranda had wanted to protest that her husband wasn't simply being pragmatic. His actions weren't all carefully calculated for the good of his position.

She wanted to rant that Zamir cared about her.

That, at least, was true. Zamir *did* care. He *was* kind as well as practical.

But had she read too much into his kindness?

Had the beautiful gleam in his eyes when he looked at her been just a reflection of her own dazzled excitement? Was she imagining what she wanted to see rather than what was really there? Was she attributing feelings to him because her own lonely heart had locked on him?

The sad truth was that her heart had imprinted on him, like an orphaned baby animal imprinting on the first living being to show it affection.

Miranda had known love as a child but after her father died her mother's love seemed tainted with disappointment. Zamir was the first person since her dad, and, to a degree, Matias, to accept her as she was, with her faults, strengths, and idiosyncrasies. The first to make her feel valued and valuable.

To make her feel loved.

Was that, as Sadia warned, an illusion? A tactic to win her over? No, Zamir never lied to her. He wouldn't stoop so low He'd never mentioned love. *She* was the one who'd extrapolated.

If he felt…more for her, he'd have said. He wasn't a man given to self-doubt or hesitation. He was a man who knew about love. It was there in his voice when he spoke about his siblings, his sister studying dry land agriculture and his brother making documentaries. His affection for them was clear.

Surely if he felt the same way she did, he'd tell her?

Of course he would. Zamir has nothing to hide.

Miranda doubled over, arms wrapped tight around her middle to hold in welling pain. But nothing could keep it back. It leaked out, growing stronger by the second.

She was in love with her husband.

A decent, kind man who tried to make her situation as easy as possible. A man who respected her but didn't love her.

Her stomach heaved and perspiration prickled her forehead. She felt she was going to be sick. But her ailment wasn't physical. She wished it were.

Dry-eyed, stomach churning, heart aching, she stared at the glittering water of their private swimming pool. She'd given herself to him there with love.

He'd given her joy and easy companionship. He had the gift of making her feel important though the fact was that she, as an individual, wasn't. He'd needed to marry a woman from her country, her family, and he had. That was the bare, brutal truth she'd forgotten in these last weeks.

Zamir was simply pragmatist enough to want a content spouse. He'd told her that for generations his family's marriages had been arranged for dynastic reasons, not love.

She was the only one foolish enough to dream of love.

The truth was so simple, she was astounded she hadn't recognised it sooner.

Miranda shot to her feet, yanking off her couture clothes as she hurried to her dressing room.

Soon after, in jeans, boots and a plain shirt, she was riding Chico, trying to ease the hurt that seemed too big for her body.

It didn't work. When finally they returned to the stables, exhausted, the pain had solidified into a hard ache in the pit of her stomach.

The only thing she'd achieved was the realisation she

couldn't live the rest of her life this way. Miranda's self-esteem had taken a battering for too many years, to the extent that her self-doubts had made her second-guess her instincts.

For most of her life she'd been second best. Not wanted or chosen for herself but out of duty. Her husband had married her as a convenient replacement for the woman he really wanted.

Her bitter laugh made Chico turn and nuzzle her questioningly as she brushed his steaming body. She leaned against his solid shoulder, murmuring reassurances as she breathed in his comforting equine smell.

'What am I going to do, Chico? This can't go on.'

While she'd been falling in love with Zamir she'd been happy, ecstatic.

Because you lived in a fool's paradise.

But now she realised the truth, she couldn't see a way to make this work. She couldn't unsee the truth or pretend everything would be okay. Zamir had shown her how much her self-doubts had held her back. He'd made her appreciate her strengths and in the process made her believe she had a right to happiness. Just as her father had always said.

Her mouth crimped at the corners as the tears she refused to shed burned her eyes and clogged her throat.

Better to know now.

Imagine if you'd had a child together.

The thought paralysed her.

She could imagine it so easily. Longing filled her, so sudden and strong she had to lean into Chico, breathing deep against the aching pleasure-pain of it.

Zamir would love their child as she would. But how would she feel watching the love between father and child grow, knowing Zamir would never love her? That she'd always be a necessary encumbrance. Not wanted for herself. What would she become then? Bitter? Needy? Desperate?

Miranda straightened, stroking Chico's cheek, his ear flicking as she spoke. 'There's only one solution. I have to leave.'

CHAPTER FIFTEEN

'I'M TIRED, ZAMIR. I'll have a bath then go straight to sleep.'

Miranda was already walking towards the bathroom, a vision in deep green silk. But there was an underlying brittleness about her tonight that worried him. Her smile didn't meet her eyes and her shoulders were too high.

No one else had noticed. Their guests at the formal dinner had been delighted and complimentary. Which confirmed how unfounded Miranda's fears had been about not measuring up to royal standards. She was a natural, warm and engaging, interested in everyone. Even if tonight Zamir sensed her mind was elsewhere.

There was something wrong. Something she wasn't sharing.

His nape prickled in alarm. 'What's wrong, Miranda? Has someone said something? Done something?'

There'd been a few grumbles after her first public appearances. A couple of busybodies drawing attention to her less formal manners and foreignness. But most, himself included, found her refreshing. If anything, Zamir was learning from Miranda how to connect more personally with his people. It was time to pull down some of the barriers surrounding the royal family.

'What could be wrong?'

Zamir's heart sank as he watched her gaze dance away from his.

Had she lost weight? Her cheekbones seemed more pronounced and the tight angle of her jaw. But they spent each night naked together. He'd have noticed any weight loss. Which meant it was tension making her look fragile.

He crossed towards her, worried yet sweeping her with an admiring glance. The diamond and emerald necklace he'd given her tonight befitted a queen. But it wasn't the trappings of majesty he responded to. He surveyed her sweet body in the silver-trimmed formal gown of deep emerald-green and need racked him.

'Miranda, I…'

His words dried as she backed a step away from him.

It felt like a stab to the belly. When had his wife ever retreated from him? He slammed to a stop before her.

'Can't it wait? I told you, I'm tired.'

It wasn't the snap of her tone that made him frown. It was the sinking feeling inside. He knew her too well now to be taken in. 'You're not tired. You're trying to avoid talking.'

If anything she looked wired, hyper-alert.

'Talk to me, Miranda. Tell me what's going on.' When she remained silent he dropped his voice to something like a plea. 'We've always been honest with each other.'

Her eyes locked on his and he felt the shock of impact right to the soles of his feet. The familiar sizzle of connection, of sexual awareness and anticipation, and something besides that gathered fear in the pit of his belly and drying throat.

Defeat. Despair. Fear.

Zamir realised that even in those desperate first hours when Miranda had learned the full cost of her decision to kidnap him, she'd never looked like this. Always there'd been a glimmer of fighting spirit in her. Now he looked beyond her show of insouciance into an endless, aching void.

He acted instinctively, covering the space between them and taking her wrists gently, his thumbs stroking her cool skin. She shivered but he couldn't tell whether it was a sensual response to his touch or something else.

'Whatever the problem, we'll fix it.' He bent his head, ensuring she read his determination. 'Between us we'll find a solution.' He curled his mouth in a smile that belied his rising worry. 'Fortunately I've got the resources to help with most things, and after next week's coronation—'

'Don't! Please.' Miranda tugged her hands free and whipped them behind her back.

Zamir frowned. 'Is it the coronation you're worried about? The ceremony is straightforward and, while there'll be a big audience, I know you'll cope. I'm proud of you, Miranda. You've done so well at all your public appearances.'

She shook her head so vehemently, her diamond and emerald earrings swung wide. Below the glittering necklace her breasts rose sharply as if she had trouble catching her breath. He knew the feeling. His lungs felt compressed.

'It's not that. Or only partly that.' She bit her lip and he wanted, so badly, to touch her there and ease the hurt. But—and it killed him to admit to it—twice now she'd withdrawn from him. Once she'd stepped back and later she'd pulled her hands from his as if his touch scalded.

Horror wound through his intestines like a ribbon of ice.

Mirroring her stance, he locked his hands behind his back, signalling that he'd give her the space she wanted.

She looked down then up again, eyes glistening bright, and he realised that for the first time Miranda was on the verge of tears. This was the woman who'd single-handedly kidnapped him. Stood proud and defiant when forced into marriage. Dared to negotiate her own terms for living here. A woman he'd believed utterly fearless.

'Are you sick?' Had she received some terrible diagnosis? 'Or is it someone at home—?'

'It's nothing like that. I'm fine.' She laughed then, a tiny sound that should have reassured yet instead sounded broken, making the fear in him notch higher.

'I didn't want to talk about this tonight when we're both

tired. But…' her eyes searched his '… I've realised I can't do this. I really can't. I've tried but it's just not possible long term.'

His voice emerged rough. 'Can't do what precisely?'

Miranda lifted her chin. She owed it to herself to make a stand but when she looked into his stunned eyes she fought the urge to reassure him and promise to try harder.

Didn't that characterise all that was wrong with this marriage? Even knowing this situation would eventually erode her soul, Miranda couldn't help wanting to do what Zamir wanted, try to be the woman he needed.

Because she cared. Too much.

'I can't be your queen. I can't be your wife. I need to get away from all this.'

She snatched a desperate breath ready to forestall his arguments but none came. Zamir stood as if turned to stone. For long seconds he didn't even seem to breathe. Then she saw his chest lift on a shuddering breath.

'It just won't work,' she hurried on. 'It's not working now and it will only get worse.'

Still he said nothing and the sight of him staring down at her, not even angry but lost for words, made her shift her weight from one foot to another.

She shouldn't feel guilty. She hadn't chosen this life. He'd forced her into it.

Yet that argument didn't work against her deep-seated guilt and concern. She had to do this for her survival but she knew her action would cost Zamir enormously. Not just in pride but perhaps in power. That haunted her, making her decision even harder.

She didn't want to hurt him, just save herself.

'I know it will take a long time to unravel this marriage. You said divorce between royals isn't possible but I know if anyone can push change through it's you. I'm willing to wait a few years while you change the law. We don't have to announce our divorce immediately. I can play my part for a while.'

Her throat closed as she imagined pretending in public to be Zamir's partner, while in private they lived separate lives. Even standing close to him now tested her to the limit. It would be easy to give in to Zamir's needs and the craving of her own body, her heart, and stay with him, *be* with him. But that would be self-destructive.

'We can negotiate some arrangement. I could live in the palace several months a year and attend functions with you.' She waved one hand vaguely. 'And the rest of the time I'll live elsewhere. You won't have to worry about me making headlines with public appearances or scandals. I can live quietly. Maybe at the old house across the border that I inherited.'

She could set up stables there. Even offer riding therapy or do freelance work with other people's horses. Her plans hadn't got that far. Whenever she imagined life after Zamir her mind went blank.

'Why?' he said finally, his voice so strained it was almost unrecognisable. 'Are you really so daunted by the public appearances? If so I could—'

'It's not that.' She didn't find them easy as Zamir did, but she was growing more confident.

'Then what? Do you miss your family? Your home in Argentina? After the coronation we could travel and in the meantime your cousin could visit here.'

Miranda goggled up at him, distracted for a moment from her misery. 'You'd have Sadia here?' The woman who'd plotted kidnap rather than marry him?

'I'll do whatever it takes to make you happy here, Miranda. To make you feel comfortable.'

Behind her back her hands twisted together. His earnest words reinforced what Sadia had said. That Zamir wanted her happy so she could play the part of his bride.

The sad thing was she'd be immeasurably happy without all the trappings of royalty, if only Zamir loved her.

She shook her head. 'Don't, Zamir. There's nothing you can say that will make things right. You're a good man. You mean well and I…like you. But being here, pretending to be happy… I just can't do it for the rest of my life.'

Miranda looked into his solemn features, the twitch of a frown between his eyebrows, the confusion in his eyes, and felt obliged to explain.

'I don't expect you to understand. You were raised to expect an arranged marriage. But I want, *need* something more.'

She smoothed damp palms down her long skirt. 'Most of my life I felt second best. The first five years of my life were gloriously happy. But after my father died I never measured up to expectations. I bounced from one place to another, one set of customs and expectations and another. I tried to be what my mother wanted but I disappointed her. I gave up trying to please my uncle years ago. In Argentina I had a career I loved. But I was still an outsider.'

She shook her head. 'Maybe I always will be. But I've learnt, and you helped me realise this, that I want and deserve respect and love. Because of who I am as a person. Not because of other people's expectations or needs.'

Miranda clasped her hands in an unconsciously pleading gesture. 'If I stay here I'll always be the wife you had to have. The stand-in bride. Not the one you chose. I'll never be *loved*.'

She ground to a halt as the words spilled out.

Then, on a surge of recklessness, she added, 'You might be able to live without love, Zamir, but I'm not made that way. When you were kind to me and caring it meant so much. It made me realise I crave genuine emotion in a relationship. It made me realise how needy I'd become and how much I'd put up with over the years. I can't be that woman any longer and I'm sorry, so sorry. I'll do whatever it takes to put an end to this farce of a marriage but I need my freedom.'

Because staying with the man she loved in this unequal relationship would turn her into a shadow of herself.

'Please, let's talk later. I need time alone.'

Miranda's eyes went to the exit to her old suite, but Zamir was between her and it. Instead she spun on her foot and hurried into the bathroom.

CHAPTER SIXTEEN

ZAMIR STARED AT the closed door, reeling.

She believed what they shared was a farce?

Pain speared him, from his chest down to feet that refused to move.

He'd tried so hard, given so much. How could she dismiss the amazing things they'd shared?

Did they really mean nothing to her?

He would have sworn on his soul that she'd also experienced those times of pure communion that transcended the reality of two separate beings. Those moments when it felt they were one, not just physically but mentally and emotionally.

Zamir had never known such a bond or such peace.

It made him realise there was far more to life than duty, despite the dictates of his uncle and his own habit of tunnel-visioned focus.

He cared about Miranda, worked hard to help her adjust, even opening up about his family life and past with her. He'd never done that before. He'd believed, despite the short time they'd been together, that they'd built an unparalleled level of trust and affection.

Now she wanted her freedom?

Anger stirred. She'd taken everything he offered and dismissed it out of hand.

Didn't she understand the freedom he gave her, the freedom she could take for herself as his queen?

But that wasn't good enough, apparently.

He wasn't good enough.

She wanted love on top of everything else. The full romantic dream.

What did she expect? Vows on bended knee? She already has his respect and affection.

But Zamir knew nothing about romantic love. It had never figured in his family as far as he could tell. It was something that happened to other people, as distant from his world as the moon.

Zamir's clenched jaw grew slack. His mind raced. His vision narrowed to the intricate inlay work on the door before him, but he didn't register it.

A great weight crushed his chest and his lungs fought to drag in enough air.

Still he stood, rooted to the spot, blood pounding, thoughts whirling, hands clenched into fists.

Miranda wanted the impossible.

The man who'd been brought up to be responsible and dutiful, bound by the dictates of the public good over personal preference, was stunned.

Yet another part of him applauded her for standing up for what she believed she needed. His heart had cracked as she'd admitted to feeling second best. To feeling she didn't belong.

Did she fear she was unworthy of the love she craved?

What would it be like to admit what it was *he* wanted from life? To build a future tailored to make that possible?

Zamir had some idea. He'd encouraged his siblings to pursue their dreams. He'd understood that neither of them wanted the burden he carried, of statesmanship and constant expectation. He revelled in their successes.

Yet he couldn't revel in Miranda's determination to plot her own course and seek her own joys.

Because you want her to find joy with you.

You want her too much to let her go.

Because even after this short time together you can't imagine going back to a life without her.

When the door opened, the room was lit by a single lamp. Miranda paused on the threshold, gripping the neckline of her robe close, cautiously surveying the room. Her face was scrubbed bare of make-up, she wore no adornment but her golden wedding band, and she'd never looked more lovely.

Was it his sharply indrawn breath that caught her attention, or did she sense him in the shadows?

One step into the room she paused, head turning unerringly to where he sat on the window seat.

'Zamir?'

'Who else did you expect?'

It hit him that, if Miranda got her way and they lived separate lives, one day some other man would share the intimacy of midnight conversations. And more, much more. His pain grew excruciating.

He rose. 'We need to speak.'

'It's very late. Let's talk tomorrow.'

Zamir rolled his shoulders, trying to unknot the tension there. 'No. This is too important. You had your say. Now it's my turn.'

For the longest time she hesitated, then with a tiny nod she crossed the room, her expression guarded. 'I'm sorry, Zamir. Truly sorry.'

Sorry! A tide of fury and fear rose at her decision to desert him. But he pushed it down. He couldn't let emotions control him now. He needed to get this right.

He gestured for her to take one end of the long, cushioned window seat. When she did, he sat at the other end, turning to face her.

The lamplight left this part of the room in shadows but the moon was out and he could see her features. They were so familiar he could almost read them in the dark anyway. One good look told him she suffered too. Regret as well as anxiety were in the way she folded and refolded the silk of her robe. And there was pain around her mouth and eyes.

His anger crumbled. Pride had no place here. He wanted to reach out to her but instinct told him she needed far more than physical reassurance.

Besides, this wasn't just about Miranda. It was about *them.* No wonder he was on edge. He had no margin for error.

'I've been thinking.' He shook his head as his carefully planned words fled, replaced by such banality.

Zamir swallowed, fighting to conquer his own apprehension. He wasn't a man given to anxiety. He was used to decision-making and high-stakes negotiation but nothing in his experience had prepared him for this.

'What you said tonight has made me reassess.'

'You're rethinking our marriage? You'll organise a divorce?' Strangely, Miranda didn't sound thrilled.

Was he grasping at straws?

'Not rethinking our marriage. Reassessing my priorities.' He paused, struggling with words to explain. Discussing emotions was new to him. 'You explained what you wanted from life, what was important. I respect you for being honest.' Even if it came as a crushing blow. 'It made me think about *my* feelings and needs.'

Silence stretched between them. Had he thought she'd help him out?

She doesn't know what you feel. How could she when you didn't even know yourself?

Zamir looked at his hands, bunched fists on his thighs. 'That's a luxury I never indulged in before.' He looked up to see her lean closer. 'All my life my role was mapped out for me. What's expected of me. The need to be strong, decisive, proud but not selfish. The need to put my nation first. But tonight I feel selfish. I want to be able to claim what *I* want. As if I were an ordinary citizen.'

'What do you want, Zamir?'

It was a whisper, so soft he couldn't read Miranda's tone. It gave no clue to her thoughts, which meant the admission he was about to make would take him into uncharted territory, putting his real self on the line, probably to be rejected.

No wonder he was petrified. These new feelings had the power to destroy.

He grimaced. 'Nothing outlandish. Probably what everyone else wants, including you. I want to be happy. But happiness doesn't come from my title or position.' Though he enjoyed helping people and was proud of his ability to do so. 'I want someone to share my life with. Not because it's decreed or because it brings political advantage. But because that person cares for me. I want love too.'

The words sounded foreign on his tongue yet they felt right.

His heart pounded like a jackhammer, making it impossible to hear anything Miranda said. But Zamir was watching her and she said nothing, though her mouth sagged in astonishment.

A good sign? Or an indication she thought it impossible anyone could love him?

'You made me think about what it is to be loved. It's not something I'd considered before, because I never saw the need. But things have changed. *I've* changed.' It astonished him how much.

'To me love covers respect, admiration, trust, and attraction…deep, deep attraction.' Despite his tension he smiled. 'It's about being there for the other person no matter what. It's about mutual support and affection. Wanting your partner to be the best version of themselves they can be, not managing them so they're forced into a mould they don't fit. It's about sharing joys and pain, whatever life brings.'

Still Miranda said nothing, but as he peered at her in the gloom he saw something silvery on her cheek.

'Miranda?' He leaned forward, brushing away the only tear

he'd ever seen her shed. His chest squeezed so hard it was a wonder he breathed. 'I didn't mean to upset you.'

He had no idea what to do. He'd thought she wanted honesty, full emotional honesty. Instead he'd hurt her.

She shook her head, drawing his hand from her cheek. 'You didn't. You just described it so perfectly it made me feel…'

Zamir heard her words through a blare of triumph because she still held his hand. Surely that was a good sign.

'There's a reason I can describe it so well,' he murmured, sliding closer. 'I'm in love with you.'

He waited for the sky to fall in or for her to laugh disbelievingly. Instead her fingers clutched his and her bright eyes held his. Hope trickled through him.

'Tell me.'

It was too soft to be a command, yet he heard his own urgency in Miranda's words.

'I didn't realise it until you said your piece then flounced into the bathroom.'

'I've never flounced.'

Her indignation settled some of his nerves, even though everything still hung in the balance. 'Flounced,' he repeated. 'Just like you sashay into a room when you're wearing something particularly sexy and you know I'm alone. Don't try to deny it. I enjoy it.' The rough, gravel note of his voice gave him away. He tried to lighten the atmosphere because his feelings were so big they threatened to overwhelm him.

What had happened to the man who kept personal emotions locked away?

'You made me wonder exactly what you meant by wanting love. I tried to define it for myself, break it down into components so I could understand.'

Zamir drew a slow breath, mustering his courage. He clasped her hand in both his.

'That's when I realised I was in love with you. I'd never thought about love and romance before, I was too busy worrying about responsibilities and expectations. But as soon as I stopped to consider I realised that you're the only woman I want in my life. It's not about being a suitable queen, though you're that and more. You have your own style and you're superb. But I'd feel the same if I weren't Sheikh. I crave you and suspect I always will, but it's more than that. I admire you. I enjoy debating with you, even arguing. I care about you.' He leaned closer, willing her to understand. 'I want to share your life and have you beside me through mine. I want…*us*.'

'Oh, Zamir!' She shook her head. 'I want to believe you. I know you'd never deliberately lie. But this revelation is very convenient. Maybe you're imagining feelings because you know I want to leave.'

His heart bottomed out. Everything went into free fall.

She wanted love, but not *his* love.

The pain was inconceivably sharp. A honed, heated blade scoring his skin before plunging deeper.

His royal education had taught him many things but rejection wasn't one of them. He couldn't even seem to let go of her hand, still clasping it in his.

With an effort, Zamir pushed back his shoulders and sat straighter. He hadn't finished. He'd come this far, he owed it to himself to continue.

'Convenient isn't the word I'd use.' Another breath, another stabbing pain. 'Contrary to what you think, I *do* mean it. So much that if there's a chance you feel the same about me, I'm willing to walk away from the coronation.'

He heard her hiss of shock but kept going. 'I don't need to be Sheikh to be happy. I can still work for my country, still contribute in other ways if it means you'll feel free to love me back.'

The world seemed to freeze with his words. Everything stilled except the quick thud-thud of his pulse and the fine tremor in Miranda's hand.

'You'd abdicate?' Her voice wobbled on the word.

'Technically it's not abdication if I haven't been formally crowned.'

Miranda clung to his hands, leaning so close he caught a drift of her sweet jasmine scent with its underlying note of warm, womanly flesh. His nostrils flared greedily.

'I don't care what it's called! You're saying you'd leave all this behind if I wanted it?'

'If you wanted me. If you loved me.'

The tremor in her hands became a shudder.

He shouldn't but he couldn't help hoping that was a positive. At least she wasn't indifferent.

'You can't do that.' She sounded angry. 'It's who you are, what you've trained for all your life. You're good at it and you enjoy it.'

Zamir shrugged. 'I told you once before that I didn't want the crown for personal reasons. It's a vocation that was thrust on me. I could be as happy working for my country in another way, if I had you.'

He'd just laid his heart, his happiness and his future bare. He'd deliberately made himself vulnerable. It terrified him yet at the same time felt incredibly liberating. Because now he and Miranda were just a man and woman, equals. That was what he craved.

'But you said your brother didn't want to be Sheikh. If you left he'd be forced to take the role.'

She was more worried about Umar than him? His tentative pleasure dimmed. 'My brother is a grown man. It would be his choice. And if he chose not then someone else would be found.'

'But they wouldn't find anyone as good as you. They need you.'

Zamir withdrew his hands and shot to his feet. If all Miranda could worry about was who led his country, it was clear she didn't return his feelings.

'They'd make do.' He paused, knowing he had to say it, yet rejecting the idea with every atom in his body. 'I told you how I feel about you, Miranda. The fact you haven't returned the favour tells me all I need to know. I wish you goodnight.'

He was halfway across the room when she rushed across to stand before him, hectic colour in her cheeks.

'You really mean it!'

Zamir scowled. 'You think I'd joke about something like this?'

'No, I don't think you would.' She planted her hands on his chest, fingers splayed, leaning so close he automatically wrapped his arms around her. Almost automatically, for he was desperate for one last hug, if that was what this was. 'I just never thought… You don't do anything by halves, do you? I like your decisiveness, but this…!'

'Oh, so there's something about me you like?'

'Love. Things I *love* about you. Why do you think I was so desperate to leave? I fell in love with you and couldn't bear to be just your necessary wife. Not when you mean everything to me.'

A great sunburst of joy exploded inside Zamir. His arms tightened around her, pulling her hard against him. As ever, they felt perfect together.

For a long time he said nothing, his throat too tight to speak, his heart overflowing.

'You *are* my necessary wife,' he managed finally. 'I couldn't go on without you, Miranda. You believe me, don't you?'

Her head tilted and her hands slid up to cup his face as if learning its contours anew. 'I really do. It's amazing, incredible, but I do.'

'*You're* amazing and incredible.'

Her laughter was throaty, spiralling through his vital organs and easing the unbearable strain in his muscles.

'So what's it to be, my love?' Had any two words ever sounded as good as those? 'Marriage to a Sheikh or an ordinary citizen?'

Her expression was warm and for the first time Zamir saw

love, complete and unfettered, reflected back at him. It was a wondrous moment he'd remember for the rest of his days.

'To a Sheikh, of course. You'll be the best leader this country has ever had.'

'Even if it means we have to live in the palace and follow protocol at least some of the time?'

Her smile was mischievous. 'I can put up with that if it means being with you. Besides, think of the perks. Sheikhs have the biggest, most comfortable beds and plenty of money to invest in the best stables.'

Gravely he nodded, fighting a grin. 'I'm glad you finally saw sense.' Then in a single, satisfying move, he lifted her into his arms.

'Not sense.' Her words feathered his chin. 'Love. True love.'

Zamir paused on the way to that big, royal bed. He looked into her lustrous eyes, his heart expanding with pure joy. 'True love.' It was a vow. 'Now and for ever.'

EPILOGUE

'YOU REALLY KNOW how to throw a party, Miranda. This is much better than any palace reception I remember.'

'Really?'

She turned from her sister-in-law beside her on the secluded balcony, to survey the crowd below them in the huge courtyard. She'd thought the space with its wide, paved areas, fragrant shrubs and decorative water features perfect for an evening reception. But it had never been used for a public event before.

After two years with Zamir, Miranda was much more comfortable suggesting changes to palace arrangements, but it was good to have her ideas endorsed so wholeheartedly.

'Absolutely. The grand reception halls are fine for state occasions but this is much more relaxed and welcoming. And I approve the more varied guest list. Not just the privileged and the powerful. In fact I had a fascinating conversation earlier with someone about irrigation improvements.' Afifa craned her neck. 'There he is. I'm just going to catch him again. There's something I want to check.'

She threaded her way past a knot of diplomats and a European prince who was in deep conversation with Miranda's stepfather, and one of the young men who had participated in that first diversionary programme in the royal stables. Far from following a career in crime, he was working with horses full-time and planning to train as a vet.

'They're probably discussing polo,' murmured a deep voice near her shoulder as a hand slid around hers.

Miranda smiled and leaned against her husband as their fingers threaded together. Her heart lifted as it always did near him. 'Of course they are. Meanwhile Afifa has met another agronomist and they're talking shop.'

'And did you notice Umar and Sadia?'

Miranda nodded, locating them, heads together, on the edge of the crowd. 'Since he decided to do a documentary on early childhood development they spend a lot of time together. Do you mind?'

She turned, looking up into the honed, proud features of the man she loved. His ebony stare caressed like velvet and promised private delight when the reception ended. A shiver of anticipation unfurled lazily inside.

Zamir shook his head, eyes not leaving hers. 'They seem well matched. Sadia's blossomed into an interesting woman these last couple of years.'

Miranda nodded but her attention wasn't on her cousin. A finger stroked the centre of her palm, making her nipples bead against her scarlet dress.

'Did I tell you how beautiful you look tonight?' Zamir's voice dropped to that intimate note that made her blood pump faster and her skin tighten.

'Only once or twice.'

He bent close, his words caressing her cheek. 'How remiss. You're utterly gorgeous. And…' His mouth curved into a sensual smile that undid something inside her. 'You're all mine.'

'And you're mine.'

'As if I'd ever forget.' His voice dropped even lower. 'I have plans for you once this reception is over…*wife*.'

A thrill passed through her. Miranda loved the way he called her that. With delicious intent and deep, abiding love.

'Excellent. I have plans for you too…*husband*. I want to renegotiate our agreement.'

Zamir lifted one eyebrow, that carnal smile still curling the corners of his mouth. 'Do you, indeed? Which part of our agreement?'

'The bit about not having children yet.'

Miranda would never forget watching his expression change from amusement to astonishment, elation and, as ever, love.

'Don't get too excited. We may not even be able to—'

'I know. Time will tell, but the fact that you want to try…' His smile was crooked and his voice gravelly. 'You really *do* trust me.'

His cheeks were warm beneath her palms as she leaned close. 'Of course I do.' How could he think anything else?

Zamir gathered her to him, his embrace gentle. 'Miranda, you're my love, the other half of my heart.'

Then, ignoring protocol and the possibility that someone might look up to the shadowy balcony, he kissed her with all the ardent tenderness she could wish for.

When finally they pulled apart, she whispered, 'You know, the best decision I ever made was to kidnap you.'

Zamir's laugh made heads turn as they walked hand in hand to join their guests.

* * * * *

A VOW TO REDEEM THE GREEK

JACKIE ASHENDEN

MILLS & BOON

CHAPTER ONE

ELENA KALATHES SURVEYED the small, unnamed Jamaican island in the middle of the Caribbean with some annoyance. All green jungle and white sand beaches, the water a crystal-clear turquoise, it was certainly picturesque. Idyllic almost and untouched. That was what the people in Kingston had told her. Off grid, they said. He has supplies delivered once a month, they said. Sometimes he visits Port Antonio but only rarely and never on a schedule, they said.

No one knows where he lives, they said.

Well, no one apart from the three Kalathes Shipping staff members she'd already sent to Jamaica to find her adoptive brother. And herself.

Not that he was her brother, not in any real sense. She hadn't grown up with him and hadn't seen him since he'd rescued her from the rubble of her home in that tiny Black Sea nation devastated by an earthquake sixteen years ago, bringing her back to the Kalathes Greek island estate, and left her there.

So no, not a brother. A fairy tale, more like. A myth, even.

Atticus Kalathes. Head of the global charity Eleos,

and who ran the whole massive enterprise from his off-grid nameless island that he never left. Or only sometimes, though no one could be entirely sure. His movements were a mystery.

The skipper had cut the engine to the boat she'd hired to get to Atticus's island and had leapt out onto the small jetty that stuck out into the clear blue sea. Once the motor died there was no sound apart from the waves lapping against the rocks and the sand, and the occasional cry of seabirds.

Sweat trickled down Elena's spine. Stupid to wear a suit in the tropics, but she'd wanted to present a strong, professional front. She'd thought the lightweight cream jacket wouldn't be too hot considering she was going to be on a boat, and the cream silk blouse she wore underneath would help keep her cool.

A mistake. The sweat was going to stain the blouse and what had possessed her to wear the matching cream skirt, God only knew.

The heels were a mistake also.

Elena glanced down at the cream kitten heels she'd brought to match her cream suit. Yes, definitely a mistake. She just…well. She liked expensive clothes. She liked to look nice. She was here as Aristeidis Kalathes representative—his adoptive daughter—and it mattered that she look the part.

The skipper tied off the boat and held out a hand to her. Elena took it and gingerly stepped onto the jetty. There were already water stains on her shoes, dammit.

‘Thank you,’ she said to the skipper. ‘Give me an hour.’

He nodded and leapt back into the boat, already getting out the first of what would no doubt be many cigarettes.

Elena turned and glanced down the small jetty then over to the beach beside it, the water lapping gently against the pristine white sand. The heat was punishing, the sun fierce even at this time of the afternoon, and the humidity was making every item of clothing she wore stick uncomfortably to her body.

She hoped an hour would be enough. The others she’d sent had lasted only ten minutes. Then again, none of them were her. None of them were the little eight-year-old Atticus had rescued from the rubble of a destroyed town, before taking her to Greece and then abandoning her at his childhood home.

She would use that abandonment if she had to. She wasn’t above a bit of emotional manipulation, not when it came to fulfilling her adoptive father’s dying wish.

Aristeidis wanted to see his son one last time, to heal the breech between them, and Elena would do anything to help him. Aristeidis had given her a home, given her his name, given her security that the traumatised child she’d once been had lost after her entire family had been killed.

He’d given her everything and for the past few years, over the course of his illness, she’d been giving back. Including bringing his estranged son home.

Atticus Kalathes was going to return to Greece, whether he wanted to or not.

She smoothed her skirt, adjusted her jacket, and walked purposely down the wooden jetty. Not far from the beach, crouched beneath the palms and tangled jungle, was a sprawling house constructed of dark wood. It seemed to be a series of boxes connected by wooden walkways, with large floor-to-ceiling windows that looked out over the beach and the ocean.

A sandy path bordered by discreet solar lighting and covered in crushed shells led from the jetty to the house. Elena started along it, only to come to a stop as a movement from the direction of the beach caught her eye.

A man walked across the sand. He'd clearly come from the rocks at the end of the beach and carried something over one muscular, tanned shoulder.

One very bare, muscular, tanned shoulder.

Elena frowned then squinted.

It wasn't just his shoulder that was bare, she realised. He didn't appear to be wearing swimming trunks of any kind.

He was completely naked.

A flush of embarrassed heat washed through her, making the sticky feeling of her clothes even worse, and she looked hurriedly away.

Of course, he would be naked. It was his island. He must think he had complete privacy and yet here she was, charging in unannounced. Well, almost unannounced. She'd sent him numerous emails and voice messages informing him of her visit, none of which he'd responded to, and she'd thought that maybe he hadn't received them. He did live off grid after all.

Or maybe he had received them, he just hadn't wanted to answer. He was famously rude, according to the various Kalathes people who'd tried to make contact with him. Though the people in Kingston had said that the rare times he did venture to the mainland, he was very charming and everyone liked him.

Elena didn't know which version of him she was going to get—she suspected the rude one—but her coming upon him naked wasn't going to endear her. Perhaps she should go back to the boat and wait until he'd got dressed.

She turned towards the jetty and the boat, and took a step.

'Stop,' a deep, masculine voice ordered.

Elena thought of herself as a modern woman, definitely a strong woman, and she didn't take kindly to being told what to do by anyone who wasn't Aristeidis, but she found that she'd obeyed the command before she'd even thought about it.

Annoyed, she turned to tell him that she wasn't a dog to be ordered around, only for the words to die unsaid on her tongue.

Atticus Kalathes stood not far away, bathed in the Caribbean sun like a male version of Botticelli's *Venus*, minus the long blonde hair and the shell.

He was very tall, very broad, and his olive skin was darkly tanned and glistening with water. Every line of him was hard, every muscle exquisitely chiselled as if out of a dark amber marble. His hips were narrow, his legs long, his thighs powerful. And between them…

Elena flushed even deeper and tore her gaze away and up to his face.

But quite frankly that wasn't any better.

She knew what he looked like, of course—Aristeidis had many albums full of photos of a laughing boy with coal-black hair and even blacker eyes. A smiling teenager with hints of the man he'd become in his strong jaw and proud blade of a nose. And she had her own memories, too, of that day so long ago now, when she'd gripped the small pocketknife she'd found in the rubble of her home, her only weapon as a crowd of looters surrounded her. They'd seen an opportunity in the lone, vulnerable child, armed with only a tiny knife.

She'd been living in the rubble for at least a week, scrounging what food she could find, not wanting to leave the ruins of her apartment building and her family lost somewhere beneath it. She'd been terrified, blood from a cut she hadn't even realised she had running down her face and getting into her eyes. But one thing surviving in the rubble for a week had taught her: the roaming packs of looters were predators and they could sense fear, so if she was caught out in the open, she mustn't ever show she was afraid. Mustn't ever look like prey.

So she'd stood there, fear like acid in her throat even as she'd gripped her knife, trying not to let any of it show. Then *he* had come out of the dark, a tall figure armed to the teeth. He'd worn a helmet and fatigues and he'd lifted his weapon, firing two shots into the air and shouting at the looters in a language she hadn't recognised. The men had scattered and then it was only her and him, and she could see his face, all stark lines and sharply cut angles, and eyes blacker the sky above her head.

A handsome man, she'd thought. A prince maybe. Because he wasn't one of the looters or the opportunists, she'd known that instinctively. He was here to save her, she'd been certain, so she'd dropped her little knife and held out her arms to him.

The eyes that looked at her now were still as black as that long ago sky, as were the uncompromising lines of his face. But she was looking at him now as an adult, not a child, and she could see how beautiful he was. Apollo come down to earth to seduce mortal women.

She'd known that though. She'd seen photos of him in the media, had read avidly all the interviews he'd given. In fact, she knew them all by heart. She could recite them in her sleep. He'd given all of four, the last one two years ago, and hadn't been in the public eye since.

Her heart thumped hard beneath the cream wool and silk of her clothing. The sun glistened in his inky hair, still wet from the swim he'd apparently just had, and there were drops caught in his long, sooty lashes.

She'd seen pictures of naked men before. It wasn't as if she hadn't. In the books in the Kalathes library, photos of paintings and sculptures and other forms of art. She'd peeked, too, on the Internet, looking at various sites out of interest, but she'd privately wondered what all the fuss was about.

Now she knew. Now she understood.

A living, breathing man, glistening in the sunlight, all damp skin, hard muscle, and glittering black eyes. He was the fuss.

He didn't seem the least bit embarrassed or bothered by his nakedness. In fact, he stood there as if he weren't naked at all or carrying some freshly caught fish still attached to a line over his shoulder. He might as well have been wearing a three-piece suit and a crown for all the notice he paid.

She really needed to say something, perhaps the little speech she'd already prepared about how his father was dying and that it was time for him to come home, but the words got jumbled up in her head and all that came out was, 'Um… I…well…'

'You don't have permission to land here,' he said, his deep voice hard.

Elena's mouth had gone dry and her cheeks felt hot. In fact, her whole body felt hot, and it wasn't only the sun or the humidity, she suspected. 'Oh, well, you possibly don't recognise me. I'm—'

'I know who you are, Elena.' He flicked an impersonal glance over her. 'You still don't have permission to land on my island.'

An electric shock went through her and she blinked. He'd recognised her, which she hadn't expected since the last time he'd seen her had been sixteen years ago, when he'd delivered her to Aristeidis and Kalifos, the Greek island where the Kalathes family lived.

She swallowed, reflexively straightening her jacket as if that would make her any cooler. 'I sent you a number of emails, and I called—'

'Yes, and did you at any point get a response from me indicating I would be pleased for a visit?'

It annoyed her that, not only did he not seem to care about his nakedness and its effect on her, he apparently hadn't cared about her emails either. 'No. But I thought they might have gone astray.'

'They did not.'

'But you—'

'My silence should have indicated my preference,' he went on as if she hadn't spoken. 'Which is to be left alone.' Despite the sun gilding his skin, his expression was cold.

It seemed she was going to get rude Atticus Kalathes.

Well, no matter. She was here on a mission for Aristeidis and she wasn't going to let anything get in the way of her goal, not even one beautiful naked man. She was determined if nothing else.

'I'm afraid I can't do that,' she said crisply, pulling herself together. 'I'm here on behalf of your father. He's dying, Atticus. He wants you to come home.'

Atticus had known exactly who the little boat carried when he'd spotted it motoring steadily towards his island not half an hour earlier. He'd been out in the water catching his dinner for the evening and the sight of the boat had put him in a foul temper.

He'd purposefully ignored Elena's emails and calls because the last thing he wanted was to have to deal with anything related to his father. He'd thought his silence would be enough to deter her. Apparently not.

Honestly, what was the point in living off grid, on an unnamed island that he'd made sure wasn't on any maps, if people could find you so damn easily?

He hadn't bothered with the niceties. If she was so insistent on coming here, to his territory, she could take him as she found him, which was naked, his preferred state on the island when he was catching his own dinner.

She was invading his home and she didn't have an invite, and he'd be damned if he stopped fishing and got dressed to accommodate her.

At least, that was what he'd thought when the boat had pulled up to the jetty at last, and he'd seen her small figure, dressed in an inappropriate cream suit, picking her careful way along the shell path to his door.

Then he'd got a closer look and hadn't been able to think of anything at all.

Sixteen years ago, she'd been a ragged little eight-year-old covered in blood, holding a knife in one small fist against the five men who had certainly meant to do her harm. Her clothes had been torn, her rich blonde hair in braids, her brown eyes full of fury.

He'd been in charge of a private army that helped

governments during times of civil unrest or disaster, and had been searching the rubble for survivors. He'd spotted her immediately and the danger she was in, and had sensed that, despite the determination in her posture and the fury in her eyes, she was terrified. As she should have been, considering she was a child surrounded by looters.

He'd fired a couple of warning shots in the air to scatter the men around her, and he'd thought she might run after that because, in fatigues and carrying weapons, he was only likely to frighten her further. Yet she'd taken one look at him, her face bloody from the cut on her forehead, had dropped her knife and held out her little arms to him as if he weren't a hardened mercenary, but her knight in shining armour instead.

He'd never forgotten that. Never forgotten the way his dead heart had given a shudder in his chest at the sight of her.

He hadn't forgotten it now as she stood in front of him, flushed and damp with perspiration in a suit that was more appropriate for the boardroom than the beach of a tropical island.

She'd changed. She'd changed completely.

That rich blonde hair wasn't in braids, but a neat bun on the back of her head, and her face had lost the roundness of childhood. She had a firm chin, a surprisingly lush mouth, a proud nose, and feathery blonde brows a shade lighter than her hair.

That tough, ragged little girl had grown up into a stunningly beautiful woman. A woman who was clearly suffering from the heat and also, he couldn't help but notice, flustered by his nakedness.

That would have made him feel satisfied if she hadn't been who she was, and he hadn't taken a lover in so long he could barely remember the last time he'd touched a woman. His libido was as dead as his heart and he felt no need to resurrect it.

Besides, she wasn't just any woman. She was the girl he'd rescued and left with his father. His father who was dying.

No, he hadn't read any of the emails she'd sent him, but, despite his anger at her arrival, he'd known deep down as soon as he'd seen her boat that if she'd come all this way to find him, it was probably about something serious.

He hadn't spoken to Aristeidis for sixteen years, and had planned on never speaking to him again, yet something unfamiliar stirred deep inside him as soon as the words 'he's dying' were out of her mouth.

Atticus ignored it.

'So?' he asked, a heartless response, which made sense considering he didn't actually have a heart.

Her warm brown eyes narrowed, making it very clear that she didn't approve of his lack of concern. 'What do you mean "so"? You heard what I said, didn't you?'

'That my father is dying and I need to come home? Yes.' He hefted the fish on his shoulder. 'One, I don't care, and two, I'm not going anywhere, so why don't you trot off back to where you came from?'

She blinked in surprise, golden lashes fluttering, and for a moment he thought she might indeed turn on one of her pretty heels and trot off back to the boat. But then those feathery brows arrowed down and that rounded chin got a distinctly determined look to it, and once again he was reminded of that eight-year-old girl, standing in the rubble, facing off five adult men as if she could fight all of them and win.

'No.' Her voice was cool and crisp as a winter frost. 'One, I promised your father I'd bring you home and two, I'm not "trotting" anywhere.'

A pulse of unwelcome electricity arrowed down his spine.

People did not talk back to him. He was head of the largest charity in the world and had a great deal of power and social standing, and he ran Eleos like a military operation. There was a strict hierarchy and he expected his staff to follow orders without question, and they did.

They certainly didn't stand there flushed and sweaty, ignoring a direct command to leave and surveying him with the most intensely disapproving look, as if *he* were in the wrong somehow.

'It was not a request,' Atticus bit out.

She straightened, a stubborn glint igniting in her dark eyes. 'And I'm not one of your employees. I don't have to do what you say.'

'You are, however, on my property. If you don't leave, I'll have you removed.'

She looked around in an exaggerated fashion. 'And

who exactly is going to be doing the removing? I don't see anyone else here.'

There was no one else here. He lived alone, which was how he liked it.

'Then I'll remove you myself.' And he went to unhook his fish from over his shoulder as if to put it on the ground in preparation for grabbing her.

It was almost a bluff. Because he'd remove her if he had to. She'd turned up here unwanted and unannounced and so she'd have to deal with the consequences.

She must have believed him though, because her hands came up. 'Wait,' she said in a breathless voice. Perspiration glistened in the soft hollow of her throat and, as he watched, a drop slid slowly down over her skin, following the curve of one full breast. 'I'm not here to fight you.'

For a second he didn't hear her, distracted by that tiny, glistening drop as it slid further down into the shadowed valley of her cleavage, before abruptly realising what he was doing and jerking his gaze back up to her face.

'Then why are you still here?' he demanded. Annoyance had sharpened his voice, but he didn't care. He didn't want her here and a curious heat was running through him. A heat he hadn't felt for a very long time and one he didn't like, not one bit. His body was a machine he kept well oiled and in peak condition, and his command over himself was total. Physical desire was an indulgence and one he didn't permit himself, so he shouldn't be reacting to her like this, not even a flicker.

'I promised him, Atticus,' Elena said firmly. 'I promised him I wouldn't come home without you and so I'm not.'

His father, Aristeidis Kalathes. Head of the Kalathes family. Owner of a multimillion-dollar shipping company. Ex-military. Proud. Arrogant. And rigid as iron.

Aristeidis, a widower left to bring up his two boys after his wife had died far too young, hadn't been any kind of father to Atticus for years, and even when he'd been a child, his father had always been about Dorian, Atticus's beloved older brother.

Dorian who'd died when Atticus was sixteen.

Still grieving his wife, his father had never got over Dorian's death either, and had never forgiven Atticus for being the reason Dorian had died, and Atticus had long since accepted that, because it was true. He *was* the reason Dorian had died, and Aristeidis had been punishing him for it for years.

His father had the right, that was clear. Yet that didn't mean Atticus was going to stay and take it either, so he'd left Kalifos for good. His father had hated him for that too.

No, if Aristeidis wanted him home, it wasn't to reconcile, no matter what he'd told Elena or what she believed herself. Atticus had no doubt the old bastard wanted to punish him some more, in which case he would be destined for disappointment. Atticus had paid for Dorian's death. He'd paid for it a hundred times over, and he was done.

He was never coming home and that was final.

'In that case—' Atticus turned towards his house '—it looks like you'll be in for a long holiday in Jamaica.'

Then he strode past her without another word.

CHAPTER TWO

ELENA STARED AFTER Atticus's taut rear as he disappeared down the shell path and around behind the house, a very real anger coiling tightly in her gut.

Aristeidis had told her that getting Atticus home would be difficult, that their relationship had been broken long ago and it was his own fault. He should have been a better father to Atticus, but he'd let grief and bitterness after Dorian's death drive his only remaining son away.

Now, as the cancer that was killing him made him sicker and sicker, all he wanted was to heal that broken relationship and tell his son how sorry he'd been for the way he'd treated Atticus all these years.

His regret and sadness had only added to the grief that Elena felt herself at his illness, and she couldn't bear the thought that the old man who'd given her a home and a family after she'd lost her own would die without reconciling with his son. She loved Aristeidis. He'd given her so much and it didn't seem like a big thing to bring his son back to him.

She'd thought that the moment she'd told Atticus about his father, he'd want to return. Not that he'd instantly drop everything, of course, but she'd thought he might be upset or at the very least be regretful.

Except he hadn't been. He didn't care, he'd said.

Her anger tightened. True, Aristeidis had made some mistakes after the death of Dorian, but still. He was Atticus's father and he was *dying*. Surely Atticus could put aside his own bitterness for his dying father? Elena didn't remember much about her own father, but she knew she would have done anything to have one last conversation with him.

If you'd managed to get the attention of someone to search through the rubble instead of running and hiding like a coward, you might have had the chance.

Elena ignored the whisper in her head. It was an old doubt that visited from time to time, but she never listened to it. There was no point. She'd been eight when her family had been killed and what could an eight-year-old have done? She'd barely survived herself.

Anyway, getting angry with Atticus wouldn't help the situation. It was a weakness she couldn't afford, and besides, it never got you what you wanted. When Atticus had left her on Kalifos she'd been furious, both at the world and at him. The world for taking away her family and then at him for abandoning her.

Aristeidis had been appalled at her arrival too and hadn't wanted anything to do with an angry child who seemed more spitting, hissing cat than human being. He wasn't a man who approved of strong displays of emotion. He was ex-military and valued strength and control, and so that was what Elena had turned herself into. A strong woman in command of herself and who never let her emotions get the better of her.

She couldn't let those emotions get the better of her now with Atticus. Though…perhaps it wouldn't hurt to let him know how much his father needed him. Perhaps even a small plea. She wouldn't allow herself to be vulnerable, not the way she'd been all those years ago, in the rubble of her devastated town, but she could allow him to think that she was.

She had no idea what kind of man he was now—she hadn't really had any idea of what kind of man he'd been when he'd rescued her all those years ago either—but he was clearly someone who responded to those in need. He ran Eleos, after all, and you didn't start up a charity then turn it into one of the world's biggest without being somewhat of a giver by nature.

Maybe if she was convincing enough he'd change his mind and come home. She'd turn on the tears if she had to. She wasn't above begging, not for Aristeidis's sake.

Taking a steadying breath and forcing her anger away, Elena started off in the direction Atticus had gone. Hopefully when she found him, he'd have put on some clothes, which would help matters.

However, when she eventually found him in a small clearing in the tangled jungle behind the house, standing at a tall wooden bench, he was still naked and in the process of gutting and cleaning the fish he'd caught. He paid her absolutely no attention at all as he stripped the scales from the fish, cut the head and tail off, then deboned it with ruthless efficiency.

And for a second all thoughts of pleading with him vanished from her head as she watched him, half mesmerised by the assured movement of his strong, scarred hands. He looked as if he'd cleaned and filleted his catch a thousand times before, every action precise and confident.

Of course he would. He's a hunter.

Where that thought came from, she had no idea. But it was true, she could see it in the hard, carved muscles of his body and the air of relaxed readiness about him. He didn't take his eyes off the fish he was preparing, but she had the sense that if prey or a threat appeared, he'd grab that knife and attack without hesitation.

'I thought I told you to leave,' he said, casually arrogant as he set aside the fish he'd cleaned and then dealt with the offal without looking up.

The tight coil of anger and grief inside her flexed and even though she was trying not to give into her emotions, what came out was, 'And I thought I told you I wasn't leaving until you came with me.'

'Get back on your boat, Elena. I'm not changing my mind.'

She tore her gaze from the distracting motion of his hands. 'Why not?'

'I'm not explaining myself either.' He looked up all of a sudden, his gaze black and glittering, the wickedly sharp boning knife held loosely in his hand. 'Make no mistake. I will forcibly remove you if I have to.'

An inexplicable shiver worked its way down her spine. Still naked, tanned by the sun, and holding a knife, there was something wild about him, something primal and, really, she should have been afraid of him.

Yet despite her anger, she found herself strangely thrilled instead.

Over the years she'd built up this idea of him, the warrior who'd saved her, the prince who'd carried her to safety. He was a fairy tale she'd embellished in her head and how could she not? At first Aristeidis had never spoken of him, not when she was growing up, that didn't happen until she'd been in her teens, so she'd had nothing real to base her imaginings on. Nothing but his rise as head of Eleos and she'd only watched that the way everyone else had—through the eyes of the media.

But this man in front of her wasn't a fairy tale and he wasn't a prince. He wasn't a myth. He was real and the reality of him was covered in scales and fish blood and holding a knife, and she found that oddly exciting, though why, she didn't know.

She wasn't leaving, though, regardless of his threats.

'Please, Atticus.' She let a thread of grief colour her voice and she didn't have to fake it. 'He hasn't even got a month. He needs you.'

'No,' he said, very obviously unmoved.

Elena clasped her hands in front of her and twisted them, making her eyes large and dark, and pouting just enough to hint at tears rather than a sulk. 'He's your father. It would mean so much to him.' She paused. 'It would mean so much to me too.'

While the hints at vulnerability were fake, she wasn't

lying. It *would* mean so much to Aristeidis and it would mean so much to her as well. She wanted him and his father to reconcile, for both their sakes.

But he was already turning away, her little performance of no interest to him. 'I've already told you my decision. I'd go now if I were you. There will be a storm front blowing in at some point this evening.'

Frustration gripped her, but she knew better than to give in to it.

You were too impatient. You should have waited for him to invite you here.

Except he was clearly never going to. No, what she needed was a bit more time and a better moment to broach the topic. Rushing him into this while he was catching and preparing his dinner, and then insisting when he was already in a bad temper, had been foolish.

Certainly the way she'd learned to endear herself to Aristeidis in those first few difficult months after she'd arrived on Kalifos was to approach him when he was in a good mood, after he'd just had a delicious meal or after a long sleep. Or in the evenings as he relaxed in the salon with his favourite brandy.

She'd kept her grief and her fear, her anger and her pain buried, letting not a hint of them show, sitting beside him quietly like a good little girl instead. And eventually, after a week of silence and her learning as much Greek as she could, he'd asked her what her name was.

He hadn't ignored her after that. He'd needed someone to take care of, she'd gradually realised, and, since she'd needed someone to take care of her, she'd turned herself into his perfect daughter.

Not that she was going to do that for Atticus, but perhaps a little neediness wouldn't go astray in the right context. First, though, she needed to give him time to finish preparing his fish, get dressed, and maybe when he was done he'd be more amenable. Especially if she got rid of her means of transport to the island. He could hardly put her on a boat back to the mainland if there wasn't a boat to put her on. And if there was a storm front coming, he wouldn't be able to take her back in any boat he might have either.

'Fine,' she said quietly. 'I'll go.' Without waiting for his response, she turned and strode off in the direction of the jetty. The skipper was sitting in the boat, casually smoking, and when Elena told him that she wasn't going to need his services for a return trip after all, he nodded and began the business of untying the boat.

It was a risk she was taking and she had no idea what Atticus was going to do when he found she'd sent her ride back to Kingston away, but it would buy her some time, that was for certain.

How she was going to convince him to return to Greece, she still had no idea, but somehow she'd find a way. She'd drag him back kicking and screaming if she had to. Though given he was at least six four and she was five two that probably wasn't going to work, but still.

Aristeidis wanted him home and she'd do anything for Aristeidis.

Elena waited until the boat had left and was on its way back to Port Antonio, then she waited a bit, giving Atticus some time to finish with his stupid fish and get some clothes on. He'd no doubt see the boat and think she was on her way back, so wouldn't be best pleased to find out she wasn't.

But that was too bad. She had a stubborn streak a mile wide and she had a sense she might need it when it came to him. In fact, she had a sense that he might equal her in stubbornness.

That should have made her wary, but it didn't. For some reason it excited her instead, which was worrying. She didn't want to be excited by him. While he was beautiful, his attitude towards his dying father—however Aristeidis had earned it in the past—still left a lot to be desired and she did not like that, not one bit.

After she'd waited what she hoped was a sufficient amount of time, she set off purposefully down the shell path again, following it back around the side of the house to the clearing and the bench where he'd cut up his fish.

Atticus wasn't there.

The path led on, however, wending through palms and shrubs, and around another of the boxes connected by glass corridors that were part of the house, following on to the beach.

She went along it until she was almost at the beach and then she saw him, standing under an outdoor shower situated beneath a shady palm.

Her mouth dried.

The water cascaded down over him, outlining the

hard ridges of every cut muscle, his body honed to perfection, his olive skin tanned and smooth, with a sprinkle of dark hair over his chest and following down his sculptured stomach and then further down…

She swallowed, but this time she couldn't stop herself from staring.

He was beautiful. He was beautiful everywhere. She almost couldn't believe he was real.

He stood for a moment, outlined in sun and water, then, obviously becoming aware of her, he shut the shower off, his black gaze colliding with hers, unmistakable anger lighting in it. His expression hardened.

Elena felt something in her harden too. Well, she knew he wouldn't be happy, but that didn't mean she'd let him intimidate her. In the first couple of months of being on Kalifos, Aristeidis would sometimes go into black moods, which were frightening. But she'd survived an earthquake that had killed everyone in her town, lived for a week on her own, facing off against looters, before being dumped on a Greek island in the care of a complete stranger. She was a survivor and she wasn't going to let one old man scare her. So she hadn't. And he'd respected her for it.

She suspected, however, that Atticus wouldn't, so she let her eyes get all big and dark and wounded, spreading her hands in a helpless gesture. 'I'm sorry, the boat wasn't there. Seemed the captain got tired of waiting and took off.' She fluttered her eyelashes, trying to be a bit pathetic. 'I'm so sorry, but… Well. It looks like I'm stuck here.'

Atticus didn't move for one long endless moment, his magnificent body gleaming like dark amber in the sun. Then abruptly he started towards her, intent in every line of him.

Alarm arrowed down her spine, all her threat senses going on high alert.

'What are you doing?' she asked, dropping the pathetic act instantly.

He didn't answer, striding towards her, the expression on his face utterly unreadable. But there was no mistaking the anger in his eyes.

Elena took a step back, her alarm increasing. 'Wait,' she began, except by then it was much too late. He took one last step and then she was swept up into his arms, his wet skin soaking her lovely cream suit.

'Atticus, what are you doing?' she repeated, too shocked to even struggle.

'I told you what would happen if you didn't leave,' he said in a hard voice.

Her heart was thumping, her pulse wild. 'Let me go,' she demanded hoarsely.

But he didn't answer, striding with her in his arms over the glittering white sand, heading towards the deep turquoise of the water.

If she hadn't been so shocked, she might have been conscious of the heat of his skin and the strength of him, and how she'd never been in the arms of a naked man before. But she was shocked and she had no time to think of those things, because then he was wading into the sea.

Every muscle in her body tightened. Oh, no, he wasn't going to do what she thought he was going to do… Was he?

'There,' he said. 'You can swim home.'

Then he unceremoniously dumped her into the ocean.

Atticus never let his temper get the better of him. He never let *any* emotion get the better of him. He'd successfully managed to detach himself from anything resembling feelings for years, firstly by joining the military in an effort to appease his father not long after Dorian's death, where he'd constantly challenged himself physically, pushing for perfection until he'd reached the peak as an elite sniper. Then once that had been achieved and it was clear that even following in his father's footsteps wouldn't heal Aristeidis's hatred of him, he'd continued his military career, assembling a private army that sold their services to governments who needed help with security concerns, peacekeeping, disaster relief, and protection for its citizens.

That might have been enough for him if he hadn't found Elena in the rubble of her town, prompting old feelings to re-emerge, and so he'd had to reassess his career yet again. He'd been independently wealthy by then, and had decided to put his military planning skills into starting a charity, and had been so successful that Eleos had become a worldwide phenomenon almost before he knew it.

Success and recognition had followed on its heels, and that should have satisfied him. Yet it hadn't. He'd been conscious instead of a growing realisation of all the things that he had that Dorian didn't. Fame. Money. Power. A life he had that Dorian didn't.

It wasn't fair and it wasn't right, not when he was the reason Dorian was dead, and he soon found he'd lost his taste for the spotlight—not that he'd ever really had it in the first place. Part of him had wanted to give Eleos up, but his name was now inextricably linked with it and he hadn't wanted to do anything to jeopardise its success. So he'd retreated to his Jamaican island and the simple life he'd found for himself there, running Eleos from his office and putting in the occasional appearance when it was demanded of him, for the good of the charity.

But the fact was, he needed the island and its simplicity, where he needed to exist only in the moment. Where he could concentrate on making sure he stayed as detached as he could from the past.

Then Elena had turned up.

Elena, bringing with her everything he'd thought he'd put behind him. Elena, all dressed in white, reminding him of the small blonde warrior with blood on her face and a knife clutched in her hand. Elena, not a child any longer…

He'd wanted her gone and out of his life, and he'd thought, when she'd walked away just before, that she'd obeyed his command and left him to it. He'd even felt satisfied when he'd heard the roar of the boat's engine, and had ignored that odd twist of what surely couldn't have been regret.

So he'd gone and showered off the remains of the fish blood and scales, only for Elena to suddenly reappear, looking at him with big dark eyes and spreading her hands helplessly, telling him the captain of the boat had just left without her.

The last time he'd seen Elena had been on Kalifos, where he'd handed her over to the Kalathes' housekeeper, Sofia, telling her that Elena was an orphan and that she was going to be living with them from now on.

Elena's brown eyes had been full of hot anger that day and as he'd handed her over into Sofia's care, she'd looked at him with complete and utter betrayal. She hadn't wanted to stay on Kalifos, she'd wanted to stay with him. And that was impossible. He was a soldier, he couldn't take care of an eight-year-old girl. Especially not a fiery, stubborn, tough eight-year-old who'd argued with him the whole long journey from her ruined country back to Athens and then to Kalifos.

A fiery, stubborn eight-year-old girl whom he suspected was just as fiery and stubborn as a woman, and not at all the helpless maiden she made out. Maybe it was that which had ignited his own anger. Or maybe it was simply because in that ridiculous white suit she was beautiful and the thought of her being in his vicinity and waking up a libido he'd thought long dead was insupportable.

His detachment had already been compromised by her mere presence, and when he'd realised she hadn't left with the boat and had actually come back, he'd noticed her watching him, a familiar look on her face.

He knew that look. It was the look of a woman who liked what she saw and she liked what she saw in him.

The male animal in him didn't care who she'd once been to him. It didn't care that she was associated with a past he'd been trying for nearly twenty years to leave behind. All it knew was that she was beautiful and it had been so long since he'd had a woman, and so his temper had frayed and his patience along with it.

He'd had to do something to teach her a lesson in obedience, so he'd shut off the shower and come towards her, ignoring the alarm on her face as he'd swept her into his arms. Then he'd turned in the direction of the sea and continued across the sand.

A mistake, and he'd realised it the moment he'd touched her. She was warm in his arms—hot even—and so soft, and it had been a long time since he'd felt a woman's curves against him. She'd made a breathless little sound and her scent had been all delicate musk and the crisp bite of apples, so sweet. He couldn't remember how long it had been since he'd experienced sweetness, or soft heat and honeyed skin.

She'd wriggled against him as he'd waded out into the water, the movement of her body exciting him. He'd wanted to hold her closer, bury his face in her neck and inhale her scent, and abruptly his control had felt tenuous.

So he'd dropped her straight into the water.

It wasn't deep, only waist height for him, but when she gave a startled cry and went under, there was a second where he felt a brief alarm, wondering if she could swim and whether he'd have to rescue her. But then she found her feet and stood up, water streaming off her.

And his mistake was compounded. Because her clothing was soaked and moulding to her curves, and her white silk blouse had gone completely transparent. He could see the delicate lace of the white bra she wore beneath it, and the soft shell-pink of little nipples gone hard in the cool of the sea.

She didn't look helpless or wounded now. Now, she looked furious, virtually quivering with rage. She spat a filthy curse at him in Greek and then her palm flashed out and she hit the water, sending up a splash that caught him full in the face.

The male animal in him growled in anger, wanting to close the distance between them and take hold of her. Perhaps dump her back in the water again or maybe something better, such as stripping off her wet clothes so she was as naked as he was, then pressing all that silky skin against him. Take her mouth, taste the salt on her lips.

His detachment, his control, wavered, and there was a moment where he had to fight to keep his grip on it. No, he couldn't do that. He'd *never* do that, not with her. Not only was she still that little girl to him, she was also now his adoptive sister and nothing was going to happen between them. If he wanted sex so badly, he'd make a trip into Port Antonio later and find a willing woman there. It didn't have to be her.

Instead, he wiped the water from his face and

turned, wading out of the sea without a word, heading towards the house.

He needed to get himself under control, get dressed, and then figure out just what the hell he was going to do with her. Because he hadn't lied when he'd told her about the storm front coming. Although the weather was perfect now, it wouldn't be for long, and there was no time to get his own boat out and take her back to the mainland.

'Atticus!' Elena shouted after him from the water, still sounding furious. 'Why did you do that? Where are you going?'

'There's a towel beside the shower,' he called back, without turning around. 'Leave your wet clothes there and once you've washed yourself off, come into the house.'

'What?' He could hear splashing behind him. 'Atticus, wait!'

But he didn't wait, striding across the hot sand and into the cool shade of the palms. He needed to get away from her and find his control again.

Inside, his house was beautifully cool—as he'd designed it to be—and the smooth dark wood of the floors was soothing after the hot sand. The ceilings were high, with exposed beams, the walls plain white. The living area featured large, louvred doors opened onto a wide deck that overlooked the lagoon. Today he had all the doors open, sunlight flooding in.

The peace and the familiarity of his home settled his frayed temper somewhat, and by the time he walked down the glass-walled corridor that led from the main living area and kitchen of the house down to another, smaller structure that was his bedroom and bathroom, he was feeling calmer.

Rinsing off in the shower, he then pulled on some clothes—worn jeans and a black T-shirt. The same louvred doors were in the bedroom too and they were also standing open, letting in the sun from the beach. He could see the outdoor shower from where he stood and Elena approaching and staring at it before glancing towards the house.

He turned away. She hadn't bothered with his privacy, but he would give her hers. God knew he didn't need any more temptation anyway.

On his way back to the living area, he made a detour down another glass-walled hallway that led to his office. It faced the jungle and the doors in this room opened onto a cool, shady deck. This was his head of operations, where he ran Eleos. There were computer screens and bookcases, one desk to work at, another that functioned as a workbench where he fixed electronics and anything else that needed fixing. Living on the ocean where the salt got into everything, there was always something that needed to be repaired.

He ran as much as he could off solar power, but he did have a back-up generator, his Internet coming from a satellite link.

Reflexively he checked the screens that were streaming news channels and social media to see if anything was happening globally that he needed to know about, but all was as usual so he directed his attention to the most reliable weather site.

The storm front would hit in about an hour, not enough time for him to get rid of Elena, and it was slow moving too, which meant she'd likely have to stay the night.

He bit off a curse. Perhaps he should just get the boat out and take her anyway. He could navigate through a storm. He'd done it before. Then again, he didn't want to risk her, and besides, why was he allowing himself to get so hot under the collar about her? She was a pretty woman, but he'd been around pretty women before without getting so wound up. And why did it matter that she stayed? He'd already told her he wasn't going back to Greece and he certainly wanted nothing whatsoever to do with his father, dying or not.

Are you sure about that?

He ignored the tug of doubt. Of course he was sure. The old man had burned so many bridges there was nothing left of them, not even a structure, and Atticus had no interest in building more.

Elena had been the last bridge he'd tried to build. She'd been an atonement of sorts for Dorian's death, not a replacement but a second chance. She'd also been something of a goodbye, since he hadn't been back to Greece since.

He'd checked in every so often with Kalathes staff to see how she was getting on, that his father was looking after her and that she was happy. And indeed, the reports had all come back that Elena was thriving on

Kalifos, getting a decent education and Aristeidis was taking an interest in her.

He'd been satisfied, pleased that the girl he'd rescued was finding happiness somehow. Then word had come a few years later that Aristeidis would be formally adopting her, and he'd been surprised by the jolt that had given him. It hadn't been pain precisely, but he'd decided he wasn't interested in finding out exactly what it was or why, so he'd ignored it.

Elena was safe and now she had a family and that was all that mattered.

It was all that mattered still.

She could stay, it wouldn't be a problem. If she kept going on about his father then he'd just tell her the subject was done and he wasn't interested in hearing any more.

His temper easing now he had a plan, Atticus turned from his screen.

He had a guest bedroom. She could sleep there and then he'd send her on her way come morning.

She wouldn't get under his skin any more than she already had.

He wouldn't let her.

CHAPTER THREE

ELENA GLANCED ONCE again towards the house then, muttering curses under her breath, she began to peel off her wet clothes.

She was furious, utterly and completely furious.

How dared he dump her in the sea? There had been absolutely no call for that kind of behaviour, none at all, and now her lovely new suit and silk blouse were ruined. She'd also lost both shoes, as well as a good portion of her dignity.

You've only got yourself to blame. He'd warned you.

Yes, he had. But she'd thought he'd settle for shouting at her. She hadn't thought he'd actually lay hands on her and throw her in the water.

A shiver ran through her at the memory of those strong, scarred hands holding her, and the heat of his skin as she'd lain briefly against his chest. He'd been so hard too; it had been like lying on sun-warmed rock.

Then had come the cold shock of the water—cold in comparison to him, at least—and the sudden surge of anger that had accompanied it. At him for not listening to her and not caring about his father, and then having the temerity to toss her into the ocean with no care for her clothes or her person. He could at least have explained his issues. He didn't have to resort to childish games.

Still, it was ridiculous to be *quite* so angry at him. She did have a quick temper, it was true, but she'd spent years keeping it in check. She shouldn't have lost it over an unexpected dunking, splashing him like a little kid. She should have been calmer, more controlled, not let him get to her.

Shivering as she pushed down her skirt and kicked it off, she glanced once again towards the house, debating whether or not to take off her wet underwear as well. But while he might be comfortable walking around naked, she wasn't, so she decided to keep it on.

She turned the shower on and stepped under the water. It was lukewarm and in other circumstances she would have enjoyed the cool feel of the water over her hot skin, but she was still too angry to enjoy it.

Keeping the shower short, she rinsed off the sea water then picked up the white fluffy towel that sat on a rock nearby and dried herself. Half the pins had come out of her bun so she took the rest out and squeezed the water from her hair, before wrapping the towel firmly around herself and making her way back along the shell path to the house.

Most of one wall of the house consisted of huge louvred doors that stood open onto a large wooden deck, so she went in a little hesitantly, finding herself in a cool room with a high ceiling of exposed beams and a few skylights. A couple of low couches and squishy, comfortable-looking chairs were scattered about, a big, brightly coloured rug covering the polished wood of the floor. A low coffee table carved out of dark wood stood near the couches, the surface cluttered with books and magazines.

There were shelves against the walls, full of books and shells and pieces of driftwood, and sea glass, as well as a few small hand-carved wooden sculptures. It felt low-key and casual and very comfortable with the sunlight dappling the floor and the warm, salty breeze coming in from the ocean.

A peaceful place. She could see why he liked it.

Until you invaded it.

Well, she wasn't going to apologise for that. His father was dying and wanted him home, and he hadn't even bothered to have a proper conversation with her. And she wasn't leaving until he had.

The living area was empty so she went through another doorway and into a large, airy hallway. There were a couple of other doorways that led off it, down the glass-walled corridors she'd seen from the outside. She peered cautiously down them but didn't see anyone, so she walked along a bit until the hallway opened up on one side to reveal a kitchen and dining area separated by a long wooden bench top.

Atticus was standing at the bench preparing what looked like a marinade for the fish that he'd put in a metal bowl.

So. Not only had he caught his own fish, he was now preparing it and would no doubt cook it too.

It shouldn't have surprised her—despite the money he'd earned from the private army he'd once owned, he was famous for his simple living, eschewing the usual trappings of wealth. He had no cars or planes. No houses in every country. He kept no personal staff. He attended no parties or galas or nightclubs or, indeed, any social occasions. He gave no interviews these days and sought no attention, which of course made everyone even more curious about him.

Yet despite all of that, she was still surprised. In her head he'd become this mythic being, not a man doing something as mundane as preparing a marinade with casual efficiency and who was, at last, mercifully wearing jeans and a T-shirt. He looked far too good in them, as attractive in simple cotton as he was in nothing but his own skin.

He didn't look up. 'I'll deal with your wet things. The second hallway on the left leads to a guest bedroom and I've put some fresh clothes on the bed for you. The storm will be here in less than an hour and it's slow moving so you won't be going anywhere tonight. I'll run you back to Port Antonio tomorrow.'

Elena opened her mouth to thank him, but he went on before she could speak, 'Also, I will not be entering into any discussion about my father or returning to Greece, and if you bring the subject up, you'll find yourself having it on your own.' Finally he glanced up, a brief glittering flash of obsidian. 'I hope you like fish. Because that's what's for dinner.'

There was an instant where she couldn't have said

whether she liked fish or not, because that brief moment of eye contact had short-circuited her brain. She swallowed, trying to pull herself together. She had no idea what was happening to her, but whatever it was, she didn't like it. Her experience of men was exceedingly limited, it was true, and that had been deliberate. Caring for Aristeidis since he'd got sick and helping him with Kalathes Shipping was far more important to her than sex and, anyway, she hadn't met anyone she'd been interested in.

Until now.

Elena ignored the thought. Atticus might be far more attractive than he had any right to be, but she wasn't going to allow herself to get distracted, not when Aristeidis was relying on her to bring him home.

'What do you mean you won't be entering into any discussion?' she asked. 'Your father is dying, Atticus.'

'Yes. You've told me so three times already.'

'But…doesn't that mean anything to you?'

He didn't look up from his marinade. 'What did I say about this conversation?'

Elena wanted to tell him what he could do with his arrogant pronouncements and almost did so, but there was no doubting the warning in his voice, so she bit down on the hot words she wanted to say. Again, she had to control her temper. If she pushed, he'd remove himself from the conversation and that wouldn't be in Aristeidis's best interest or hers. No, she had to play along for now. She'd figure out a way to get through to him, and at least, from what he'd said about the storm, she had a whole night to try to convince him.

Maybe she could even find out exactly why, even after all the time that had passed, he was still so angry with his father, and why returning to Greece was so out of the question.

'Fine,' she said, quelling her impatience. 'Yes, I like fish.' She was tempted to add that she'd often had it on Kalifos, but decided that would be too pointed. 'Thank you for cooking for me.'

Again, he glanced at her, his black gaze oddly searing. 'I'm not cooking for you, Elenitsa. You just happen to be here while I'm cooking.'

Elenitsa.

What he'd called her all those years ago, after he'd rescued her and she'd told him her name. After he'd discovered that she was all alone, that everyone she knew and everyone she'd loved had died in the earthquake. That she'd been surviving for a week on her own, with no one and nothing.

She hadn't known Greek or English, but he'd had a smattering of the Russian that was her birth language, and so he'd taught her a few words of both so they could communicate. He'd told her that he would take her away and find her a family, but all she'd wanted then was to stay with him. He was her saviour, her protector. He'd cared for her when no one else had and she didn't want or need anyone else.

Abruptly, she didn't want him to call her Elenitsa.

He'd abandoned her; he didn't have a right to it. Only Aristeidis did.

'Don't call me that,' she snapped, her temper already on a short leash. 'Only your father gets to call me that.'

Atticus looked up, something gleaming in his gaze. 'How quickly you forget who saved you all those years ago. And it was not my father.'

A strange, hot thrill chased along her skin and she found herself lifting her chin in response, as if he'd challenged her. 'And how quickly you forget who you abandoned all those years ago. Who you left alone in a foreign country, with complete strangers.'

He didn't look away. 'I did not forget. Are we going to have the same argument now as we did back then? When you were eight years old?'

She felt a flush creep over her cheeks. She didn't want him reminding her of the child she'd once been, and she didn't want him treating her like that either. The angry, abandoned child who'd been left by everyone who'd cared about her. The needy, desperate child…

Well, she wasn't that child any more. She wasn't needy or desperate or vulnerable in any way. Aristeidis loved her and had told her that he'd made provision for her in his will so she wouldn't be left with nothing after his death. It mattered to him that she was looked after once he was gone.

From out of nowhere came a sudden surge of the grief that had become her constant companion since Aristeidis's health had declined. It was nice that he'd thought of her, but money was a poor substitute for a person. He was her only family and once he was gone, she'd have no one.

Again.

The grief must have showed on her face because Atticus frowned abruptly, his gaze sharpening. 'What is it?' he asked.

But she wasn't going to explain her grief, not to him, not when it was still too close to the surface. It made her feel too vulnerable and she couldn't bear the thought of being vulnerable in front of this hard, uncompromising man. The man who'd once praised her bravery and strength, making her feel as if she was indeed brave and strong and not just a coward who'd run and hid instead of getting help for her family.

Grief wrapped its cold fingers around her throat, squeezing tighter.

Elena turned away, clutching her towel around her. 'I'm going to get changed,' she muttered and fled.

Atticus watched Elena's small figure disappear back down the hallway and frowned. For a second there she'd looked almost distraught and he couldn't think what he'd said to upset her. He'd only mentioned the argument they'd had when she'd been a child and he'd left her on Kalifos, but that had been years ago. Surely she couldn't still be angry about that? She was an adult now and should understand why he hadn't been able to take her with him.

Or perhaps leaving a traumatised child in the com-

pany of complete strangers wasn't such a great idea after all?

Doubt tugged at him again, but he pushed it aside and looked back down at the marinade he was preparing.

What else could he have done? He'd been twenty-three, a mercenary soldier growing his small private army, and there had been no way he could have looked after a child. Not that he could have even if he'd wanted to. He would never be father material and he'd already had ample proof that he wasn't big brother material either. On Kalifos she'd wanted for nothing. So why would she still be angry that he'd left her alone? If that was even what she was upset about.

Why are you so curious? Does it matter why?

He didn't know and it didn't matter. She wasn't his responsibility and hadn't been for some time, and, apart from anything else, she was an adult now. Her reasons were her own and they were none of his business.

Irritated with himself for even bothering to think about it, Atticus concentrated on finishing up the marinade, putting his fish into it, then putting the bowl into the fridge.

Yet his thoughts kept straying back to Elena and how she'd looked wrapped up in that white towel, with her blonde hair hanging damply over her shoulders and curling as it dried. She'd clearly kept her underwear on since he'd seen the delicate straps of her bra, and that beast in him had wanted to pull her towel away, pull that bra away too so that nothing marred the smooth perfection of her skin.

It had liked her snapping at him when he'd called her Elenitsa, as well, and then when she'd lifted her chin, responding to his challenge about their old argument. There had been electricity in the air between them, he'd felt it, and he was pretty sure she'd been aware of it too, though maybe she hadn't known what it meant.

Again, though, that was something he shouldn't be thinking about, most definitely not.

Even more irritated at himself and the direction of his thoughts, Atticus busied himself with getting her wet clothing. He rinsed her skirt, jacket and blouse, and hung them out to dry in a covered area near the house, though he was pretty certain the items were ruined, in which case he'd buy her some replacements.

After he'd finished dealing with that, he went back into the living area to find Elena standing in front of one of the shelves and looking at the items on it.

The only clothing he had in the house was his, so he'd found an old white T-shirt and a pair of loose, linen drawstring trousers that would have fitted her. Except all she wore now was the T-shirt, which hung down almost to her knees, leaving a pair of shapely calves and ankles bare.

It made something twist hard inside him, something hot and almost…possessive. As if he liked seeing her wearing nothing but a T-shirt. *His* T-shirt.

'What happened to the trousers?' The words came out more like a demand than a question, but he didn't bother to temper it.

She glanced at him then down at her bare legs. 'I

had to roll them up so much it was ridiculous. The T-shirt is fine.'

The T-shirt was *not* fine. It left far too much of her bare skin on show, though why he should even find that troubling, he had no idea.

His control over himself and his environment was perfect, so he had no excuse for getting hot and bothered over the potential glimpse of one pretty woman's thighs. Certainly not enough to get her to change.

'You'll have to wear them tomorrow when I take you back,' he said shortly. 'I've hung your other clothes out, but they're unlikely to be dry by morning, not in this humidity or with the storm coming. I'll have to buy you some replacements.'

She'd turned back to the shelf, studying a small wooden sculpture of a rearing horse. 'Yes, please. Considering you were the one who dumped me in the sea without warning.'

'I gave you plenty of warning.'

'Not that you were going to make me swim back to my boat.'

'If you'd actually left with your boat instead of coming back to lie about it, then I wouldn't have made you swim back to it.'

She glanced at him again, her brown eyes glittering with anger. 'They said you were rude. I had no idea just *how* rude.'

Perhaps that should have made him feel ashamed or at least a little bit embarrassed. It did not. Most people knew that coming to his island unannounced would ensure an unpleasant reception and he didn't apologise for it.

'If you'd wanted a different reception then perhaps you should have waited for an invitation,' he said coldly.

'If you don't want people to turn up unannounced then perhaps you should try replying to your emails,' she snapped back.

Theos, the woman was impossible. She'd been tough, he remembered that, but had she always been such a little spitfire? And how had his father handled that? Aristeidis had been stern and quite the disciplinarian and hadn't put up with what he'd termed 'nonsense'. Surely he wouldn't have been so indulgent of her? How could he? When he'd cut Atticus off so completely after Dorian's death?

Perhaps he mellowed?

No, he shouldn't even be thinking about his father. Yet another reason why Elena's presence here was an irritant that he needed to get rid of as soon as possible.

Except you like her being an irritant. You like fighting with her.

He did not. It was a mistake and if she couldn't keep control of her temper then it was up to him to stay in control of his own, no matter how much she annoyed him.

'Peace, Elena,' he said. 'You're here for the night so let's not make it any more unpleasant than it already is.'

She bristled and looked as if she might snap at him again, then her lush mouth compressed and she turned back to the shelf again. 'I like this horse,' she said after a moment. 'Where did you get it?'

Trying to relax his tight muscles, Atticus thrust his hands into his pockets. 'I didn't get it anywhere. I made it.'

Her brown eyes went wide and she glanced at him again. 'You did?'

'Yes. Carving occupies my hands and I find it relaxing.'

She reached out and touched the horse's head with a delicate finger. Her nails were short and painted the same kind of shell pink as he'd glimpsed through her bra in the sea, and for some reason the way she touched the sculpture sent a bolt of heat through him. 'It's beautiful.'

The bolt of heat intensified, though he wasn't sure why. He didn't need her praise. He carved because it focused him and, as he'd said, relaxed him. He didn't do it for any other reason and he wanted to tell her that, but he was trying to control his raw temper, so all he said was, 'Thank you.'

Elena stared at the horse a moment longer then she turned around and stared at him, her gaze very direct. 'Look, I know you said you didn't want to talk about your father, but I—'

'No,' he interrupted flatly. 'I told you we would not be having this discussion.'

'But—'

'No,' he repeated, and turned to the doorway. He'd told her he wasn't going to talk about this and he'd meant it He'd made his decision and there would be no changing it.

Are you sure? Do you really want to leave things as they are?

He absolutely could. The old man had never cared to talk to him before Aristeidis found out he was dying, so why should Atticus be the one to make the effort now? Did his father really want to mend things between them or was it only the prospect of having a clean soul before he faced his heavenly reckoning?

Either way, Atticus wasn't going to help him.

He started for the doorway to the hall, but found that Elena had nipped past him and was now standing directly in his way.

She wasn't very tall—the top of her head only came up to his chest—and she seemed delicate, especially wearing his T-shirt. However, determination radiated from her and there was a stubborn look in her deep brown eyes.

'No,' she said. '*You* listen to me, Atticus. We will be having this decision and we'll be having it now. I want to know why you won't come home. Why you're insisting on putting what you want ahead of your dying father's wishes.'

He ignored her, sidestepping and intending to go around her, but she sidestepped too, again in his way. 'Have a conversation with me,' she insisted. 'Give me something I can tell Aristeidis.'

His patience frayed, the threads on it snapping one by one as once again he tried to go around her. Again she blocked him. 'You can try and avoid me all you want. But I'm not going to let you.'

'Get out of the way,' he ordered through gritted teeth. 'If you continue to be a nuisance, I'll put you on that boat and the storm be damned.'

She gave him the most dismissive look. 'Don't be childish. Give me one good reason why you don't want to come home. I think you owe me that at least.'

And just like that his temper snapped completely.

He was tired of her being here, reminding him of the past. Reminding him of all the painful things he'd put behind him. Reminding him that he still had a heart whether he liked it or not, and that he still felt things even though he didn't want to. Reminding him that his body was hungry for a woman's touch and that she was beautiful, and he didn't like that. Not at all.

'I *owe* you?' he demanded, closing the gap between them, getting close to her, looming over her. 'I owe you for what? I rescued you. I gave you a home. I gave you a family. I gave you a future. I owe you *nothing*.'

Another woman might have found him intimidating and backed away. But not Elena. She didn't give an inch, staring straight up at him as if he weren't taller than she was and much bigger, much stronger. 'You left me alone in a country I didn't know, in the care of man who was a stranger to me, who didn't speak my language and didn't want a child dumped on him.' Bright golden sparks of anger glittered deep in the warm brown of her eyes. 'And this was *after* I'd lost everything and everyone I'd ever loved. So yes…' She lifted a finger and jabbed him hard in the chest. 'You *do* owe me.'

He didn't know what came over him in that moment, a sudden rush of fury and, beneath it, a flood of pain he hadn't realised he still felt, and he raised his hands so he could lift her and put her out of his way. Or at least that was what he intended.

Yet the moment his hands settled on her hips, all he could feel was the heat of her body beneath the T-shirt, and how seductive it was. How lush her sulky mouth looked and how he could think of a much better way to get her to be quiet.

'Atticus,' she said, her feathery blonde brows descending. 'What are you doing? We need to talk about—'

But she never got to tell him what it was they needed to talk about, because by that stage Atticus had got tired of listening too.

If she wouldn't get out of his way or be quiet, then he'd do something else to silence her.

He bent his head and covered her mouth with his.

CHAPTER FOUR

ELENA KNEW WHAT he was going to do—the flare of heat in his eyes had been warning enough. Not that she needed it, given the electricity in the air that had surrounded them just before his hands had settled on her hips. An electricity composed of anger, grief, pain and a deep, physical desire unfamiliar to her, yet that had caught her by the throat all the same the moment she'd looked into his black eyes.

She'd never been kissed before. She'd never even come close and the thought that her first kiss would be from *him*…

Perhaps that was what she'd unconsciously wanted the moment she'd seen him walking across the sand to her a couple of hours earlier, magnificently naked and so beautiful. A myth made real. Perhaps that was why she'd kept pushing him, telling herself all the while that it was for Aristeidis's sake, when all along it had been because of him. Because the raw, primal power of him had thrilled her, the heat in his black gaze exciting her. The sense that he was dangerous, that he was a threat, was intoxicating and she'd wanted to see how far she could push him before he broke and that threat was made real.

And what a delicious threat he was. His hard mouth on hers, so hot and demanding. She could taste his anger and his desire, and it was thrilling to know it was because of her. Because he wanted her.

She'd spent years viewing him through the lens of her own dim memories and then through that of the media. An enigmatic, brilliant, ambitious man, who'd then retreated from the world stage, whispered about only as rumours and hearsay.

But he was here now and real, so real. His hands were on her hips, holding her fast, his palms burning through the cotton of the T-shirt she wore. His T-shirt. She'd shivered when she'd put it on and smelled his scent, salt and sun and something deliciously musky and masculine.

She shivered again now, surrounded by that same scent, tasting salt as he kissed her, along with a heat that stole her breath. His tongue touched her bottom lip and then pushed inside her mouth, and her head went back, giving him access.

Warmth was beginning to spread through her, a heavy ache gathering between her thighs. She lifted her hands to his chest and spread her fingers out, feeling him, testing his strength beneath the warm cotton of his T-shirt. So hard, like rock.

He deepened the kiss, taking more, like a marauder, and she followed his lead, kissing him back, rewarded when he growled and his hands slid from her hips to the backs of her bare thighs and then up again, moving beneath the hem of her T-shirt. His fingers slipped beneath her underwear, those large, warm palms covering her rear and squeezing, then lifting her up onto her toes as he pulled her hips against his. The hard ridge behind his fly was pressed to the softness between her thighs, making the ache worse and sending a pulse of the most delicious pleasure spiralling through her.

Oh, this felt so good, so much better than the grief and the ache of impending loss she'd been mired in for the past couple of months. This was heaven and she wanted more of it.

She leaned into him, her fingers curling into the soft material of his T-shirt, shifting her hips against his in a blind attempt to get more of that bright, electric pleasure, and he made another deep growling sound in his throat.

He took his hands from her rear, but only to pull the T-shirt off her and discard it onto the floor. Then he ripped her bra off before dealing with his own T-shirt. She didn't stop him—it didn't even occur to her—gasping as he pulled her back for another deep, demanding kiss, her sensitive breasts pressing against his hard, bare chest.

The heat of him was astonishing. His skin felt smooth as oiled silk, with a sprinkle of crisp black hair, and she couldn't stop touching him.

His mouth had made its way down the side of her neck and her head fell back as he found the tender hollow of her throat, his tongue tasting the beat of her quickening pulse. Chills were chasing themselves all over her body, jolts of white-hot electricity making her tremble. His hands slipped down her back and beneath her underwear again, kneading her, pressing her harder against his groin.

In the back of her mind, Elena could hear alarm bells ringing, warning her that this was a terrible idea, that letting grief and anger do her thinking for her was a mistake and life would only get more complicated if she did this with him—especially with him—not less.

But then he made another growling sound and there came a sharp pull and a tearing as he ripped her underwear clean off. His fingers slid through the damp curls between her thighs, fingertips touching her slick flesh, stroking her, sending an intense surge of pleasure through her. And she forgot completely why this was a bad idea, forgot why she was even here.

There was only him and his fingers touching her, gently, delicately, weaving threads of ecstasy through her and making her pant.

'Atticus…' Her voice had become husky and ragged. 'Oh…please…'

He moved again, his hands gripping her hips, and then she was being lifted and carried to the low, comfortable-looking sofa and laid down on it. He ripped off his jeans and his underwear and then that magnificent body was over hers, settling between her thighs. His mouth was at her breasts, his tongue teasing one sensitive nipple before drawing it into the heat of his mouth and sucking hard.

Arrows of pleasure lanced through her and she closed her eyes, trembling as he transferred his attentions to her other breast. She threaded her fingers through his hair, the strands thick and silky against her skin, gasping as he began to work his way down her body, his hot mouth exploring, nipping and licking as he went.

Oh, God, he was going there, wasn't he? He was going to taste her there. She should stop him, she really should, but she didn't want to. She wanted him to keep going, to keep bringing her this blinding pleasure, because she wanted to lose herself in the moment. She didn't want to think.

His strong hands were demanding as they pushed her thighs apart and then she felt his breath against her sensitive skin, his fingers pressing apart her sensitive flesh, baring her for the lick of his tongue.

An intense bolt of ecstasy burst through her as she felt him and she cried out, pushing herself up onto her elbows and looking down, because she wanted to see. She wanted to see what he was doing to her.

His dark head was between her spread thighs, his fingers on her pale skin, and then he glanced up at her, his black eyes full of a dark flame that made her tremble all over again. He looked hungry; he looked like a predator. He looked like a hunter having secured his kill and now he was going to feast. On her.

She couldn't look away as he found the sensitive bud between her legs and teased it, nipping at her and licking. She groaned, her whole body shaking. And when his tongue pushed inside her, tasting her deeply, she screamed as the climax hit her in a white-hot burst.

Elena sagged back onto the sofa, shaking, her mind reeling from the force of it. She couldn't think, every part of her felt deliciously sensitive and raw, as if the pleasure had hollowed her out, leaving nothing behind but a shell.

Dimly she heard him move and the sounds of a packet ripping, and then he was above her, that magnificent rock-hard body settling down on hers. And she found herself looking up into black eyes full of flames, all that dark, predatory hunger focused on her.

She couldn't tear her gaze away as he positioned himself and then he was pushing into her, the unfamiliarity of the feeling making her groan. He was so big, she felt as if there wasn't room for him and her as well, her breath catching in her throat. Sensitive flesh burned as it parted for him and another groan escaped her.

He pushed deeper, his hands sliding beneath her rear, cupping her, lifting her, tilting her hips so he could slide even deeper. 'Elenitsa,' he murmured, his deep voice roughened and full of heat, his gaze on hers. 'Take me.'

And she did, her sex slick and ready for him, and there was no pain, only a feeling of fullness that made her pant. He waited for her to adjust, her hands pressed against his chest, and she was desperate for him to move. 'Please,' she gasped. 'Please… Atticus.'

He must have known exactly what she meant, because he did, deep and slow at first, then getting faster.

More pleasure spread out inside her, along with a

sense of rightness she didn't understand, but didn't question. Because it was him, and he was inside her, and she felt as if this was where he was always meant to be.

This myth become a man. Her saviour become her lover.

His beautiful face was taut and she could see her own pleasure reflected back in his eyes. He felt this too, she knew it deep in her soul.

'Atticus.' She touched his face gently, and then he moved harder, deeper, and the moment was gone, an urgent need replacing it.

His hands encouraged her to move with him so she did, matching his rhythm as if born to it, and the spiralling heat began to gather tighter and tighter.

She lifted her hands to his shoulders, nails digging into his skin, and then she wrapped her thighs around his waist, lifting her hips. He made another of those deep, masculine growling sounds and lowered his head, taking her mouth, his kiss as hot and as raw as the movement of his sex within hers.

He moved faster, harder, and she gripped him tight, pleasure building, a pressure that was getting too intense to bear. And then just when she thought she couldn't handle it another second, his hand moved and she felt his fingers slide down between her thighs, to where they were joined, and he slicked his finger over that sensitive bundle of nerves there.

And as if her body were his to command, the pressure fractured and shattered, and she was screaming his name, dimly aware of his own roar of release, as the sky fell down around her and covered her with light.

Atticus lay on the couch, his mind for the first time in years utterly blank, his body full of a delicious lassitude that he hadn't felt in far too long. Years for that too, perhaps? He couldn't remember.

For a moment he didn't move, letting himself drift in blissful silence and enjoying the moment, until slowly awareness began to trickle through him.

Of who the beautifully soft and hot woman lying beneath him was, and why she was here, and that he'd fully lost control of himself, taking her like a beast…

Just like that all the blissful warmth disappeared to be replaced by solid ice.

He'd lost control of himself. He *never* lost control of himself. Never, *ever.*

You remembered a condom at least.

Atticus abruptly shoved himself up and away from her, getting off the couch. His brain was still spinning so he didn't say a word as he went down the hall and into the bathroom to deal with said condom. Then he paused a moment at the basin and splashed some water on his face, trying to get his head clear.

What had he done? What the *hell* had he done?

He'd only wanted to end the conversation, do something about the crackling, fizzing electricity that arced in the air between them. Get rid of the anger inside him that he couldn't seem to leash.

The kiss had been a huge mistake, though at the time

it had seemed the only option, and he'd told himself just before his lips met hers that he'd take the kiss, silence her, then push her away. And yet…

The moment he'd felt the softness of her mouth and tasted the sweetness of it, every thought had gone out of his head. There had been only hunger, a raw aching need that had slipped straight through his fingers and out of his control.

It had been so long since he'd felt the soft heat of a woman, so long since he'd touched silky skin and tasted salt and sweetness. She'd been hot, her passion flaring as he'd kissed her, and when he hadn't been able to stop himself from sliding his hands beneath her T-shirt and taking a hold of her satiny giving flesh, pulling her hard against him…

Theos.

She'd shivered, her hands on him, as hungry for him as he was for her, and he'd…lost all sense. His anger had transmuted into sexual desire so quickly and he'd gone up in flames just as she had.

The taste of her was still in his mouth, the slick feel of her sex around his, making him hard again already…

It's Elena. The girl you rescued. The girl your father adopted.

Atticus gripped the sides of the basin, his knuckles white, staring down at it unseeing.

She was the last woman he should have taken, the very last. His father was dying and she was here to bring him home, and he hadn't seen her for sixteen years. And he should have put her on that damn boat the minute she'd got off it, not let her stay, not argue with her, not let the undeniable chemistry between them burn so hot and so bright. And definitely *not* lose his head and take her on the couch in his living room.

She'd been unpractised too, he'd been able to tell, and that was something else he'd conveniently pushed to the back of his mind.

Now you're just going to leave her alone on the couch?

He cursed. He couldn't remember the last time he'd taken a lover—which had obviously been part of the problem—but even when he had, it had only ever been for a night, two at most. He didn't do relationships. A wife and a family would never be in his future. Eleos was and would always be his main concern, which was exactly how he liked it.

Elena was special. She was sacrosanct, and yet…

And yet you took her like a beast.

The porcelain of the basin dug into his fingers. He knew what happened when he lost control of himself, when he allowed his emotions to get the better of him. He made mistakes. How could he have forgotten that?

Taking Elena had been a mistake. A terrible mistake.

And you want to do it again.

No. He couldn't risk it, no matter how much his body might want to. He'd thought his control was perfect, but she'd just blown that little comforting lie to smithereens. Taking her again would only compound the error and further compromise his command over himself. Besides, she was Elena. His Elenitsa. Or at least, she once had been.

Slowly, Atticus forced his fingers to release their grip on the basin. There was no point castigating himself. What was done was done. He'd be a gentleman, though. He wouldn't pretend it never happened or kick her out, but he'd definitely make it clear that it would not be happening again.

Turning from the basin at last, he strode back into the living area. Elena had pulled the T-shirt back on and was now standing once again at the shelves, studying them as if nothing untoward had occurred.

He could almost believe it too if it weren't for the white scraps that littered the floor near the couch, the remains of the underwear he'd torn off her, and the fact that her hair was in a wild golden tangle down her back.

Beautiful...so beautiful...

He gritted his teeth and strode over to where his own clothing lay on the floor, pulling on his jeans and T-shirt as Elena examined the shelves intently.

'Are you okay?' he asked as he pulled up the zip of his fly.

She glanced at him, looking surprised. 'What? Oh, yes, I'm fine.' Except her cheeks were deeply flushed and her mouth was full and red from his kisses, and there was something glittering in her dark eyes. Something that looked like shock.

He came over to her and before she could pull away, he took her face between his hands, tilting her head back slightly so he could study her. 'You are not fine,' he said. 'I'm sorry. That was a mistake.'

She flushed a deeper red. 'If you regret it, I'd really rather not—'

'I didn't say I regretted it,' he interrupted, because, rather to his own surprise, he didn't. 'But it was still a mistake.'

Her expression shuttered and she pulled away, turning to gaze at the shelves again. 'It's fine, Atticus.' The words were casual but it sounded forced. 'It was just sex. No big deal.'

But he suspected it was a big deal all the same.

Another reason why you can't let your control falter, not even for an instant. You are too susceptible to making mistakes.

As if he needed the reminder.

He shoved his hands into his pockets. 'Are you hurt? Do you need—?'

'Like I said, I'm fine.' She gave him another glance and smiled. 'Honestly.' Yet the smile was as forced as her casual tone. There was nothing honest about it.

'You were a virgin, weren't you?'

Another blush stole through her cheeks and her blonde lashes came down, hiding her gaze. 'That's none of your business, but no. I'm not.'

Another lie, he could tell. Which meant she had, indeed, been a virgin.

And you took her brutally fast and hard on the couch.

A thread of shame wound through him.

Theos. He knew what happened when he allowed his emotions to get the better of him, he *knew.*

Excitement. Inattention. His finger on the trigger. A

movement in the trees and a surge of adrenaline. The sound of the gun firing in his ears...

He shoved the memories away, trying to find the obsessive focus that was his normal state of being, the fierce homing-in of his attention that allowed him to detach himself from the past and all the emotions that came with it.

He'd allowed her into his private space, allowed her to distract him from the tasks that normally consumed him here on the island, and that had been his first mistake. He couldn't allow it to continue. The longer he stayed here talking to her, the more distraction would happen, and since he was stuck with her for the night, perhaps it was best for him to absent himself.

'Fine,' he said, allowing her the lie. 'If you need to use the shower, there is one next to the guest bedroom.'

'Thank you.' Still not looking at him, she turned back to her study of the shelves. 'And just so you know, I don't regret it either.'

Another bolt of heat shot through him and he could feel himself getting hard again, wanting more. He could still smell her, taste her, feel the tight, wet heat of her, and the urge to take her stubborn chin and turn her face towards him, to cover her lush mouth with his again, get rid of her T-shirt and take her down onto the floor, was almost too much for him. It took him at least a full minute to wrestle his hunger back into submission.

He didn't say anything, merely turning and heading for the door.

'Don't think I've forgotten what we were discussing,' she said from behind him. 'I still need to talk to you about your father.'

They would not be discussing his father. Not tonight. Not ever.

Atticus ignored her, heading out of the room and into the kitchen, and he forced all thoughts of her and the astonishing pleasure she'd given him from his head, turning his focus onto the dinner he was preparing.

That occupied him fully until he had the fish cooked and a salad prepared, some fresh bread rolls ready to go. By that stage the storm front was nearing, the wind whipping up the palms. He went around the house, closing windows and doors and making sure everything was secure, a process he'd done a thousand times before. The familiarity of the routine soothed him, and by the time dinner was ready and he'd put it on the dining table, he felt more like himself. Cold and focused and intent.

He was just about to call Elena to dinner when his mobile went off. The number was Greek and looked to be from a Kalathes staff member, which was unusual enough that he hit the answer button. 'Kalathes,' he said shortly.

'Mr Kalathes?' a man said. 'I'm afraid I have some bad news.'

Everything inside him tightened. 'What bad news?'

'Your father's health declined quite markedly two days ago, and while the medical staff did everything they could for him, they were ultimately unsuccessful. I'm sorry to say that he died half an hour ago.'

CHAPTER FIVE

ELENA STOOD IN the large, airy salon in the Kalathes villa, the deep blue of the sea through the windows almost aching in its beauty. In fact, the whole island was achingly beautiful, as was the villa that sat on it, all whitewashed stone, with many terraces and cool courtyards shaded with vine-covered pergolas.

Kalifos was as far removed from the dusty mountainside town Elena had grown up in as it was possible to get, and she loved it completely. Aristeidis had loved it too.

She and Atticus had just finished scattering some of his ashes in the ocean—as per his request—while the rest had been interred in the Kalathes vault inside the tiny island's church. It had been a beautiful funeral, but there had been no wake. There had been too much media interest and Atticus had been adamant that he wanted none of them anywhere near the island.

Elena hadn't cared. She'd only wanted to be sure that Aristeidis had the send-off he'd both wanted and deserved, since his last wish—reconciling with his son—hadn't been fulfilled. Atticus had attended the funeral so there was that at least.

The lawyer would be here any second to read the will—Atticus had insisted this be done as soon as possible—and already Elena felt exhausted.

She'd been feeling exhausted the whole of this past week, in fact. Ever since Atticus had come into the living area of his house in Jamaica, his face white, to tell her that Aristeidis had passed away.

Her adoptive father's health hadn't been good when she'd left Greece, but he'd insisted that she go to find Atticus. He'd be fine until she returned. She shouldn't have listened to him. She'd been worried about leaving him, but he'd been so insistent on her finding Atticus that she hadn't been able to refuse when he'd told her to go.

So she had. She'd gone in search of his son and while she'd been fighting with Atticus and then having sex, the only person who'd loved her in the entire world had died, and now she was alone. Again.

She hadn't even had a chance to say goodbye. Again.

At least, Atticus hadn't wasted any time or argued about the need to return to Greece. They'd left Jamaica the next day, and upon arrival on Kalifos, he'd gone straight into organisation mode. He'd been in meetings most of the week with people from his father's company, sorting through what needed to happen with the business, and then more meetings to deal with Aristeidis's finances, and she'd barely seen him. Not that she'd wanted to see him.

She felt as if part of the foundation of her life had fallen away and now everything was unsteady and precarious, and he made everything feel even more so. He was a stranger to her, a fierce, demanding stranger, and now Aristeidis had gone, it was as if she were that eight-year-old girl once more. That girl Atticus had rescued, who'd lost everyone and everything, and who'd been cast on the mercy of someone she didn't know.

Alone in the world yet again.

Her heart tightened and ached. It hadn't helped that she'd had nothing to do since she'd returned, because Atticus had taken over all the organisation. That had galled her, since she'd been handling Kalathes Shipping for a couple of years now due to Aristeidis's illness, but she didn't feel she could protest. Atticus *was* his son after all. She didn't like not having anything to do, however. It left her with too much time to think.

She'd demanded the right to arrange Aristeidis's funeral at least, and Atticus had granted her that. But he hadn't seemed to care that she'd been the one who'd been taking care of Aristeidis for years, who'd become, in essence, his assistant. In fact, Atticus hadn't seemed to care about anything at all. He left the Kalifos villa early in the mornings, taking a helicopter into the Kalathes offices in Athens, and not coming home till late at night, long after she'd gone to bed.

She'd tried to talk to him the few times they'd been in the same room at the same time, but the beautifully carved lines of his face had been hard and set, and his expression forbidding.

A hard, uncompromising man who apparently felt no grief at the death of his father. No grief at not being able to reconcile with him the way Aristeidis had wanted. He didn't seem to let grief touch him at all.

She did, though. She grieved, nursing the thread of anger that ran through her grief. Anger at Atticus. That he hadn't given his father the opportunity to talk, to say goodbye. That he hadn't been able to put a sick, old man ahead of his own issues.

Voices in the hall made her turn from her contemplation of the sea as Atticus and a shorter, older man, silver-haired and in a perfectly tailored suit, entered the salon.

Atticus wore a suit too, black for the funeral and tailored to emphasise his perfect physique. His wide shoulders and broad chest, his narrow waist, lean hips and powerful thighs. Even in a suit, though, there was no hiding the primal vitality of the man who wore it. He radiated it as the sun radiated heat.

Her mouth dried and she tried to ignore the sudden rush of desire that always seemed to occur whenever she was in his vicinity. Just as she tried not to remember that half an hour on the couch in Jamaica, when he'd been inside her, moving deep and hard, giving her the most exquisite pleasure she'd ever experienced.

You can try to forget it, but you'll never succeed.

It was true. Those moments were burned in her brain for ever, hot and bright and overwhelming. She hadn't known what to do when he'd suddenly pushed himself away from her and left the room, her mind still reeling from the effects of that orgasm. She'd never slept with a man before, and she'd felt…devastated in a way she couldn't articulate. As if he'd taken her in those strong, scarred hands of his, broken her into pieces, and then put her back together again in a way that felt wholly new and wholly unfamiliar.

When he'd come back from wherever he'd been and told her it had been a mistake, making it obvious he hadn't felt that same sense of devastation, the only thing that had mattered was that she protect herself. That she give no hint of her own vulnerability.

So she had. She'd told him it was fine, that it was just sex, no big deal.

He hadn't argued. Clearly to him, that was all it had been too.

Yet knowing all of that didn't stop the intense rush of physical desire every time she got close to him. She hated it.

'Elena,' Atticus said in his usual peremptory way, gesturing to the elegant couch upholstered in white linen and scattered with cushions in varying shades of blue. 'You should sit. This won't take long, but you look exhausted.'

The lawyer had already sat himself down in one of the matching armchairs near the couch and was pulling papers out of his briefcase.

Annoyance gripped her, Atticus's high-handedness abrading a temper already rubbed raw with grief and tiredness and a fear she couldn't shake. But snapping at him wouldn't help and she was actually tired. She hadn't been thinking of the will, but, now the time for it to be read was here, part of her didn't want to hear it.

Aristeidis had provided for her, or so he'd said, and she had no idea how and, quite frankly, she wasn't interested. Money seemed like a paltry thing to have instead of Aristeidis himself. She'd rather have had him, rather have had her life here on Kalifos back, than any amount of money.

Atticus sat on the couch beside her, though at the other end, leaving a good amount of distance between them. She tried not to notice that as well.

'Proceed,' he ordered, gesturing at the lawyer.

'Well,' the man said. 'It's all very straightforward. Everything the elder Mr Kalathes had has been left to you, Mr Kalathes.'

'I see,' Atticus said without any discernible expression.

Elena gripped her hands together in her lap. She hoped he'd leave her a few little mementos; that was all she wanted. Some photos perhaps, and maybe one of his handkerchiefs. He'd worn a heavy gold signet ring too, and she wouldn't mind that, though obviously that would probably go to Atticus.

'There's just one tiny complication,' the lawyer went on, 'and it involves Miss Kalathes here.'

Elena frowned. 'What complication?'

The lawyer gave both her and Atticus a rather embarrassed smile. 'Your father stipulated that inheriting his estate, Mr Kalathes, is contingent on you marrying Miss Kalathes.'

A hot shock went through Elena. She stared at the lawyer, conscious of Atticus's tense figure down the other end of the couch. 'Excuse me?' she asked faintly, her brain struggling to process what he'd said. 'He mentioned that he'd provided for me, but he'd never said anything about marriage.'

The lawyer spread his hands, looking apologetic. 'I'm sorry, Miss Kalathes, but he amended the will just before he died. He was very concerned that you be taken care of and because of your…past, he thought Mr Kalathes should be the one to take care of you.'

Elena blinked and opened her mouth, to say what she wasn't sure, but Atticus got in first. 'So in order to inherit, I must marry Elena?' he asked shortly.

'Yes, that's what it says.' The lawyer looked down at the papers held in his lap, shuffling through them. 'He specified that the estate will pass to you once you are married, but keeping it is contingent on you staying married for at least five years and that children were to be part of it. Two at the least, either biological or adopted. Mr Kalathes was very clear that he wanted Miss Kalathes to have a family of her own.'

Another shock washed through her. Marriage. Children. A family…

Aristeidis had wanted her to have all the things she'd lost.

Her vision swam, her throat aching. He'd thought of her, he really had. He'd said he'd make sure she was provided for…except he wanted Atticus to be her husband.

She didn't dare look at the man at the other end of the couch. He'd gone very still. 'And if we decide not to marry?'

'In that case the estate is to be sold.'

Atticus's features were expressionless. 'Thank you, Mr Georgiou. That will be all.'

The lawyer nodded and Elena was conscious of Atticus rising and talking to him as the man put his papers back in his briefcase, the two of them then walking to the door. Except she wasn't listening, the shock of the will still resonating through her.

There didn't seem to be any end to the shocks she'd been given the past week. First the shock of Atticus's presence and then their one blistering encounter, followed by the bombshell of Aristeidis's death.

She still remembered Atticus's hoarse voice as he'd informed her that Aristeidis had died, seeing the same shock in his eyes that she'd felt and the same grief. Yet his had been momentary. Within five minutes, while she'd shattered, he'd seemed to turn to stone.

He'd made her sit down then too, and had poured her a glass of brandy as she'd wept. But he didn't touch her, not once. And he hadn't touched her since.

She swallowed, another surge of grief hitting her, but she forced it back. She didn't want to cry again in his presence, not when it left her feeling so vulnerable. The marriage idea, while nice that Aristeidis had thought of her, was impossible. She didn't want to marry him, didn't want a family with him, and especially not if the only reason Atticus agreed was because he wanted to inherit his father's estate.

It was true that she longed for a family of her own and always had, but she didn't want anyone forced into marrying her. She wanted what she'd had before her family had died, before Aristeidis had died. She wanted someone to care about her. She wanted someone to love her. And Atticus didn't seem like the kind of man who even knew what love was.

The door shut behind the lawyer and Elena became aware that Atticus had come to stand in front of her, his black handmade leather shoes shiny against the pale wood of the floor.

There was a tight band around her chest, making it difficult to breathe. She didn't want to look up into his face, see that cold, set expression in his eyes. She was used to being strong, yet what she wanted passionately, right in this moment, was someone to hold her. Except she didn't want him to know that.

She couldn't be weak. Back in Jamaica, she'd allowed herself to weep in front of him, but that had been the shock getting to her. She couldn't allow that to happen, not now. Once, long ago, she'd trusted him and he'd abandoned her. And even though she was an adult now and she knew why he had, she still couldn't bring herself to let her guard down with him, not again.

She couldn't rely on him, couldn't trust him as she once had. She only had herself, and the only course left to her was to pull herself together and get on with it. Obviously, she'd have to leave Kalifos. Atticus wouldn't marry her, which meant the entire island and the house with it would go up for sale, and she couldn't afford to buy it. Why Aristeidis had believed his son would fulfil his wishes and marry her, she had no idea. Either way, though, she had nothing.

The thought of losing the only home she'd known for the past sixteen years twisted the knife in her heart, but she ignored the pain. Instead she clasped her hands tightly in her lap and forced herself to look up into Atticus's cold black eyes. 'That's unfortunate,' she said. 'I hope you don't think I had anything to do with it. I had no idea Aristeidis would want to put that in his will.'

Atticus said nothing for a long moment, studying her face. 'No,' he said, his tone impossible to read. 'I'm sure you didn't.'

'Good. Then there's really nothing further to say. I'll collect my things and—'

'No,' he repeated in the same expressionless tone. 'You will not.'

She frowned. 'What are you saying? I can't stay here. The island will have to go up for sale and I—'

'The house will not be going up for sale,' Atticus interrupted. 'And you will not be going anywhere. This is your home, Elena.'

Her throat closed and she had to force herself to swallow. 'But…but if you want to keep the island, you'll have to…'

'Yes,' he said steadily. 'I'll have to marry you.'

As soon as the lawyer had said the words Atticus had known there was no other option. Even through the shock, and he *had* been shocked—he'd been sure his father would have cut him out of his will the way he'd promised after Dorian had died. Yet apparently not.

Apparently his father had decided to make life even more difficult for both him and Elena. The old man could have just left everything to her and it would have been fine. Atticus wouldn't have cared. He had all the money he'd ever need and Eleos to concern himself with. He didn't need the family shipping company on top of all of that.

But no, Aristeidis had wanted Elena to have a family and expected his son to provide her with one.

Fury at his father had grabbed Atticus by the throat, and his first, reflexive thought had been to refuse. He'd never wanted a wife and he'd never wanted a family. The island and everything on it would be sold, as would the company, and he'd donate the proceeds to charity as they should, his father be damned.

Yet even as the thought had occurred to him, he knew he couldn't refuse. Elena had spent the past sixteen years here, this was *her* house more than it had ever been his, and she'd already lost her home once. She'd already lost her family, too, and besides, the day he'd rescued her, he'd promised her that he'd look after her.

So while this was a responsibility he hadn't asked for and he was furious about it, he had to accept it. She was his responsibility. She'd always been his responsibility.

He looked down at Elena now, sitting on the couch. She wore full mourning, a black dress with a black veil covering her rich blonde hair. Her attention was on her hands clasped in her lap, her face pale, shadows under her eyes. She looked so small sitting there. Fragile.

This whole week since they'd been back in Greece, she'd been outwardly calm, giving no sign of the grief he'd seen back in his house in Jamaica, where she'd wept on his couch, the glass of brandy he'd given her clutched in her hand. She hadn't been calm then, or the stubborn, challenging, passionate woman he'd taken on that same couch, but a woman fractured by grief.

Something tight had shifted in his chest then, like boulders shifting after a landslide, his own grief stirring. Yet he'd ignored it. He wouldn't cry for his father. He wouldn't grieve. For years he'd tried to reach the old man after Dorian had died, needing his comfort and his reassurance, and he hadn't got it. No, instead all he'd had from Aristeidis was blame.

'You should have died,' Aristeidis had flung at him in those first, terrible days afterwards. *'It should have been you, not him. You.'*

The worst part had been that Atticus had agreed. Yes, it should have been him. But it hadn't. Dorian had been three years older than him. Dorian had known his way around a gun. Dorian had told him all about safety when hunting and to be careful and yet…

All of that had meant nothing, because Atticus had let the excitement of a hunting trip in the countryside with his adored older brother overwhelm him. He'd seen a movement in the trees and he'd pulled the trigger without thinking. But it hadn't been a deer. It had been Dorian.

He shouldn't hold his father responsible for all the years of blame, for all the years of distance, yet he did. He'd been sixteen when Dorian had died and ill equipped to deal with loss of any kind, let alone to bear the responsibility of killing his own brother. He should have been helped, not accused. Yet his father, still grieving the wife he'd lost nearly fifteen years earlier, hadn't been able to get past it, and he hadn't allowed Atticus to get past it either.

So no, the old man was dead and all he felt was fury. But as he looked at Elena sitting on the couch a ghost of the same protectiveness that had gripped him when he'd first spotted her in the rubble all those years ago gripped him again. Back then she had had a knife in her hand and blood on her face, determined and brave in the face of the threats around her.

She should look like that, not defeated and…broken.

He'd rescued her once and given her a home and a family, and it wouldn't cost him anything to give her another one.

Are you sure about this? Marriage and *fatherhood?*

The thought of fatherhood particularly had unsettled him, which hadn't done his temper any good. Then again, children were part of the stipulation and so why not? He didn't have to be involved in their lives. In fact, it was probably best for all concerned if he wasn't. And as for the getting of said children… Well, he knew that wouldn't be an issue, not with their chemistry.

'You can't be serious,' Elena said, her deep brown eyes still full of shock. 'You can't actually marry me.'

There were definite shadows under her eyes and he could see pain and grief in the tight lines around her lush mouth. She was very pale, the black making her seem even paler, and yet…

Still so beautiful.

'I can,' he said, ignoring the kick of desire inside him that wouldn't seem to leave him alone. There was a reason he'd avoided her since coming back to this place and all the memories associated with it, and, while he had himself under tight control, there wasn't any need to make things any more difficult than they already were. 'And to be clear, it's not the inheritance I want. In fact, once you're my wife, I'll sign ownership of this island and Kalathes Shipping over to you. I have Eleos and don't need anything else filling up my already limited time.'

Those feathery golden lashes fluttered as she blinked yet again. 'So, what? You'll just marry me and give me children and I'll get to stay on Kalifos?'

'Why not? You can manage the company if you so choose, or sell it. I don't care what you do with it. And you'll have the family you always wanted.'

'But…it's marriage, Atticus. We have to stay married for five years. And do you really want children?'

He wasn't sure why she was arguing with him, a bad idea with this knot of temper still sitting in his gut. 'I don't, no. But you want them, I'm assuming?'

'Yes, but—'

'Then what's the problem? I can give you children and you can bring them up on Kalifos. You'll have a family of your own.'

She took a little breath. In her hands was a damp tissue that she'd wadded up and was in the process of tearing apart. 'A family that won't include you.'

'No,' he agreed. 'But I'm not the one who wants a family.'

'And my idea of a family includes the father of my children.'

He lifted a shoulder. 'We can compromise on a few things.'

'You can't *want* to marry me,' she insisted.

'I don't want to marry anyone.' He paused. 'But you should be provided for.'

She glanced away, giving a strange, bitter-sounding laugh. 'So, what? You care about me all of a sudden? After sixteen years? The sex must have been really good.'

Another sharp pulse of anger went through him, though since he'd spent the whole week gripping his emotions by the throat, he certainly wasn't going to release it now.

There was no point giving in to his fury at his father, or at himself for those sixteen years of no contact with her, not even once. He'd thought she would have forgotten about him, but it was clear she hadn't.

And then you had sex with her, before telling her it was a mistake. She was a virgin, you heard her lie about that, and you let that go, treating her like you'd treat any other of your lovers. She deserved more from you.

He didn't like the feeling that sat inside him, the defensiveness and beneath it the shame. Firstly that he hadn't contacted her while she was growing up and then that he'd let her lie. That he'd taken her on the couch and even now couldn't get the memory of the feel of her skin and the taste of her body out of his head. Her passionate kisses and the way she'd called his name.

You'd like her to be your wife. You'd like to give her children.

He ignored the voice in his head, ignored the desire that still gripped him and the anger that lay burning in his gut. Ignored the way his attention kept focusing on the beat of her pulse in the hollow of her throat and the way the deep V neck of her black dress revealed the soft shadows between her breasts.

'The sex was good,' he said, because she deserved that truth from him at least. 'In fact, the sex was phenomenal. And you're wrong to think I didn't care. I kept tabs on you while you were growing up. I wanted to make sure Aristeidis was looking after you properly.'

She gave him a sudden, piercing look. 'But you never contacted me, not once.'

'No. I…thought it would be better if I didn't.' It was the truth. He had thought that. He'd wanted her to forget him, to forge a relationship with his father instead. 'And I expected you to forget me.'

Emotions flickered over her face, gone so fast he couldn't read them all. But he thought he saw pain and grief and the sparks of something hotter, probably anger. 'Yes, well,' she murmured. 'I didn't forget.' She was still tearing up the tissue in her hands and his gaze kept getting drawn to the neckline of her dress, and he could smell her scent, the tart sweetness of apples. It made him want to take a bite right out of her…

He gritted his teeth. 'Regardless of the past, we need to sort this out now. My offer stands. I rescued you all those years ago, Elena. I wanted to give you a family and a home, and it's not your fault that you've now lost that family and home. You deserve to have another chance at one.'

'So, it's your guilty conscience talking, then.'

Another flicker of anger caught at him, loosening the stranglehold he had on his detachment. 'Does it matter?' He didn't bother hiding the impatience in his voice. 'You need to stay here, where you grew up, and if that means marrying me then I don't see the issue. I can give you everything you ever wanted, Elena. It's only a couple of signatures on a piece of paper. It's no big deal.' He hadn't consciously imitated her saying sex was no big deal, but he heard the echoes of it all the same.

It didn't matter, though. And it *wasn't* a big deal. His focus would always be Eleos, and marriage wasn't going to change that. He wouldn't live here, not in this house full of memories. Memories of the big brother he'd lost and the father who'd turned his back on him. A father who was now gone and good riddance to him.

Don't you regret, even for a moment, not having the chance to speak with Aristeidis before he died?

Something tugged at Atticus, but he ignored it. No, he didn't regret it. Not at all. He'd leave here and go back to Jamaica and his island once he'd married her, and all this was cleared up.

His parents' own marriage had been a loving one, though his mother had died when he was small and he didn't remember her. Sometimes he'd wondered, after Dorian had died, what would have happened if she'd still been alive. Whether his father would have been quite so grief-stricken and determined to take it out on him. Whether he might have had one person who wouldn't have blamed him so completely. But those thoughts weren't productive, since the past was the past and you couldn't change it.

Dorian remembered her though.

Ah, yes. Yet another thing to lay at his door. Dorian's memories of their mother that he had destroyed when he'd mistakenly pulled that trigger. His father had never ceased reminding him about that, either.

Elena was silent. Then, abruptly, she pushed herself up from the couch and moved restlessly over to the windows, looking out over the sea for a moment. Then she turned back to him, her eyes very dark. 'And love? What about that?'

The question caught him off guard. What did love have to do with any of this?

'I don't believe my father mentioned love,' he said coolly. 'He only mentioned marriage. Love has nothing to do with this.' Not that love mattered to him anyway. He'd got rid of that and all the rest of his agonising, useless emotions when he'd turned his back on Kalifos and his father and joined the army.

Love was something that turned on you when you least expected it. Love was unforgiving. Love was vengeful and full of retribution and he wanted nothing whatsoever to do with it.

Elena glanced back out of the window. 'In that case, if it's all the same to you, I'd rather not marry you.'

For a second, all Atticus could do was stare at her. He'd not expected her to refuse him. 'What do you mean you'd rather not marry me?'

'I think it's obvious what I meant. I know your father wanted to provide for me, but I don't want to marry someone who's been forced into it. And I certainly don't want to have a child by that someone.'

His anger pulled against his grip on it. She was *his* responsibility. She had nothing and no one, and he knew what that was like. To have no family at all. But he could provide her with one and he would.

She's right; it is your guilty conscience talking.

Maybe it was, but did that matter? He wasn't going to change his mind. The past week he'd found out from various Kalathes staff members that Elena had taken over managing various aspects of Kalathes Shipping as his father's health had declined. It had been with his blessing and she'd been an astute and capable manager. Whether she enjoyed the work, he wasn't sure, but, regardless, all the more reason it should be in her name.

'It was not a request,' he said. 'If you want Kalifos, if you want the company, there's only one way for that to happen and that's by marrying me.'

'You're assuming I want those things.'

Atticus opened his mouth to send back a sharp reply, but then bit down on it. Her temper sparked too easily off his and he was allowing it. He liked arguing with her, but that wasn't helping.

Anger isn't the only thing you spark, remember?

A thick, hot feeling shifted inside him. That was true. Perhaps there was…another way to get her agreement. A way that would end up being far more pleasurable for both of them than bickering.

'I know what you want, Elenitsa,' he murmured, letting his voice drop.

She gave him a glance. 'Oh, yes? What?'

He held her melted-chocolate gaze with his. 'Me.'

CHAPTER SIX

THE WORD SPOKEN in his deep, dark voice sent a lightning strike of heat straight down Elena's spine. His gaze was electric, full of sparks and black flames, as if he'd suddenly thrown open a door and all the light and heat inside were spilling out.

There had been nothing but that tight band of grief locked around her chest and yet, looking at him now, she forgot all about it.

He dominated the room, filled it with the intense, primal energy she'd felt back on his island. The black suit he wore fitted him so perfectly, yet he might as well have been naked. It couldn't contain him or his presence.

He's right. You do want him.

She swallowed, her mouth gone dry. 'No,' she said, lying through her teeth. 'No, I don't.'

He raised one dark brow. 'I see. So you don't want me just like you weren't a virgin?'

Did you really think he wouldn't know what a liar you are?

She could feel the flush creep up her neck and into her cheeks. She'd suspected he knew that she'd lied to him about her virginity, but since he hadn't called her on it, she'd told herself that maybe her suspicions were wrong.

Sadly they were not wrong.

She wanted to deny it, tell him she wasn't lying, but, with that black gaze holding hers, she knew that would only be making the hole she was digging for herself even deeper.

'Fine,' she snapped. 'I was a virgin. But I'm not lying about wanting you. We had sex and it was great, but I don't necessarily need to revisit it.'

He said nothing for a long moment, still studying her. Then he took a few casual steps in her direction and every muscle in her body tightened in response, her heartbeat thumping hard in her head.

'Don't you?' His voice was just as casual as the slow way he approached her. 'Are you sure you couldn't be tempted to revisit it?'

He wasn't being threatening. His hands were in the pockets of his trousers, his posture relaxed, and yet… She could feel the intense sexual energy he was radiating and it made her go hot with reaction. There was a pulse of heat between her thighs, a dragging ache. She couldn't seem to get a breath.

'N-no,' she said, hating the way she stuttered and how breathy her voice sounded. 'I mean… I'm… I'm sure.'

His black gaze settled on hers, full of intent and a dark hunger that she knew he was letting her see on purpose. It made the ache inside her get worse. 'There's no purpose in lying, Elena,' he murmured. 'Because I can see what I do to you. I *know* what I do to you. I was there, remember? I heard the way you called my name as you climaxed. Twice, wasn't it?'

She knew she should look away, turn and walk from the room, get out of his vicinity somehow, but she couldn't seem to move. She was caught in his gaze like a deer in the headlights of a car, utterly frozen. And not just caught by her own need, but by the need she saw in his face too. Need for her.

'I'm not the only one,' she said huskily. 'I do the same to you.'

'That's true.' He moved again, coming even closer, until he was mere inches away. And she could smell him once again, salt and sun and masculine spice, so delicious. He wore a deep blue silk tie with his black shirt, the colour highlighting the tanned olive skin of his strong neck, and suddenly all she could think about was undoing that tie and taking it off, pulling at the top buttons of his shirt and uncovering his skin. Tasting the hollow of his throat the way he'd tasted hers.

'In which case…' He reached out, putting one long finger beneath her chin, tipping her head back, and she didn't pull away, trapped by the force of her hunger and by the sheer charisma of his presence. 'Why not give us what we both want? Marrying me wouldn't be all bad, Elenitsa. You'd get the island, the company, and, while I have no plans to live here, I could certainly spend some time consummating our marriage.'

Her heartbeat got louder and louder. She couldn't

tear her gaze from his. The heat from his finger beneath her chin felt as if it were burning into her, the warmth of his body and the scent of him making every part of her go weak with hunger.

Would it really be so bad? No, it's not love, but then you don't love him. You don't need him to stay here on Kalifos, either. And you'd be fulfilling Aristeidis's last wish, which is to make sure you're provided for.

It was true, she would. Aristeidis had wanted to give her a family and it seemed petty of her to deny him that just because Atticus unsettled her and because she was holding out for love. Especially after Aristeidis been denied a reconciliation with his son. Also, she hadn't been there when he'd died; she hadn't even been able to say goodbye. Surely she couldn't refuse to fulfil at least *one* of his dying wishes. Besides, they didn't even need to be together for ever, since the will stipulated they had to stay married for only five years. She could find the love she wanted with someone else after that.

'I… I don't know.' Her voice had become so husky, giving her away. 'Do you even want to consummate our marriage?'

His hard mouth curved and abruptly she could see the desire that burned hot and strong in his gaze. 'I wouldn't have offered if I didn't want to. For the record, there isn't one person on this planet who can force me into doing what I don't want to do.'

Something about that half-smile made her breath catch. He'd been nothing but focused and very intense since the day she'd met him, and she wouldn't have thought he'd even known what a smile was, but it seemed that he did. And it was mesmerising. She couldn't stop looking at it.

'Yes,' she heard herself say. 'I think I already know that about you.'

His thumb moved, tracing her bottom lip, pushing gently against the softness, making her heart beat even faster. 'Good. Then you'll know that there isn't anything I'd like better than to give you a suitable wedding night.'

She swallowed, her bottom lip feeling acutely sensitised. 'Atticus…'

He gripped her chin and bent his head, his mouth brushing over hers, and her brain blanked, the electricity of the kiss making even the air around her crackle and spark.

His fingers tightened and he kissed her again, as if he couldn't help himself, his mouth lingering, coaxing her to open. And she did, unable to stop herself, letting him deepen the kiss.

He tasted so good and she was tired of grief, tired of looking into the future and seeing nothing but loneliness, nothing but having no one and nowhere to call home, no connections with anyone or anything. She wanted this, the heat of his mouth and the glory of his touch. The need she saw in his eyes. And she could stay on Kalifos, which was home to her, and where she had a purpose.

So why not marry him? Why not have this? She could have him. He would be her husband for a few years and he'd give her children. She'd have a family in the end. It was what she'd always wanted and what Aristeidis had wanted for her too, so why not?

Elena opened her mouth, let the kiss get hotter. Let him tip her head back further, explore her deeper. She kissed him back, the rich taste of him filling her head, dark chocolate and mint. It felt like balm to her wounded soul, and she found her hands lifting, reaching for him.

Abruptly, though, he released her, lifting his head and looking down into her eyes. 'Is that a yes?' His voice was rough, and she could hear the edge of demand in it.

She swallowed, her fingers itching to touch him, her whole body aching with desire. Part of her didn't want to give in so easily, though, still half angry with him over so many years of silence, a silence that she hadn't thought she'd care about and yet apparently still did. Angry, too, that he had the power to unsettle her, to make her feel vulnerable when she didn't want to be.

'I don't know,' she said huskily. 'Is that a proposal?'

His black eyes glittered and suddenly his hands dropped to her hips and she was being pushed firmly but gently up against the wall. The breath went out of her as he looked down into her eyes. 'If it's a proposal you want, then here it is. Marry me, Elenitsa.'

It wasn't a request, it was an order; she could hear the edge of command in his voice. The stubborn part of her wanted to refuse, the lost girl who'd been abandoned by him and still felt that abandonment even years later. But she wasn't that girl any more. She wasn't a child. Marrying him wouldn't mean anything, not if she didn't want it to, and if it would get her what she wanted then why not?

He'd been the soldier who saved her, the prince, a fairy tale, a cipher. He'd never been a person to her, only a stranger. She didn't know him now either, and so why she was letting him get to her so intensely, she had no idea.

Still, she didn't see why all the power should be with him. She liked pushing him, liked testing herself against him. Found the sensual threat he presented and the sparks they created between them intensely exciting.

He unsettled her and she didn't see why she shouldn't return the favour. If she could…

She looked up at him from beneath her lashes, wanting him to know that he wasn't going to get it all his own way. 'Convince me,' she said, then reached up and began to undo his tie.

Atticus stared down into Elena's darkening brown eyes. They were liquid with desire and her cheeks were flushed. The pulse at the base of her throat was fast and getting faster, and the heat of her body against his was rapidly making it impossible to think.

He wasn't sure why she was so determinedly holding out against him, because he knew she wanted him and badly. He hadn't been wrong about that. So was it only because she liked arguing with him, or was it really about the past still? Or was there more going on here than he thought, something else?

Her fingers tugged at his tie, pulling the silk out of its knot, and he let her. He was still in command of himself and he'd stay in command, no matter how hot her mouth tasted or how soft her body felt.

She dropped the tie onto the floor then began undoing the top buttons of his shirt, pulling open the cotton and baring his throat.

'Seems like you're already convinced,' he murmured.

'But I haven't said yes yet.' She put her hands on his chest and rose up onto her toes, putting her mouth at the base of his throat.

All his muscles tightened, desire pulsing like a giant heartbeat inside him. Her little tongue touched his skin, tasting him, and her lips were so soft. The pressure of her hands on his chest felt maddening. He wanted to feel her bare skin on his, because he could still remember how silky it had been and how hot. How sweet it had tasted, too.

And why not? If she was going to be his wife, there wasn't any reason why they couldn't fully indulge in the sexual attraction that burned between them. If they had to stay married for five years and there was a stipulation for children, then they were even obligated to indulge themselves. He certainly wasn't going to remain celibate all that time, not when he very much wanted her.

She's already made you lose control once. She'll do it again if you're not careful.

No, she wouldn't. True, he'd been taken off guard a week ago when she'd first turned up and he hadn't managed himself well. But he was prepared for his attraction to her now, he could control it. In fact, it would be easy. No doubt after five years it would burn itself out. In fact, he'd be surprised if it lasted beyond a year. Sexual infatuations always did, not that he'd ever been sexually infatuated with anyone.

Still, maybe this would be a good test for himself, and he did like testing himself. He did it constantly on the island, testing himself physically against the elements. He'd done so in the army too, after Dorian had died, applying to join the elite sniper unit. Handling a gun again had filled him with dread and yet he'd forced himself to become comfortable with it. He'd wanted to master his fear, wanted to master himself, so he'd never again be in a situation where he wasn't in control. Where he wasn't in complete command of the situation and of himself.

Becoming a sniper had been hard, both physically and emotionally, but he'd pushed himself to become the best they'd had. The coldest, the deadliest. No life was taken except when he willed it and he made no mistakes. Mistakes were unforgivable.

He'd made a mistake back in Jamaica in allowing his physical hunger to overcome him, but he wouldn't make the same mistake now. She could do whatever she wanted to him. He wouldn't break.

If he could pick up a gun again after Dorian had died, he could do anything at all.

She undid another button and then another, baring his skin to her kisses. He could hear her breathing getting faster and faster, could feel his own hunger tightening. He was getting hard, the beast in him urging him to push her against the wall, haul her dress up and get inside her as quickly as he could.

He ignored the feeling, putting his hands to the wall on either side of her head and pressing against it.

She pulled open the buttons of his shirt completely, baring his chest, her hands stroking him, following the lines of his pecs and down to his abs, caressing him as if he were a work of art and she were breathless before him.

Her fingertips were cool and he could smell her scent, sweet musk and apples, and a possessive growl formed in his throat. Then her fingers stroked lower, to the button of his trousers, and the growl rumbled in his chest, a low, rough sound.

It was getting harder not to touch her, not to rip away her veil and loose her hair. Not to force her head back and kiss her, taste her sweetness and heat. But no, he could bear this. There was no rush. He wasn't going to take her like an animal the way he had last time. In fact, he might not take her at all. He wanted to, badly, but his body didn't get to decide his actions. Only his mind did.

Her fingers were undoing his trousers now, finding the tab of his zip and taking hold of it.

'What are you doing, Elenitsa?' he asked in a voice that was much rougher than it should have been. 'I thought I was supposed to be the one convincing you?'

'I changed my mind.' Slowly she drew down his zip, glancing up at him from beneath her thick golden lashes. 'I think I need to convince myself.'

He gritted his teeth against the sudden rush of hunger. 'Convince yourself of what? If it's that I'll give you pleasure, then you found that out pretty thoroughly last week.'

She held his gaze as she slid her hand into his trousers, caressing the hard length of him through the cotton of his underwear. Electricity crackled through him at her light touch, making his breath catch. It was maddening.

He had his hand over hers, pressing her palm harder against him before he'd even thought straight, and when he saw an answering flare of heat in her eyes, he suddenly realised exactly what she was doing.

'What do you want?' he demanded roughly. 'To push me? Is that what you're doing?'

'No.' She didn't pull her hand away. Instead she squeezed him gently, making him give another helpless growl, her dark eyes full of determination and heat. 'I only wanted to give you a taste of your own medicine.'

Ah, so that was it. She didn't like how hungry she was for him and so was hoping to return the favour. Little witch.

It's working.

Well, he was hungry for her, yes, but not beyond all

sense. He was in control of this and his own body. He wasn't going to lose it. He could pull away from her whenever he wanted, and, in fact, maybe he should do it now. Just to prove his point.

Except he didn't.

'If you really want to give me a taste of my own medicine,' he heard himself say, 'then perhaps get down on your knees.'

It was a challenge, he couldn't say it wasn't. Since she was challenging him with her maddening touch and her soft mouth, then he would do the same to her. He told himself that she wouldn't do it, that she'd baulk. She was inexperienced, after all, and perhaps this would be a step too far for her.

But deep down, he knew she wouldn't baulk. Not Elena. Elena, who'd held five men at bay with a knife, at eight years old. Who'd survived on her own in the ruins of her village for a week before he'd found her, somehow finding food and water, and managing to avoid looters and all kinds of other people who'd do her harm.

Something hot lit in her gaze and slowly she obeyed, going down onto her knees in front of him.

He couldn't take his eyes off her as electricity crackled through him, desire tightening its grip. She looked perfect kneeling on the floor, gazing up at him, her eyes dark, her mouth full and lush and red. Her hands went to his underwear, pulling it down and taking him out without hesitation. Then her cool fingers were on him, stroking him.

Atticus reached for her veil without thinking, pulling it off so he could push his fingers into the silky wealth of her hair. She shuddered as he did so, but didn't hesitate as she leaned forward to take him in her mouth.

He couldn't stop the groan that escaped, or the fierce rush of pleasure that flooded through him as the heat of her mouth enveloped him.

She will *make you lose control. You can't stop her.*

No, it was worse than that. He didn't want to stop her. He wanted her to keep going. He wanted the heat of her mouth and the pressure, the feel of her teeth against his aching shaft and the exploration of her tongue.

'Elena,' he growled as she began to explore, licking him, teasing him.

She only looked up, her eyes dark, the flush in her cheeks creeping down her neck and down beneath the neckline of her dress. It was the most erotic sight, watching her swallow him as she knelt in front of him, her own hunger for him blazing in her eyes.

He gripped her hair tighter, murmuring to her, and she set up a rhythm in response with a confidence that left him breathless as the pleasure began to tighten inside him.

Her mouth was hot and felt so good, and he couldn't think why he'd wanted to hold out against her. He couldn't seem to think at all. Nothing was working right, only the heat of her mouth and the pleasure she was giving him mattered. Only the silky feel of her hair between his fingers and the thrust of his hips.

She made a soft throaty sound, as if she was enjoying this as much as he was, and then the pressure increased as she took him deeper. Then he was thinking about nothing but the ecstasy she was giving him, indescribable, unstoppable, and dimly he was aware that somehow, at some point, the control he was so proud of had escaped his grip. But by then he didn't care.

He roared her name as abruptly the pleasure contracted like a fist around him and crushed him into dust.

CHAPTER SEVEN

ELENA ADJUSTED THE drape of the wedding gown and stared at herself in the bedroom's full-length mirror. She couldn't speak, a complicated knot of emotion sitting heavy in her chest and closing around her throat.

She would be marrying Atticus tomorrow, a week to the day since she'd knelt for him in the salon and taken him in her mouth. A week since she'd made him lose control. And a week since he'd hauled her to her feet, pushed her up against the wall, pulled her dress up and had taken her again within minutes.

They hadn't spoken afterwards yet that night there had come a knock on her door, and when she'd opened it, she'd found him standing on the other side. He hadn't said a word, but his gaze had been fierce and hot, making it obvious what he'd wanted.

She'd had a half-second where she'd considered refusing him and then that half-second had passed and she'd thrown the door open, stepping aside to let him enter. Because she'd wanted what he'd wanted and every bit as badly.

He'd come to her door every night since and every night she hadn't refused him. They didn't talk. There wasn't any need to. The only language they needed was that of passion and pleasure, hunger and desire.

During the day, they barely saw each other. He was busy dealing with Eleos, so she took over handling the intricacies of Kalathes Shipping, as well as planning the wedding, which they both wanted to occur as quickly as possible.

She'd asked him if he had any preferences on the type of wedding he wanted and he'd told her that he didn't care as he had no one he wanted to invite, though he did insist on no media coverage.

She was fine with that. She had no one to invite either, though she'd decided she wanted more than the register office wedding that Atticus had suggested. She'd lost many important things in her life, but a lovely wedding gown, a beautiful church, wedding rings and a ceremony weren't going to number among those things. They weren't marrying for love, but for a will, it was true, but she wanted the trappings of a true wedding all the same. She'd even insisted on a honeymoon.

Atticus hadn't argued. The only thing he seemed to want was her, at least physically. He'd been insatiable, glutting himself every night on her, keeping her up until the small hours of the morning. She hadn't minded, not when she'd been just as obsessed as he was. The things he'd taught her, the things they did together...

They made her feel hot to think about, they made her feel hungry. *He* made her feel hungry. As if the more she had of him, the more she wanted. She hadn't realised sex could be like that, and she wasn't sure she liked it. It made her feel vulnerable, as if she needed him, and she didn't like the idea of needing him. Then again, she didn't want to stop and there was no reason to anyway. He was going to be her husband and since children had been part of Aristeidis's will, they had to be conceived somehow.

The emotion that constricted her throat tightened further as she looked in the mirror. She couldn't tell if what she felt was grief, regret, happiness or anger. Maybe it was a combination of all of them. Grief that her long-ago family weren't around to see her get married. That her father wouldn't be able to give her away, neither would Aristeidis. Regret that Aristeidis was gone, that he wouldn't see her marry his son.

Happiness that here she was in the most beautiful wedding gown she'd ever seen, and she felt good in it, and she would have a veil and flowers, and it would be the wedding she'd always dreamed of.

Anger that she was wasting all of this on a man she didn't love and who didn't love her.

Then again, without that man, she wouldn't even be having a wedding, let alone a wedding dress like this, with acres of white silk and frothy tulle, rising up into a strapless bodice with a deep V neckline that showcased her pale shoulders and breasts. There were tiny crystals embroidered onto the skirts that glittered and sparkled whenever she moved, as if stars had fallen all over her and had become caught in the fabric.

Do you really deserve this? After you let a complete

stranger take you away to a pampered life in Greece, while your family lay dead beneath the rubble?

The old doubts whispered unexpectedly in her head, chilling her, but she forced them aside. What was she supposed to have done? She'd been eight and all alone. She'd had to leave them behind; she'd had to.

Anyway, what was done was done, and she couldn't think about it now.

Elena stared at her figure in the mirror, blinking fiercely against the prickle of silly emotional tears.

Atticus would like it, she was sure, but there wouldn't be any other, deeper emotion attached to it for him. He wasn't marrying her because he loved her and wanted her to be his wife. He was marrying her to provide for her, because he felt obligated towards her due to his father's will, and that wasn't the same.

You weren't supposed to care whether he loved you or not.

And she didn't. Not at all. It was only that a wedding was supposed to be a celebration of love and theirs wouldn't be a celebration of anything.

So what's the point of all this? The dress and the church? The rings and flowers? You might just as well have got married in a register office.

Elena tore her gaze from the mirror and adjusted the bodice needlessly. There *was* a point to this. The gown and the little church on Kalifos where they were going to be married, the rings…all of those things were for her, because she wanted them. She'd lost everything that mattered to her once and then she'd lost it again after Aristeidis had died. She wasn't going to let it happen again. She wanted a home and a family and everything that went with it, and that included a proper wedding. That mattered to her.

You won't have a proper husband though.

Elena forced the thought away as a knock sounded on the bedroom door.

Gathering her skirts, she went over to it, opening it a crack, not wanting anyone to get a glimpse of her gown.

It was Atticus.

The sight of him sent first a shock, then a shiver of pure heat straight through her. She wasn't expecting him, not now, not so early in the evening. He wasn't supposed to come until well after dinner had been finished and the sky was dark.

Yet here he was and her pulse was already beginning to pick up, her mouth getting dry. He wore one of the handmade suits that looked so stunning on him, this one in a deep, dark blue wool, bordering on black. The colour was fantastic against his tanned skin, as was the white of his shirt. He wasn't wearing a tie and the top buttons of his shirt were undone and immediately all she wanted was to press her mouth to his throat.

His eyes glittered—clearly he knew exactly what she was thinking.

'You're early,' she said, feeling herself blush, which was ridiculous considering all the things they'd done together over the past week.

'I need to talk to you.' His gaze dropped to her bare

shoulders. 'Though, if you're naked, I can think of something else I'd much rather do first.'

Much to her annoyance, she could feel her blush deepen. 'I'm not naked, but I need a minute to change.'

'I can help with that.'

A strangely vulnerable feeling stole through her. She didn't want him to see her in her gown, not yet, which was silly considering he wouldn't care. But still, she'd wanted a proper wedding and the groom not seeing the bride in her gown before the wedding was a tradition.

'No,' she said, not wanting to explain it to him. Her emotions and reasons were too complicated and she didn't want to go into it.

He frowned. 'Why not?'

'Because you'll only...distract me. Give me five minutes.' And she closed the door in his face before he could get another word in.

She managed to get the zip down and then carefully stepped out of the gown, making sure to put it back in its protective garment bag and hang it back in her wardrobe. She half expected Atticus to ignore her and come in anyway, but he didn't.

Finally, pulling on some soft yoga pants and a white cotton T-shirt, she went back over to the door and opened it wide, standing aside to let him enter. '*Now* you can come in.'

He went past her into the room, his gaze narrowing as he looked around, as if she'd been hiding something from him and he wanted to know what it was.

'I don't have a lover stashed under the bed or in the

wardrobe,' she said tartly, still feeling vulnerable and not liking it one bit. 'If that's what you're worried about.'

His black gaze settled on her and once again she felt the build-up of electricity, the intense static charge of their attraction in the air around them. Surely it shouldn't still be so intense by now? They'd slept together every night for the past week; she couldn't still be so hungry for him, could she?

'No.' His voice had deepened with a very male kind of satisfaction. 'That's the very last thing I'd be worrying about.'

Excitement and annoyance knotted inside her. Excitement at his presence and annoyance at his arrogance, as if he was completely and utterly confident that the last thing she'd have was another lover somewhere.

He was right, though, she didn't. In fact even the thought of being with another man left her cold, which he didn't need to know since he was already arrogant enough as it was.

'I might have another lover,' she said, unable to help herself. 'You don't know.'

'I do know and if you want me to prove it, I'd be happy to.' He was already taking a step towards her, flames in his eyes, but she held up her hand, discomfited by the sudden burst of desire she felt.

She had to give him some boundaries somewhere, otherwise she'd let him have everything he wanted, and she wasn't starting off their marriage like that. In fact, come to think of it, she really should talk to him at some point about what their marriage *would* look like, especially since they were supposed to stay married for five years.

She didn't want him thinking she'd give in every time he wanted her. She wasn't *that* available.

Elena was just about to open her mouth to tell him not now, when he stopped his advance towards her. 'As much as I'd like to put your bed to good use, that can wait. I have something to give you.' He put his hand into the pocket of his trousers and brought something out of it. A small black velvet box.

She stared, the thick weight of emotion in her chest getting even thicker, even heavier, because that was a ring box. Why would he be giving her a ring box? She'd got one of the best ring designers she could find to design their wedding rings and he knew that. So this couldn't be a wedding ring.

'What is it?' she asked after a couple of moments.

Atticus merely continued to hold it out to her. 'Open it.'

Slowly, she took the box from his hand and lifted the lid. A man's heavy golden signet ring gleamed against the black velvet.

Aristeidis's ring.

Elena lost her voice completely, staring at the ring then meeting his gaze.

The expression in his dark eyes was very direct. 'Aristeidis wanted you to marry me so that you could be taken care of, and it seemed appropriate, since he isn't here, that you have his ring as an engagement ring. Unless you'd prefer something more feminine?'

Another rush of emotion took her, so intense she couldn't have spoken even if she'd wanted to. Helpless, pathetic tears filled her eyes, her vision swimming, and she had to blink them back fiercely, because she didn't want to cry in front of him, not again.

'I'll have something else made if you don't like it,' Atticus went on, frowning as if he'd spotted her tears. 'You shouldn't have to buy your own engagement ring at least.'

It was clear he thought she didn't like it, when in fact the opposite was true. It was Aristeidis's ring, the one she'd hoped to have passed on to her when his will had been read, but she'd thought Atticus might want it. It was a man's ring after all.

'How did you know?' Her voice was way too hoarse and the question revealed more than she wanted it to, but she couldn't help it. 'How did you know I wanted this?'

Atticus's dark gaze flickered, the frown disappearing. He studied her for a long moment. 'He meant a lot to you, I know that. He brought you up, he was a father to you. And you meant a lot to him. I think he would have wanted you to have his ring and I can't think of a more appropriate occasion than to have it as an engagement ring.'

She was shocked that Atticus had thought about it. That he'd thought of her and Aristeidis, of what he'd meant to her and she to him, and had come up with a gesture so lovely and so meaningful that her heart ached with a bittersweet grief.

'He wanted to give me away at my wedding,' she said huskily, staring at the ring. 'And I wanted him to.'

Atticus was silent a moment, then he came towards her and took the box from her shaking hand, extracting the ring. He put the box back in his pocket and then took her hand.

'It'll be too big,' she said, suddenly feeling horribly fragile. 'It'll be too big and I—'

Without a word, Atticus slid the ring onto her finger. It fitted perfectly.

'I had it resized for you,' he said.

Despite her best efforts, a tear slid slowly down over her cheek as she stared at the ring, but she resisted the urge to brush it away. Perhaps if she ignored it, Atticus wouldn't notice. 'You don't want it for yourself?' she asked, keeping her gaze on the soft glow of gold around her finger.

'No. He was a better father to you than he ever was to me.' After a moment, he went over to her dresser, where there was a tissue box. Taking a couple of tissues out, he came back then took her chin in one hand and tilted her head back so she was looking at up him.

She didn't want him to see her tears, to see her vulnerability, but his hold was gentle and she didn't resist as he began to carefully wipe her tears away.

Elena trembled. She felt raw all of a sudden, yet his touch was very kind, with none of his usual sexual demand in it, and, strangely, she found herself relaxing in his hold. She still couldn't meet his gaze, though. Her instinct was to say something sharp or pull away to protect herself, but part of her liked the gentle way he was touching her far too much.

Aristeidis had cared about her, but he'd never been physically affectionate. He'd never given her hugs. And he'd never known what to do when she cried, so she'd soon learned that if she wanted something from him, it was best not to cry. It was best not to look as if she needed anything at all. It wasn't that he was negligent or cruel. He just wasn't physically affectionate and outward displays of emotion made him uncomfortable.

So Atticus taking care of her like this, giving her a gift that meant something to her and then wiping her tears away… It set up a painful ache deep in her heart, the tug of a need she hadn't realised she still felt, a weakness she couldn't allow herself.

Yet still she stood there, letting him touch her.

'You know that, not only will the island be yours,' he murmured, giving her face a critical examination as he wiped away the last of her tears, 'but everything in it will also be yours, too.'

She swallowed, half sad when he finally released her chin, half relieved. 'There must be something that *you* want here, though,' she said.

He put the tissue in a waste basket near her dresser. 'No. I don't want any of it.'

'Why not?' It wasn't the best thing to be discussing now, but she still felt overly emotional and she didn't want to answer any questions he might ask her. Much better to turn the conversation back on him. 'I would have thought you might—'

'I said no.' The concern he'd shown her just before was gone, only annoyance snapping in his black eyes.

'It's because of Dorian, isn't it?' She wasn't going to regret the loss of that concern. His anger she could deal with far better than his tenderness. 'And because of what happened afterwards?'

Instantly Atticus's expression went hard then it blanked completely. 'I don't want to discuss this now.'

She shouldn't push. It would only ruin the moment and make things difficult between them, which, considering they were getting married in the morning, wasn't a great start. And anyway, she was suddenly tired of arguing with him, tired of things being difficult between them.

'Okay,' she said simply, dropping the subject.

Surprise flickered over his features. Clearly he'd expected an argument, and it gave her a brief thrill of satisfaction that she could upset his expectations and take him off guard in a way that wasn't sexual.

In fact, she wanted to do it again.

'Wait there,' she said, holding up a finger. Then she went over to her dresser and pulled open a drawer. She'd been saving the small wedding gift she'd had made for him until tomorrow, but he'd given her Aristeidis's ring and she wanted to give him something in return now.

Taking out the small box in the drawer, she turned and came over to him. His gaze narrowed as she approached, and a wave of unfamiliar shyness overcame her. What if he didn't like it? Or what if it wasn't meaningful to him? She didn't know him, that was the issue.

Oh, she knew about his boyhood here on Kalifos, because Aristeidis had told her all about it, stories of him and Dorian and the things they used to get up to, the scrapes they got into. Atticus loved the outdoors, and was always the more boisterous of the two, Aristeidis used to say. The naughtiest, the more high-spirited, and the one who took the most risks. A typical youngest child, whom, by his own admission, Aristeidis had been harder on than Dorian.

'I have something for you, too,' she said and held out the box.

He stared at it as if he'd never seen a box before in his entire life. 'Something for me?' The disbelief in his voice was palpable.

She smiled, pleased that she'd managed to shock him, because there was no doubting the shock on his face. 'It's a wedding gift. I was going to give it to you tomorrow, but you may as well have it now.'

'A wedding gift,' he repeated, as if the words were foreign to him. 'But…this isn't a real wedding, you know that, Elena.'

'I know. But that doesn't mean we can't have the trappings of one. And you're still going to be my legal husband, whether it's real or not, and so I wanted to get you a gift.'

He stared at her for a long moment, then reached out and took the box from her hand. Her heartbeat sped up, nervousness kicking in. She hadn't realised how much she wanted him to like this, but she did. His opinion mattered.

Slowly he took the box in his large hands, the scars standing out whitely against his olive skin, and he opened it, staring down at the small item sitting in the black velvet.

It was a pin crafted out of platinum, of a small child with their arms lifting up as if for someone to carry them. The Eleos symbol.

He stared at it, his face utterly unreadable, and nerves crowded in her throat. 'It's just a little thing,' she said quickly, desperate to fill up the silence. 'It's probably silly. You've probably got hundreds of them and you don't—'

'I don't,' he interrupted, still staring down at the pin. 'I don't have a single one.' Then he looked up at her, an emotion she didn't understand burning in his black eyes. 'Where did you get this?'

'I had it made. I wanted to give you a gift that meant something to you, but I don't know you well enough and I…' She trailed off, because he was still staring at her, a fierce storm in his eyes.

'Do you know what this is?' he asked.

Her heart was beating faster and she didn't know what to say, because she wasn't sure whether he liked it or not, or whether she'd somehow offended him. 'Yes, it's the symbol of your charity.'

'It's not just the symbol of my charity.' A bright, intense flame glowed in his eyes. 'It's also you, Elena.'

Perhaps he shouldn't have said it. Perhaps he shouldn't have revealed something so personal. But it was too late now. He'd told her, he hadn't been able to help it. She'd given him this pin, a symbol of his charity, a symbol of hope. Because she'd been his hope.

That night in the rubble of that town, surrounded by death and hopelessness, he'd wondered what the point of it all was. He'd been involved in the business of violence for years and he was starting to lose himself. He was starting to think that maybe there was no difference between himself and those he was protecting people from. After all, he was a killer just as they were. What made him different? What made him a good person? He'd killed his brother, been repudiated by his father… Was there anything good in him at all?

A black despair had been creeping up on him, and that was when he'd seen her, a small figure fighting back against impossible odds. Indomitable. Unbroken. Her braids had been lit by the setting sun, gleaming gold, and the blood on her face had made her look fierce. She'd been so small and yet there she was, fighting back against the dark.

He'd felt something leap inside him in that moment and he'd known immediately that he had to save her and that if he had to die to do so, then die he would. He'd lifted his weapon and fired the warning shots and her attackers had scattered, and he'd been expecting her to run from him too.

Yet she hadn't. She'd lifted her arms to him as if she'd been waiting for him, as if she wasn't afraid of him. As if she knew completely that he would pick her up and take care of her.

As if she could see that there was some part of him that was still good.

She'd had no idea what she'd meant to him that evening. No idea how she'd turned his life around. After he'd taken her back to Kalifos and to his father, he'd turned his private army into Eleos. Mercy. Dedicated to saving people throughout the world, no matter what they needed. All because a little girl had given him hope and he'd wanted to pass that hope on to others.

Now that same little girl was giving him a pin crafted in her likeness. Giving him the gift of hope once again.

He'd never been one for signs or portents, and he'd never believed in fate. He'd never believed in anything much at all, but this gift of hers…it meant something. Hope for the future maybe, or perhaps something else, but it was something.

She stared at him now and he could see anxiety in her eyes, as if she was she worried he wouldn't like it. 'What do you mean, it's me?' she asked.

He ignored her for the moment, holding out the box in her direction. 'Come here. Pin it on for me.' It came out sounding more like an order than anything else, but she came over to him and took the pin out of the box. Then she came in close and slid her fingers beneath his lapel, lifting it so she could pin the small Eleos symbol to his jacket.

He could smell her luscious scent, apples and musk, that never failed to get him hard, and could see the sparkle of a tear still caught on her golden lashes. His gift had meant something to her, too, something that had affected her every bit as deeply as hers had him.

Aristeidis's ring had seemed like the natural thing to give her since he'd been concerned she hadn't had an engagement ring. Why exactly he'd been concerned, he wasn't sure. He only knew that she'd wanted the trappings of a real wedding and if she wanted to organise them, he wasn't going to get in her way. Except it had bothered him that she hadn't had a ring and he didn't like the thought of her ordering one for herself.

He was the groom; it was his job to find one. So when he'd discovered Aristeidis's ring in amongst his father's belongings, knowing what his father had meant to her, it had seemed like the perfect ring for her. If she wanted something more feminine, he could get her something later.

But as soon as she'd seen it, it was clear to him that he wasn't going to need to get her another one. There had been tears in her eyes when he'd presented it to her, and that had made something shift inside himself too. A deep pleasure that he could do that for her, that he could give her something meaningful.

Perhaps that was why her gift to him had affected him so deeply. He'd already been moved by her reaction to the ring.

None of this should mean anything at all to you.

It was true, it shouldn't. Ever since that day when she'd got on her knees and made him lose control, he'd let her somehow get under his skin in a way he shouldn't have. He'd been thinking that he'd give himself a week, up until their marriage, to indulge himself, and then, after the wedding, he'd take himself back to Jamaica, find his detachment and his focus again. So perhaps it didn't matter if he let this be important to him now.

She finished with the pin, the platinum gleaming against the dark blue wool of his suit. It looked good there, a little reminder of the hope she'd always brought to him.

Her eyes were very dark as they looked up into his and he could see that she was still anxious. She wanted him to like this and it gave him a peculiar thrill to know his opinion mattered to her.

'Do you remember when I first saw you?' he asked. 'You were standing in the rubble and you had a knife in your hand. There were about five men who were going to attack you and you looked as if you could take on each and every one of them.'

A small crease appeared between her brows. 'Yes, I remember.'

'I fired my gun and they scattered. And I thought… I thought you'd run, too. But you didn't. You held your arms up to me instead.'

'I wasn't scared of you,' she said. 'I just…knew you were here to save me.'

Atticus touched the pin. 'This is you, Elena. That night I'd felt I'd come to a dead end. That I was no different from the men I was trying to protect people like you from. Then you appeared, and you seemed to see something in me that I'd thought had died a long time ago. You gave me hope. So when I started Eleos and I wanted a logo, all I could think about was you. You in the rubble, lifting your arms to me.'

Her eyes widened, a flush creeping over her skin. 'I… I had no idea. I didn't even realise you remembered that.'

'Of course, I remembered that.' Perhaps it had been a mistake to tell her what she represented to him, a ceding of power he hadn't been prepared for. Then again, if anyone should know the story behind the Eleos child, it should be her. She had been that child, after all.

Elena glanced at the pin then up at him once more. 'You like it?'

He put his hand over it, feeling the cool metal warm against his palm, and held her gaze, let her see what her gift had meant to him. 'Yes,' he said simply.

She smiled, so warm and sweet it stole his breath, and the glow that suffused her face made something inside him tighten.

You like making her smile.

And he wanted to do it again.

'I'm so glad,' she said, a little shyly. 'I love the ring too. Just before the will was read out I was hoping I'd get a few keepsakes from him. I thought you'd probably want the ring though.'

He hadn't known she'd actively been hoping for the ring. He'd just thought she might appreciate it.

You should tell her why you don't want anything from him. She deserves to know.

A cold thread wound through his pleasure. He'd been harsh when she'd asked him why he hadn't wanted anything of his father's, because harsh was his usual response when anyone asked him about Dorian. Harsh made sure no one ever questioned him again.

But…she knew already what had happened to his brother. It wasn't as if he was going to be telling her things she wasn't already aware of. Also, she was really the heir of the Kalathes fortune, not him, so why shouldn't she know the truth?

'You wanted to know why I didn't want anything of my father's?' The words came out roughly, but he didn't try to soften them. 'Because after Dorian died, he cut me off. Both emotionally and financially. He told me that he wished I had been the one to die, not Dorian. He told me that I had to leave Kalifos, and that he never wanted to see me again. I was sixteen.'

Shock then sympathy flickered over her face. 'Oh, Atticus…'

'So I left home and, since there was nothing else for me here, I joined the army. Over the years I tried periodically to make contact with him, but he always refused. He didn't want to talk to me and he didn't want to see me. He'd meant it when he said he never wanted to see me again.'

She'd gone pale, her eyes darkening. 'That was unforgivable of him,' she said quietly but with some force.

That surprised him. He'd expected her to come to Aristeidis's defence. 'He had reason,' Atticus said.

'He was wrong.' Her chin came up. 'He told me that he'd treated you badly and that he'd said some terrible things, but he was never clear on what exactly he'd said. He just didn't blame you for not wanting to see him.'

Unexpected grief twisted inside him. He didn't want to know about Aristeidis's regrets, especially when it was too late to do anything about them.

You let your own bitterness eat you alive the same way he let it eat at him.

Atticus gritted his teeth. Well, if he was bitter, didn't he have a right to it? The days, weeks, months and years after Dorian's death, he'd been suffering in his own private hell and had been desperate for someone to save him. Yet the one person who could had left him there to suffer instead.

Memories rose inside him, memories he'd been struggling to keep at bay while he'd been back here. Memories of his childhood here, with Dorian. Of playing chase in the villa and hide and seek in the gardens. Games of war with sticks for swords and the time he'd tied a towel around his neck as a cape and tried to jump from the window in this very room, thinking he could fly. Only for his brother to stop him, saving him…

A suffocating feeling rose inside him, the memories drowning him.

He had to get out of the room, go somewhere else. Perhaps to the pool or to run along the island's beaches. He needed fresh air, the scent of salt and the sea. He needed to push himself to exhaustion, needed the burn of his muscles as he pushed himself physically instead of the ache in his heart.

He went to turn, but then Elena reached out and gripped his arm. 'Wait.'

He could have pulled away, but somehow her touch

eased the constriction in his chest so he stopped and glanced at her.

Her expression was full of painful sympathy. ‘He was a good father to me,’ she said. ‘But he wasn’t a good father to you, I can see that. He shouldn’t have said all those terrible things to you. He should have been there for you, and I realise why you didn’t want to talk to him.’

He hadn’t known he’d needed her understanding until he saw it glowing in the depths of her eyes. ‘Like I said. He had a right to it.’

‘No,’ Elena said quietly but very firmly. ‘No, he didn’t.’

How strange that it was he who now felt defensive of the man he’d felt nothing but bitter anger towards for the past twenty years.

‘I killed my brother,’ he said harshly. ‘You don’t think he had a right to be angry with me for that?’

‘Not angrier than you were at yourself,’ she said, as if she knew. As if she knew exactly what it was to be responsible for the death of another person. A person he’d loved. As if she knew exactly the depth of his bitterness and his self-loathing, because that was still there, deep down inside him.

A morass of pain and grief and fury and hatred.

At himself.

The sense of suffocation increased, making it feel as if there were hands around his throat, choking him. Abruptly he couldn’t stand it.

He ripped his arm from her grip and strode out without a word.

CHAPTER EIGHT

ELENA STEPPED INTO the cool of the tiny Kalifos church that had only recently hosted Aristeidis's funeral and would now be hosting her wedding.

She adjusted her bouquet of calla lilies, while the woman she'd hired to help her dress, apply her make-up and do her hair fussed around with her gown.

She would have had a bridesmaid if she could, but growing up on Kalifos, which had isolated her anyway, and then looking after Aristeidis had left her little time for cultivating friendships. She could have done the make-up and hair herself, but she'd wanted to indulge herself on her wedding day, so she had.

After a few more twitches of her dress and a quick touch to her veil, the woman gave her a smile then disappeared through the door into the church, to tell Atticus that she'd arrived.

Elena took a couple of breaths to calm the twisting anxiety in her gut and to ease the tight band of emotion that had closed around her chest.

She wished Aristeidis were here. She wished her long-dead family were here. She wished she were marrying a man who loved her and whom she loved.

But none of that was to be. She was marrying Atticus to fulfil Aristeidis's last wish, and so she could stay in the home she loved, and to one day have the family of her own that she so longed for.

Not that you deserve to have that.

The doubt felt like a thorn sliding through her, but she ignored it, the way she always did. The wedding was happening and she would have all those other things too, irrespective of whether she deserved them or not. And she was grateful, that was what she was.

Her husband-to-be was beautiful and there was a lot of pleasure to be had in his bed. They hadn't discussed living arrangements or anything, but she'd assumed that once they were married he'd be living elsewhere, while she stayed on Kalifos. He'd clearly have to visit on occasion so she could conceive the children Aristeidis had specified, but he wouldn't otherwise impede her in any way. And she'd thought that she'd be happy with that.

Except…he was a difficult man, it was true, but she'd caught glimpses of another man beneath his hard shell. A man who'd dried her tears gently, then looked at her with shock and a fierce rush of emotion as he'd opened the box with the pin in it. Who'd then also given her a glimpse of the deep, sharp pain that lived inside him when he'd pulled his arm from her grip and had left the room so suddenly.

Behind the silk of her bodice, her heart ached. Both for the pain she'd seen in him and for the calm way he'd dried her tears. For how he'd put his hand over the pin she'd given him, as if he'd never had anything so precious, and told her that the symbol of Eleos was her.

She could still feel the echo of the shock that had caused her reverberating through her now. She'd had no idea that he'd even remembered the day he'd found her, let alone that she'd changed something in him. That she had been the reason he'd started his charity.

She'd had no idea that she'd represented hope for him.

The ache in her heart deepened into a bittersweet pain. Bitter that he'd been so despairing and yet so sweet that she'd helped him. She'd never helped anyone except Aristeidis before, and it mattered to her that the person she'd helped had been him. That she'd given him hope when he'd had none.

You can't let this—him—mean anything to you.

She shouldn't. He'd already told her that love wouldn't be a part of this marriage, so getting further involved with him, letting him mean something to her, letting herself be vulnerable to him, would only be setting herself up for further pain.

But...he was clearly still tormented by the death of his brother—the brief flash of pain and rage in his eyes before he'd walked out the night before had been clear evidence of that—and that made her hurt for him. That made her want to help him, too.

Aristeidis had told her what had happened to Dorian, and he'd also told Elena that he 'hadn't handled it well'. An understatement, apparently.

The death of Dorian had fractured an already tenuous relationship, Aristeidis letting grief overwhelm him, causing him to alienate his youngest son, piling more salt onto what was already an open wound.

Atticus blamed himself for his brother's death, that was obvious. He was already angry and his father had made things worse by blaming him too. Instead of helping them both grieve, Aristeidis had broken their relationship entirely. And he'd regretted it deeply.

She'd helped him with his regrets, but it had been he who'd decided that he needed to talk to Atticus. To try and rebuild what he'd broken.

Too late.

The music was starting, signalling her entrance, but she had to take another moment as yet more tears prickled, making her have to blink hard so they wouldn't ruin her make-up.

Well, Aristeidis had gone, but his son was still here and she was going to marry him. He'd given her a glimpse of the pain that lay in his heart and maybe he wouldn't reveal more. Or maybe that was the start. But she wanted to help him, maybe rebuild the relationship that Aristeidis had destroyed. That was the least she could do, surely?

Decision made, Elena gripped her flowers tightly as the doors were pulled open. Then she walked down the aisle of Kalifos's small, ancient stone church, smelling of incense and old stone, hand-carved wooden pews on either side of her.

At the other end of the aisle, Atticus waited.

He wore a morning suit of dove grey, with a crisp

white shirt that emphasised his tanned skin and the darkness of his eyes. The pure planes and angles of his face were set in hard lines, yet the moment his gaze settled on her, something fierce and hot leapt in it.

A wave of heat washed over her as he took in her dress and the veil that covered her hair and face, the flames in his eyes leaping higher. It was very, very clear he liked her wedding gown.

She took a little breath, unable to help noticing that in place of flowers on his lapel, he had the pin she'd given him the night before. It gleamed softly in the dim light.

He was so beautiful.

You can't fall for him. He'll never give you what you want.

Good thing that she wasn't falling for him then. He made her ache, but it wasn't with longing. It was sympathy for what he'd gone through, for the pain he still felt for his brother's death, and for the fact that his father had died and there would never be a reconciliation for either of them.

It wasn't for herself and some old longing that she'd put behind her years ago, the longing of a child for someone to protect her, someone to trust, someone to love. Because she couldn't love him. He'd left her, he'd abandoned her all those years ago and, while she knew he'd had to, she couldn't trust that he wouldn't do so again. Especially when there was nothing tying him to her but the last wish of a dying man.

She would never allow herself to be so vulnerable to him again.

Elena finally came to a stop at the altar, her heartbeat thumping in her chest, nerves gathering inside her despite the fact that this was simply a legal procedure. It didn't mean anything.

Atticus was still staring at her as if he couldn't look away, and somehow it made her nerves both worse and better. Then he frowned slightly and held out his hand to her and automatically she took it. His fingers curled around hers, warm and strong, and abruptly the flutter inside her settled. Relieved, she gave him an instinctive smile through her veil and her nerves settled even further when he smiled back.

You should be worried, not calmed.

Elena ignored the thought as the priest began the ceremony and when it came time to say her vows, she was able to speak levelly and without a stutter or nervous tremble. Atticus said his too, his deep, dark voice as calm as hers, though there was nothing calm in the look he gave her. It just about burned her to the ground.

He kept holding her hand throughout, the warmth of his touch soothing, yet at the exchange of rings she could feel the electric shock that crackled over her skin as he slid the wedding band onto her finger. Then it was her turn, his large hand in hers, the white scars on his fingers standing out against his skin as she did the same with his ring.

Then the priest pronounced them husband and wife and Atticus was lifting her veil and putting it back.

There was an intense light in his eyes, some strange emotion glowing there that she didn't understand. It was sexual heat, she was familiar enough with that by now to recognise it, but there was also something else there, something deeper.

He took her chin in his hand the way he had the night before, his touch just as gentle, and tilted her head back. For a moment he said nothing, only looked at her as if she were a prize that he'd worked long and hard for and had now won. It made her own heart twist, full of the same longing she'd already told her herself she didn't feel. And then she had no more time to think, because he bent his head and kissed her. His mouth was hot, yet unexpectedly gentle and his kiss was sweet, deepening the ache in her heart.

How much sweeter all of this would be if they loved each other, if they'd chosen each other. If their future were a life spent together and the family they'd create.

You can't want more, not with him, and you know it.

Yes, she did. If she was ever to have the future she really wanted for herself, she wouldn't have it with him. She could *never* have it with him.

Elena was shaking a little by the time he lifted his mouth, the fierce expression still burning in his eyes. And abruptly she wanted to know what it was that made him look at her that way. She wanted to know what he was feeling and whether this was as emotionally complicated for him as it was for her. Whether this mattered to him and whether the future he'd envisioned for himself featured her in any way.

She knew she shouldn't be thinking things like that, but she couldn't help herself. Even though they'd been sleeping together for the past week, he was still a stranger to her, despite all the stories she'd heard about him, and despite her knowing the tragedy that had shaped him. Yet those stories had been about the boy he'd once been, not the man, and it was the man who was her husband now. It was the man she wanted to know more about.

And why not? Five years, Aristeidis had stipulated, that was how long they were supposed to be together, so why couldn't they have some kind of relationship during that time? They would be lovers, yes, but why not friends too? She should know more about the father of her children, she really should.

Atticus threaded his fingers through hers and then she was being led out of the church and onto the bright sunlight.

She'd organised for their honeymoon to be in a villa along the Adriatic coast in Italy, and a helicopter would take them to Athens and to the Kalathes jet that would then take them to Italy. Atticus had agreed to it all without question when she'd told him about it and she was already planning in her head the questions she was going to ask him once they'd got there, when he said, 'I have cancelled the Italy trip.'

They were walking up the small rocky path that led from the church back to the Kalathes villa, and she stopped in shock, her veil flying out behind her as the wind caught it.

'What?'

He'd stopped too, the burning look that he'd given her back in the church in his eyes once again. 'We will not be going to Italy. I've decided we'll be going to Jamaica instead.'

Elena stood there in the bright sunlight, the crystals in her wedding gown glittering, her veil fluttering out behind her like a flag, her eyes dark and smoky. Her golden hair was in a beautiful arrangement on top of her head, all soft curls and threaded through with wildflowers. There were lilies in her hand and on the other hand glowed his father's ring. His wedding band was there too, the wedding band she'd designed.

She was so beautiful it almost hurt to look at her.

Your wife. She's your *wife now.*

Being here on Kalifos, where he'd grown up, had triggered memories he didn't want, memories he'd been trying to escape. He'd been plagued by them the past week, and even up until last night all he'd been able to think about were all the moments his brother had missed, all the firsts Dorian would never have. He'd never marry, for example. He'd never get to see his bride standing in the sun, sparkling like a fall of stardust.

It should have been you who died and it should be him standing here now, looking at Elena.

It should, but it wasn't, and normally that would feel like a knife sliding directly into his heart. Yet all he felt now was a savage satisfaction that it *wasn't*

Dorian standing here, looking at Elena. That it was *him* instead.

You don't deserve this.

No, of course he didn't. But he wasn't going to turn away from it either and he'd realised that the moment the music had started and the church doors had opened, and Elena had appeared, glowing like an angel fallen to earth.

He'd spent all night trying and failing to forget about the discussion they'd had about Dorian. Trying and failing to forget about the understanding he'd seen in her eyes and how she'd told him that his father had been too hard on him. How she'd seemed to know about the anger that lived in his heart. The anger at himself that he couldn't seem to outrun.

He'd never known what to do with that anger except bury it so far down he forgot it was there, and he didn't know what to do with her understanding either. It felt dangerous, though he couldn't have said why, so he'd spent the entire morning as he'd prepared for their wedding battling to find his usual detachment, his usual focus, pushing all the thoughts of the past to one side.

Until she'd walked down the aisle towards him. And he'd realised that all his attempts at detachment, his burying of the tragedy of Dorian's death, were useless. He couldn't outrun the past or the memories. He couldn't bury those terrible, painful emotions, just as he couldn't bury or outrun his intense desire for her.

She made it impossible. Because right from the first moment he'd seen her, she'd brought all his bitter emotions to the surface. She'd brought them out into the open and then she'd eased them.

She was his hope. That was why he'd rescued her from the rubble and given her to his father to look after. That was why he'd started Eleos. That was why millions of people now had better lives and it was all because of her.

She was his hope for the future, his hope of redemption. His hope of healing. She'd given him that pin and now she was giving him herself, and he knew he couldn't refuse her.

He hadn't given much thought to what form their marriage would take, half thinking that he'd live in Jamaica while she lived on Kalifos, and every six months or so he'd visit her to conceive the children his father had specified. There had been no stipulation, after all, that they were to live as husband and wife.

But as she'd walked down the aisle to him in that church and the realisation had hit him of what she was to him, of what she represented, he'd changed his mind. They *would* live together as husband and wife, and he'd be her husband in all ways. He'd be a father to her children. He'd give her the family she'd always wanted.

Love was still out of the question, but he could make her happy without it, he was sure. No, he *would* make her happy. She was the hope he clung to and, because of that, he couldn't let her go. He wouldn't. There would be no hope at all if he did.

They'd need to discuss where they'd live, naturally, since he didn't want to be on Kalifos, but perhaps she'd like his island in Jamaica. Or perhaps they'd find somewhere else. Either way, she was his now.

She'd changed his life all those years ago, and now she was changing it again. She was giving him back the hope he'd lost and he couldn't turn away from it, not again.

She's more than just a representation of hope. She's also a woman with her own dreams and needs.

Well, of course she was, and he'd treat her as such. He wasn't that much of a monster.

'Jamaica?' she repeated blankly.

Of course, Jamaica for the honeymoon. It made sense. He wanted to bring her back to the island that meant something to him. He'd kept himself alone and apart from people for so long, but he didn't need to with her. She already knew the worst parts of him and he was done with hiding them.

'Italy is beautiful,' he said. 'But my island is home to me. More of a home than Kalifos. And I'd like to show it to you, spend some time with you there.'

The shock vanished from her face, her brown eyes glowing. 'Oh, yes,' she breathed, as if she couldn't think of anything better. 'Yes, I'd love to go in that case.'

Satisfaction gripped him, along with a rush of intense desire at the obvious delight on her face. He'd expected her to argue about the sudden change of plans, not look thrilled at the thought of returning to a place she'd already been. 'Good. It's a bit of a trek, so I've organised for us to leave tomorrow. Tonight, though…'

he gripped her hand, pulling her gently but firmly close '…it's our wedding night and I want to make sure it's one you won't forget.'

Colour swept through her cheeks, which he found adorable. It made him bend to kiss her, a light brush of his lips against hers that only incited him further. Impatient, he stepped back and turned, pulling her along with him up the path to the villa.

As they reached the entrance, he swept her up into his arms and carried her over the threshold, and he knew she loved the gesture, because her eyes sparkled and she smiled, her head back against his shoulder.

He didn't take her to the master bedroom, or to the bedroom that he'd once had as a child. He didn't take her to the guest room he'd been using either; there were too many memories associated with all of them. Her room, though, the only memories he had of it were of pleasure.

It overlooked the sea and a white terrace, and best of all the bed was big and wide, covered in a thick white quilt and blue cushions.

He set her down in the middle of the room and pulled the veil from her hair, before carefully laying it out on the couch near the window. Then he took her by the shoulders and turned her around so he could undo the many tiny buttons on the back of her dress.

As the heavy fabric fell away, it revealed pale, silky skin. She wore nothing underneath her gown except a pair of lacy knickers and high-heeled sandals.

Desire gripped him, his satisfaction deepening, and

he let it run through him, sharpening his hunger to a fine point. She was his wife. She was *his* and he'd never had anyone of his own before. He hadn't known how deeply that would matter to him.

The male beast in him wanted to gorge itself on her as soon as possible, but he'd already decided he wasn't going to rush it. This was her wedding night and she was his wife, and savouring her was no less than she deserved.

She had given him hope and so he would give her pleasure.

He helped her to step out of her dress and then he laid that out over the couch too, before coming back to her. She'd gone the prettiest shade of pink, the wild-flowers still woven in her lovely hair.

This time it was his turn to kneel, he decided, and he did so before her, lifting his hands to run them up her thighs, stroking the warm satin of her skin, and making her tremble. Her eyes were dark and smoky as she looked down at him, and he held her gaze as he hooked his fingers into the lace of her underwear, slowly drawing it down. She swallowed, the pulse at the base of her throat beating fast, her cheeks flushed.

He helped her step out of the lacy fabric and then got rid of it, so that all she wore were her high-heeled sandals and nothing else.

She was the most beautiful thing he'd ever seen in his life.

Another moment Dorian will never get to have: a wedding night.

The thought was a knife, cutting him open, but he shoved it aside. He wasn't going to think about his brother, not now, not here. This was for him. *She* was for him. She was his hope and he had to believe in the future she represented. He had to.

He ran his hands up her thighs again, leaning in and pressing kisses against her stomach, stroking her softly rounded curves, filling himself with her delicious, sweet and musky scent. She was getting aroused now, he could smell it, so he explored lower, nuzzling against the soft curls between her thighs.

She shivered in his hands, a sound escaping her as he kissed down to the sweet heat that lay between her legs. He leaned in further, tasting her with his tongue, filling his hands with softness of her rear and squeezing gently as he held her still for his mouth. He pushed his tongue inside her, tasting her deeper, licking her and making her gasp. Her fingers were in his hair, twisting, gripping him tightly as he gorged himself on her flavour and the way she shivered and gasped against him.

He brought her to climax quickly and hard, and she cried his name, sagging against him as if she couldn't hold herself upright any longer. He rose to his feet, picking her up in his arms and taking her to the bed. Then he put her down on the mattress and with slow care removed her sandals. He took his time, undoing the strap of each one, cradling her small foot as he slipped them off.

She lay back on the white sheets, her skin beautifully flushed, her hair a golden veil across the pillows with wildflowers scattered everywhere, her eyes glowing like banked coals from the pleasure he'd just given her. There was pleasure in this too, in taking her shoes off, in stroking her feet and making her giggle and squirm.

That made him smile, which surprised him. He couldn't remember the last time he'd smiled during sex. He couldn't remember the last time he'd smiled at all, at least not when it hadn't been at her.

And then her shoes were off and his clothes felt too tight. He wanted her bare skin against his, and so he clawed them off, discarding them carelessly on the floor before joining her on the bed. He moved over her, settling himself between her thighs and lowering his head to kiss her, deep and hot. Letting her taste herself on him.

She gave a soft, throaty moan, her hips lifting against his in blatant demand. But he was still taking his time, so he teased them both, rubbing the hard length of his shaft against the tender flesh of her sex, making her gasp and clutch at him. But soon he too lost patience, easing her thighs wide and pushing inside her in a long, slow, deep glide.

'Atticus…' Her back arched, her eyes gone liquid and dark as the night sky. She felt so good around him, tight and wet and so hot his brain momentarily blanked.

She was beneath him, taking all of him, looking up at him as if he was the best thing she'd seen all day. As if he was the best thing she'd ever seen in her entire life.

No one had ever looked at him like that. No one.

Then she lifted her arms to him the way she had all

those years ago, her hands on his shoulders, gripping him as if she never wanted to let him go, and he began to move inside her, deep and slow.

Pleasure was a dark pulse inside him, so strong and getting stronger, and he could see it reflected in her eyes too. Her nails dug into him and she didn't look away. 'Atticus,' she whispered as he slid his hands beneath her, lifting her hips so he could move deeper. 'Oh, my God…'

She was electric around him, fierce ecstasy arcing through him and spitting sparks, the trail of a comet flying in a night sky.

'Elena.' He could taste her name. It had a flavour all its own and that was something else he wanted to savour. 'My Elenitsa.'

She shuddered, staring up at him as he moved inside her, fast and getting faster, twisting everything tight and making it desperate. Her legs closed around his waist, her hips moving with his, falling into his rhythm as if born to it.

There was ecstasy between them, a fever that grew with every thrust of his hips, and he had one moment's fleeting doubt that he was perhaps feeling all this a lot more strongly than he should have, when it all exploded in a wild flame, and he let them both burn until they were nothing but sparks and ash on the wind.

CHAPTER NINE

'THIS IS VERY UNFAIR,' Elena protested. 'Let me see.' Atticus had his hands over her eyes and she couldn't see a thing. It was very annoying.

'It's a surprise,' he said from behind her, guiding her across sand still warm from the day's sun. 'And if I let you see, it would spoil the surprise.'

She sighed. 'Your logic is both irrefutable and deeply irritating.'

'I know.' He finally stopped and took his hands away. 'You can look now.'

Elena blinked as her eyes adjusted.

It was night, the sky above studded with stars, but in front of her, set on a platform of smooth inlaid rock that faced the beach, was a big white porcelain claw-foot bath. A rock wall sat behind the bath, the taps inset into it, and small tea lights in coloured glass holders had been placed on ledges that looked custom made for that purpose. The flames leapt and flickered and danced, casting shadows everywhere. Around the bath were small trees to give a bit of privacy, and they had been strung with small solar fairy lights, bathing everything in a warm glow. The bath itself was full of gently steaming water, and there were even petals floating in it.

Atticus had said he'd prepared a surprise for her early that afternoon, but she'd never guessed it would be an outdoor bath. They'd been here a few days already and she hadn't even known it was there.

Then again, they hadn't ventured much beyond the house, too busy with exploring each other, let alone the island. He had taken her out fishing earlier that day, showing her the rocks in the lagoon and the best places to cast a line. She'd loved it and had been especially excited when she'd caught a fish of her own. He'd prepared it and cooked it for her for dinner that night, and it had been delicious.

In fact, everything about being here with him was delicious, from the long, lazy mornings in bed, to a swim in the clear waters of the lagoon, and lunch in the deck facing the sea. Then usually some more lazy, sun-drenched sex on the deck or on the sand, or in the water, depending on when and where they were at the time, before dinner, that Atticus insisted on preparing himself.

He was also a joy to be with. As soon as they'd arrived it was as if a heavy weight had lifted from him. He was still intense and sharp and focused, but there was an easiness to him, as if something coiled tight inside him had relaxed. He smiled. He laughed. He teased her as if they'd known each other for years, grinning as she teased him back.

He asked her what she'd been doing over the years,

listening to her speak as if he'd never heard anything more important in his life. Then he told her about his own past, stories from his days in the army and then as a mercenary in his own private security force. She found it fascinating. She found *him* fascinating, everything about him, and she hadn't expected that. Sex and as much pleasure as she could handle, yes. But talking deep into the night with Atticus about Eleos and his mission to save as many people as he could? Telling him about the intricacies and challenges of Kalathes Shipping? Giggling like a schoolgirl as he tickled her feet and then laughing as she poked him in the sides, trying to find out where he was ticklish? No. Not at all.

And then there was how he did everything for her, waiting on her hand and foot, ignoring her completely when she told him she wasn't helpless and that she could do some things herself. She didn't mind. After the years of caring for Aristeidis, she secretly loved having someone take care of her for a change.

Tomorrow, he'd promised they'd go snorkelling in the lagoon and then he'd take out the yacht and he'd teach her to sail. And maybe the day after that they'd go into Port Antonio so she could look around and maybe get dinner there.

She loved it. She loved him showing her around the island, taking her to all his favourite places, showing her pieces of himself that no one else knew. He was such a caring man, the evidence not just in how he believed totally in his charity and his mission, but also in how he treated with care the nature he lived in. He showed her how he collected rainwater for the house and recycled the grey water. How he used solar power for everything, collecting sun the way he collected the rain. He showed her the garden where he grew herbs and other greens. He showed her the office where he ran his charity, linked to the rest of the world from this peaceful, quiet place by satellites.

Several times she wondered why he'd taken himself away from society quite so completely, when it was apparent from his visit to Greece that he had no problems actually being around people. She wanted to ask him, but the moment was never quite right. She was loving being with him like this and she didn't want to destroy the mood with questions that he wouldn't want to answer.

You wanted to help him find his way back to his father.

She did, but as she stared at the outdoor bath, at the dancing tea lights and the stack of towels on the stone pad, she knew that this was another moment she didn't want to destroy with questions.

Instead, she turned to him with shining eyes. 'I love it. It's amazing.'

He smiled, the flickering flames of the tea lights and the fairy lights overhead casting shadows over his beautiful face and the hard, carved lines of his body. They were both naked and she'd become used to wandering around the island either wearing nothing or merely a light wrap. There was no one to see them and it was too hot for clothes most of the time.

'Get in,' he said. 'The water's warm.'

So she did, delighted when he got in too, sitting behind her so that she could settle back in his arms, the warm water lapping around them. The night was quiet as most of the nights here were, the only sound the waves on the beach and the wind in the palms.

‘I want to talk to you about our future,’ Atticus said unexpectedly as she felt him pour water over her hair.

She tried not to tense. The future was an unwelcome subject and one she’d been deliberately not thinking about for the past three days, wanting to enjoy the moments she had with him. She knew eventually they’d have to decide what their future would look like and she was pretty sure it would be apart. And she didn’t like the little lurch in her heart the prospect of that gave her. She was supposed to enjoy her honeymoon and then equally enjoy living on her own on Kalifos. She wasn’t supposed to feel a sharp pang of loss at the thought of leaving him.

‘Oh?’ she asked, hoping it sounded casual and not as tense as she felt.

Behind her he turned, reaching over the side of the bath for the bottle of shampoo that stood on a small stool. He put some in his hands and then began lathering her hair. It felt soothing. Over the past couple of days, she’d learned he wasn’t a man who liked to sit still. He always had to be doing something with his hands. She liked that too since what he did with his hands was either something interesting or intensely pleasurable for her.

A deep, animal pleasure stole the tension from her

now as those hands moved in her hair and she relaxed back against him.

'I think we should live together,' he said. 'As husband and wife. It can either be here or somewhere else, I don't mind where as long as it's not Kalifos.'

Elena's muscles locked up in shock. She had *not* expected that he'd want them to live together, especially when he'd been so clear that their marriage was merely for Aristeidis's will.

'Why?' she asked blankly. 'I thought that—'

'I know, but I've changed my mind.' He eased her back further against him, then urged her deeper into the water so her hair was submerged. She found herself looking up at him, his black eyes holding hers, the same ferocious expression in them as there'd been the day of their wedding. 'I want us to have a real marriage,' he went on. 'To have a family together. Bring up our children together.'

A shiver went through her. He began squeezing out her hair, rinsing away the shampoo, and she couldn't stop staring up at him.

A real marriage. Having a family with him. Living with him as his wife…

Her heart ached with a longing she'd tried to ignore for a long time now. The longing to be with someone, to have someone of her own, someone who wouldn't leave her.

It can't be him. It can't.

A thread of panic wound through her, making her feel as if she'd made a mistake somewhere along the line, a mistake that it was now too late to fix.

She sat up abruptly, water streaming from her hair, her back to him. She didn't want to look at him, didn't want him to see her panic. The water was warm but she felt cold. 'I see,' she said, trying to sound as neutral as possible. 'What made you change your mind?'

If he'd picked up on her tension he gave no sign, his hands in her hair again, squeezing the water from it gently. 'You did,' he said. 'The day of our wedding. Or maybe it was even the night before, when you gave me that pin.'

Her heart thumped loudly in her ears and she was suddenly full of fear though, again, she wasn't sure why. She leaned forward in the water, wrapping her arms around her knees. 'How did I do that?'

'I told you that the night I found you in the rubble, you gave me hope.' His voice was a deep rumble at her back. 'And when you gave me that pin, I was reminded of it. Then in the church, when you appeared in your wedding gown, it was as if you were giving me yourself. You've always been hope to me, Elenitsa, and on our wedding day, you gave me hope again.' His hands stroked down her spine and she shivered helplessly. 'Hope for a future I didn't know I wanted. A future I thought I couldn't have.'

His words made her heart clench. They should make her feel good, she knew, because who didn't want to be someone's hope? But there was only a kind of lurching disappointment. This wasn't about her. This wasn't about who she was. It was about what she represented to him. Of course, she liked being his hope, but…

You want to be more than that to him.

Her feelings tangled and knotted inside her, cold fear and disappointment, that terrible aching longing and a sharp kind of sadness. No, she hadn't wanted to be more to him, she hadn't wanted him to matter to her at all, and yet… Part of her knew the truth. That he did matter to her. That the past three days with him had been the happiest of her life, happier than she'd ever been as Aristeidis's daughter.

You're falling for him.

No, no. No, she couldn't do that. The was the very last thing in the world that she should do.

Too late.

Elena gripped the side of the bath tightly, the cold fear inside her winding deeper. 'Oh,' she said, sharper than she'd intended. 'So it's not really about me, then?' As soon as the words were out of her mouth, she knew she shouldn't have said them. They revealed far too much. But like most things to do with Atticus, it was too late.

He'd gone still behind her. 'What do you mean?'

'I mean, you don't really want to live with me.'

'Of course I want to live with you.' There was a puzzled note in his voice. 'Wasn't that what I just said?'

She turned her head, glancing at him from over her shoulder. 'You said you wanted to live with me because of what I represent. That's not about me, Atticus. That's about you.'

His black brows drew down, the flames from the tea lights leaping in his night-dark eyes. 'It's you I want to live with, Elena. Is that not clear?'

'No, it's not clear. You said I represented hope for you. Hope is what you want to live with, it's not me.' Her throat had tightened. She didn't want to argue with him, but it felt as if the conversation had got away from her and she didn't know how to get it back.

His gaze became edged, focusing on her in that abrupt way he had that made her feel as if he could read every thought in her head.

He'll know how you feel about him. He'll be able to see it.

The thread of panic constricted and abruptly she didn't want to be here any longer, in the warm water with him and his seductive hands and his sharp gaze. She felt far too vulnerable, far too open, and she hated it. She'd always hated it.

He'll know about how you left them, too. He'll know what a coward you are.

The water surged as Elena pushed herself up and out of the bath, splashing onto the stone pad.

'Elena?' Atticus sounded shocked. 'Elena, what is it?'

But she didn't answer. She felt cold, the kind of chill that had nothing to do with the temperature, and she had to get away from him. She couldn't be around him a second longer. Picking up a towel, she wrapped it around herself, then stalked back into the house without a word.

Atticus sat for a moment in the bath, staring after her. He had no idea what had happened, but something had upset her. And she was upset, that was obvious. He'd thought she'd enjoy the outdoor bath and she certainly had been doing before he'd mentioned living together as husband and wife.

He'd been planning on having the conversation since they'd arrived on the island, but he'd thought he'd give them both a few days to get comfortable with each other, and to take the edge off the seemingly bottomless well of desire he had for her.

He'd thought to surprise her with the bath since she was such a sensual creature, and he knew she'd enjoy it. Then he'd bring the subject up when she was relaxed and in his arms. He hadn't thought it would be a big deal, especially not given the past couple of days.

Being with her had been a revelation. She'd fallen into the rhythms of the island as if born to them, seemingly delighted by everything he showed her. She was up for anything he suggested, even demanding that he show her how to fillet and prepare the fish she caught. She was fascinated by how he recycled everything he could because he wanted to leave as minimal a footprint on the island as possible, which had then led to a discussion about sustainable housing, which was something he wanted to develop with Eleos.

She was so interesting. She had a quick mind and could see the big picture in a way that he sometimes struggled with, since he was so detail oriented. She also had the sweetest laugh that he soon found himself obsessed with, and coaxing her glorious smile out made him feel as if he'd won a gold medal.

He wanted more of that and his suggestion of them

living together was merely a natural extension of what they were already doing. So what was it about it that she hadn't liked? Did it really matter why he wanted them to live together? She'd seemed upset about him calling her his hope, that it meant it wasn't really her that he wanted, and clearly that mattered to her. But why? What more did she want from him? They'd married for the will, that was all, but surely that didn't mean they couldn't live together or raise a family together. He wanted that and he knew that she wanted it too, so what was the issue?

Annoyance collected inside him. He hadn't handled this well, it was clear, otherwise she wouldn't have walked off, but if she thought he'd leave it at that, she was mistaken. This was important, their future was important, and he wanted it sorted out sooner rather than later.

Getting out of the bath, Atticus gave himself a cursory dry-off with a towel and then strode back along the path and into the house.

He found Elena in the bedroom, in the process of belting a long silk robe of blue Chinese silk very firmly around her. It annoyed him unreasonably.

He'd loved how she'd become so comfortable with him and with herself that she wasn't bothered that they didn't wear clothes most of the day. It was a far cry from the prissy cream suit she'd worn the first day she'd come here and he'd dumped her in the ocean.

But now the fact that she wore a robe, covering up her beautiful body, felt as if she was putting distance between them. As if she was armouring herself, and he didn't like that, not at all.

'What's wrong?' he asked, trying not to make it sound like a demand. 'Why are you upset?'

Her expression was very set and she half turned away from him, squeezing her hair out with the towel she had wrapped around it. 'It's nothing,' she said dismissively. 'Forget it.'

She was lying through her teeth and that annoyed him as well. He was tempted to provoke her into an argument, since they sparked so completely off each other that it would likely end up in bed. She'd probably forget all about whatever was upsetting her then, so maybe it would be worth it.

This will take more than just sex and you know it.

Doubt shifted inside him and an odd desperation he didn't know what to do with. This had to be discussed, whatever it was, because he had the sense that if it wasn't, the future he wanted with her would slip through his fingers. He couldn't have that; he just couldn't.

'No,' he said flatly. 'I'm not going to forget it. Tell me what's wrong.'

She squeezed the towel one more time then dropped it, her hair falling around her shoulders in damp, pretty golden curls. Her eyes were very dark and he could see pain glittering in them. 'I told you what was wrong. You say I'm your hope, Atticus, but I'm not. I'm your wife. I'm a person, not a…a talisman.'

A flicker of surprise cut through his anger and frustration. He didn't see her that way. How could she think that? After the past few days?

Don't you? Isn't that exactly how you see her? How you've always seen her?

'What makes you think that?' he demanded, ignoring the thought.

'You said I was your hope for the future.' Her chin came up, her dark eyes full of anger. 'That's not about me, is it? That's all about you, Atticus.'

Something in his chest twisted hard. 'It's not about me,' he snapped before he could stop himself. 'It's about Dorian.'

Her gaze flickered, her expression softening. 'What about Dorian?'

He didn't want to talk about this—he never wanted to talk about this—but back in Greece he'd decided he couldn't outrun the past. And that she was the one person in this world who knew all about the tragedy that had taken Dorian's life. He didn't have to explain it to her. Yet still, the words were hard to find.

'He...will never have this,' Atticus said roughly. 'He will never have a wife and he'll never have a family. And so since I have the opportunity, I...owe it to him to have both.'

Pain flickered in Elena's eyes for a moment, then her lashes lowered, veiling her gaze. 'I see. So this future you want, this life you're planning on, is for him, not for you.' It wasn't a question.

There was a heavy sensation in his chest as if a boulder had fallen on him and he were lying pinned beneath it, struggling to get a breath. 'It's not just for him. Elena, I… I haven't seen a future for me, not one that includes a wife and children. But… I told you, Aristeidis's will, marrying you, it was as if fate was trying to tell me something. That perhaps I deserved after all to have the things that I took from Dorian.'

She stared at him for a long moment, her brown eyes soft with an emotion he didn't understand, sympathy almost and a terrible kind of understanding. Terrible, because it hurt, as if she'd slid a sharp knife between his ribs. 'You think you don't deserve those things?' she asked.

The harsh laugh escaped him before he could stop it. 'Of course I don't deserve them. I killed my own brother. Why would I deserve anything of the kind?'

'Atticus…' She took a step towards him then stopped. 'It was an accident. You were very young and—'

'I still killed him,' he interrupted roughly. 'Yes, I was young. But I was unfamiliar with the gun he gave me and I didn't bother to listen to his safety instructions, because I was excited. Because I wanted to go hunting with my big brother.' It felt as if his heart were full of ground glass, every beat causing him agony, but he made himself go on, because now he'd started he couldn't seem to shut himself up. But she had to know. She had to know the ugly truth.

'We saw a deer and Dorian told me to wait while he got a bit closer. But I couldn't wait. I was impatient and excited and nervous. I wanted to prove myself to him. There was a movement in the trees and I pulled the trigger thinking it was the deer.' The beat of his heart was so full of agony, it would never be any less painful, never. 'But it wasn't the deer. It was Dorian.' And just like that, he was back in the dusty hills, surrounded by brush and short scrubby trees, suffocating in horror when he'd discovered what he'd done…

'Atticus.' Soft hands cupped his face. 'Atticus, come back to me.'

He blinked at the sound of his name, his heart racing, for a moment still lost in the horror of it all. Then his vision cleared, and instead of Dorian's wide unseeing gaze, it was Elena's warm brown eyes looking at him, full of concern. 'You're here,' she said softly. 'You're here on the island with me.'

He felt cold, as if he'd been plunged into a snow drift. 'Baba blamed me,' he said hoarsely. 'He was right to. I pulled that trigger, no one else. Dorian was the oldest. He should have lived, not me. But… Aristeidis was my father and he should have helped me. I needed him and he left me to suffer.'

Elena's arms were around him, all the soft warmth of her body pressed to his, surrounding him in her scent, and for a second all he could do was stand there trying to hold onto the present while all the past wanted to do was drag him down and suck him under.

When he was in despair, she always seemed to be there when he needed her, holding him.

But what have you done for her? Nothing.

He shoved the thought away, because he had too much weighing him down already. He didn't need anything more. Instead he concentrated on her and her heat, grounding him in the here and now.

Her hair was silky against his skin, her face pressed to his chest, her arms holding him tight. 'I'm sorry,' she said in a muffled voice, threaded through with pain. 'I'm so sorry, Atticus.'

'Sorry?' he repeated blankly. 'Sorry for what?'

She lifted her head and looked up at him, her eyes darkened, and he could see the gleam of tears on her cheeks. 'For what you went through. And for what your father put you through too. You didn't deserve that. You *didn't*.' Her gaze turned fierce. 'It *was* an accident, Atticus. But you can't keep blaming yourself for it for ever. You can't keep torturing yourself, either. There comes a point where you have to let it go.'

He lifted a hand, touched one of the tears on her cheeks. Tears she'd cried for him. 'Does there come a point? Tell me, have you been able to let go your tragedies?'

He'd never asked her about her family and she'd never spoken about them. When he'd rescued her, she'd been a traumatised child and he hadn't wanted to visit more pain on her by questioning her. And it seemed, despite what she'd told him about letting go and despite all the years that had passed, that pain still lived inside her.

She glanced away, golden lashes veiling her gaze. 'I... I'm trying to.'

He let his fingers trail down her cheek to her jaw and then along to her chin where he gripped it gently. 'Your family, hmm?'

She kept her gaze averted but didn't pull away. 'I had to let them go. I had to let them lie in the rubble of my home. Because if I kept them with me, I'd never have been able to settle into Kalifos. I would never have been able to connect with Aristeidis. I would have been constantly wishing for something I could never have again, and there's no point in that.'

But there was an uncertain note in her voice, as if she didn't believe what she was saying herself. 'And did you do that, Elenitsa?' he asked, allowing himself to be distracted from his own pain so he could concentrate on hers. 'Were you able to leave them in the past?'

Her throat moved and, to his shock, more tears seeped from beneath her lashes. 'After the earthquake, I woke up to find myself surrounded by rubble. I was alone. I thought… I thought I could hear my father shouting. I thought he was still alive. I tried to get to him, but there were people yelling and screaming and the aftershocks… I was so afraid. I ran and hid in the ruins.' Another tear slid down her cheek. 'There were rescue workers helping dig through the rubble to find survivors, and I tried to tell them about my family, but they were so busy. They didn't listen to me and I was so terrified I ran and hid again.'

His heart contracted at the hurt in her voice, a dull ache in his chest, and he stroked her chin gently, wanting to soothe her however he could.

'I shouldn't have left them,' she went on, her voice raw. 'I should have tried harder to get help. They might have been alive and they might have—'

'No,' he interrupted, appalled that she'd been carrying this pain and doubt around with her for so long, and clearly torturing herself with it too. He was appalled at himself as well, because he could have given her this relief years ago and he hadn't thought of it. He'd left her alone instead. 'No, Elena.'

Her lashes lifted slowly, her dark eyes meeting his.

'Your family died instantly,' he went on. 'I checked. I made sure. You couldn't have saved them even if you'd managed to get the rescue teams to search through the rubble. You didn't leave them, sweetheart. They were already gone.'

She didn't speak, again just staring at him, tears gleaming on her cheeks. Then a tension went out of her, as if she'd been relieved of a load she'd been carrying for far too long. 'I knew that,' she said. 'Or at least, I told myself I knew that. But there was always this doubt. And when you came and took me to safety, I didn't even look back. I just…left them there with no memorial, no one to remember them, no nothing.' She paused and swallowed. 'It feels wrong that I was the one who got to walk away. Do you…do you think I'm a coward for leaving?'

He stared down at her, conscious of a growing, ferocious need to soothe her, comfort her, reassure her, and he didn't question it. All he knew was that he'd do anything to ease her pain.

'No,' he said, letting her see the conviction in his gaze. 'You're as far from a coward as it's possible to get. You survived for a week on your own in a very dangerous place. You were brave and stubborn and resourceful. You stayed with your family as long as you could, but in the end you had to leave. I think your parents would have been proud of you, and very glad that you found safety.' He ran his thumb along the side of her jaw in a featherlight caress. 'Also, while you might think that I rescued you, it was you who rescued me.'

She blinked. 'I rescued you?'

'From the darkness. From despair. You gave me hope, Elena, I told you that.' He let go of her chin and brushed away her tears. 'You saved me as much as I saved you.'

She searched his gaze for a long moment, though what she saw there, he had no idea. 'I'm glad I did, in that case,' she said hoarsely. 'I'm glad I was there. And, you know, I didn't totally leave them behind. My family, I mean. I kept some parts of them with me. The parts that make me happy. The good memories.' She paused. 'Do you have good memories of Dorian?'

The change of subject took him off guard and for a minute he couldn't think. Did he have good memories of Dorian? He'd avoided thinking of his brother for so long, he wasn't sure. 'I…' He stopped.

'No, go on,' Elena said. 'Tell me about him.'

He didn't want to revisit that particular agony, yet she'd told him about her family and her own painful doubts, and it seemed wrong not to give her something in return.

'He…was a rule follower,' Atticus began haltingly. 'But he could be persuaded to break the rules sometimes. He taught me how to sail in the sea around Kalifos and he taught me how to swim. When I stole cookies from the pantry and the housekeeper found out, he took the blame.' It was painful to think of him, exquisitely so, and yet…there was a sweetness to the memories that eased the pain. 'He told me ghost stories that terrified me so much I couldn't sleep, and he let me play with his toys when I was sick. He taught me how to fish…'

Elena's mouth had softened and it was curving in one of her beautiful smiles. 'He sounds like a good brother.'

'He was.' Atticus's voice was hoarse and he knew he should give her more, but all of a sudden he'd reached the end of what he could deal with right now. The combination of her loss and his own was too much, and he didn't want to talk any more. But she knew and she must have been feeling the same way, because abruptly she went up on her toes and pressed her mouth to his.

Desire leapt high and he was powerless to resist it. He didn't want to resist it. It was a fire that cauterised all wounds and he wanted to throw himself into the conflagration and let himself burn.

Clearly Elena was in agreement, because she got rid of her robe with a shrug of her shoulders, letting it slip to the ground. Then she was bare as she should always be with him, and his hands were on her hips, propelling her to the bed then taking her down onto it.

He pinned her beneath him, desperate for her, and she didn't deny him. She closed her legs around his waist, put her arms around his neck, kissing him hungrily. Then her hands stroked down his back, her hips lifting against his, encouraging him and so he sheathed himself in her welcoming heat.

He looked down at her as he began to move, locked in the moment, all thoughts of the past fading, the ground glass in his heart loosening, the pleasure she gave him blunting the edges.

Her dark eyes were full of heat and yet beneath that heat lay something else, an emotion that burned hotter and fiercer, and he couldn't look away.

She had given him so many things he'd never had from anyone else. Understanding and sympathy. Kindness and comfort.

She's not just hope to you. She's something more.

But he didn't want to think about what more she was, not now, not with the ghosts of his brother and her family still in the room, so he pushed the thought away and lost himself in the darkness of her eyes and the heat of her body, until there was only her and the fire they created between them, and the rest of the world ceased to exist.

CHAPTER TEN

ELENA WOKE THE next morning to find herself wrapped around Atticus's hard, hot body. The sun was already shining through the big windows, the sea gleaming a deep blue through the glass.

He'd kept her up all night, taking her again and again as if he couldn't get enough of her, as if he were escaping his terrible past and all the pain that came with it by gorging himself on pleasure. She couldn't blame him. She'd felt the same way after she'd told him about her family and her doubts about how she'd left them. She'd thought she'd regret telling him and yet…

'You're as far from a coward as it's possible to get.'

There had been so much conviction in his eyes and in his voice that she couldn't help but think that maybe she'd been too hard on herself. Maybe she didn't have to listen to those doubts after all.

'You saved me.'

She shut her eyes, going back over the memory of his confession about his brother. She'd known all about that tragedy, but she hadn't known how deeply it still ate away at him. And it really wasn't any wonder. Atticus was a good man, a man with a deep need to care for people, and the accident that had taken his brother's life had scarred him deeply.

She'd known as she'd stood in front of him the night before and seen his gaze look through her, full of a horror that only he saw as he relived the moment of that terrible hunting accident. She hadn't meant for the conversation to take that turn, but he was the one who'd brought Dorian up, and then had told her all about what had happened that day.

No wonder he still felt the pain. He'd had the responsibility of his brother's death on his shoulders, the unbearable weight of it only made more unbearable by his father's blame too.

She could forgive Aristeidis many things, but she almost couldn't forgive him that. Except, Aristeidis's own regrets had eaten away at him, and he'd wanted to apologise to his son, so the intention had been there at least.

But she could see now why Atticus hadn't wanted anything to do with him.

Her heart still aching, she opened her eyes and shifted in his arms, turning to face him, expecting him to be asleep only to find his black eyes on hers.

'Good morning, Elenitsa,' he said in a sleep-roughened voice. 'I'm sorry, I kept you up far too late last night.'

'It's okay.' She searched his face, hoping she wouldn't see the pain that had been there last night, but his expression was clear. 'I'm sorry for last night too,' she went on impulsively. 'I shouldn't have got out of the bath so abruptly and left without talking to you. And I'm sorry you felt you had to explain what happened—'

'It's all right,' he said quietly. 'I wanted to tell you. I wanted you to know.'

Her heart twisted at the look in his eyes. 'Thank you for sharing the memories of Dorian with me.'

His mouth curved. 'It was good. I need to remember him more like that and less…' He stopped, but she didn't need him to elaborate, she knew what he meant. 'I would like to hear about your family,' he went on. 'Tell me your good memories of them.'

A little burst of surprise went through her. 'You really want to hear?'

'Of course.' He lifted a finger and brushed a curl from her forehead. 'Will you share them with me?'

She felt stupidly shy and yet she loved that he'd asked her. It had always been difficult to remember, because whenever she did, it was always accompanied by a dragging sense of shame. As if she didn't deserve to have even the good parts of her family. But that shame had lessened now, as if her confession to him the night before had drained the bulk of it away.

'Oh, it's just little things,' she said. 'Dad used to take me skating on the lake in winter and he'd lift me up in his arms, making me feel as if I was flying. And my mother used to make the best hot chocolate.' She smiled, remembering. 'I hated waking up in the mornings so she'd tell me that if I was a good girl and got up on time, there would be a mug of hot chocolate in the kitchen for me. And there always was.' They were small memories of little moments, and now, robbed of the shame, they were joyful and it felt good to share them with him. 'My little sister used to steal my toys and it would drive me crazy and I'd get so angry with her. But after we argued, she'd always throw her arms around my waist and beg me to forgive her.'

Atticus's dark gaze didn't move from hers. 'And you did?'

'Yes. Always.' A familiar bittersweet grief wound through her. 'We used to have the loudest family dinners and we'd argue with each other a lot, but we also laughed a lot too. My dad had the most ridiculous sense of humour, while my mother's was more sarcastic and sly.'

Atticus shifted against her, pulling her more firmly into his arms. 'And you're somewhere in the middle, I think. Though erring towards sarcastic.'

There was an amusement in his voice that almost sounded tender and it made her chest feel tight. 'How would you know?' she asked, realising as soon as she said it that it sounded more like an accusation than the joke she'd been meaning it as. 'I mean, you don't know me that well.'

His dark eyes held hers, the amusement fading from them. 'I know that you love swimming naked in the sea. I know that you don't like to talk when you're eating something delicious because you want to savour the taste. I know that you're quick to learn, and your mind and the way you think are fascinating to me. I know that you smell of apples and that when you come, you say my name.'

A flush crept over her. She hadn't known he'd been paying attention, that he'd been collecting pieces of her all this time. He'd called her his hope and she'd thought that was how he saw her, as an ideal, a cipher, not as a woman.

'I know that your anger is quick to rouse,' he went on. 'And yet you let it go just as quickly, and that your eyes are full of sparks when you're sharpening your claws on me. And I know that you're very strong and very stubborn and I find that maddening.'

She flushed deeper. 'Atticus…'

'Yet I also know that arguing with you is one of life's pleasures and that it excites me. I know that you like trying new things, that you ask a lot of questions, and are very competitive. I know that in the evening, in the last rays of the sun, when you're lying on the sand, you look like you've been dipped in gold.'

Her throat closed and she couldn't speak.

'And I know that for some reason you're afraid of something,' he went on in the same quiet voice. 'And you won't tell me what it is or why.'

She looked away. 'I'm not afraid.'

'Yes, you are,' he said, quietly insistent. 'You were afraid last night, that's why you got out of the bath.'

Elena lifted her hands and pushed against his chest, needing some space. Because of course she was afraid, she just didn't want to explain it to him, when she barely knew herself what was making her so afraid. Only that it had something to do with wanting more from him, wanting something she knew she was never going to have.

And you know all about that, don't you?

That was why she tried to remember only the good parts of the time she had with her family, the parts that didn't hurt. Not the terrible ache of grief that had never left her, the wanting of something she would never have.

Atticus let her push him away, not making any move as she sat on the side of the bed, catching the sheet protectively around her, needing the distance.

All those things he'd said about her, all those things he'd noticed… They were all her, all parts of herself that Aristeidis had never seen, because for him, she suspected, she'd always been a sign that his son wasn't completely gone from him. A second chance he hadn't thought he'd have, and while those weren't bad things, they weren't entirely about her, either.

But Atticus had noticed them. Atticus had seen deeper into her, and it made her feel vulnerable.

'I'm fine.' She forced out the words. 'There really wasn't anything—'

But she didn't get to finish, because Atticus abruptly grabbed her and she found herself hauled back and pinned beneath him on the bed once again.

She put up a cursory resistance, but then he took her wrists and pinned them to the mattress on either side of her head.

'No,' he said flatly, his black gaze burning into hers. 'You're not doing the equivalent of walking out on me, not again. Not after last night. Tell me what's bothering you and tell me now.'

Oh, she wished she didn't like it when he got insistent like this, when he held her so she couldn't escape. When he made it obvious that he wouldn't let her avoid his questions, because he wanted to know. Because she mattered to him.

She wished she had the willpower to shove him away. It would be so much easier than having to tell him the truth.

And what is the truth?

Her mouth dried. 'It's stupid. I just…wanted to be more than a cipher to you. I wanted…'

'What? What do you want?'

Love. You want him to love you.

The thought struck her like a bullet from a gun, a direct hit, and for a moment she couldn't breathe. She'd asked him at the reading of Aristeidis's will whether love came into any of this and he'd looked at her with his fierce black gaze and had said love had nothing to do with it.

That had been her first warning, and she hadn't listened. She'd thought that sleeping with him, that a wedding and a honeymoon, wouldn't impact her intentions not to let him get under her skin. She'd thought she was strong, that she could hold out against him, and yet…

He was a combination of arrogance, fierce primal beauty, along with a protectiveness, a gentleness and a kindness she hadn't expected. And last night he'd shown her that there was a vulnerability to him too that had crept under her defences and laid waste to her heart. The tragedy that shaped him, that ate away at him, that had propelled him to create his charity that changed the lives of so many people in the entire world… That took drive and focus, and ambition, but fundamentally it took a deep caring for people and a need to help them, and that was what he had in abundance.

She'd been silly to think she could hold out against him, that he wouldn't change her just as deeply as she'd changed him. Silly to think that she could forget the deep sense of trust she'd felt the moment he'd seen her in the rubble and had saved her. Had altered the course of her life for ever.

Except how could she tell him that? When love was the one thing he'd told her very firmly was out of the question?

And why would he love you anyway? No one stays. Everyone leaves you in the end.

'Elena.' Atticus was frowning now as he studied her. 'What is it?'

Her sense of vulnerability deepened and she really did want to pull away then, but his grip on her wrists was too strong and the weight of him pinning her too great for her to shift. She was surrounded by his heat and his sunshine and salt scent, and the feel of his body on hers… He made her feel safe and yet threatened at the same time.

'Elena,' he insisted.

And she knew that there was no escape. That she'd have to tell him. And that once she had, everything would change. She would lose him the way she lost everyone else who'd ever mattered to her.

'I love you,' she burst out. 'That's what the problem is.

I love you and I can't think of anything better than living with you as your wife. Of creating the future we both wanted, with children, having a family. But a family to me means love, Atticus, and if we don't have that between us…' Her throat closed, but she forced the words out. 'I don't want to be your hope. I want to be your love.'

At first Atticus wasn't quite sure what she'd said. And then, as he stared down into her dark eyes, seeing the fear in them along with her usual fierce stubbornness, the words finally penetrated.

She loved him.

She *loved* him.

It felt as if something had grabbed him hard by the throat and refused to let go.

Love wasn't supposed to be a part of this, it was *never* supposed to be a part of this. He didn't want it. Love was the horror of seeing your brother dead on the ground and knowing it was because of you, and that your life would never be the same again. Love was the anger in your father's eyes, and the blame too. Love turned to hate in the blink of an eye. Love wanted revenge.

He never wanted anything to do with it again, not even from her.

He let go of her and pushed himself off the bed.

Elena sat up, her hair cascading around her head in a long golden fall. Wrapped in the white sheet, her pale shoulders revealed, she looked heartbreakingly beautiful and so fragile he wanted to wrap her up and hide her away so no one could ever hurt her.

Someone like you, perhaps?

He was already cold and that thought made him go even colder. She couldn't love him, it was impossible. One day he'd make a mistake, do something unforgivable, and that love would turn to hate. That love would destroy what relationship they'd managed to build and he couldn't allow that to happen. He just couldn't.

'No,' he said flatly. 'I'm sorry, Elena, but no.'

'What do you mean no?'

'I told you. Love can't be part of this. Not at all.'

Her chin lifted, her backbone straightening. 'Well, that's too bad, isn't it? Because I love you.'

He found himself shaking his head. 'Why? What on earth about me is there to love?'

She just stared at him. 'Didn't you hear yourself saying all those things you noticed about me? All those things you know about me that no one else ever has. You…you make me feel good, Atticus.'

He gave a bitter laugh. 'That's just the sex talking.'

Anger flickered in her eyes. 'No, it's not. I might be inexperienced but I know the difference between sexual obsession and love.' Her gaze focused abruptly on him. 'Do you?'

Of course he knew. Did she think he'd never felt love before? 'I know what love is,' he spat. 'It's the horror of finding out you killed the person who was most important to you in the whole world. It's the hate in your father's eyes whenever he looks at you. It's having the people you care about slam doors in your face and cut you off without recourse and all because you made a mistake. One simple mistake.' He was breathing very fast now, all his muscles tense, the pressure inside him building and building. 'I don't want anything to do with love ever again.'

There was a long moment of silence where he was conscious of his harsh, ragged breathing, as if he'd run a long race. Then Elena slid off the bed, leaving the sheet behind her and coming over to him. She was naked, her body all soft pink and cream curves. The look in her eyes was soft and that terrible understanding was back, as if she knew his pain. As if she'd experienced it herself.

She stopped in front of him, her expression full of a fierce tenderness. 'I won't do that to you, Atticus,' she said. 'I won't ever do that to you.'

But he was shaking his head, his heartbeat loud in his ears. 'You don't know that. Aristeidis, I'm sure, thought he would never do that too, and then I killed Dorian and all that love he had for me was gone. It didn't matter that I was his son, Elena. Love didn't matter at all.'

Her eyes were very dark, tenderness burning in them like a flame. 'I can see why you'd think that,' she said. 'Believe me, I can see. But don't you think it can be different with us?'

'No, I don't. And why would I ever take that chance anyway?' He wanted to touch her very badly, but he knew that would be a bad idea, so he kept his hands to himself. 'I could hurt you, Elena. I could...hurt any children we have. And that...would destroy me.'

Her gaze turned liquid, tears glittering in her eyes, but she didn't look away, her expression still fierce.

They made everything worse, those tears. They made that ground-glass feeling in his heart return, a burning agony that he could never outrun.

'You won't do that though,' she said passionately. 'You won't. You're the most caring, the most protective, the most gentle man I've ever known. You saved me all those years ago, Atticus. You brought me home to your father. You gave me a life I'd never thought I'd have. And you'd never hurt me, you'd never hurt our family either.'

He searched her beautiful face. 'But aren't I? Aren't I hurting you right now?'

She didn't look away, the vulnerability in her eyes so painful it made him catch his breath. She was always so strong and so determined, but he could see the need in her. For him. 'Yes,' she admitted.

'It'll pass,' he ground out. 'Give it time.'

But she shook her head. 'I never wanted to need anyone. I never wanted to be vulnerable, not after the earthquake. Not after I lost my family. Then you came and you made me feel safe for the first time since my family died, and I thought… I thought I could trust you. But then you took me to Kalifos and you left me there, and I felt abandoned. So I decided that day that I wasn't going to ever need you again.'

Her voice thickened even more, but the burning look in her eyes didn't waver. 'But I do, Atticus, I need you. I always have, right from that moment you saw me in the rubble. And I think I always will.'

He remembered that moment. When he'd left her with the housekeeper on Kalifos and there had been tears streaming down her face. 'Don't go,' she'd whispered in the Greek she was already getting very good at. 'Please don't leave me here.'

But he'd had to and he couldn't stay. That was when he'd had to harden his heart, to detach himself from his emotions.

He had to do that now, because he'd made a mistake, he could see that so clearly now. Yet another mistake. He'd let her mean something to him. He'd let her matter and now he was hurting her. He'd never wanted to hurt her.

'I'm sorry,' he said, and he meant it. 'But this is something I can't do. Love can't be part of our marriage, Elena, and that's final.'

For a moment, she stared at him. Then abruptly she took a step closer, all pink and golden nakedness, and she went on her toes and pressed a kiss to his mouth. But it was so brief, so achingly brief, and he knew it was a goodbye.

'Then I'm sorry,' she said, her gaze ferocious. 'But I can't do a marriage without love.'

And before he could say a word, she walked past him and out of the bedroom.

CHAPTER ELEVEN

ELENA CALLED THE Kalathes staff and organised a helicopter to come to the island. Atticus didn't follow her. After she'd arranged her transport, she went back to the bedroom to tell him she was leaving, but he wasn't there.

Her heart felt as if it were shattering in her chest, but she ignored the pain as she went around the room, packing up her belongings, tears running down her cheeks.

She let them fall. It didn't matter if she cried and it felt cathartic. Even her tears hadn't been enough to make him stay, even baring her heart. He was right after all, love didn't matter. Perhaps it never had.

Then again, why she thought it would, she had no idea. She should never have told him how she felt, but he'd demanded the truth from her and so she'd given it to him. Then when she'd said it and when he'd recoiled, she'd felt the oddest sense of calm wash over her.

He couldn't do this—she knew he wouldn't—and even her honesty, even her tears, even her anger and her passion weren't enough. But the pain in her heart was sweet despite it all. The love she felt for him, a bright glow, a ball of sunshine that she knew would never dim. She could feel its strength, its peace. It wasn't a weakness at all, and yes, there was pain, but the feeling itself was calm and strong and right as a heartbeat.

If ever there was a man who needed love in his life, it was Atticus Kalathes. And while he might not accept it, she wasn't going to deny loving him. And she wasn't going to stop. She would just have to love him in other ways, from afar, and it would have to be from afar. While she might love him, she wasn't going to compromise on what she needed, not this time.

He was in agony, she could see that, but she couldn't deny what was in her own heart. It was dishonest. She couldn't bring her children into a world with a father who thought love was destructive, who didn't want anything to do with it. She couldn't create a family without it. She remembered her own family, those bright moments of joy that she kept close to her heart, and in every single one of them was evidence of love. Evidence of the caring they'd had for each other.

She wanted that again. She wanted it desperately. She'd tried to have it on Kalifos with Aristeidis, but it had been so one-sided. She, giving everything to Aristeidis, while he had been so caught up in his own grief he hadn't noticed.

She couldn't do that with Atticus, not again.

Perhaps it was cutting off her nose to spite her face, but if that was the case then so be it. She couldn't build a life and a family with a man who didn't love her. She wouldn't.

Tears dripped slowly down her face as she doggedly finished packing and then got dressed in simple jeans and a T-shirt. The clothing felt rough and uncomfortable after the days of having nothing on her bare skin but sun, yet she ignored the discomfort just as she ignored everything else.

Once she was packed, she debated trying to find Atticus to tell him where she'd gone, and then decided not to. He'd deliberately taken himself away from her and there wasn't any benefit to going after him. He'd see the helicopter when it landed and know she was leaving anyway.

Her heart aching, Elena picked up her bag and walked out of the house to the jetty to wait.

Atticus watched her from the other end of the beach, a small figure sitting hunched over on the jetty, her hair blowing around like a golden flag in the breeze that came off the sea.

Every part of him was in agony. He'd tried very hard to detach himself, running hard along the beach, hoping physical exercise would help him find that space where he could be free of the pain. Where his focus would subsume everything, the past lost in the moment of the present.

But he couldn't lose himself. All he could see was Elena's pale face and the fierce light in her eyes. All he could hear was her voice telling him how much she needed him.

How can you let her leave?

He had to, that was the issue. He couldn't insist she stay. She wanted something from him that he didn't want to give, and it was too much. He couldn't ask her not to love him and he couldn't keep on insisting on a marriage that wouldn't give her what she needed.

He wasn't that man.

If she wanted to leave, he had to let her go.

If you let go of her, you let go of hope.

He sat on the rocks, ignoring the sting of rough granite against his bare flesh, watching her. He'd called her his hope, but she'd wanted to be more than just an ideal, more than a talisman, and she was.

Over the past couple of weeks she'd become so much more. Warmth and comfort and a source of strength. Understanding and sympathy. And laughter. Joy. So many things he'd never thought he'd find again until she came into his life. All the things that were intrinsic to her, and weren't merely a representation in platinum. A child reaching up their arms.

She wasn't a child. She was a grown woman, with thoughts and feelings and dreams of her own, and she had to be free to live them. He couldn't keep hold of her just because of what she'd once represented to him.

If she's more than that to you, why are you giving her up?

He shook his head, trying to get rid of the voice inside him. But it wouldn't go away. He *had* to give her up. He couldn't, wouldn't have anything to do with love again.

If you give her up, you also give up all the good things that came with it. The joy, the happiness, the comfort, the strength...

His jaw was tight, his shoulders tighter. He tore his gaze from the jetty where she sat, hoping if he didn't see her, he wouldn't remember his arms around her, her laugh in his ears, the smiles she gave him. The peace in his heart when she was in his arms. The comfort of her touch…

'Do you have good memories of Dorian?' she'd asked.

And he had remembered. So many good things that had been lost under his grief and his pain.

Love is pain, but it's also all those other things too. Comfort and joy and happiness. Love is charity too.

Atticus shut his eyes. His charity was a business and he ran it as such. He'd wanted to give people hope.

Where do you think hope comes from?

A strange feeling coiled inside him, a powerful intensity that he didn't understand. Hope came from… well, it came from a little girl in the rubble. It came from finding a moment of brightness in the midst of the darkness. It came from…

It comes from love.

Atticus took a breath and another, the feeling like a pressure starting to burst. He'd loved his brother and he'd loved his father, and there had been good things in those relationships. It hadn't all been horror and pain and grief.

She found happiness in the midst of despair. Why can't you? She showed you the way. All you have to do is follow her.

Every part of him felt as if he were going to burst apart. Was it that simple? Could he just accept the pain, the agony, the horror again?

You already have. And it's as simple as picking up a little girl in the rubble.

He couldn't breathe. Could he do this? Could he accept what she wanted, what she demanded? Could he open himself up to what he'd been avoiding all these years?

Except…he'd never avoided it, had he? All that feeling he was trying to deny, all the pain and grief, were locked up tight in his heart. But all the joy and the happiness were locked up there too.

You can't have one without the other. But it's easier to have the pain when she's around to help you bear it.

It came to him, in a bolt from the blue, that he'd spent years detaching himself. Years telling himself he felt nothing, distracting himself from the storm inside him. But he hadn't distracted himself. He'd started a charity, for God's sake. And it wasn't because he felt nothing. It was because he felt *everything.*

It rushed through him then, the pain and the agony, but also the joy, the happiness. The bright moments that Elena had talked about, and treasured. Her beneath him, her eyes full of desire. Her laughing as he tickled her foot. Her face flushed with pleasure as she held up a fish she'd caught…

He couldn't have one without the other, and he realised all of a sudden that he didn't want to. She embraced both parts of love and so could he.

Where she led, he would follow. He had to. He couldn't do anything else.

He shoved himself off the rocks and ran hard across the beach, across the hot sand to the path to the jetty and then down it.

She lifted her head as he approached then stood up. 'The helicopter is coming,' she began.

'I'm cancelling the helicopter,' he said.

She blinked then glanced behind her as if she wanted to back away, but there was only the sea behind her. He didn't stop coming.

'Atticus,' she said, but then he was right in front of her and this time it was he who lifted his arms to her, putting them around her and sweeping her up in them, holding her where she was always meant to be. Against his chest, against his heart.

She pushed against him once then stopped, going lax as if she was too tired to struggle any more. A tear slid down her nose, her dark eyes full of pain. 'What are you doing? I told you I couldn't—'

'I know what you told me.' He looked down at her, seeing how she hurt and knowing it was his fault, but also knowing that he was going to spend the rest of his life healing that hurt. 'But I was wrong. So I changed my mind. Or rather, you helped me change it. You made me see that love doesn't have to be destructive. That it's not only about pain and grief, but also about happiness and joy and I… I want that. I want more of that. I want you to teach me more, show me more. More happiness. More joy. More laughter. I want bright moments and precious memories, and I want to create them with you. I want memories we can treasure for the rest our lives, because…' His heart thundered in his head and the only thing that was real was her lying in his arms. 'I love you, Elenitsa. It feels as if I've loved you for ever.'

Her mouth had opened in shock, her eyes going wide. She searched his face as if looking for the truth and he made sure she saw it. He let her see all the love in his heart that he'd denied for too many years. He let it out.

'Oh, Atticus…' There were more tears in her eyes, but they weren't of sadness, not this time. 'I just…want happiness for you more than anything in the whole world.'

'Then let's find it,' he said. 'Let's find it together.'

'Are you sure?' she whispered. 'Are you sure this is what you want?'

'I'm sure.' And he could feel the certainty settled down inside him, and he already knew that this would be one of those bright moments, a precious memory that he would look at later in life and treasure for ever. 'You're not my hope after all, Elena. All this time, you were my love.'

She reached up to him then, and put her arms around him, and her mouth was on his and there was so much warmth and sweetness in her kiss that he wondered how he could ever have walked away from her.

Well, he wasn't going to any more. He never would again.

He turned with her in his arms, and he carried her back to the house, and together they started making those moments, moments full of happiness, moments full of joy. Moments full of love, that would last them the rest of their lives.

EPILOGUE

ATTICUS THREW THE wreath Elena had made out of wildflowers into the sea, and then pulled her in close to his side. She held their son in her arms, his dark head on her shoulder. Dorian Aristeidis Kalathes was quiet now, but he'd proved himself to be a handful right from the moment of his birth.

Atticus wouldn't have it any other way.

The wreath was for his father, the first anniversary of Aristeidis's death, and it had been Elena's idea to mark the occasion with flowers cast on the sea and then, like counting a rosary, he would remember the good moments, the treasured moments that Atticus had of his father, and of Dorian.

He spoke the words now without faltering, the pain bittersweet yet bearable, because there had been some good moments. Some very good moments. Moments he wanted to remember so he could rebuild the relationship between them that had been broken. His father wasn't around to help, but Atticus couldn't help feeling that somehow, wherever he was, Aristeidis knew and approved.

He had a feeling that Aristeidis would approve of the

little family he and Elena had created for themselves over the past year too. They'd set about incorporating parts of Kalathes Shipping into Eleos, making their own shipping network that greatly facilitated delivery of important supplies to various needy countries around the world. Elena was a proven genius when it came to logistics and supply-chain issues, and she'd already improved some of Eleos's operations immeasurably.

She'd improved his life immeasurably, too, bringing to it a lightness and joy he'd never experienced before. A happiness he'd never thought he'd have.

The wreath drifted over the water, two seabirds hovering over it, their wings motionless in the air. Then they flew into the sky, circling Atticus and Elena and their son once before disappearing.

'I think he and Dorian liked our gesture,' Elena murmured as they watched the birds disappear into the sky.

Atticus hadn't ever believed in signs or portents. He'd never believed in fate. And once, he hadn't believed in love.

But he was different now. He'd changed. And now, he believed.

He believed in love with every beat of his heart.

'I think they did,' he said, his heart finally free of the chains of guilt and grief and bitterness.

Then he put his arm around his wife and his son, and they all went back to the villa. Ready to create yet more memories, yet more moments of joy, a never-ending chain that would last them all the days of their lives.

* * * * *

MILLS & BOON®

Coming next month

CINDERELLA'S ONE-NIGHT BABY
Michelle Smart

Skimming her fingers up his arm, Gabrielle placed her palm on his chest.

He sucked in a breath. His grip on her hip tightened. The thuds of his heartbeat perfectly matched the thuds of her own.

Andrés was a strictly short-term relationship man. He wouldn't want more than she could give, and all she could give him was one night. It was all she could give to herself.

This was meant to be, she realised, staring even deeper into his eyes. It had been from the start. If she'd known he was single, she would have refused point blank to attend the party with him, would have spent the night alone in her tiny apartment unaware that he held the key to unlocking all the desires she'd kept buried so deep she'd hardly been aware they existed.

For this one night she could put those desires first, and do so with the sexiest man to roam the earth, the man who had the power to turn her to liquid without even touching her.

A man who wouldn't want anything more from her.

She moved her face closer. Their lips brushed like feathers. The heat of his breath filled her senses.

Continue reading
CINDERELLA'S ONE-NIGHT BABY
Michelle Smart

Available next month
millsandboon.co.uk